Hattie Tyng Griswold, Frederick William Gookin

Personal sketches of recent authors

Hattie Tyng Griswold, Frederick William Gookin

Personal sketches of recent authors

ISBN/EAN: 9783337281458

Printed in Europe, USA, Canada, Australia, Japan

Cover: Foto ©Andreas Hilbeck / pixelio.de

More available books at **www.hansebooks.com**

PERSONAL SKETCHES

OF

RECENT AUTHORS

BY

HATTIE TYNG GRISWOLD

AUTHOR OF "HOME LIFE OF GREAT AUTHORS," ETC.

CHICAGO

A. C. McCLURG AND COMPANY

1898

PREFACE.

"THE HOME LIFE OF GREAT AUTHORS," written by me and published in 1886, was an attempt to give, in readable and interesting form, some of those intimate and personal details of the lives and characters of a few popular authors which prove so welcome to readers who are acquainted with the books rather than the writers, and the knowledge of which invests the books themselves with an added charm.

The success of the former book showed that it supplied a popular want, and its author is now encouraged to extend the series of lives by treating in the present volume certain other great authors, some of whom have attained fame and favor since the former series was written, and some of whom, for lack of space, could not find places in that work. In one or two instances, also, such as the lives of Tennyson and Ruskin, such a flood of light has been thrown of late years upon the personality of authors that entirely new sketches of them have seemed to be demanded, and have accordingly been prepared and included in this volume.

In the hope that these sketches will render the works of the authors treated more vital and human by revealing the men and women behind the masks, this book is submitted by

THE AUTHOR.

COLUMBUS, WIS.,
 September, 1898.

PAGE

ALFRED TENNYSON 11

ERNEST RENAN 32

CHARLES DARWIN 54

MATTHEW ARNOLD 78

GEORGE DU MAURIER 96

ELIZABETH BARRETT BROWNING 114

JOHN RUSKIN 136

THOMAS HENRY HUXLEY 152

HARRIET BEECHER STOWE 168

ROBERT LOUIS STEVENSON 191

WILLIAM DEAN HOWELLS 209

LOUISA MAY ALCOTT 229

LYEFF TOLSTOI 251

RUDYARD KIPLING 266

CHRISTINA ROSSETTI 281

HENRY DAVID THOREAU 298

BAYARD TAYLOR 316

JAMES MATTHEW BARRIE 336

PORTRAITS.

		PAGE
ALFRED TENNYSON	*Frontispiece*	
ERNEST RENAN	*Facing page*	32
CHARLES DARWIN	„ „	54
MATTHEW ARNOLD	„ „	78
GEORGE DU MAURIER	„ „	96
ELIZABETH BARRETT BROWNING	„ „	114
JOHN RUSKIN	„ „	136
THOMAS HENRY HUXLEY	„ „	152
HARRIET BEECHER STOWE	„ „	168
ROBERT LOUIS STEVENSON	„ „	191
WILLIAM DEAN HOWELLS	„ „	209
LOUISA MAY ALCOTT	„ „	229
LYEFF TOLSTOI	„ „	251
RUDYARD KIPLING	„ „	266
CHRISTINA ROSSETTI	„ „	281
HENRY DAVID THOREAU	„ „	298
BAYARD TAYLOR	„ „	316
JAMES MATTHEW BARRIE	„ „	336

PERSONAL SKETCHES OF RECENT AUTHORS.

ALFRED TENNYSON.

WHEN the news of the death of Tennyson was flashed along the wires, many hearts echoed his own words in the " Ode on the Death of the Duke of Wellington," " The last great Englishman is low." Many more would have echoed them had they read, "The last great English poet is low," for it is a fact that no one remained whom the people deemed worthy of the succession to the Laureate's high position. It had been filled too long by a man of consummate genius, whose faultless taste had added new lustre to its honors, to be handed down to any minor poet of the day whose talents elevated him a little " above the unlettered plain, its herd and crop." Swinburne could not be placed in such a category as that, but for many reasons there was little real enthusiasm for Swinburne. Had Robert Browning been alive, there would have been no hesitation. He was born to the purple, and the world had at last acknowledged it.

> "He was a man born with thy face and throat,
>   Lyric Apollo;"

and though he met many rebuffs, he flung at the world the scornful message,

> "Leave Now for dogs and apes!
>   Man has Forever!"

and continued his upward climb. Alfred Tennyson had no such years of weary waiting for recognition as Browning endured. His lyric sweetness and dulcet melody caught the ear of the world quickly, whereas the harsh dissonance of Browning's voice repelled all except those who sought for the thought beneath the words. But Tennyson, after he had well proved the fact that he possessed some power other than the twanging of a tinkling lute, held the attention of thoughtful minds, even as Browning did, and thought and music were blended as one. Both men devoted their lives to poetry, hardly considering the possibility of any other course. Both were poor, but chose to live modestly, even sparingly, in order to follow the bent of their natures. Browning lived the greater part of his life on three hundred pounds a year, and Tennyson waited for twelve years before he could marry the woman of his choice, yet neither ever seemed to have any temptation to sell his birthright for a mess of pottage. The quick returns of literary notoriety were unknown in those days, and poets in particular were accustomed to have their books remain long on the bookseller's shelves. Even now, of course, their wares are less remunerative than those of their fellow-craftsmen, the writers of prose; yet now a poet who catches the popular ear does not need to starve in a garret, as Browning and Tennyson would have done had they been entirely dependent upon their own work. One wonders whether a poet like Longfellow, could he have been endowed, and relieved from the drudgery of teaching and lecturing to college boys, would really have achieved much finer results; or should we have had merely a greater quantity of poetry, with no corresponding difference in quality? One must give up many things in this world who determines to follow his dream; but happy is the land where many men are content to live humbly, that they may strive, unhampered by worldly cares, toward a high ideal. May our poets, at least, be free from too many corroding cares! May they be able to live, as Tennyson did, secluded lives amid beautiful surroundings, and free from the intrusion of that commonplace crowd which throttles genius by too close contact! For a high man with a great thing to pursue, the kingdom of heaven does not come with observation. Alfred Tennyson was born in the seclusion of a country parsonage, in that far away time, 1809, when men did not live and strive in the public eye to the extent they do in these later days. His father, a Lincolnshire clergyman, lived almost an ideal scholar's life in that beautiful country, where seldom the " chimney glowed in expectation of a guest." Alfred and his brothers passed their quiet years here, reading and studying, and trying their hands at poetry at a very early age. Two of his brothers seemed as promising as he, in childhood, and indeed were possessed of real poetic gifts. One is reminded of the Brontë sisters on the Yorkshire moors, with their early attempts at literary production, and their keen interest and sympathy in each other's labor. All had a true vocation, but time and circumstance permitted but one to attain to an excellence which the world acknowledged. So Charles and Frederick Tennyson remained as lesser lights in this constellation of genius; but each had the poetic temperament, to say the least, and that is a gift of exceeding great value. Samuel Longfellow is another case in point, with his rare poet's soul and exquisite touch within the limits to which he has confined himself. When Charles Tennyson was eighteen, and Alfred only seventeen, they published their first verses. A local bookseller paid them one hundred dollars for them, expecting, no doubt, to sell the book mostly in the parish, where the father was very influential, and the boys favorites. When Alfred went up to Cambridge at nineteen and entered Trinity College, his father was already in failing health, and the resources of the family quite meagre. At Cambridge the boy had been heralded as one of mark. If he had not written three books on the soul, proving absurd all written hitherto, like Cleon, he had at least written one book, and at seventeen that is some distinction. There were a number of youths there at that time, of commanding talent, nearly a dozen of whom became distinguished in after years in their chosen lines; so from his early years he mingled with men not only of great ability, but of the highest character and standing. His own early life was pitched conspicuously high, his religious feeling being innate, and well developed by his early training. Some of the companions of his college life met him on this ground, and his lofty attitude toward life was not lowered by the influence of companions who mocked at it. His habit of referring all questions of conduct to the higher elements of his nature was already established, and he never lost it throughout life. His scorn for low ideals was very genuine, and his delight in the " heart affluence of discursive talk" on noble themes was enduring. He met here for the first time Arthur Hallam, the friend whose name has been handed down to coming time in " In Memoriam." Here began that happy intercourse,

> " When each by turns was guide to each,
>   And Fancy light from Fancy caught,
>   And Thought leapt out to wed with thought
> Ere Thought could wed itself with Speech;

> " And all we met was fair and good,
>   And all was good that Time could bring,
>   And all the secret of the Spring
> Moved in the chambers of the blood;

> " And many an old philosophy
>   On Argive heights divinely sang,
>   And round us all the thicket rang
> To many a flute of Arcady."

Though he made lifelong friends of many of the men he met at Cambridge, Arthur Hallam endeared himself to him above all others; and though it might have been the early death of the favored friend which made " former gladness loom so great," he never replaced him with another quite as near and dear. The acquaintance of Arthur Hallam with the Tennyson family, which consisted of twelve children of whom Alfred was the third, resulted in his engagement to

Miss Tennyson, and in his being a very constant visitor at the home at Somersby. These days are commemorated by the poet: —

> "While now we talk as once we talked
>   Of men and minds, the dust of change,
>   The days that grow to something strange
> In walking as of old we walked
>
> "Beside the river's wooded reach,
>   The fortress, and the mountain ridge,
>   The cataract flashing from the bridge,
> The breaker breaking on the beach."

After his friend's too early death at Vienna, he writes thus of the sister who is bereaved: —

> " Her eyes are homes of silent prayer,
>   Nor other thought her mind admits,
>   But, he was dead, and there he sits,
> And he who brought him back is there.
>
> " Then one deep love doth supersede
>   All other, when her ardent gaze
>   Roves from the living brother's face,
> And rests upon the Life indeed.
>
> " All subtle thought, all curious fears,
>   Borne down by gladness so complete,
>   She bows, she bathes the Savior's feet
> With costly spikenard and with tears."

This poem has seemed sacred, seemed the supreme poem, to all who love and grieve, ever since in his young manhood he embalmed such love and grief in that imperishable verse. When but twenty-one years old he published the volume called " Poems, Chiefly Lyrical," and in 1832 another volume which contained some of his best-known poems, — " The Lotos-Eaters," " The Lady of Shalott," " The Palace of Art," " The Dream of Fair Women," among them.

From " The Palace of Art " several verses were omitted at the time of publication which are given in his Memoirs. He intended to introduce sculpture into it, and had written two descriptions, as follows: —

> " One was the Tishbite whom the raven fed,
> As when he stood on Carmel steeps
> With one arm stretched out bare, and mocked and said,
> 'Come, cry aloud, he sleeps.'
> Tall, eager, lean and strong, his cloak wind-borne
> Behind, his forehead heavenly bright
> From the clear marble pouring glorious scorn,
> Lit as with inner light.
> One was Olympias ; the floating snake
> Rolled round her ankles, round her waist
> Knotted, and folded once about her neck,
> Her perfect lips to taste."

As is the case usually when surviving friends collect and publish the work rejected by a poet himself, the new poems given in the Life prepared by his son will not add much to his reputation. Many such instances might be pointed out. The case of Christina Rossetti is a recent and notable one. Her own fine critical taste had culled from the mass of her poetical work what she was willing to submit to posterity, but the mistaken affection of her brother gave to the world a volume of New Poems, which to say the least were not up to the highest mark reached by her in life. The searching of the diaries and notebooks of dead friends, and the thrusting of their unimportant contents on the world, has certainly been carried far enough in recent years, yet the tendency is still further to exploit such private miscellanies for the gratification of the morbid curiosity of modern readers.

In the summer of 1831 Tennyson and Arthur Hallam, in all the glow and ardor of early youth, became absorbed in the interest they felt in a conspiracy against the rule of Spain, and started off for the Pyrences to carry money to the insurgent allies of Torrijos, who had raised the standard of revolt against the inquisition, and the tyranny of Ferdinand, the King of Spain. They held a secret meeting with the heads of the conspiracy on the Spanish border, and caused great alarm among their friends by sending no news of themselves for several weeks. One is glad to have this glimpse of the poet as a man of action, and to count him among those young men who risk something for a noble cause. Byron's enthusiasm for Greek liberty has always been the brightest spot in the record of his clouded life. That Tennyson's soul was capable of a righteous wrath he proved many times in life. As early as his first university years he was stirred to indignation by the lethargy and selfishness of the college life and the narrow limits of thought there. He had higher ideals of what a scholar's life should be, and of the inspiration he should receive from the men who guided it. The following lines written in 1830 will show his feeling : —

> "Therefore your Halls, your ancient Colleges,
>   Your portals statued with old kings and queens,
>   Your gardens, myriad-volumed libraries,
>   Wax-lighted chapels, and rich carven screens,
>   Your doctors, and your proctors, and your deans,
>   Shall not avail you, when the Day-beam sports
>   New-risen o'er awakened Albion. No !
>   Nor yet your solemn organ pipes that blow
>   Melodious thunders thro' your vacant courts

> At noon and eve, because your manner sorts
> Not with this age, wherefrom ye stand apart,
> Because the lips of little children preach
> Against you, you that do profess to teach
> And teach us nothing, feeding not the heart."

Soon after Arthur Hallam's death he wrote "Ulysses," one of the noblest of his poems. He tells us that "it gave his feeling about the need of going forward and braving the struggle of life, perhaps more simply than anything in 'In Memoriam.'" He sees even as early as that

> "How dull it is to pause, to make an end,
>   To rust unburnished, not to shine in use!
>   As tho' to breathe were life.   Life piled on life
>   Were all too little, and of one to me
>   Little remains ; but every hour is saved
>   From that eternal silence, something more,
>   A bringer of new things; and vile it were
>   For some three suns to store and hoard myself,
>   And this gray spirit yearning in desire
>   To follow knowledge like a sinking star,
>   Beyond the utmost bound of human thought."

Again he says, —

> "Death closes all : but something ere the end,
>   Some work of noble note, may yet be done,
>   Not unbecoming men that strove with Gods."

The volume of 1832 placed him at the head of the poets of his generation, though there were critics who cavilled, as they had done at the two small preceding volumes.   Of the little volume published by Charles and Alfred, Coleridge is said to have remarked that only the poems signed C. T. gave promise of a coming poet, and other reviewers sneered at some of the early poems in a manner showing how little insight they really possessed. We who consider that some of the poems of that period were never surpassed by him, can but wonder at the obtuseness which saw in them only the rhymes of mediocrity.

The failing health of his father recalled him from Cambridge to Somersby before he had taken his degree, and he never resumed his studies there. But he began reading, soon after, many books on physical science, and meditating much on the problems they presented to his mind. In the years in which he was composing "In Memoriam" he read metaphysics a good deal also, and began to doubt some things he had been taught; but though his opinions changed somewhat from his early beliefs, he retained his firm faith in the existence of a Deity who guided the destinies of men. His religious attitude at that time is very clearly depicted in the poem. It was perhaps summed up as nearly in the lines which follow as anywhere: —

> "Oh, yet we trust that somehow good
>   Will be the final goal of ill,
>   To pangs of nature, sins of will,
> Defects of doubt, and taints of blood;
>
> "That nothing walks with aimless feet;
>   That not one life shall be destroyed,
>   Or cast as rubbish to the void,
> When God has made his pile complete;
>
> "That not a worm is cloven in vain;
>   That not a moth with vain desire
>   Is shrivelled in a fruitless fire,
> Or but subserves another's gain.

> " Behold, we know not anything ;
>   I can but trust that good shall fall
>   At last — far off — at last to all,
> And every winter change to spring."

This poem, or series of poems, which had been so long in the writing, was not published until 1850. Previous to this, he had published " English Idylls and other Poems," and in 1847, " The Princess," a medley. In 1850 his circumstances permitted him to marry Miss Emily Sellwood, to whom he had been engaged so long. In 1845 he had been granted a pension of two hundred pounds a year, and the sale of his books had become considerable. At the death of his father he also received a small annuity. But his means were still very limited wherewith to maintain a household. He had continued to live with his mother and sisters after his father's death until his marriage, though the establishment at Somersby had been broken up. Carlyle described him in those years after this manner :

"One of the finest-looking men in the world. A great shock of rough, dusty-dark hair ; bright laughing hazel eyes ; massive aquiline face, most massive, yet most delicate ; of sallow brown complexion, almost Indian looking ; clothes cynically loose, free-and-easy ; smokes infinite tobacco. His voice is musical metallic, — fit for loud laughter and piercing wail, and all that may lie between ; speech and speculation free and plenteous ; I do not meet in these decades such company over a pipe. We shall see what he will grow to. He is often unwell ; very chaotic — his way is through Chaos and the Bottomless and Pathless ; not handy for making out many miles upon."

We may insert here a description of his personal appearance in late life, as a foil to the other.

Thomas Wentworth Higginson has recently written in the "Atlantic Monthly" some very interesting reminiscences of famous men in England, which contain this description of Tennyson: —

" He was tall and high shouldered, careless in dress, and while he had a high and domed forehead, yet his brilliant eyes and tangled hair and beard gave him rather the air of a partially reformed Corsican bandit, or else an imperfectly secularized Carmelite monk, than of a decorous and well-groomed Englishman."

After his marriage he removed to Farringford, Freshwater, in the Isle of Wight, where he continued to live exclusively until 1869, and at intervals all his life.   Here his love for country life and for seclusion were completely gratified.   Here he made those fine observations of nature which are detected in many of his poems, and passed much of his time in the open air.   He had no fondness for sport, and did not affect the country for the same reason that so many Englishmen do, but from a real poetic delight in its pomps and shows.   The friends he loved were invited to visit him here, and he had great pleasure in entertaining them.   His favorite time for exercising this hospitality was from Saturday until Monday, and many of his guests were thus invited.   Then they wandered by the wild sea, or out upon the downs, where the gorse flamed like a conflagration, or in the lanes, which were crowded with anemones and primroses, or climbed up to the beacon-staff, or to the Needles, or sat on the lawn with the gentle invalid, Mrs. Tennyson, who could not walk without support, and was often wheeled about by her husband and sons in a chair. She is described as a very lovely woman, gifted and appreciative, who held the devotion of her husband to the last days of his life. The house was completely hidden from the view of passers-by. The interior was very attractive, with a glow of crimson everywhere in the old time, and a " great oriel window in the drawing-room full of green and golden leaves, of the sound of birds, and of the distant sea." Here the poet frequently entertained his friends by reading his poems to them. The honor was very highly esteemed by them, but sometimes proved a little wearisome, when he became so much interested himself that he read the whole of " Maud " or " The Princess " to them at a sitting. Mrs. Browning tells in one of her letters of his having read " Maud " entire to her and her husband, and evidently considered it a rather exhausting entertainment. " Maud " was one of his favorite poems, despite the fact that it received more unfavorable criticism than any of the others. His son describes the reading of " Maud " quite at length, and especially the last reading of it, when he was eighty-three years old. He was sitting in a high-backed chair fronting a southern window, which looks over the groves of Sussex. His head was outlined against the sunset clouds seen through the window. His beautifully modulated voice had retained its flexibility, and he threw great feeling into the lines. He called the poem " a little Hamlet," and the hero was evidently much loved by his creator. The passion of the first canto was given in a sort of rushing recitative. No one who had heard it could ever forget the voice singing

> "A passionate ballad gallant and gay,"

or

> " Oh, let the solid ground not fail beneath my feet,"

or

> " Go not, happy day, from the shining fields."

But the most memorable part was when he reached the eighteenth canto beginning, —

> " I have led her home, my love, my only friend,
>   There is none like her, none.
>   And never yet so warmly ran my blood,
>   And sweetly, on and on
>   Calming itself to the long-wished-for end,
>   Full to the banks, close on the promised good."

II

> " None like her, none.
>   Just now the dry-tongued laurels' pattering talk
>   Seem'd her light foot along the garden walk,
>   And shook my heart to think she comes once more;
>   But even then I heard her close the door,
>   The gates of Heaven are closed, and she is gone.

III

> " There is none like her, none.
>   Nor will be when our summers have deceased.
>   O, art thou sighing for Lebanon
>   In the long breeze that streams to thy delicious East,
>   Sighing for Lebanon,
>   Dark cedar, tho' thy limbs have here increased,
>   Upon a pastoral slope as fair,
>   And looking to the South, and fed
>   With honey'd rain and delicate air,
>   And haunted by the starry head
>   Of her whose gentle will has changed my fate,
>   And made my life a perfumed altar-flame;
>   And over whom thy darkness must have spread
>   With such delight as theirs of old, thy great
>   Forefathers of the thornless garden, there
>   Shadowing the snow-limb'd Eve from whom she came."

One is tempted to quote the whole canto; and we do not wonder that the old poet's voice broke over it, and that tears came to the eyes of the listeners. The pathos of deep joy can go no further. Tennyson's love poetry is always perfect, and puts to shame such writers as Rossetti and Swinburne, who prostitute their genius to write only of the baser element of passion. What verse have they written, with all the license they have given themselves, which can compare with many of this nobler poet, written not in youth, but some of them away on in middle age? What have they to match this verse, for instance?

> "She is coming, my own, my sweet:
>   Were it ever so airy a tread,
>   My heart would hear her and beat,
>   Were it earth in an earthy bed;
>   My dust would hear her and beat,
>   Had I lain for a century dead;
>   Would start and tremble under her feet,
>   And blossom in purple and red."

The "Ode to the Duke of Wellington" and "Guinevere" were also poems which he was fond of reading to his friends. The Ode was written after he was appointed Laureate, upon the death of Wordsworth, in 1850, and was severely criticised at the time of its appearance, as were many of his poems written in an official capacity. All will recall "The Charge of the Light Brigade," and the various odes written on the deaths or marriages in the royal family, in this connection. In 1859 appeared the "Idylls of the King," and there was little but applause for this crowning work of the poet's genius. He left some notes on these poems which are interesting. Of "Morte d'Arthur" he says: —

"How much of history we have in the story of Arthur is doubtful. Let not my readers press too hardly on details, whether for history or allegory. Some think that King Arthur may be taken to typify Conscience. He is, anyhow, meant to be a man who spent himself in the cause of honor, duty, and self-sacrifice; who felt and aspired with his nobler knights, though with a stronger and clearer conscience than any of them, 'reverencing his conscience as his king.' There was no such perfect man since Adam, as an old writer said."

What would not the jaded readers of too many books to-day give for the thrilling interest with which their elders read the wonderful Idylls when they appeared? Four stories — "Enid," "Vivien," "Elaine," and "Guinevere" — comprised the first series. They were followed by "The Holy Grail," "Gareth and Lynette," "Pelleas and Ettarre," "The Last Tournament," and "The Passing of Arthur." It was twelve years before we had the completed work, and Guinevere had passed

> "To where beyond these voices there is peace,"

but there was no flagging of interest, and every loyal lover of "Arthur's Coming" read with equal delight of his "Passing." How they still come

> "As from beyond the limit of the world,
> Like the last echo born of a great cry,
> Sounds, as if some fair city were one voice
> Around a king returning from his wars."

And how we still see

> "the speck that bare the king,
> Down that long water opening on the deep
> Somewhere far off, pass on and on, and go
> From less to less and vanish into light."

Tennyson published many poems after this, notably his dramas; but he wrote nothing from this time on that really added to his fame.

"The Princess" was one of the most popular of his poems; and even as good a judge as Dean Farrar so delighted in it that he could repeat the larger part of it, without ever having consciously committed it to memory. The poet himself said he had put some of his best work into it.

He was very fond of discussing his own work, and easily led to tell the history of any poem. His work was in reality his life, so entirely had he been absorbed by it throughout his fourscore years. Friends occasionally suggested to him a subject for a poem, but they were usually evolved after long brooding over a particular theme. Dean Farrar had the honor of suggesting to him the subject of his poem "St. Telemachus," which appears in one of his later volumes.

One of the most noticeable of his personal peculiarities was his love of privacy and distaste for personal notoriety. The intrusions of the vulgarly curious he resented almost savagely. The manners of these later years he looked on with an ineffable disdain, and he defended himself from the forward and the pushing, by himself assuming a demeanor so hostile that even the most brazen were repelled. Particularly did he dislike the exploiting of a dead man's faults or foibles or eccentricities. On one such occasion he wrote the well-known lines: —

> " Proclaim the faults he would not show ;
> Break lock and seal ; betray the trust ;

> Keep nothing sacred ; 't is but just
> The many-headed beast should know."

He was so carefully guarded from the intrusion of strangers by his family and servants, that one day Prince Albert himself was refused admission at his door. But he met the Prince frequently after that informal call, and visited the Queen at Windsor on many different occasions. But he was no courtier, not even after he was created a peer of the realm. The fawning ways of flattering fools were supremely distasteful to him, and he greeted the great ones of the earth with a simple dignity that betokened his sense of equality with them. This was taken note of on the occasion of his signing his name to the list of peers, and on other important occasions. But although he would not flatter, he was very susceptible to flattery himself, and liked people who talked to him principally of his poetry and his fame. He never became satiated with praise, and probably never heard much adverse criticism. One wonders what effect the opinion of Carlyle, expressed in 1867 in a letter, would have had on him: "We read at first Tennyson's 'Idylls' with profound recognition of the finely elaborated execution, and also of the inward perfection of vacancy — and to say truth, with considerable impatience at being treated so very like infants though the lollipops were so superlative." Matthew Arnold, too, acknowledged that Tennyson was not a poet to his taste, though of course recognizing his consummate workmanship.

Tennyson's own favorites among poets were Shakespeare, Homer, Virgil, Dante, Milton, Wordsworth, and Keats. These he read throughout life with increasing

love and pleasure, and often expressed his delight in
them. Byron he was less fond of, though he knew
his poetry very thoroughly. Among American
writers he ranked Edgar A. Poe very high, both in
verse and prose. Of Keats he said, " There is something of the innermost soul of Poetry in almost everything he wrote."

His friends were naturally the most distinguished
men of his day, though he lived so apart from the
world. He had residences at Petersfield, Hampshire,
and at Aldworth, Hazlemere, Surrey, in addition to
his Farringford estate, and in all of these places he
was somewhat isolated, and saw comparatively little
company. Carlyle was one of his early friends, and
notwithstanding his opinion of " The Idylls " remained
so to the end, though in the later years they did not
meet often. With Browning he enjoyed an ideal
friendship, and also with Edward Fitzgerald, perhaps
the dearest companion of all. He was naturally of a
somewhat melancholy temperament or habit of mind
himself, and the hearty cheerfulness of a man like
Browning had a pleasant tonic influence upon him.
But his own moods of depression were rather infre-
quent, and his life a happy one as the world goes.
The death of his son Lionel, in 1886, was the only
great grief of his later years. This son was a young
man of great promise, who had not been married
long when his death occurred, in India, and the
deepest sympathy was expressed throughout the
reading world, both for the bereaved parents and the
young wife. His son Hallam, the present Lord
Tennyson, was in close attendance upon his father
during the last years of his life, and has published

his Life and Letters, the work having been done
with great care and exquisite taste. There is no
doubt that the poet's old age was rather a sombre
one, though he had all that should attend on age,
— honor, love, obedience, and troops of friends. The
weight of years oppressed him; and all who saw him
in the last months of his life felt when they left him
that they should never see his face again. He died
in October, 1892. His last volume of verse was published in that year.

Life ebbed but slowly, and he was long in dying,
and would lie repeating the dirge from " Cymbeline,"
saying softly to himself at intervals : —

> " Fear no more the heat o' the sun,
>   Nor the furious winter's rages ;
>   Thou thy worldly task hast done,
>   Home art gone, and ta'en thy wages."

And again,

> " Quiet consummation have,
>   And renowned be thy grave."

In his own youth he had written a dirge almost as
frankly pagan as Shakespeare's, beginning, —

> " Now is done thy long day's work ;
>   Fold thy palms across thy breast,
>   Fold thy arms, turn to thy rest.
>   Let them rave.
>   Shadows of the silver birk
>   Sweep the green that folds thy grave.
>   Let them rave."

But in his old age he had written "Crossing the
Bar."

> " Sunset and evening star,
>   And one clear call for me !
>   And may there be no moaning of the bar,
>   When I put out to sea,

" But such a tide as moving seems asleep,
    Too full for sound and foam,
When that which drew from out the boundless deep"
    Turns again home.

" Twilight and evening bell,
    And after that the dark !
And may there be no sadness of farewell,
    When I embark;

" For tho' from out our bourne of Time and Place
    The flood may bear me far,
I hope to see my Pilot face to face
    When I have crost the bar."

The picture is a beautiful one of the great poet lying in his stately chamber, on that memorable moonlit night, when the family were gathered about him awaiting the end. He had ordered away the lights and lay dying there in the moonlight. Messengers had long been waiting about, to send the news of his departure on the four winds of heaven. Long he lay there in that solemn state, before the quiet consummation came. Then he knew what the flower in the crannied wall could not tell him.

ERNEST RENAN.

" TRÉGUIER is an ancient cathedral city set high upon a hill at the confluence of two rivers," in the Côtes du Nord.   In all Brittany there is not so beautiful a Gothic cathedral as this of Tréguier, with its lofty spire at once so delicate and so simple. About it is a green churchyard containing the tomb of St. Ives, the patron saint of Brittany, and surrounding that are the ancient cloisters.   The seaport of Tréguier is not far away, on an estuary between two wooded promontories.   The town traffics in fish and grain, and the inhabitants are chiefly concerned with the sea.   Brittany mans the navy of France to a large extent, and from this very port many men have gone forth to the service of the state.

The ancestors of Ernest Renan had been among these sailor folk for several generations.   They had lived in a house on the hill near the cathedral, and not down by the water with the sailors, who had not means enough to buy a fishing-smack.   His grandfather was a true Breton, religious, melancholy, pleasure-loving, garrulous, capable of passion, and with a genius for superstition.   His father, Captain Renan, had married the daughter of a Lannion trader.   She was an ardent Catholic and an Orlean-

ist, while her husband was a Republican. Ernest was born on the 28th of February, 1823, and being a small and fragile child it was feared he could not live. We are told that "Old Gude, the witch, took the babe's little shirt and dipped it in a country holy-well. She came back radiant: ' He will live, after all,' she cried; ' the two little arms stretched out, and you should have seen the whole garment swell and float; he means to live.' " And live he did, to be the pride of his fond, vivacious mother, and one of the most illustrious of the sons of France in these later days.

The Breton coast near Tréguier is incomparably soft and lovely, and the gray mists wrap it all in a delicate veil much of the time. Their filmy tracery is over everything, and their dampness induces a scanty verdure where barrenness would otherwise have reigned. It was up and down this coast that Ernest Renan wandered when a boy, enamoured of the sea, like all his race, and knowing it in every varying mood. And he loved the animated port between the promontories where the seamen brought their boats, and where loading and unloading went on constantly before his eyes, and where he saw men of many various climes come and go. He was a quiet, dreamy boy, not very active in work or play, but full of questions and devoted to his family. He had an older brother, Alain, and a sister, Henriette, who was twelve years old when he was born. She was almost a second mother to him in his boyhood, and found her chief delight in his presence. She was not a favorite with her gay and vivacious little gypsy mother, who loved beautiful and attractive children, — for she was very plain, her face marred by a birth-mark, though she had tender eyes and a certain look of distinction. So she lavished all her love on her baby brother, and made herself so necessary to his happiness that they were hardly ever separated. His father was lost at sea when he was five years old, and the little mother and serious-minded sister were left not only without means, but in debt. He knew from that time not actual destitution, but poverty with all its limitations. At this time Henriette began to teach him. She had herself been taught by noble ladies, who after the Revolution had come back and were trying to earn their living by giving lessons in towns like Tréguier. There were many such in France in those days. Henriette was naturally thoughtful and serious, and she had so well improved her opportunities that an excellent foundation had been laid for that exquisite culture for which she was noted later in life. She also had an air of good breeding very noticeable amid such surroundings as hers, though her mother was not without refinement and grace. She found Ernest an apt and faithful pupil, if more eager for fairy tales and old legends and the poetic superstitions of the country than for his more prosaic lessons. Brittany is the very home of myths and legends, and he was fed on these to his heart's content. It was near by Lannion that Arthur held his court and fought the dragon, and here his knights had wandered and fought, and there was scarce a lonely spot the country through on which some Arthurian legend was not founded. Henriette, who was herself of the poetic temperament, enjoyed telling these tales quite as much as little Ernest enjoyed hearing and then repeating them. He knew very well in his boyhood the land of Cameliard,

> "Thick with wet woods, and many a beast therein,
> And none or few to scare or chase the beast;"

and the

> "wolf-like men, worse than the wolves;"

and

> "the heathen horde
> Reddening the sun with smoke and earth with blood;"

and Uther and Merlin, Gorloïs and Bedivere, were familiar names.

As the boy grew older, his first serious grief was the avowed intention of Henriette to become a nun. Pensive by nature, and brought up an ardent Catholic, she seemed to herself to have a true vocation; and Ernest, who was very fond of the Church himself, and very early decided to become a priest, never questioned the desirability of her entering the convent. But he could not part with her, that was all. So the matter was put off from time to time, and in the end abandoned, because Henriette had really become the head of the family and must earn money to supply its wants and to pay her father's debts, which hung like a millstone around her neck. She at first taught a school at Tréguier, and afterwards went up to Paris, where she was governess in a girl's school. Ernest was sent to the priests at the Seminary. They taught him mathematics and Latin, and, as he used to say long afterward, "the love of truth, the respect for reason, the earnestness of life." He was rather a slow lad, and utterly unobservant, but he was recognized as gifted from the first, and his idea of becoming a priest was early encouraged, and became his fixed desire. Nearly all the clever boys in the Seminary were designed for the priesthood, and Ernest was fully persuaded that no other life was beneficent or noble. The little mother was completely in accord with the idea, the sister also.

In the summer of 1838, he carried off all the prizes of the college, and made his mother and sister the happiest of women. Henriette's feelings could not be concealed from her co-workers in the school, and soon the fame of the gifted brother was spread abroad. It finally reached Monsieur Dupanloup, the superior of a Parisian seminary which he had founded. Always on the lookout for talent, this brilliant ecclesiastic conceived the idea of sending for the boy to come to him. He did so; and Ernest, at the age of fifteen, went up to Paris to pursue his studies. He thus describes the event: —

"I was spending the holidays with a friend near Tréguier. On the afternoon of the 4th of September, a messenger came to fetch me in great haste. I remember it all as if it was yesterday! We had a walk of about five miles through the country fields; then, as we came in sight of Tréguier, the pious cadence of the Angelus, pealing in response from parish tower to parish tower, fell through the evening air with an inexpressible calm and melancholy. It was an image of the life I was about to quit forever. On the morrow I left for Paris. All that I saw there was as strange to me as if I had been suddenly projected into the wilds of Tahiti or Timbuctoo."

But into this strangeness soon came Henriette, and the homesick boy was content. But apart from her, he yearned constantly for home and mother-love. The professors were disappointed in him. He had no life, no spirit for his work; he seemed not only dull but unfeeling. But one day the priest, whose duty it was to read the letters sent away by the boys, read one from Ernest to his mother, in which he poured out his whole heart in fervent love and longing, and he showed it to Monsieur Dupanloup, who saw that no mistake had been made, that they had a boy of original genius in the Seminary, however unpromising his present aspect.

From that hour he became the friend, counsellor, and patron of the boy; he cured his homesickness, awakened his ambition, and gave a new charm to his life. The boy had loved the priests at Tréguier; he had loved the life there; he had believed implicitly all he had been taught. He learned after a time to love the priests at St. Nicholas du Chardonnet and the life he led there; but there was a difference, — here he began to think, and whosoever thinks, changes. Here he was first introduced to secular literature, here first heard the names of Michelet, Lamartine, Victor Hugo, his contemporaries, whose renown had not yet reached Brittany. The great world of books opened before him, and its enchantment bewildered him. He knew not where to turn amid such sudden riches. Henriette also read, and she became his guide for a time; for the brother and sister grew, if possible, nearer to each other than ever, in the strangeness of Paris. He had not read very much before he discovered that there were things in life of which he had not been told, that all men did not believe with the good priests, his friends and patrons.

At first he was simply shocked and frightened. After a while he appealed to Henriette. She who had wished to be a nun, to have him a priest, what did she say to him? She too had changed, had read, had grown, and she was not so greatly shocked as he had feared. She said only, "Study and wait." And he studied and waited. He read philosophy as he grew older with the greatest ardor, and thought unceasingly. Henriette too began to read philosophy, and they talked together of Malebranche, Hegel, Kant, and Herder. "I studied the German," he writes, "and I thought I entered a Temple." He had a passionate love of study, and he stopped at nothing. Month by month he waded deeper into the great sea of speculation. And his sister did not linger behind. Even before her brother she questioned the idea of his becoming a priest. She would not have him an insincere one, and she had found that he had an inquiring mind. In this mood of questioning he left the Seminary at Issy and went to the great College of St. Sulpice to take his degree in theology prior to entering the Church. Here he began to study Hebrew, and to develop his taste for Semitic philology. The plan was soon made for him to be a professor of Oriental languages in a Catholic seminary. He was now twenty-two years old, and the world of study seemed to open very fair before him. But he was beset by doubts he could not stifle, and he became more unhappy than he had ever been in his life. His sister was now far away, but their correspondence was incessant. She had gone with a noble Polish family to their own country as governess to their children, and she had promised to

remain with them for ten years. From the gloomy
forests of that savage land she wrote back almost
heartbreaking letters, she was so consumed with
homesickness. But she never thought of giving up
to it. She thought only to earn money to care for
her mother, and to pay her father's debts. Her own
intellectual struggle was now over. Out of the ashes
of her old belief, we are told, "reverently lifted on
to the high places of the soul, there leapt a brighter
flame, a new religion, imprecise, without text or
dogma, and almost wholly moral; a belief in the
vast order of the Universe, speeding through cycles
of time towards some Divine intent, and furthered
in its grand and gracious plan by every private act
of mercy or renouncement, by all the tendency of
effort which makes for righteousness."

From this new standpoint she advised her brother.
She was now strongly against his becoming a priest;
his own strong desire was to become one. It was
the only vocation in life toward which he inclined
with his whole heart. He loved his friends, the
priests, almost passionately; he loved the Church
itself and its ministries. It satisfied his artistic
instincts and his tender sensibility. He thought
he should love the parish work of a priest, had
always thought so. But that was not necessary now.
He could become a great professor, a scholar, an
ecclesiastic — if he would. He had been appointed
already to a professorship in the Archbishop of
Paris's new Carmelite College. From that on, the
way was clear; the Church has always had use for
her men of genius. The struggle was a very sore
one. There was but one thing in his way, — his

conscience. What would he do with that? Being an honest man, he went to his superiors and told them the simple truth. The fathers were deeply astonished and grieved, but they had nothing but kindness for him, as from the beginning.

He went to Stanislas College, which is a Jesuit institution participating in the examinations and other advantages of the lay public schools of Paris. He thought he might honorably teach there, when his position had been made known. But he was very miserable. He wrote to a friend: "There is no more happiness for me on earth. . . . I remember my mother, my little room, my books, my dreams, my quiet walks at my mother's side. . . . All the color seems to have faded out of life." The priests treated him with the utmost friendliness. Monsieur Dupanloup offered him money to live upon. But his sister had already provided him with that. The little governess in the Polish forest meant to count for something in this battle. She knew that her brother still confessed and received absolution; she knew how her brother loved the old ways, and she feared he might go back to what she deemed bondage. But she was mistaken. He at first enjoyed his new work very greatly; but when he was required to wear a cassock and conform in outward things to his ecclesiastical environment, he saw his false position, and went away, still with love in his heart. It was November, 1845, when he began his new work at M. Crouzet's school. It occupied only his evenings, and he had his day for literary work. He made here a lifelong friend in the person of M. Berthelot, who introduced him to the physical and natural sciences. He was astonished and delighted at the new vistas they opened to his vision. He began at that time his passionate worship of the universe, which lasted him all his days. He walked in a new world outwardly as well as in spirit. He felt in every atom of his tingling frame the splendor upon which he gazed, the magnificence of the work of God's hand, upon which the world gazes unmoved. His eyes had been unclosed, and he wished to open the eyes of the whole world. Science had completed what philosophy had begun. No persecution had followed his renouncement of the priesthood. He continued to study, and passed at various times his examinations for his degrees. He was first Bachelier, then Licencié. He was made Fellow of the University, and offered the Professorship of Philosophy at the Lycée of Vendome. He visited his mother for a season, and wrote his thesis on Averroës for his doctor's degree.

But he was not contented away from Paris, and soon returned there. He had been so immersed in study that he had scarcely heard the mutterings of the Revolution. But one day he had to climb a barricade to get to the College of France, which was found full of soldiers. The king and his family went into exile, and civil war again reddened the streets of Paris. The dreamer was awakened at last. One of his letters at this time reads thus: —

"The evening and last night were worse than ever. There was a massacre at the Gate of St. Jacques, another at the Fontainebleau Gate; I spare you details. The St. Bartholomew offers nothing like them. There must be in human nature something naturally cannibal which bursts out at certain moments. As for me, I would willingly have fought with the Garde Nationale, until, in their turn, the guards became murderers. No doubt they are guilty, these poor mad insurrectionaries, who shed their blood and know not what they ask ; but are they not guiltier who by system have deadened in them every human feeling?"

Again he writes : —

" Horror of exact reprisals. I am always for the massacred, even though they be guilty. The National Guard has been guilty of atrocities I scarcely dare recount. After the battle was over, posted on the terrace of the École des Mines, they amused themselves by 'potting' at their leisure, as a form of recreation, the passers-by in the adjacent streets, where the thoroughfare was still open. That may have been the last flicker of the fury of the fray. But what is awful to think of, is the hecatomb of prisoners sacrificed several days later. During whole afternoons I have heard the ceaseless firing in the Luxembourg Gardens — and yet the fighting was over. The sound and the thoughts it suggested exasperated me to such a degree that I determined to see for myself, so I went and called on one of my friends whose windows overlook the gardens. It was too true. If I did not see the murderers with my own eyes, I saw what was worse, what I never can forget, and what, if I did not try to lift myself above personal sentiments, would leave in my soul an everlasting hate. . . . The unhappy prisoners were packed in the garrets of the Palace under the leads, in the stifling heat of the roof. Every now and then one of them would thrust his head out of the dormer window for a breath of air. Every head served as a target for the soldiers in the gardens below ; they never missed their aim ! After that, I say the middle class is capable of the massacres of the Terror."

A young man of the nature of Renan could not witness scenes like these without being profoundly stirred, and fired with the desire to add his mite to the solution of the problems involved in the Revolution of 1848. It was a bulky sermon, called "L'Avenir de la Science." Science he believed to be the new religion which alone could answer the questions which were agitating the heart of the world. Science would reconstitute the states on new lines; science would reform the degraded lives of men. Ten years later Darwin, in the "Origin of Species," gave the precise data upon which what were considered the visionary conclusions of a young enthusiast could be based. Now many things which Renan said in 1848 are the merest commonplaces.

The next year he went to Rome, and found a new world once more, — the world of art. The visions of science had enraptured him, now the visions of art cast a new spell over him. Art was to remain one of the permanent interests of his life. The ten years of Henriette's exile were now finished, and she returned to Paris, and took charge of the little home Ernest was able to offer her. He had written to her: "We shall be so happy, dear! I am easy-tempered and gentle. You will let me lead the serious, simple life I love, and I will tell you all I think and all I feel. We shall have our friends, too, — refined and elect spirits, — who will beautify our life." And his prophecy became true. They loved each other, and they were happy together. She helped him much in his literary labors, besides attending to domestic affairs, and she sympathized with every movement of his mind and heart. She was a sharp critic also, and always held him to his best. His style of writing was materially improved under her supervision. He had by this time become a writer for the " Revue des Deux Mondes " and to the " Débats," and gained many surpassing excellences of workmanship. These reviews did not remain long uncollected, and when given to the world in book form, as " Études d'Histoire Religieuse," placed him in the front rank of modern French writers. A second volume followed almost immediately, the " Essais de Morale et de Critique." His next book was the " General History of Semitic Languages." This, which had unpublished won him the Volney prize, several years before, now opened to him the doors of the Institute. Soon after he was elected a member of the Academy of Inscriptions and Belles Lettres. The repression which followed 1848 was very severely felt by journalism. The papers were placed under all sorts of restraint, and scarcely dared represent Liberalism openly. But Renan continued to hold up an austere ideal, and to belittle as much as he dared the material good, upon which the Empire laid such stress. " No good," cried he. " What material progress can compensate a moral decadence? Will a steam-traction engine make a man happy? Will a Universal Exhibition make him nobler or better? In taking the triumphs of mechanical ingenuity for the sign of an advanced civilization, you mistake the mere accident for the essential." So he continued to cry throughout the fifties, while they were rebuilding Paris.

Among his friends at this period of his life was Ary Scheffer, and after a while the ladies of his

family. Renan was a singularly unattractive man
in personal appearance. He was small, had heavy
sloping shoulders, a very large head, and heavy
jaws. The eyes and smile were sweet and helped
to redeem the face. He was also awkward, silent,
except at excited intervals, and reserved. But he
had a charming gentleness, and with those he loved
a tender way, which was winning. He had known
very few ladies when he first met Camélie Scheffer,
the Dutch painter's niece, but he fell in love with
her, and she reciprocated his affection. Previous
to this, Henriette, who feared she was selfishly
keeping her brother from the blessings of family
life, had proposed to him a suitable marriage; but
he had refused to consider it, and had gone on in
apparent content. She had now become accustomed to have him to herself, and she was bitterly
opposed to the marriage he proposed. This caused
him intense pain and a great struggle in his heart
between love and what he regarded as duty. In
the duel between these two love went down, and
he bade farewell to the young girl whose love he
had won, with the greatest solemnity and sorrow.
Then he told his sister what he had done, and she
became so conscience-stricken that she went to his
betrothed and entreated her to take him back. She
promised, and all was well again. Their marriage
soon took place, and it was a happy one despite
Henriette, who regarded the wife somewhat jeal-
ously, and loved too well to hold the reins of authority. But the new sisters loved each other sincerely,
and united in worshipping Ernest. Soon there was
a son in the house, and this united the women more

completely. Then came little Ernestine, who lived but a few months, but bound them all together with a sacred bond. Madame Renan had joined the family circle by this time, and her son, who had always been passionately fond of her, regarded his happiness as complete. The evening hour which he spent with her, and when she talked with him of Tréguier and Lannion, was one of the happiest of his day.

In 1860 the Emperor, despite Renan's Liberalism, offered to send him on an archæological expedition to Phenicia. He immediately accepted, and looked forward with delight to the change of scene. Henriette was to accompany him as secretary. They went out on a vessel which carried a division of French troops to Syria. Just previous to their departure, a massacre of Christians had taken place at Mount Lebanon, and Napoleon was sending out troops to protect the Maronites. They landed at Beyrout, and Renan began his excavations at Byblos. The brother and sister entered upon their work with singular enthusiasm. Henriette could spend ten hours a day on horseback, and both seemed to renew their youth. The East had always had a fascination for Renan, and now he was face to face with her mysteries and her charms. The autumn was beautiful. He dreamed over the dreams of his youth amid the flower-strewn plains, the leaping brooks, and the mountains which encircled all. Just over their blue tops was Palestine, whither he should soon go and see the sacred places whose names had been household words to him so long. He should follow in the very footsteps of that Jesus to whom he had devoted his young life.

Bethany and Galilee and Jerusalem would deliver up
to him their secrets. Even in Gethsemane he might
stand, and on Calvary. His head swam and his
heart was hot within him. In January Madame
Ernest Renan came out to join them, and in the
spring they at last went to Palestine. Renan had
long ago conceived the idea of writing a " Life of
Jesus," one of a series on "The Origins of Christianity," and here the project took on a tangible
form. He read constantly the New Testament,
and felt its charm more than ever, in this new
environment. Jesus seemed ever with him, whether
he waked or slept, whether he meditated or was
actively engaged; and every spot he visited became
engraved upon his memory, so that he recalled it
minutely afterward. All the glowing pictures which
he soon painted in words, were impressed upon his
mind in these few months of impassioned observation. In May the heat became unbearable, and they
started back to Beyrout. The fever attacked nearly
every member of the expedition, but at first the
Renans were excepted. In July Madame Renan
returned to France. Ernest and Henriette fled to
the hills. At Ghazir they took a little house, and
he began to write "The Life of Jesus." He had
no books, but that was all the better. The East
was spread open before him, a living book, and from
his mountain-top he looked over the sacred country
spread out before him like a scroll. Through the
long hours of the day he labored, and when evening
came, he sat with his sister under the alien skies and
gazed up at the strange stars, telling her of his work,
and filling her heart with joy by his appreciation of

her labors in his behalf and of her society. Once more she had him all to herself. It was doubtless the happiest period of her life. When the book was nearly finished they were obliged to return to Beyrout. Henriette had been afflicted with neuralgia ever since she arrived in Syria, and of late the pains had been cruel and protracted. She was not well, but she was brave and determined. For some reason their ship was delayed a week, and they went to Byblos to see to the shipping of some sarcophagi. They rested at the little village of Amschit, where they had spent the first weeks after their arrival. Here Henriette was taken ill with fever aggravated by neuralgic pains. In a day or two her brother was also down with the same fever. The surgeon of the ship did not understand the terrible malaria of the Syrian coast, and apprehended no danger. But one evening when he arrived, he found both his patients apparently dead, laid out on the floor, watched over by their manservant. Henriette never recovered consciousness. Her brother woke from his long swoon about an hour before she died; but he was too ill to realize what had befallen him. When he did realize, he was out at sea, and Henriette was sleeping under the palms of Amschit. "The Life of Jesus" was finished without her, but finished religiously as he thought she would have liked it. She influenced him even more after her death than she had done throughout her life. He writes: —

"The loss of my brave companion attached me closer than ever to the studies which had cost so dear. . . . I have looked death in the face. The pygmy cares which eat

our lives away are henceforth meaningless to me. I have
brought back from the threshold of the infinite a livelier
faith than I ever knew in the superior reality of the world
of the Ideal. . . . The older I grow the dearer I have at
heart the one problem which ever keeps its profound significance, its enchanting novelty. The Infinite surrounds
us, overlaps us, haunts us. Bubbles on the surface of existence, we feel a mysterious kinship with our Father the
Abyss. God is revealed by no miracle, but in our hearts,
whence, as St. Paul has said, an unutterable moaning goes
up to him without ceasing. And this sentiment of our
obscure relationship to the universe, of our Divine descend-
ance, graven in fire in every human heart, is the source of
all virtue, the reason we love, and the one thing that makes
our life worth living. Jesus is in my eyes the greatest of men,
because he developed this dim feeling with an unprece-
dented, an unsurpassable power. His religion holds the
secret of the future. . . . To transport religion beyond the
supernatural, to separate the ever-triumphant cause of Faith
from the forlorn hope of the Miraculous, is to render a service to them that believe. Religion is necessary, as eternal
as poetry or love ; Religion will survive the destruction of
all her illusions. I say it with confidence : the day will come
when I shall have the sympathy of really religious souls."

Soon after his return to Paris he received the
long-delayed appointment of Professor of Hebrew at
the College of France. The Catholics were unitedly
opposed to this appointment, and had been able to
delay it thus long; the students of the Latin Quarter,
his most violent friends, were indignant that he
should accept it from the Emperor. So there was a
stormy time expected at his opening lecture; and
that expectation was fulfilled. Excited by opposition, he went a little beyond the moderate bounds

he had proposed to himself, and the tumult almost amounted to a riot.   Upon the fact that his lecture had disturbed the cause of public order was based the excuse for suspending the new professor from his functions.   He was afterward officially removed, it was supposed through the influence of the party of the Empress.

"The Life of Jesus" appeared the last of June, 1863.   Before November sixty thousand copies were sold.   It was a magnificent success for that day; but it was accompanied by a perfect storm of harsh criticism and partisan abuse.   The beauty of its style, the mildness of its spirit, its literary charm, were admitted, but the believers in Christianity could not forgive its leading proposition.   The incomparable *man* was not their Jesus, their Lord. The other six books in the series of "Origins of Christianity" were met in the same spirit.   His partisans were wildly enthusiastic over them, the Church consistent in its opposition.   "The Apostles" and "St. Paul" were as successful as the "Life of Jesus;" "The Antichrist" perhaps a little less so, though it contains some of the most brilliant writing of the series.

During the excited period preceding the Franco-Prussian war, the Liberal opposition asked Renan to stand for Meaux.   He felt it his duty to do so, and he was defeated.   He had always loved Germany next to France, and he passionately deplored a war which to his mind seemed a war between brethren.   But no words of warning could avail when madmen were at the helm.   France was destined to drain to the very lees the bitter cup of disappointment and humiliation; and he was destined to feel to the uttermost every iota of her sorrow and her shame. Exposed to the long agony of the siege, unpopular through his early opposition to the war, in danger from violent factions as well as from the enemy at large, he came out of the dreadful contest a changed, almost an embittered, man. He had lost faith in the people. After the Commune he could not believe that the ideal state would be attained through Democracy. For the moment he believed in the government of the Élite. Give over the masses, find your strong and wise men and let them govern the country. But how to find them? The old question did not fail to harry him, and a sad and cynical philosopher retired from the contemplation of public life, and resumed his studies. In his " Philosophic Dialogues " he now elaborated his doctrine of the Élite. He was valiantly met by the Church, whose ideal is the good of the masses, and who felt the impracticability of his schemes. His next works, " The Christian Church " and " Marcus Aurelius," showed him again reconciled to Democracy, and full of faith in the progress of the world. His despair was but a passing mood born of overwhelming grief and dismay; and in writing of the Church much of his old love and tenderness returned, and he felt all the appealing charm of the faith which had once been his own.

When nearly sixty years old, he wrote the " Souvenirs d'Enfance et de Jeunesse," one of the most charming of his many books. It was hardly a biography, but it was a looking back on his life from the standpoint of age, and rediscovering all the charms of youth. He took the world into his confidence, and the world appreciated the honor. None of his books had been received with greater popular acclamations. His egotism was so frank and childlike that it had a charm for the learned as well as the simple, and all classes could unite almost for the first time in enjoying his matchless prose. Then followed the "History of Israel," a history of the religious Idea, read almost exclusively by scholars. Renan did not live to see the publication of the two concluding volumes, the last of which appeared in 1891. He had not been well for several years, but had continued to labor at this last great work, spite of the neuralgia which tortured him for months. He loved life and remained cheerful to the last. His wife and children and grandchildren were with him, and hosts of devoted friends. He had completed his task, he had loved, he had thought, he had done. Perplexed in faith, but pure in deeds, he had beat his music out, and

> " Power was with him in the night,
>   Which makes the darkness and the light,
>   And dwells not in the light alone ;

> " But in the darkness and the cloud,
>   As over Sinai's peaks of old,
>   While Israel made their gods of gold,
>   Altho' the trumpet blew so loud."

With a sentence of his own we may fittingly close this paper : —

" He, at least, is not wholly mistaken who fears lest he be in the wrong and treats no one as blind ; who, ignoring the goal of man, loves him as he strives, him and his work ; who seeks the Truth in doubting of heart, and who says to his opponent: ' Perchance seest thou clearer than I.' He, in fine, who accords his fellows the wide liberty he takes for himself, — he surely may sleep in peace and await the judgment of all things, if such a judgment there shall be."

CHARLES DARWIN.

CHARLES DARWIN came of a family of yeomen who had lived for many generations in Lincolnshire, close to Yorkshire. His father and grandfather were doctors, and practised medicine throughout their long and useful lives. His father, Charles always considered a remarkable man, and he writes at some length about him in his "Recollections." This Dr. Darwin, although a very successful practitioner, at first hated his profession so much that he afterward declared that had he been assured of the merest pittance in any other line of work, he would never have practised medicine for a day. To the end of his life, the thought of an operation sickened him. He was vehement against drinking, and was convinced of both the direct and inherited evil effects of alcohol when habitually taken, even in moderate quantity, an opinion in which he was much in advance of his time, and one in which his son afterward came to share. Dr. Darwin's "mind was not scientific, and he did not try to generalize his knowledge under general laws." His son did not think that he gained much from him intellectually, but that all his children were much indebted to him morally. Charles was born in 1809, and was one of six children. Of these brothers and sisters, we hear most of the eldest, Erasmus, who died un-

CHARLES DARWIN.

married at the age of seventy-seven. The picture painted of him by Charles in his Autobiography is a very pleasant one; and there is also a fine sketch of him in "Carlyle's Reminiscences." Carlyle preferred Erasmus to Charles for intellect, and Mrs. Carlyle was exceedingly fond of him. Charles, in speaking of him, says: "Our minds and tastes were so different, however, that I do not think I owe much to him intellectually. I am inclined to agree with Francis Galton in believing that education and environment produce only a small effect on the mind of any one, and that most of our qualities are innate."

Mrs. Darwin died when Charles was eight years old, and he was sent at once to a school, where he stayed a year. At that time his taste for natural history and his passion for collecting were already well developed, and he thinks were clearly innate, as none of his brothers or sisters ever showed any fondness for these things. He had also at this time quite a passion "for inventing deliberate falsehoods for the sake of causing excitement." By the example and instruction of his sisters he was humane as a boy, even in collecting his much prized specimens, and he remembered even to his old age the one exception to this rule, when he beat a puppy, and "remembered the exact spot where the crime was committed." He had a passion for angling when a boy, and for shooting as he grew older. For many years, when he was a young man, he took the greatest delight in hunting, and it is characteristic of the man that he finally gave it up because one day, after he had been shooting the previous day, he found a bird on the ground — not yet dead — which he had shot. The cruelty of the sport which could cause such innocent suffering as this, seemed so wicked to his mind that he resolved to forego it altogether, and did so.

As a boy, he had almost no home life. Until he was sixteen years old he was left at a school in Shrewsbury, which, to be sure, was only a mile from home; and he "often ran there in the longer intervals between the callings-over and before locking up at night." The school was a strictly classical one, and Darwin always felt as if his time was thrown away there, as he had no taste whatever for the study of language. He was a favorite among the boys, and deeply attached to some of them. He engaged much in collecting minerals at this time, and a little later was fascinated by beetles. He was fond of general reading also, especially of Shakespeare; and he read other poetry, such as Thomson's "Seasons," and Byron and Scott. In 1825 he was sent to Edinburgh University, where he remained two years engaged in the study of medicine. The operations which he was forced to see (before the days of chloroform) were so distressing to him that he says they fairly haunted him for many years. He had no liking for medicine, but got in with several young men here who had tastes for natural history, and liked them much, and learned something from them. He considered in after life that his time was thrown away at Edinburgh the same as at school, and even the three years he afterward spent at Cambridge he deemed very badly spent indeed. Mathematics and the classics were the all in all at that time everywhere in England, and although he had some lectures on Geology and Zoölogy at Edinburgh, he found them "incredibly dull." At Cambridge he got in for a while with a sporting set, from his great fondness for hunting and riding, and the little interest he took in his studies. He afterward regretted very much the time thus wasted, as he placed in later years the utmost value upon every moment of his time. It seems strange to us now that with the decided bent he showed for natural science he should not have had opportunities for such study as he would have delighted in, and that he should not have been released from the traditional construing and verse-making. But even as strong a man as Dr. Darwin appears to have been, did not dare to break away from the conventions of his day, and lay out an original course for his son, and so, much precious time was lost before he entered upon his real life-work. Before going to Cambridge it had been decided that he should enter the Church, so great was his disinclination to practise medicine. In order to do so, he must take a degree, and he seems to have studied just enough to accomplish his object, and in a merely perfunctory manner. Paley's "Evidences of Christianity" and his "Moral Philosophy" were the only studies which gave him any pleasure. The logic of these books delighted him; and as he did not at all trouble himself about the premises, he easily accepted the results of the line of argumentation. At this time he seems to have had no hesitation about taking holy orders on the grounds of disbelief; and even when he did begin to hesitate, it was on the ground that he could not conscientiously affirm that he thought he had been inwardly moved by the Holy Spirit. This was about the time when he says he did not in the least doubt the literal truth of every word in the Bible, and he thought the Creed of the Church arose quite naturally from the teachings of the Scriptures. The intention of becoming a clergyman was never formally given up; even when he went on board the Beagle as naturalist, he expected to return in due time and take orders. But that voyage was really the turning-point in his life, and determined his career. It came about in this way.

While quite undecided as to his future, and engaged only in some passing geological studies and explorations, he was informed by Professor Hunslow "that Captain Fitz-Roy was willing to give up a part of his own cabin to any young man who would volunteer to go with him without pay as naturalist to the voyage of the Beagle." Delighted beyond measure at the prospect of the adventurous voyage, and not considering very seriously the length of time the voyage might occupy, or the bearing the loss of this time might have on all his future life, he would instantly have accepted the offer but for his father, who strongly objected. But his uncle supported him in his desire to go, and his father had great respect for his brother's opinions. So the eager young naturalist was finally allowed to go up to London to see Captain Fitz-Roy, who came very near to rejecting him on account of the shape of his nose. He was an ardent disciple of Lavater, and doubted whether any one with a nose like Darwin's could have sufficient energy and determination for the voyage. But he was finally persuaded to

overlook the nose, and never regretted his decision.
He was a man of rather singular character, made
up of many conflicting elements; bold, generous, of
remarkable energy, and ardently devoted to his
friends, yet possessed of a temper which made it
difficult for any one to live with him without great
annoyance, and even serious difficulty. To share
his cabin for five years was not a light matter, as
Darwin speedily found out. They had several quar-
rels, one of which Darwin describes: —

" Early in the voyage at Bahia in Brazil, he defended and
praised slavery, which I abominated, and told me that he
had just visited a great slave-owner who had called up many
of his slaves and asked them whether they were happy and
whether they wished to be free, and all answered ' No.'
I then asked him. perhaps with a sneer. whether he thought
that the answer of slaves in the presence of their master was
worth anything? This made him excessively angry, and he
said that as I doubted his word we could no longer live
together. I thought that I should have been compelled to
leave the ship ; but as soon as the news spread, which it did
quickly, as the captain sent for the first lieutenant to assuage
his anger by abusing me, I was deeply gratified by receiving
an invitation from all the gun-room officers to mess with
them. But after a few hours Fitz-Roy showed his usual
magnanimity by sending an officer to me with an apology
and a request that I would continue to live with him."

Before the end of the voyage these two men became warmly attached to each other, and Darwin
writes that Fitz-Roy's character was in some
respects one of the most noble he had ever known.
Darwin's duties on board the Beagle were at first
somewhat indefinite, but gradually settled them-

selves to his satisfaction. He had brought with
him Lyell's "Principles of Geology," and was at
first a most enthusiastic geologist, considering Lyell
as his master and following his method. Soon, however, he began collecting animals of all classes,
briefly describing and roughly dissecting many of
them. His lack of a knowledge of drawing was a
serious difficulty in his work, and he continued to
feel this throughout life. He wrote every day in
his journal, describing carefully and vividly what he
saw.   In his Autobiography he writes : —

"The glories of the vegetation of the Tropics rise before
my mind at the present time more vividly than anything
else ; though the sense of sublimity which the great deserts
of Patagonia and the forest-clad mountains of Tierra del
Fuego excited in me, has left an indelible impression on my
mind.   The sight of a naked savage in his native land is an
event which can never be forgotten. Many of my excursions on horseback through wild countries, or in the boats,
some of which lasted several weeks, were deeply interesting : their discomfort and some degree of danger were at
that time hardly a drawback, and none at all afterwards. I
also reflect with high satisfaction on some of my scientific
work, such as solving the problem of coral islands, and
making out the geological structure of certain islands, for
instance, St. Helena. Nor must I pass over the discovery
of the singular relations of the animals and plants inhabiting
the several islands of the Galipagos archipelago, and of all of
them to the inhabitants of South America.

" As far as I can judge of myself, I worked to the utmost
during the voyage from the mere pleasure of investigation,
and from my strong desire to add a few facts to the great
mass of facts in Natural Science. But I was ambitious to
take a fair place among scientific men, — whether more am-

bitious or less so than most of my fellow-workers I can form no opinion."

His first real conception of what his life-work was to be came to him one day while resting beneath a low cliff of lava, with the sun glaring hot, a few strange desert plants growing near, and with living corals in the tidal pools at his feet. Here he first thought of writing a book about the geology of the various countries visited, and he says it gave him a thrill of real delight. Later in the voyage the suggestion was made by Fitz-Roy that the journal would make a valuable book, and he began to plan for that also. These new hopes and plans enlivened the tedium of the latter part of the long voyage, which had grown almost intolerable to Darwin. He was very much afflicted with sea-sickness during much of the time he was afloat. "It is a lucky thing for me that the voyage is drawing to its close, for I positively suffer more from sea-sickness now than three years ago," he wrote in June, 1836, and there is much testimony to the fact of his serious affliction in this way, by officers and companions. He was also impatient to be at his work, and to see his family, from whom he felt his separation more and more. As the time of his release drew near, he wrote: —

"It is too delightful to think that I shall see the leaves fall and hear the robins sing next autumn in Shrewsbury. My feelings are those of a schoolboy to the smallest point; I doubt whether ever boy longed for his holydays as much as I do to see you all again. I am at present, although nearly half the world is between me and home, beginning to arrange what I shall do, where I shall go during the first week."

In October, 1836, he reached home after an absence of five years, the most memorable of his life. These years determined his whole future, and laid the foundations of his fame. He had found his life-work, and he never wavered for a moment in its pursuit afterward. Scientific research became the aim and object of his life from this time on, as well as its joy and pride. Nothing was allowed to interfere with it, nothing else gave him such pleasure. It determined his friends and associates, his residence, and his habits. He would have found his work and have done it in any event, but the voyage of the Beagle led him to it while young and full of energy and enthusiasm, and held him to it steadily and inexorably during several years of his life, and its importance to him cannot be overestimated.

In 1839 his "Journal of Researches" was published as part of Fitz-Roy's work. A new edition was published in 1845, and became a very popular book. He says: "The success of this, my first literary child, always tickles my vanity more than that of any of my other books. Even to this day it sells steadily in England and the United States, and has been translated for the second time into German, and into French and other languages." In the year 1844 his observations on the volcanic islands visited during his voyage was published. In 1846 his "Geological Observations on South America" appeared. Four and a half years' work was given to his three Geological works, including his "Coral Reefs." In the same year he began his exhaustive study of the Cirripedia. He continued to work upon this for eight years, though he lost much time from illness. Two large volumes were ultimately published on the known living species, and two small ones on the extinct species. He had some doubts about the propriety of spending so much time on this work, but was reassured by his friends, and indeed recognized himself the valuable training it had given him, both in observation and in expression. Sir J. D. Hooker, always one of his most valued friends, writes to Darwin's son of the matter in these words: —

"Your father recognized three stages in his career as a biologist: the mere collector at Cambridge; the collector and observer in the Beagle and for some years afterwards; and the trained naturalist after, and only after, the Cirripede work. That he was a thinker all along is true enough, and there is a vast deal in his writings previous to the Cirripedes that a trained naturalist could but emulate. . . . "

Professor Huxley says of it: "In my opinion your sagacious father never did a wiser thing than when he devoted himself to the years of patient toil which the Cirripede-book cost him." During the progress of the book his letters were filled with it. Indeed it seemed to completely occupy his mind. In 1849 he writes to Lyell: —

" I work now every day at the Cirripedia for 2½ hours, and so get on a little, but very slowly. I sometimes, after a whole week employed and having described perhaps only two species, agree mentally with Lord Stanhope, that it is all fiddle-faddle; however, the other day I got a curious case of a unisexual instead of hermaphrodite cirripede, in which the female had the common cirripedal character, and in two valves of her shell had two little pockets, in *each* of which she kept a little husband ; I do not know of any other case where a female invariably has two husbands. I have one still odder fact, common to several species ; namely, that though they are hermaphrodite, they have small additional, or, as I shall call them, complemental males ; one specimen itself hermaphrodite had no less than *seven* of these complemental males attached to it. Truly the schemes and wonders of Nature are illimitable."

During this long preliminary work the first dawning in his mind of the great theory of evolution took place. In writing to J. D. Hooker, in 1844, he probably mentioned it for the first time. He says: "At last gleams of light have come, and I am almost convinced (quite contrary to the opinion I started with) that species are not (it is like confessing a murder) immutable." In 1845 he writes to L. Jenyns: "The general conclusion to which I have slowly been driven from a directly opposite conviction, is that species are mutable, and that allied species are co-descendants from common stocks. . . . I shall not publish on this subject for several years." He in time drew up a sketch of his new doctrine, if such it could be called, of about two hundred pages; and also began to mention his audacious new theories to his most trusted scientific friends, and to beg for their opinion of them. He wrote to one of these: "I am a bold man to lay myself open to being thought a complete fool, and a most deliberate one." But his own convictions were strengthened by his attempted statement of them, and by the arguments he had with friends, and his tone grew more confident as opposition strengthened. In 1856 he began writing out his views on a large scale. But at this moment he received from Mr. A. R. Wallace, who was then in the Malay Archipelago, an essay which contained almost exactly the same ideas which he was trying to embody. The consequence was that, by the advice of his scientific friends, he permitted an abstract of his own views to be published at the same time with Mr. Wallace's Essay. Neither attracted much attention, which was rather mortifying to both writers. The only prominent reviewer ended his essay with the conclusion that "all that was new in them was false, and what was true was old." In 1858 he began the "Origin of Species," and it was published in 1859. It was a decided success. The first edition went off in a day, and the second almost immediately. It was an epoch-making book, and was recognized as such from the first day of publication. During the twenty years that he had been considering his subject he had anticipated almost every objection which would be made to his views, and answered it. Every fact which came under his observation which told against his theory had been written down and studiously considered, and usually discussed with one or more friends. The size of the book was a factor in its success, no doubt. Had he written at the length which he at first proposed to himself, very few people would have read his book, even scientists would have shrunk from it appalled. The training of the eight years wasted, as some thought, on the Cirripedia, counted for much in this later work, the crowning one of his life. The immense amount of labor that had been expended upon it will never be fully realized by the reading world. Material sufficient for a work five or six times as large as the one that finally appeared had been collected, every fact most laboriously verified, and much time spent in preparing it for the press in that shape. His correspondence upon the subject with scientific men alone had been a vast labor, and his original experiments almost the work of a lifetime. He writes to a friend during the progress of his book: "I am like Crœsus, overwhelmed with my riches in facts." And in regard to style, he writes to Hooker: "Thank you for telling me about obscurity of style. But on my life no nigger with lash over him could have worked harder at clearness than I have done. But the very difficulty, to me, of itself leads to the probability that I fail." How very weary he got before it was finished he intimates thus: "I fear that my book will not deserve at all the pleasant things you say about it; but, Good Lord, how I do long to have done with it!" While reading the proofs, he was completely prostrated for a time, and wrote to Hooker: "I had great prostration of mind and body, but entire rest, and the douche, and ' Adam Bede,' have together done me a world of good." He wrote to his publisher at this time of weariness and discouragement:—

"I get on very slowly with proofs. I remember writing to you that I thought there would be not much correction. I honestly wrote what I thought, but was most grievously mistaken. I find the style incredibly bad, and most difficult to make clear and smooth. I am extremely sorry to say on account of expense, and loss of time for me, that the corrections are heavy, as heavy as possible. But from casual glances, I still hope that later chapters are not so badly written. How I could have written so badly is quite inconceivable, but I suppose it was owing to my whole attention being fixed on the general line of argument, and not on details. All I can say is that I am very sorry."

To Lyell he writes also at this trying time: "I have tried my best to make it clear and striking, but very much fear I have failed, — so many discussions are and must be very perplexing. I have done my best. If you had all my materials, I am sure you would have made a splendid book. I long to finish, for I am nearly worn out." Again to Hooker: "I had a terribly long fit of sickness yesterday, which makes the world rather extra gloomy to-day, but I have an insanely strong wish to finish my accursed book, such corrections every page has required as I never saw before." After the work was fairly launched, his interest was intense in what the scientific world would think of it, and particularly the few men whose opinion he valued most highly. Their verdict he thought would make or mar the success of his book, and, more important far than that, the acceptance of his opinions. To Lyell he wrote: —

"You once gave me intense pleasure, or rather delight, by the way you were interested, in a manner I never expected, in my Coral Reef notions, and now you have again given me similar pleasure by the manner you have noticed my species work. Nothing could be more satisfactory to me, and I thank you for myself, and even more for the subject's sake, as I know well that the sentence will make many fairly consider the subject, instead of ridiculing it. Although your previously felt doubts on the immutability of species may have more influence in converting you (if you be converted) than my book, yet as I regard your verdict as far more important in my own eyes, and I believe in the eyes of the world, than of any other dozen men, I am naturally very anxious about it."

To Huxley he writes, October 15, 1859: —

" I am here [at Ilkley] hydropathizing and coming to life again, after having finished my accursed book, which would have been easy work to any one else, but half killed me. . . . I shall be *intensely* curious to hear what effect the book produces on you. I know that there will be much in it which you will object to, and I do not doubt many errors. I am far from expecting to convert you to many of my heresies ; but if, on the whole, you and two or three others think I am on the right road, I shall not care what the mob of naturalists think. The penultimate chapter, though I believe it includes the truth, will, I much fear, make you savage. Do not act and say, like Macleary versus Fleming, ' I write with aqua fortis to bite into brass.' "

Lyell was soon ranked as a supporter of Darwin, though he entered some exceptions. Hooker became a vigorous adherent, Sir John Lubbock an influential friend, and Huxley a brilliant advocate. Asa Gray fought the battle in the United States, at first almost alone. Among the most powerful critics of the book and of the theory of evolution, were numbered Agassiz, Murray the entomologist, Harvey, a noted botanist, and many writers of unsigned articles in the Reviews. But the advances of the doctrine of evolution from that time on are known of all the world, and do not need further elucidation in this brief sketch. Nor shall we dwell at length upon the various books afterward published by Mr. Darwin.

Among them were "The Movements and Habits of Climbing Plants," in 1875; "The Variation of Animals and Plants under Domestication," in 1868; "The Descent of Man, and Selection in Relation to Sex," in 1871; the "Expression of the Emotions in Man and Animals," in 1872. Several other volumes, and many papers upon important subjects were issued from time to time. But we pass from this hurried account of the production of his chief works, to a condensed glance at the chief features of his life, and his personal characteristics.

After Darwin's return from the voyage of the Beagle, he settled down in London, where he lived nearly four years. He was married in 1839 to his cousin, Emma Wedgewood, and in 1842 removed to the country, where he resided until the time of his death. The life of the family after they were settled at Down, was one of the quietest possible. Here the children were born, and here the great books were written, and here came an occasional visitor in the person of some distinguished man of science; but usually the family life was as quiet and uneventful as any of which we can possibly conceive, in the heart of a populous district, and in a family of wealth and position. Darwin owed it to the fortune left him by his father, that he was never obliged to work for money, and could live the life of a man of leisure, giving all his time to his scientific work. It is one of the surprises of the story of his life to discover that the great naturalist was so much of an invalid. So great were his achievements in science, so great the mere physical labor of his researches and his writings, that one can scarcely imagine him as otherwise than strong and well. But he had much sickness to contend with, after his return from the famous voyage, sometimes losing months at a time in this manner; and even when he was nominally well, suffering greatly from weakness, lack of sleep, and many painful ailments. He bore his illness with such uncomplaining patience that his friends hardly realized what he suffered habitually. His son writes that "for nearly forty years he never knew one day of the health of ordinary men, and thus his life was one long struggle against the weariness and strain of sickness."

The deep devotion and unwearied care of his wife alone made his existence endurable. She gave up her whole life to this care, and thus enabled him to do the great work which he did, oftentimes through the greatest suffering, but always with a brave heart. One by one the great books were written, and his fame grew until it spread through the earth; but the same quiet life went on at Down, and there was no change in this to the last. All but one of his children lived to maturity, and no evil fortune ever assailed him, so that in spite of ill-health his life was calm and happy throughout, filled to the brim with love and reverence and kindliness. No evil word was ever spoken of him, but all who ever knew him dwell upon his kindness and his tenderness. Many anecdotes are told in his "Life and Letters" of the affectionateness of his nature, of his gentleness and generosity, which make us love the man as much for what he was as we admire him for what he did. His relationship to the village people was always one of paternal kindness, and he was much beloved by them. He founded for them a Friendly Club when he first settled among them, and remained connected with it for thirty years; and he gave them kindly advice and assistance whenever it was possible to do so. To his children he was the kindest and most indulgent of friends, and lived in the sweetest intimacy with them all. In serving a friend, he gave generously of his time and strength, and he had the faculty of attaching these friends very warmly to him. Of Mr. Huxley he was especially fond, and often employed the expression, " What splendid fun Huxley is! " in speaking of him. Of Sir Joseph Hooker he writes, " I have known hardly any man more lovable than Hooker." He was very fond of rallying his friends, and very charming when doing so, his spirits rising to the greatest heights, and he becoming really boyish in his manner. He was also very delightful in his intercourse with women, having so much of gentleness and deference in his manner, and yet being so amusing and jovial. As he grew older, it grieved him that he could not feel quite the enthusiasm of his youth for his friends, but he retained all the old loyalty and helpfulness, and never lost one from the number of his real friends throughout life, unless by death. He was not fond of meeting strangers, and his manner toward them was rather formal, though always polite.

He had no respect for books as such, and would cut a big volume in two, for convenience in handling, or tear out the leaves he required for reference, in the most heartless manner, causing a real lover of books a shudder to behold. His library from this cause presented a very remarkable appearance. But he had great respect for authors, and generous praise for those who interested him. In later life he entirely lost his taste for poetry, and said he could not read a page of Shakespeare, it had grown so intolerably dull. He much regretted this change in his mind, and said that his taste for fine scenery was the only one of the higher tastes which he retained, and even that had become dulled. He was fond of music when young, but had absolutely no ear for it. In later life music set him to thinking too intently, and his struggle had come to be, to cease thinking long enough to procure the necessary sleep. He was exceedingly fond of novels, and, like Macaulay, liked poor ones almost as well as good. Those of Walter Scott, Miss Austen, and Mrs. Gaskell were great favorites, and were read and reread with the greatest pleasure. He could not read a story with a tragical end without great discomfort, and said that writing a novel with a bad ending ought to be made a capital offence. He took the keenest interest in the plot of a book, and would never allow any one to give a hint as to its ending. He was also fond of books of travel, and of essays and other light literature. When young, he was fond of art, particularly of engravings, but used in later life to laugh at his own ignorance, and amuse himself much in telling how Ruskin asked for his opinion on certain pictures. He claimed that he could see absolutely nothing which Ruskin saw in his "Turners." Of nicety of touch he had a great admiration, and grew very enthusiastic over fine dissections, always lamenting his own clumsiness in this department, which he doubtless exaggerated, as he must have done some good work in this line in earlier life. He bestowed great praise upon the illustrations of his books, which were done by his children, — sometimes exclaiming over a clever bit, " Michael Angelo is nothing to it."

Much of Darwin's scientific reading was done in German, which was a great labor to him, as he never really mastered the language. He was not alone among his scientific friends in this, for he remarks that when he told Sir Joseph Hooker that he had begun German, Hooker replied, " Ah, my dear fellow, that 's nothing; I 've begun it many times." He kept up his interest in all branches of science, and used to say that he got a kind of satisfaction in reading the treatises upon subjects which he could not understand.

He was the most industrious of men, and the most regular in his habits of work. He never rested for a day unless forced to do so by sickness. Week days and Sundays passed off alike, each with its stated amount of work and rest, and he seldom took a holiday or made a visit, unless over-urged by his friends, who saw his need of it. Then, he would drive hard bargains about the time, and usually get off with a day or two less than was prescribed. He was very careful and economical in money matters, yet very generous to his children. He was exact and methodical in all his affairs, and thoroughly understood his business matters. But he did not trouble himself about the management of the garden, the cows, and such things, and " considered the horses so little his concern that he used to ask doubtfully whether he might have a horse and cart to send to Keston for Drosera, or to the nurseries for plants."

The change in his religious belief came about very gradually and was without pain. At the end, he had lost everything except his belief in a First Cause. He writes in 1879: "In my most extreme fluctuations I have never been an Atheist, in the sense of denying the existence of a God. I think that generally, and more and more as I grow older, but not always, an Agnostic would be the more correct description of my state of mind." And again: "I cannot pretend to throw the least light on such abstruse problems. The mystery of the beginning of all things is insoluble by us; and I, for one, must be content to remain an Agnostic." The whole chapter in his Life, which is given to the subject of religion, is of intense interest, showing as it does the candor and extreme sincerity of the man, and his genuine modesty, for he frequently disclaims the power to reason or to think deeply upon this great theme, and never makes the least effort to justify his opinions or to impress them upon others.

The Duke of Argyll records a conversation with him during the last year of his life, in which he said to Mr. Darwin with reference to some of his remarkable works on the Fertilization of Orchids, and upon the Earthworms, and various other observations he had made of the wonderful contrivances for certain purposes in nature, that it was impossible to look at these without seeing that they were the effect and expression of mind. "I shall never forget," he says, "Mr. Darwin's answer. He looked at me very hard, and said, 'Well, that often comes over me with overwhelming force; but at other times,' and he shook his head vaguely, adding, 'it seems to go away.'"

His attitude upon the subject of vivisection was much discussed at one time, and his own summing up of the matter will be read with interest, as the question is still a burning one. He says in a published letter upon the subject in 1881 : —

"Several years ago, when the agitation against physiologists commenced in England, it was asserted that inhumanity was here practised, and useless suffering caused to animals ; and I was led to think that it might be advisable to have an Act of Parliament on the subject. I then took an active part in trying to get a Bill passed, such as would have removed all just cause of complaint, and at the same time have left physiologists free to pursue their researches, — a Bill very different from the Act which has since been passed.

" It is right to add that the investigation by a Royal Commission proved that the accusations made against our English physiologists were false. From all that I have heard, however, I fear that in some parts of Europe little regard is paid to the sufferings of animals, and if this be the case, I should be glad to hear of legislation against inhumanity in any such country. On the other hand, I know that physiology cannot possibly progress except by means of experiments on living animals, and I feel the deepest conviction that he who retards the progress of physiology commits a crime against mankind. Any one who remembers, as I can, the state of this science half a century ago, must admit that it has made immense progress, and it is now progressing at an ever-increasing rate."

Another letter upon this subject to Mr. Romanes illustrates the difficulty he often found in expressing his ideas, and the labor that serious writing was to him to the end of his life. He writes : —

" I have been thinking at intervals all the morning what I could say, and it is the simple truth that I have nothing worth saying. You, and men like you, whose ideas flow freely, and who can express them easily, cannot understand the state of mental paralysis in which I find myself. What is most wanted is a careful and accurate attempt to show what physiology has already done for man, and even more strongly what there is every reason to believe it will hereafter do. Now I am absolutely incapable of doing this, or of discussing the other points suggested by you. . . . I do not grudge the labor and thought; but I could write nothing worth any one reading."

Although his general health improved somewhat during the last ten years of his life, there was apparent a loss of physical vigor, and an almost permanent sense of weariness. In 1879 he writes: " My scientific work tires me more than it used to do, but I have nothing else to do, and whether one is worn out a year or two sooner or later signifies but little." In 1881 he says: " I am rather despondent about myself. . . . I have not the heart or strength to begin any investigation lasting years, which is the only thing which I can enjoy, and I have no little jobs which I can do." In July, 1881, too, he writes to Mr. Wallace: " We have just returned home after spending five weeks at Ullswater; the scenery is quite charming, but I cannot walk, and everything tires me, even seeing scenery. . . . What I shall do with my few remaining years of life I can hardly tell. I have everything to make me happy and contented, but life has become very wearisome to me."

Rest was near at hand. Some affection of the heart began to trouble him the last of February, 1882, and on the 19th of April he died. He was buried in Westminster Abbey, in the north aisle of the nave, a few feet from the grave of Sir Isaac Newton. The last words of the manuscript of his Autobiography, written in 1879, read thus : " As for myself, I believe that I have acted rightly in steadily following and devoting my life to Science. I feel no remorse from having committed any great sin, but have often and often regretted that I have not done more direct good to my fellow creatures."

MATTHEW ARNOLD.

UPON the fine historic background of the Arnold family, the figure of the poet is drawn in clear outlines and carefully shaded in. No name is more highly honored in England than that of the great head master of Rugby, and his son bears the honored place in the succession; indeed he has added new lustre to the name. The world has begun to laugh at the claims of long descent, but the harshest scoffer of all would value the lineage of an Arnold. Culture and courage, unspotted purity and lofty ambition, would satisfy even those who covet earnestly the best gifts. Of Dr. Arnold, Browning might have written with the utmost applicability the lines so often inappropriately quoted, —

"One who never turned his back, but marched breast-forward,
  Never doubted clouds would break,
  Never dreamed, though right were worsted, wrong would
      triumph;
  Held we fall to rise, are baffled to fight better, sleep to wake."

His son Matthew was born on Christmas Eve, 1822, at Lalcham, in the valley of the Thames. Dr. Arnold had not yet been appointed to Rugby, but received pupils in his own house at that time. His son entered Rugby in 1837, living under his

father's own roof at the School-house. In 1840 he was elected to an open classical scholarship at Balliol. In 1842 he won the Hertford Scholarship, and in 1843 the Newdigate Prize, with his poem on Cromwell. Thus early he showed his bent toward poetry, and his capability of winning scholastic honors. He was elected Fellow of Oriel in 1845, and in 1847 was appointed Private Secretary to Lord Lansdowne, then Lord President of the Council. These facts are given in the introduction to the Life and Letters which his family have given to the world in the place of any formal biography, as Mr. Arnold had expressly forbidden the preparation of such a work. It is not plain to us just how families of distinguished men justify to their consciences the keeping of the letter, but entirely contravening the spirit of such requests, or positive orders, as in some cases. To our mind the publication of the most intimate letters of a man's lifetime, written carelessly for the most loving eyes, and with no suspicion of after publicity, is only to be justified by the knowledge that such action would not be offensive to the taste of the departed friend. But such letters are eagerly sought and read, and furnish perhaps the best means of determining the real character of the man. This volume gives the reading world for the first time an opportunity to become acquainted with a great man who had been before the public in his capacity of author for forty years at least. The events of his life were few, and can be easily summed up with the help of the letters. But though uneventful, it is a beautiful life that is revealed in them, — a life of absolute self-denial, of loving service, of great disappointment and discouragement, hero-ically borne, of unremitting drudgery in an uncongenial occupation, of lofty endeavor and aspiration, of the gentlest human kindness to every living thing, of serenity amid things evil, and of deep religious feeling under the outer guise of dissent against prevalent dogma. In 1851 he was appointed to the Inspectorship of Schools, and began what proved to be his life-work, though that was far from his expectation at the time. He was married in that year to Frances Lucy, daughter of Sir William Wrightman, one of the judges of the Court of Queen's Bench. To her he writes about the schools soon after his appointment:—

"I shall get interested in the schools after a little time; their effects on the children are so immense, and their future effects in civilizing the next generation of the lower classes, who, as things are going, will have most of the political power of the country in their hands, may be so important."

A little later he writes his sister, after he has been appointed Commissioner to report on the systems of elementary education in the French-speaking countries:—

"I like the thought of the mission more and more. You know I have no special interest in the subject of public education, but a mission like this appeals even to the general interest which every educated man cannot help feeling in such a subject. I shall for five months get free from the routine work of it, of which I sometimes get very sick, and be dealing with its history and principles. Then foreign life is still to me perfectly delightful, and *liberating* in the highest degree, although I get more and more satisfied to live generally in England, and convinced that I shall work best in the long run by living in the country which is my own. But when I think of the borders of the Lake of Geneva in May, and the narcissuses, and the lilies, I can hardly sit still."

He went to the Continent as planned, but his pleasure was turned to pain in Paris by the news of the death of his brother William at Gibraltar. He was returning home from India. His death was afterward commemorated in the poem, " A Southern Night," and also in "Stanzas from Carnac." The wife of this brother had been buried in India, and is alluded to in the lines: —

> " Ah me! Gibraltar's strand is far,
>   But farther yet across the brine
>   Thy dear wife's ashes buried are,
>   Remote from thine.
>
> " For there where Morning's sacred fount
>   Its golden rain on earth confers,
>   The snowy Himalayan Mount
>   O'ershadows hers.
>
> " Strange irony of Fate, alas,
>   Which for two jaded English saves,
>   When from their dusty life they pass,
>   Such peaceful graves."

To his mother he writes after this stroke of fate, at the close of a letter, thus: " Poor Fanny! she at Dhurmsala, and he by the rock of Gibraltar. God bless you. What I *can* be to you, and to all of them, I will be." " All of them " included the four young children of his brother, now so helpless and so alone. The affection shown in all his family letters is very remarkable, and his constant fine and tender feeling. His family seem to have been very congenial companions to him, one and all. They shared his intellectual tastes, and were capable of appreciating his best work, — yea, sometimes of inspiring it. He returned to London in October, 1860, and prepared and delivered three lectures on Homer the following winter. He had already begun his literary labors, and his poem on "Obermann" had been translated and praised by Sainte Beuve, greatly to his pleasure. But he was soon attacked in the "Saturday Review" for his lectures on Homer, which caused him some annoyance.

His poems and essays all had to be written in the short intervals between the drudgery of his school inspections. The pity of it all, the almost shame of it all, to England is unbearable. That one of the first literary men of his time, one of its most original thinkers and polished poets, perhaps its finest educator, should have been left throughout his life to the deep drudgery of inspecting schools, looking over the examination papers of boys and girls, and other routine work, was a sad commentary on the intelligence of his native land. Only late in life did the government recognize him to the extent of giving him a pension of two hundred and fifty pounds. Like Longfellow, who throughout the long years of his professorship at Harvard was constantly lamenting his lack of time to write the poems which were ringing in his brain, Arnold was pressed at all times by the literary work he wished to do, but which must be put by for his school work. He complains but little, but the irksomeness of it all told upon his spirits as the years went by. His books never became popular, nor was this to be expected, and consequently the returns from them never relieved him of the need to prosecute his uncongenial work.

He lived in and about London the greater part of his life, making his journeys from that point. That sort of travelling was wearisome, and it kept him away from the home he loved so much, with its numerous children and devoted wife. Toward the close of his life he retired to Harrow, where he was much happier, being enthusiastically fond of all country sights and sounds. He was especially fond of Fox How in Westmoreland, the home of his mother, where he revelled in country pleasures for a few weeks every year. He took the deepest interest in all that went on there, and no changes were made without his approval. He writes at one time from another country place at which he is visiting: —

" This place is very, very far from being to me what Fox How is. The sea is a fine object, but it does not replace mountains, being much simpler and less inexhaustible than they, with their infinite detail, are; and the country about here is hideous. Then the place as a place is so much less pleasant than Fox How, and the grounds so inferior, and it is melancholy to see the pines struggling for life and growth here, when one remembers their great rich shoots at Fox How. But I have been much struck with the arbutus in the grounds of a villa near by, and it seems to me we do not turn that beautiful shrub to enough account at Fox How. You ask me about shrubs. On the *left* hand of the path, as you go from the drawing-room window to the hand-bridge, nothing is to be put in except one evergreen, to make a sort of triangle with the little cypress and the odd-leaved beech. On the other side are to be rhododendrons, with a few laurels interspersed, but neither the one nor the other thick enough to make a jungle."

His attitude toward America has been much discussed, and the following extract will show where he stood in December, 1861 : —

" Every one I see is very warlike. I myself think that it has become indispensable to give the Americans a *moral lesson*, and fervently hope that it will be given them ; but I am still inclined to think that they will take their lesson without war. However people keep saying they won't. The most remarkable thing is that that feeling of sympathy with them (based on the ground of their common radicalness, dissentingness, and general mixture of self-assertion and narrowness) seems to be so much weaker than was expected. I always thought it was this sympathy, and not cotton, that kept our Government from resenting their insolences, for I don't imagine the feeling of kinship with them exists at all among the higher classes ; after immediate blood relationship, the relationship of the soul is the only important thing, and this one has far more with the French, Italians, or Germans than with the Americans."

He uses this tone in nearly all his references to America until after his visit to us late in life. Our faults seemed to be peculiarly exasperating to him, he had many entirely false ideas concerning us, and our virtues had not become apparent to him. In 1860 he writes thus : —

" I see Bright goes on envying the Americans, but I cannot but think that the state of things with respect to their *national character*, which, after all, is the base of the only real grandeur or prosperity, becomes graver and graver. It seems as if few stocks could be trusted to grow up properly without having a priesthood and an aristocracy to act as their schoolmasters at some time or other of their national existence."

In writing to Rev. F. B. Zincke, who had written a pamphlet about America, he said in 1883: —

" You bring out what is most important, — that the real America is made up of families, of owners and cultivators of their own land. I hope this is true ; one hears so much of the cities, which do not seem tempting, and of the tendency of every American, farmer or not, to turn into a *trader*, and a trader of the 'cutest and hardest kind. I do not think the bulk of the American nation at present gives one the impression of being made of fine enough clay to serve the highest purposes of civilization in the way you expect ; they are what I call Philistines, I suspect, too many of them."

In 1849 he had published " A Strayed Reveller and Other Poems ; " in 1852, " Empedocles on Etna and Other Poems ; " in 1853, " Poems by Matthew Arnold ; " and in 1855, a " Second Series of Poems ; " in 1858, " Merope, a Tragedy." He also published several volumes of Essays, and " Literature and Dogma," and " God and the Bible, a Review of Objections to Literature and Dogma." In the preface to the latter book he writes :—

" In revising the present volume, the suspicion and alarm which its contents, like those of its predecessor, will in some quarters excite, could not but be present to my mind. I hope, however, that I have at last made my aim clear, even to the most suspicious. Some of the comments on ' Literature and Dogma ' did, I own, surprise me ; . . . but however that judgment may go, whether it pronounce the attempt made here to be of solid worth or not, I have little fear but that it will recognize it to have been an attempt conservative and an attempt religious."

The former book had been fiercely attacked by the Church for its plea to have the Bible read as literature,

not as dogma.   This plea came from a heart filled
with love and admiration for the Scriptures, and a
desire to have other readers share his admiration and
delight.   Nowhere in literature is such admiration
for the Bible expressed as in his letters.   He read
and studied it constantly, and refers very often to
such reading in his home letters.   Of course he read
it as literature, but his poetic nature was deeply
stirred by its sublimity, and he never tired of re-read-
ing what was already as familiar to him as household
words.   Orthodox Christians to whom "Literature
and Dogma" has been a book tabooed, would be
blessed indeed, could they get a tithe of his pleasure
and profit from the Bible.   And he loved the Church
and her stately service, and if he had a bit of con-
tempt and dislike in his heart, it was probably for
dissenters of all sorts and conditions.   Among his
nearest friends were high officials in the Church,
Arthur Stanley being perhaps the closest.   In later
life his opinions upon all points in Biblical criticism
were much sought after; in literary criticism they
had become authoritative.

His poems were read and prized by scholars and
by the literary class.   They had few of the elements
of general popularity.   But it was his high ambition to
be a poet, and to have his meed of admiration and applause.   Upon this subject he wrote quite early in life,
speaking of a letter he had received from Froude
"begging him to discontinue the *Merope* line," but
praising his poems.   He says : —

"Indeed, if the opinion of the general public about my
poems were the same as that of the leading literary men, I
should make more money by them than I do.   But, more

than this, I should gain the stimulus necessary to enable me to produce my best, — all that I have in me, whatever that may be, — to produce which is no light matter with an existence so hampered as mine is. . . . Wordsworth could give his whole life to it ; Shelley and Byron both could, and were, besides, driven by their demon to do so. Tennyson, a far inferior natural power to either of the three, can ; but of the moderns, Goethe is the only one, I think, of those who have had an *existence assujettie*, who has thrown himself with a great result into poetry."

There are other opinions of his concerning his contemporaries which may be of interest to some readers. He asks in one place : " Why is ' Villette ' disagreeable ? Because the writer's mind contains nothing but hunger, rebellion, and rage, and therefore that is all she can in fact put into her book. No fine writing can hide this thoroughly, and it will be fatal to her in the long run." He speaks elsewhere of meeting Charlotte Brontë with Miss Martineau, and his impression of her did not appear to have changed much. Of " My Novel " he writes : " I have read it with great pleasure, though Bulwer's nature is by no means a perfect one, either, which makes itself felt in his book ; but his gush, his better humor, his abundant materials, and his mellowed constructive skill, — all these are great things." Of Renan he writes, speaking of German critics : " Their Biblical critics, who have been toiling all their lives, with but a narrow circle of readers at the end of it all, do not like to be so egregiously outshone in the eyes of the world at large, by a young gentleman who takes it so easy as they think Renan does. . . . The book, however, will feed a movement which was inevitable, and from which good will in the end come; and from Renan himself, too, far more good is to be got than harm." Of Swinburne he writes: "His fatal habit of using one hundred words where one would suffice always offends me, and I have not yet faced his poem, but I must try it soon." Of Morley he says: "You should read Morley's Life of Cobden. Morley is, when he writes, a bitter political partisan; when you meet him in society he is the gentlest and most charming of men." Of Forbes he thinks: "An evening of Bulgaria is too much, and of course Forbes knows nothing else, and Gladstone can go on for hours about that or any other subject." Ruskin appears thus to him: "Ruskin was there, looking very slight and spiritual. I am getting to like him. He gains much by evening dress, plain black and white, and by his fancy's being forbidden to range through the world of colored cravats." Beaconsfield he sums up thus: "I cannot say I much regret to see the Liberal party in a state of chaos, but I am sincerely sorry that a charlatan like Dizzy should be Premier now." At another time he writes: "Macaulay is to me uninteresting, mainly, I think, from a dash of intellectual vulgarity which I find in all his performance." Of Kingsley he was fond, and says: "I think he was the most generous man I have ever known; the most forward to praise what he thought good, the most willing to admire, the most free from all thought of himself in praising and admiring, and the most incapable of being ill-natured, or even indifferent, by having to support ill-natured attacks himself." Of his own poems he says: "It might be

fairly urged that I have less poetical sentiment than
Tennyson, and less intellectual vigor and abundance
than Browning; yet because I have perhaps more
of a fusion of the two than either of them, and have
more regularly applied that fusion to the main line of
modern development, I am likely enough to have
my turn, as they have had theirs." These extracts
throw great light upon the character of their author,
though it should not be forgotten that they are taken
from private letters to his family, which have been
allowed to see the light.

Mrs. Arnold, his mother, died in 1873, at the age
of eighty-two. He felt her loss very deeply, and
made many allusions to it in letters of that period.
He says in one: "She had a clearness and fairness
of mind, an interest in things, and a power of appreciating what might not be in her own line, which
were very remarkable, and which remained with her
to the very end of her life. . . . To many who knew
my father, her death will be the end of a period, and
deeply felt accordingly. And to me and her children how much more must it be than this!" Again
he writes: "You may believe that I thought of you
and of Fox How, and of all the past on Wednesday.
We call it the past, but how much one retains of it;
and then it is not really the dead past, but a part of
the living present. And this is especially true of
that central personage of our past, — dearest mamma. We retain so much of her, she is so often in
our thoughts, that she does not really pass away from
us. She constantly comes to my mind."

He also knew death in his own family; his invalid
boy, Tom, to whom so many touching allusions are

made in the letters, passing away, after much suffer-ering, in early manhood. Of his son's death he wrote in 1868 : —

" Everything has seemed to come together to make this year the beginning of a new time to me: the gradual settlement of my own thought, little Basil's death, and then my dear, dear Tommy's. And Tommy's death, in particular, was associated with several awakening and epoch-making things. The chapter for the day of his death was that great chapter, the 1st of Isaiah ; the first Sunday after his death was Advent Sunday, with its glorious Collect, and in the Epistle the passage which converted St. Augustine. All these things point to a new beginning, yet it may well be that I am near my end, as papa was at my age, but without papa's ripeness, and that there will be little time to carry far the new beginning. But that is all the more reason for car-rying it as far as one can, and as earnestly as one can, while one lives."

In 1883 he undertook the first long journey of his life, sailing for New York in October. He had made frequent visits to the Continent, and was espe-cially fond of Italy, but an ocean voyage was to him a new experience. His wife and daughter accom-panied him. They were received with great cordial-ity, and enjoyed the hospitality of the best people wherever they went. He had prepared three lec-tures to be given throughout the North, in all the larger places. They were " Numbers; or the Major-ity and the Remnant," " Literature and Science," and " Emerson." The last he wrote after his arrival in America. The kindness of the people seemed to be a constant astonishment to him, as was the knowledge of his books displayed by all the people he met. If not quite up to what had been promised him by a railway contractor before starting from home, it was sufficient. This gentleman had told him that all the railway porters and guides had read his books. What came nearest to this was perhaps in New York, where, he says, " the young master of the hotel asked to present his steward to me last night, as a recompense to him for his beautiful arrangement of palms, fruit, and flowers in the great hall. The German boys who wait in the hair-cutting room and the clerks at the photographer's express their delight at seeing 'a great English poet,' and ask me to write in their autograph books, which they always have ready."

In his first lectures he was not well heard, not being accustomed to speaking in large halls; but he soon overcame this difficulty, and his lectures were highly enjoyed.

Almost his only complaint of us after he had seen America was of the blaring publicity of our life, and of the defects of our newspapers. These journals were the subjects of constant vituperation, and the interviewer the one person upon whom he emptied the vials of his wrath. He had expected to find our natural scenery " monotonous," but after he had enjoyed a New England autumn, had seen the Hudson and Niagara, Washington and the Great West, — or what he called the Great West, for he did not go beyond the Mississippi, — he said nothing of the monotony of the landscape. The trees and flowers were a perpetual delight, though he found the streams and mountain brooks, — not the great rivers, poor. He writes at one time : —

"'The great feature in Pennsylvania was the rhododendron by the stream sides and shining in the damp thickets,—bushes thirty feet high, covered with white tresses. I was too late for the azalea and for the dogwood, both of them, I am told, most beautiful here. The cardinal flower I shall see ; it is not out yet. A curious thing is our garden golden-rod of North England and Scotland, which grows every-where, like the wild goldenrod with us. What would I give to go in your company, for even one mile, on any of the roads out of Stockbridge? The trees too delight me. I had no notion what maples really were, thinking only of our pretty hedgerow shrub at home ; but they are, as of course you know, trees of the family of our sycamore, but more im-posing than our sycamore, or more delicate. The sugar maple is more imposing, the silver maple more delicate. The American elm I cannot prefer to the English, but still I admire it extremely."

He found Quebec the most interesting thing by much that he had seen on this continent, and thought he "would sooner be a poor priest in Quebec than a rich hog merchant in Chicago." At another time he wrote: "Lucy is in bliss in New York, but she is a goose to prefer it to Canada."

More seriously he writes to another : —

"What strikes me in America is the number of friends 'Literature and Dogma' has made me, — amongst ministers of religion especially, — and how here the effect of the book is conservative. The force of mere convention is much less strong here than in England. The dread of seeing and say-ing that what is old has served its time and must be dis-placed, is much less. People here are therefore, in the more educated classes at least, less prone to conceal from themselves the actual position of things as to popular Protestantism than they are in England, and the alarm at my book, simply as a startling innovation, is not considerable."

The following paragraph has apparently become historic, it has been quoted so often: —

"I proceeded to Chicago. An evening paper was given me soon after I arrived; I opened it and found . . . the following picture of myself: 'He has harsh features, supercilious manners, parts his hair down the middle, wears a single eyeglass and ill-fitting clothes.'"

And the following is almost as often seen: —

"The universal enjoyment and good nature are what strike one here. On the other hand, some of the best English qualities are clean gone; the love of quiet and dislike of a crowd is gone out of America entirely. They say Washington had it . . . but I have seen no American yet, except Norton at Cambridge, who does not seem to desire constant publicity, and to be on the go all the day long. I thank God it only confirms me in the desire to 'hide my life,' as the Greek philosopher recommended, as much as possible."

After his return to England he said a great deal of how inconceivably kind every one had been, and one heard no more of harsh comments on America. His daughter, Lucy, had been married to Mr. F. W. Whitridge of New York, and after that pleasant international event he was linked to us by very strong ties.

In 1886 he came again to America for a visit to his daughter and granddaughter, and friends he had made over here, and spent a summer most delightfully in New England and New York. He was awaiting the arrival of this daughter and her baby, in April, 1888, at Liverpool, when his sudden death took place, from that heart complaint which we hear of first while he was in America. A brave, true life had come to an end gently and painlessly.

> " And he is now by fortune foiled
>   No more ; and we retain
> The memory of a man unspoiled,
>   Sweet, generous, and humane —
> With all the fortunate have not,
>   With gentle voice and brow.
> Alive we would have changed his lot,
>   We would not change it now."

Will the world learn the lesson which his life should teach, — not to relegate to worlds yet distant our repose, not to toil too strenuously in the morning, if we would also see the placid evening hours? He died at sixty-five, when at last he might have rested, and enjoyed the fruit of his labors and the increasing splendor of his fame. Still, life had been rich and full to him, as it is to poets, whatever their outward lot.

> " Is it so small a thing
>   To have enjoyed the sun,
>   To have lived light in the spring,
>   To have loved, to have thought, to have done ;
>   To have advanced true friends, and beat down baffling foes,"

that we must cry out for a few more years for him, in which to live, and so to suffer, in which to work, and so grow weary, in which to aspire, and so to be unsatisfied?

Will he survive as a poet? Let us see what he says of the fame of a greater than himself: "I do not think Tennyson a great and powerful spirit in any line, as Goethe was in the line of modern thought, Byron even in that of passion, Wordsworth in that of contemplation; and unless a poet at this time of day is that, my interest in him is only slight, and my conviction that he will not stand, is firm." Was Matthew Arnold this great and powerful spirit? We who have known him long and loved him well, believe that he was, and that his influence has been great and will be enduring.

GEORGE DU MAURIER.

AS a cartoonist for " Punch " for thirty years, Mr.
Du Maurier had made himself known to half
the world; as the author of " Trilby," he, a few years
ago, made himself known to the other half. To be
sure, the halves were not entirely separate; the people
who had so long watched for and smiled at the cari-
catures were probably the first readers of the novel;
but the readers became a great multitude which no
man could number, while the lovers of his pictorial
work were but a clique, although a large one.

A few had known him even before " Punch " had exploited him, in the old " Once a Week," where some
quaint and whimsical drawings had appeared, in
which a few artists and critics recognized a new
touch. But the work all had a certain individuality;
on even to the end of it all, there could be no mistak-
ing the hand that did those slight, exquisite things,
whose charm no one could ever describe, and only
the like-minded feel.

How constantly the types were repeated all his
admirers knew, but there was still variety in same-
ness, and a unique delight in finding now and again
that all were not gone, — the old familiar faces. After
one had seen Du Maurier's millionaires and swells and

singers and artists a sufficiently long time, he preferred them to other people, for it is undeniable that there was a bit of chic about them that could not be readily picked up in the shops. The facility in caricature which is now so common, was a development after he first began his labors, not perhaps owing to him very much, but a part of the development of art taste in the people during the time in which he had been working.

Born in Paris in 1834, he had known fully the ups and downs of an artist's life both there and in England. His mixed blood and his residence alternately in the two countries had given him a keen insight into the characters of both the French and English people. He had lived also in Berlin and in Belgium in his youth, and retained some of the pictures there stamped upon an immature mind.

One can but smile at the thought of Du Maurier as a chemist, yet that was the business for which he was first designed by his father. Even in the shop it is said he began to caricature every sort of customer who appeared before him, and his text-books were covered with all sorts of grotesque representations. Some of these were prodigiously funny, and their originality attracted some attention even at that early day. He began to publish first in the "Cornhill," but as early as 1864 began his contributions to "Punch." He lived for many years at Hampstead, and every feature of the landscape which could be seen from his windows entered constantly into his drawings, and was recognized year after year by his friends. Henry James, who always writes of him lovingly, almost caressingly, says on this point:

" I like for this reason, as well as for others, the little round pond where the hill is highest, the folds of the rusty Heath, the dips and dells and ridges, the scattered nooks and precious bits, the old red walls and jealous gates, the old benches in the right places, and even the young couples in the wrong. Nothing was so completely in the right place as the group of Scotch firs that in many a ' Punch ' had produced for August or September a semblance of the social deer forest, unless it might be the dome of St. Paul's, which loomed far away, through the brown breath of London."

Here were passed the middle years between his sweet eccentric youth and the time when the world claimed him for its own, after he had published his books which dealt so patiently and so faithfully with his own early life. They were perhaps his happiest days, for they were largely given to the friends of his heart, those artists and literary men, those musicians, and those people of unclassified genius, who sat in the light of his smiles and heard those quaint and merry and pathetic revelations of his inward life, which so enthralled the reading world when they were afterward given in his novels. His intimates had heard them, bit by bit, through all the years of their acquaintance. Here had been told to loving and eager listeners all the dreams of " Peter Ibbetson," all the experiences of his boyhood in a French school, which so fascinated the readers of " The Martian ; " and here the descriptions of life in the Latin Quarter which were the charm of " Trilby " had been repeated many times to his cronies, through clouds of smoke. That new note which he struck in his writings, as in his drawings, had long been known to his special Bohemia, as the personal note, struck

only by Du Maurier, though oft repeated. He had
no imitators, as every one knew instinctively that
any kind of imitation would be pinchbeck, and
could not pass where he was known. Nor will he
have imitators in his writings. Their first fine careless rapture will never be caught by any other hand.
The place he had taken on the staff of " Punch "
in those far-away days which now belong to ancient
history, was that of John Leech, who had just died.
Leech was also one of the best beloved men of his
day, and deeply missed and mourned by his associates.
Du Maurier himself tells of his funeral : —

"There were crowds of people, Charles Dickens among
them ; Canon Hole, a great friend of Leech's and who has
written most affectionately about him, read the service ; and
when the coffin was lowered into the grave, John Millais
burst into tears and loud sobs, setting an example that was
followed all round : we all forgot our manhood and cried
like women ! I can recall no funeral in my time where simple
grief and affection have been so openly and spontaneously
displayed by so many strangers as well as friends, — not even
in France, where people are more demonstrative than here.
No burial in Westminster Abbey that I have ever seen, ever
gave such an impression of universal honor, love, and regret."

Du Maurier was also bidden to fill Leech's empty
place at the weekly dinner, and to carve his initials
on the table by those of his lost friend, and near to
the W. M. T. which Thackeray had cut there so long
ago. And if Leech's mantle fell on his shoulders
while he was yet young, there are those who think
that the mantle of Thackeray also rested there when
at sixty he began to write his inimitable books.
Certainly there has been nothing so much like

Thackeray, done since the time when "the angel came by night." Then began the long list of drawings illustrating the follies and foibles of London society, which sustained the reputation of " Punch," and increased that of " Harper's Monthly Magazine " — that is, of course, in the line of caricature. Henry James tells us : —

" Immemorial custom had imposed on the regular pair of ' Punch ' pictures an inspiration essentially domestic. I recall his often telling me — and my envying him as well as pitying him a little for the definite familiar rigor of it — that it was vain for him to go, for holidays and absences, to places that did n't yield him subjects, and that the British background was, save for an occasional fling across the border, practically indispensable to the joke."

No doubt other artists, notably Leech, had a greater variety of observation, but on his limited ground Du Maurier saw all the comedy, all the farce and fun, that were to be found.

From the time of his marriage in 1863, he lived practically in this limited environment, Hampstead, Whitby, and the other so well-known localities which his drawings represent. He was often urged to enlarge his circuit, — to see the great panorama of the North, — the midnight sun, the fiords, the cliffs, and the ice-fields which would have so entranced his soul, — to sail in Venetian waters, to watch the sunset over the Adriatic or the moonlight on the lagoons, to see the Illyrian hills, the Hellespont, — all the great sights which his friends felt would so inspire him and enlarge his vision; but he always insisted upon his need to do his work at home, and if there was any sadness in his renunciation of wider horizons, none were permitted to know it. His need, like that of most of his fellows, was to earn money; and if he could continue to do that in his rut, then he would stay in it, with that sweetness of temper which was his distinguishing charm. How he emerged from his quiet semi-obscurity at last, into the full glare of a pronounced literary success, is known to all who read. It was primarily the need of money which led to it, as it had led to an effort to lecture on the subject of his connection with " Punch," which was soon discontinued. With the publication of " Peter Ibbetsen " the need of lecturing was forever put away from him, and that brief era of pecuniary prosperity which lasted till his death set in. This book is regarded by many as his most exquisite work, and it attracted wide attention; but its success was overshadowed by the far more tremendous one of " Trilby," when that appeared. His own early childhood is closely and lovingly depicted in " Peter Ibbetsen," as are his boyhood and youth in " The Martian " and " Trilby; " and his exquisite literary touch alone made it to differ from the talk to which his friends had listened through all the years of their acquaintance with him. It filled them all with wonder that they had not long before seen the possibilities in it, and urged him to leave the narrow field of illustration for the wider one of literature. Mr. Henry James is credited with insisting upon the writing of " Trilby," when Du Maurier, having unfolded its plot to the novelist, urged him to make a novel out of it. But no one but Du Maurier could have written it, the plot itself being nothing but a bare framework over which the trailing vines of the artist's fancy ran in wild luxuriance. Whether Du Maurier could have written much outside of his own experience, is a mooted question. In point of fact he did not do so. Only his closest friends know how completely he revealed himself in his books. The most trivial incidents of his life, every opinion he has cherished, almost every fancy in which he has indulged, are enlarged upon and made to assume a seductive interest, in his writings. All his friends contribute their share also, — traits, peculiarities, poses, and dramatic situations. Mr. Whistler was not the only one who recognized himself, or whom his friends recognized. There were features of almost every one whom he knew, in the *tout ensemble*. In some hands this sort of thing would have made him master of the gentle art of making enemies, but it does not appear that any one save Mr. Whistler took exceptions to his course. The situations in all the books are like instantaneous photographs in their realism, although of course the stories themselves are by no means taken from real life. Still there are portions of these, like the episode of threatened blindness in "The Martian," which are transcripts out of his own life. The descriptions of school life also in that book are almost literal pictures, from the moment when the narrator exclaims: "Oh crimini, but it was hot! and how I did hate the pious Æneas!" through the surreptitious reading of "Monte Cristo," the appearance of the white mouse, and the disappearance and re-appearance of the pocket-handkerchief, the chocolate drops, and all the accessories to the first appearance of Barty at Monsieur Bonzig's school; through to the very end

of that quaint recital. Barty did not make any great
mark in scholarship at Monsieur Bonzig's, or indeed
anywhere else. We are told, however, that he "got
five marks for English history because he remembered a good deal about Richard Cœur de Lion, and
John, and Friar Tuck, and Robin Hood, and especially one Cedric the Saxon, a historical personage of whom the examiner (a decorated gentleman
from the Collège de France) had never even heard."
Very naturally we are told he was good at all
games, and that he could actually turn a somersault
backwards with all the ease and finish of a professional acrobat; and that he brought back with him
to school after vacation a gigantic horned owl with
eyes that reminded him of Bonzig's; also that
"every now and then, if things did n't go quite as he
wished, he would fly into comic rages, and become
quite violent and intractable for at least five minutes,
and then for quite five minutes more he would
silently sulk, and then, just as suddenly, he would
forget all about it, and become once more the genial,
affectionate, and caressing creature he always was;"
and that at one time he felt called upon to become
a sportsman, and, seeing a hare running at full tilt
before him, fired at it. Then he says: "The hare
shrieked, and turned a big somersault and fell on its
back and kicked convulsively, its legs still galloping,
and its face and neck covered with blood; and to
my astonishment Barty became quite hysterical with
grief at what we had done. It's the only time I ever
saw him cry." And the narrator remarks that Barty
never went shooting again, and that he himself inherited his gun, which was double-barrelled. He

sang charmingly at this time, and his songs were in great demand, as they were on convivial occasions for many, many years after. Music was a passion with him his life long, and one of his never-failing sources of pleasure. A tune or a snatch of melody would sometimes charm him for years. He tells us in one place: —

" Many years ago a great pianist to amuse some friends (of whom I was one) played a series of waltzes by Schubert which I had never heard before, — the ' Soirées de Vienne,' I think they were called. They were lovely from beginning to end ; but one short measure in particular was full of such extraordinary enchantment for me that it has really haunted me all my life. It is as if it were made on purpose for me alone, a little intimate aside *à mon intention*, — the gainliest, happiest thought I had ever heard expressed in music. For nobody else seemed to think those particular bars were more beautiful than all the rest ; but oh ! the difference to me."

One point upon which all his friends remarked, was the acuteness of his senses. With his one eye he saw more than any one else with two, as we are frequently told, and his other senses were also acute in the extreme, and a never-failing source of wonder to his intimates. His love of Bohemia was of life-long duration. He was never quite at home anywhere else, and said in the latter days: " It is not a bad school in which to graduate, if you can do so without loss of principle, or sacrifice of the delicate bloom of honor or self-respect." Next to this, Barty, we are told, " loved the barbarians he belonged to on his father's side, who, whatever their faults, are seldom prigs or Philistines ; and then he loved the proletarians, who had good straightforward manners, and no pretensions, — the laborer, the skilled artisan, especially the toilers of the sea." Again we are told that —

"in spite of his love for his own sex, he was of the kind who can go to the devil for the love of a pretty woman.

" He did not do this : he married one instead, fortunately for himself and for his children and for her, and stuck to her and preferred her society to any society in the world. Her mere presence seemed to have an extraordinarily soothing influence on him ; it was as though life were short, and he could never see enough of her in the allotted time and space ; the chronic necessity of her nearness to him became a habit and a second nature, — like his pipe, as he would say.

"Still, he was such a slave to his own æsthetic eye and ever-youthful heart that the sight of lovely woman pleased him more than the sight of anything else on earth ; he delighted in her proximity, in the rustle of her garments, in the sound of her voice ; and lovely woman's instinct told her this, so she was very fond of Barty in return."

And further : —

" He was especially popular with sweet, pretty young girls, to whom his genial, happy, paternal manner endeared him. They felt as safe with Barty as with any father or uncle, for all his facetious love-making ; he made them laugh, and they loved him for it, and they forgot his Apollo-ship and his Lionhood and his general Immensity, which he never remembered himself. It is to be feared that women who lacked the heavenly gift of good looks did not interest him quite so much, whatever other gifts they might possess, unless it were the gift of making lovely music."

While speaking of his domestic relations, and it is well understood that in this matter Du Maurier and

Barty are not to be separated, we will quote one or two more paragraphs from " The Martian " : —

" How admirably she [Leah] filled the high and arduous position of wife to Barty Josselin is well known to the world at large. It was no sinecure ! But she gloried in it ; and to her thorough apprehension and management of their joint lives and all that came of them, as well as to her beauty and sense and genial warmth, was due her great popularity for many years in an immense and ever-widening circle, where the memory of her is still preserved and cherished as one of the most remarkable women of her time.

" With all her power of passionate self-surrender to her husband in all things, little and big, she was not of the type that cannot see the faults of the beloved one, and Barty was very often frankly pulled up for his shortcomings, and by no means had it all his own way, when his own way was n't good for him. She was a person to reckon with, and incapable of the slightest flattery, even to Barty, who was so fond of it from her, and in spite of her unbounded admiration for him."

Again he says : —

" She developed into a woman of the world in the best sense, — full of sympathy, full of observation, and quick understanding of others' needs and thoughts and feelings ; absolutely sincere, of a constant and even temper, and a cheerfulness that never failed, — the result of her splendid health ; without caprice, without a spark of vanity, without selfishness of any kind, generous, open-handed, charitable to a fault ; always taking the large and generous view of everything and everybody ; a little impulsive, perhaps, but not often having to regret her impulses ; of unwearied devotion to her husband, and capable of any heroism or self-sacrifice for his sake."

That such a marriage as this played a very important part in the life of a struggling artist, is not to be questioned. It in fact constituted the happiness of that life to a very great extent, and, we may almost say, its success; for it left him, as all men of genius must be left, free to pursue his own aims, without that attention to the details of living which is so burdensome to men whose thoughts roam forever abroad and cannot brook confinement. She married him when "he was a very impecunious and stricken young man of genius, who at the time did n't know if he were English or French, a chemist or a painter, possible or impossible, blind or seeing, alive or dead," as another has put it; and she helped him in all the days that followed, until he emerged famous and wealthy and beloved, and enjoyed for a brief time his own success. It was not until after the publication of "Trilby" that he ever felt that he could rest, or forego his weekly labors as an illustrator. But the phenomenal success of that engaging book gave him a sense of independence. In the matter of autobiographic detail, "The Martian" should have come first, and we have so considered it; but "Trilby" showed him the mine, and afterward he had only to return to it to pick up the rich nuggets. "Trilby" is undoubtedly the most charming of the books, as it was the most unstudied. It was the work of love; "The Martian," of consideration and elaboration. Almost all authors put forth one book that writes itself; "Trilby" was Du Maurier's. One will readily think of "Uncle Tom's Cabin," "David Copperfield," "Ramona," "Little Women," "The Bonnie Brier Bush," and "The Autocrat of the Breakfast Table," and the list might be almost indefinitely extended. It is not always the first book, though it is apt to be that one. That life of the studios which he sketched in "Trilby" was the life he knew so well; he simply gossiped about it, as he had been in the habit of doing with his cronies. And for such naïve chat about the old Latin Quarter, the literary and moral world has always had a relish, even when less charmingly done. One soon begins to find traces of the Du Maurier we know, and there is no lack of them all through. For instance : —

"But then, to make up for it, when they all three went to the Louvre, he did n't seem to trouble much about Titian either, or Rembrandt, or Velasquez, Rubens, Veronese, or Leonardo. He looked at the people who looked at the pictures instead of at the pictures themselves, especially at the people who copied them, — the sometimes charming young-lady painters — and these seemed to him even more charming than they really were ; and he looked a great deal out of the Louvre windows, where there was much to be seen ; more Paris, for instance, — Paris, of which he could never have enough."

Then how soon the musical strain comes in ! Little Billee adored "all sweet musicianers," and when Svengali played "his heart went nigh to bursting with suppressed emotion and delight." He had never heard Chopin before, and, in fact, nothing but "innocent little motherly and sisterly tinklings." Imagine the delight of such an one in "little fragmentary things, sometimes consisting of but a few bars, but these bars of *such* beauty and meaning ! Scraps, snatches, short melodies meant to fetch, to charm immediately, or to melt or sadden or madden just for a moment, and that knew just when to leave off, — czardas, gypsy dances, Hungarian love plaints, — little things little known out of Eastern Europe in the fifties of this century." And how often the hard-worked and rather care-full artist of " Punch " used to refer to " the happy days and happy nights, sacred to art and friendship ! " " Oh, happy times," he exclaims, " of careless impecuniosity, and youth, and hope, and health, and strength, and freedom, — with all Paris for a background, and its dear old unregenerate Latin Quarter for a workshop and a home ! " And what could be more characteristic of our artist than such friendships as he thus apostrophizes : " Oh, ye impecunious, unpinnacled young inseparables of eighteen, nineteen, twenty, even twenty-five, who share each other's thoughts and purses, and wear each other's clothes, and swear each other's oaths, and smoke each other's pipes, and respect each other's lights o' love, and keep each other's secrets, and tell each other's jokes, and pawn each other's watches, and make merry together on the proceeds, and sit all night by each other's bedsides in sickness, and comfort each other in sorrow and disappointment with silent, manly sympathy, — wait till ye get to forty year. Nay," he adds with another personal touch, " wait till either or each of you gets himself a wife." Du Maurier was no preacher, but who, save him, could have so delicately put the change which came over Little Billee after he had first over-indulged in the wine that was red, that gave its color in the cup : —

" In all his innocent little life he had never dreamed of such humiliation as this, — such ignominious depths of shame and misery and remorse. He did not care to live. . . . And when, after some forty-eight hours or so, he had quite slept off the fumes of that memorable Christmas debauch, he found that a sad thing had happened to him, and a strange ! It was as though a tarnishing breath had swept over the reminiscent mirror of his mind and left a little film behind it, so that no past thing he wished to see therein was re-flected with quite the old pristine clearness ; as though the keen, razorlike edge of his power to reach and re-evoke the bygone charm and glamour and essence of things had been blunted and coarsened ; as though the bloom of that special joy, the gift he unconsciously had of recalling past emotions and sensations and situations, and making them actual once more by a mere effort of the will, had been brushed away. And he never recovered the full use of that most precious faculty, the boon of youth and happy child-hood, and which he had once possessed, without knowing it, in such singular and exceptional completeness."

There is more than a sermon in this ; but he was to lose " other precious faculties of his over-rich and complex nature — to be pruned and clipped and thinned " — till out of the sensitive and impassioned and high-aspiring youth, should come the man of the world, *blasé*, cynical, and somewhat earthy.

The marvel of the success of " Trilby " is still dis-cussed by the literary world, and no one was so much surprised at it as its author. He was in a way dis-turbed by it too. It changed his whole outlook upon life, and he had a difficulty in adjusting himself to it. Sudden fame has its penalties as well as its joys and triumphs. It is a drain upon the vitality that is felt afterward, if not so much realized at the moment. All the penalties of greatness were suddenly thrust upon him, the glaring publicity, the too numerous calls upon

time and strength and income, the wearisome adula-
tion, and the harsh criticism, the innumerable army
of bores epistolary and in the flesh, the great expectations of one, which he feels can never be fulfilled,
because his heart has grown so humble in those
hours, — all these told from the first upon the very
life of this gentle, modest man, who, although he
had been a semi-celebrity for many years, was much
overcome by the sudden blaze of glory in which he
found himself. He had less heart to enjoy what was
tendered him by fortune than ever before in his life.
This is the most caustic irony of fate, — to grant us our
desire after the burning wish has expired, and when
the blackened embers proclaim to all that it is too
late. The relaxation from the absolute necessity of
labor is of itself debilitating for a time, and the new
care of a fortune a heavy weight to the uninitiated.

How he would once have enjoyed the leisure and
the opportunity to write as uninterruptedly as he did
in his last work! But there are marks of strain
in this, and in all his later artistic work, which
show that the day had passed for light-hearted
unconscious production. He felt now an unnatural
need of doing his best, of keeping up to the highest
pitch, of even outdoing himself, which wearied him
supremely. There is no actual falling-off in the first
half of "The Martian." It is perhaps as charming as
the first half of "Trilby," and possibly the last half of
it can be favorably compared with the corresponding
part of that book; but it shows fag. The bouquet is
lacking, has somehow been dissipated, and the wine,
though good, is not so dulcet, delicious, and dreamy as
the same brand of the years before.

All of his nearest friends saw that he was not quite equal to his triumph, but hoped he might rally, and live to enjoy his new honors and emoluments. He grew even more gentle and mild than was his wont, and would scarcely show irritability when the great army of bores worried him day by day for interviews, for sketches, for mementos. The day is coming, and now is, when a man like Stevenson or Du Maurier cannot live in his own house and among his own people unless he has a moat and a drawbridge, and defends himself after the manner of the robber barons of an elder day. Or, perhaps the coming man will be so constituted that he will like all this publicity, and will dine and dress and eat and sleep, like some king, in the eye of the multitude, and hire some poor man of genius to live in solitude and write his books for him. As our dear friend would have said, May the present scribe be dead! In the last days he turned more than ever away from the things he had never cared for, and grew more devoted to what he had always loved. He rode more than ever on the top of omnibuses and road-cars, a favorite diversion at all times, looking down on the sea of faces and amusing himself with them as of old. And he visited all the old haunts, — Whitby, among others, where the hill had grown too long and the blasts too searching for his strength. The collapse was sudden at the last, but it had been led up to by many months of failing strength, and waning enjoyment of the dear accustomed things. He made no sign, but who can doubt that a man of his insight knew all it meant. At such a time, as Browning says, —

> "Life will try his nerves,
> When the sky, which noticed all, makes no disclosure,
> And the earth keeps up her terrible composure."

But who shall say it was not well? Our own thought is expressed in the lines that follow,—

O thou swift runner of the olden days,
Who sped to tell the tale of Marathon,
And, flying fleetly till the set of sun,
Passed through the gates of Athens, as his rays
Set all the white Acropolis ablaze,
And shouted, dying, that the day was won,
Then fell triumphant when thy work was done,—
I hold thy lot was blest ; I sing its praise.
In all the fulness of thy boundless joy,
In all the rapture of victorious rage,
To die amid the Grecian world's acclaim ;
How better far, than wait for time's alloy,
Or disillusion of oncoming age,
Or fruits of envy of thy hard-won fame.

ELIZABETH BARRETT BROWNING.

UNTIL last year the student of literary biography sought in vain for details of Mrs. Browning's life, there having been no biography of her written. Her own expressed wish was that no such life be given to the world. Mr. Browning also expressed a like wish in regard to himself. But a few years ago a life of Mr. Browning prepared by Mrs. Sutherland Orr was published in response to the steady demand for such a work; and now we have two volumes of Mrs. Browning's letters, held together by a thread of narration, that practically give us the interesting story of her life.

It has been thought that the prohibition of a biography applied only to her own lifetime, and that she would be willing to have the letters published after the passage of so many years. These letters are the simple familiar ones written to her nearest friends, and contain a complete revelation of her inner personal life, and all the little homely details of social and domestic affairs in which the reading public seems to have so absorbing an interest. No book of the last decade was read with more avidity than the Letters of Jane Carlyle, or called out more of sympathetic interest, although there was

scarcely anything in them but minute personal details of her every-day life. The tragedy of that long life of repression and blighting disappointment moved the strong heart of the public, as few such revelations have moved it, partly from the charm of her graphic writing, but more largely from the relationship she bore to the popular idol of at least a portion of the reading world. In Mrs. Browning's letters the revelations are all of peace and love, and increasing happiness year by year, in beautiful contrast to the dark picture of Mrs. Carlyle's life. The unhappiness of Mrs. Browning passed away with her marriage instead of beginning at that time, and only the unavoidable sorrows and losses of a life darken these pages.

Elizabeth Barrett was born on March 6, 1809, the eldest child of Edward and Mary Moulton Barrett. The family had been connected for some generations with the island of Jamaica, and owned considerable estates there. Robert Browning was likewise, in part, of West Indian descent. Mr. Barrett's family was a large one, consisting of three daughters and eight sons, and the mother died while they were very young, leaving to him the bringing up and education of the little troop. While Elizabeth was still an infant, they removed to a newly purchased estate in Herefordshire, among the Malvern Hills, and only a few miles from Malvern itself. Here she lived for twenty years, in all the enjoyment of that country life she so loved, and of which she was destined to know so little for the remainder of her life. But she began to live early in the realm of books. The Greeks out of Pope's Homer haunted her, and she tells us that she dreamed more of Agamemnon than of Moses, her black pony. When eleven or twelve years old she wrote an epic poem in four books called the "Battle of Marathon;" and her father had it printed for distribution among his friends, so proud was he of her signal ability. The life at Hope End was as quiet as possible, and she was very seldom interrupted in her study of Greek and her reading of Plato and the dramatists. For lighter reading she had Pope and Byron and Coleridge. At the age of fifteen she had a very serious illness, and was never quite well again; but she did not allow this to interfere with her intellectual work, and at twenty published her first volume of verse. In 1835 the family removed to London; and Elizabeth, whose health had not been good before, broke down entirely in the bad air of the great city, and from that time came to be regarded as an invalid, and after a while a hopeless one. Some injury to the spine was the cause of her long years of confinement and suffering. She of course made few acquaintances, though it was from this time that she dated her friendship with her distant cousin John Kenyon and with Miss Mitford. She began now to contribute poems to the periodicals, and thus made some literary friends, very few of whom, however, she saw personally.

In 1838 she published "The Seraphim and Other Poems," the first book published under her own name. The older poets were by this time ceasing to be productive; Wordsworth's flowering season was long over, Landor, Southey, Rogers, and Campbell were all past their prime. The masters, Shelley, Keats, Byron, and Scott, were dead. Tennyson was in his youth, and Robert Browning just beginning to sing. The "Seraphim" was received with moderate favor by the people, and with great favor by the critics, although they did not fail to point out its very obvious faults. She was said to lack discriminating taste, though her genius was allowed to be active, vigorous, and versatile. She was thought to lack equipoise, and "to aim at flights which have done no good to the strongest," and of falling infinitely short of what a proper exercise of her genius might reach. Some critic also objected to her "reckless repetition of the name of God," and others to her technique, — a point on which she was then, as afterward, very much open to criticism.

In 1840 she spent the summer at Torquay, and while there, where she thought she was gradually improving in health, her brother Edward was drowned. Accompanied by two friends, he went out in a sailboat, and, not returning when expected, the greatest anxiety was felt in regard to them. It was three days before definite information was obtained concerning them, and this period of suspense was so dreadful, and was followed up by such an appalling catastrophe, that his sister was so much overcome by it that it was years before she recovered from its effects, and the sound of the sea was ever after a horror to her. In the fall of 1841 she was at last able to leave Torquay, and returned to London. Her life was simply that of an invalid, confined to her room the greater part of the year, and seeing only a few intimate friends, but doing some literary work. During this year occurs the first mention of Mr. Browning in her letters. She says: —

"I do assure you I never saw him in my life — do not know him even by correspondence — and yet, whether through fellow-feeling for Eleusinian mysteries, or whether through the more generous motive of appreciation of his powers, I am very sensitive to the thousand and one stripes with which the assembly of critics doth expound its vocation over him, and the ' Athenæum,' for instance, made me quite cross and misanthropical last week. The truth is — and the world should know the truth — it is easier to find a more faultless writer than a poet of equal genius. Don't let us fall into the category of the sons of Noah. Noah was once drunk, indeed, but once he built the ark."

A picture which she gives of her life at this time runs thus : —

"I am thinking, lifting up my pen, what I can write to you which is likely to be interesting to you. After all I come to chaos and silence, and even old night — it is growing so dark. I live in London, to be sure, and except for the glory of it I might live in a desert, so profound is my solitude, and so complete my isolation from things and persons without. I lie all day, and day after day, on the sofa, and my windows do not even look into the street. To amuse myself with a vain deceit of rural life, I have had ivy planted in a box, and it has spread over one window, and strikes against the glass with a little stroke from the thicker leaves when the wind blows at all briskly. *Then* I think of forests and groves ; it is my triumph when the leaves strike the window-pane, and this is not a sound like a lament. Books and thoughts and dreams (almost too consciously *dreamed*, however, for me — the illusion of them has almost passed) and domestic tenderness can and ought to leave nobody lamenting. Also God's wisdom deeply steeped in his love *is* as far as we can stretch out our hands."

Her own poem, "My Heart and I," must have come near to expressing her own feeling at this dreary season of her life: —

> "How tired we feel, my heart and I !
> We seem of no use in the world;
> Our fancies hang gray and uncurled
> About men's eyes indifferently ;
> Our voice which thrilled you so, will let
> You sleep ; our tears are only wet ;
> What do we here, my heart and I ?
>
> "Tired out we are, my heart and I.
> Suppose the world brought diadems
> To tempt us, crusted with loose gems
> Of powers and pleasures ?   Let it try.
> We scarcely care to look at even
> A pretty child, or God's blue heaven,
> We feel so tired, my heart and I."

But in those dreary years, notwithstanding her depression, she had been busy with her pen, and in 1844 she published two volumes of Poems which lifted her at once into the foremost ranks of living poets. They contain that part of her work which has always remained most popular, if we except the "Sonnets from the Portuguese" and "Aurora Leigh." Among them were "The Drama of Exile," the longest and most pretentious poem, and "The Vision of Poets," "The Cry of the Children," "The Dead Pan," "Bertha in the Lane," "Crowned and Buried," "Sleep," "Lady Geraldine's Courtship," "The Romaunt of the Page," and the "Rhyme of the Duchess May."

Browning had just published his "Bells and Pomegranates," and in "Lady Geraldine's Courtship" she had made an allusion to his poems, which perhaps attracted his notice, and led to a desire for an acquaintance with her. Chancing to express his interest to Mr. Kenyon, a life-long friend, he was urged to write to Miss Barrett and tell her of his pleasure in her work. He did so, and the letter was received with the greatest pride and pleasure. The correspondence was regular after that, and equally enjoyed by both. After a few months, in the early summer, when she was usually better than at any other time in the year, they met for the first time. She received only a few of her most intimate friends in her room, but made an exception in his case, feeling so strong a desire to see him face to face. He came not only once, but many times, bringing books and flowers, and cheering her greatly by his admiration and appreciation of her best work. This acquaintance lasted for about two years. At the end of that time, if not long before, they loved each other with absolute devotion. Her own record of her feelings can be read in the " Sonnets from the Portuguese," for it is set down there line for line. But when he spoke to her of his love she did not dare to think of such a thing as accepting it. She tells of her feeling in a letter written soon after her marriage to one of her oldest friends : —

" So then I showed him how he was throwing into the ashes his best affections — how the common gifts of youth and cheerfulness were behind me — how I had not strength, even of *heart*, for the ordinary duties of life — everything I told him and showed him. ' Look at this — and this — and this, throwing down all my disadvantages. To which he did not answer by a single compliment, but simply that he had not then to choose, and that I might be right, or he might be right,

he was not there to decide; but that he loved me, and
should to his last hour. He said that the freshness of youth
had passed with him also, and that he had studied the world
out of books, and seen many women, yet he had never loved
one until he had seen me. That he knew himself, and knew
that, if ever so repulsed, he should love me to his last hour
— it should be first and last. At the same time he would not
tease me, he would wait twenty years if I pleased, and then,
if life lasted so long for both of us, then when it was ending
perhaps, I might understand him, and feel that I might have
trusted him. For my health, he had believed when he first
spoke that I was suffering from an incurable injury of the
spine, and that he could never hope to see me stand up before his face, and he appealed to my womanly sense of what
a pure attachment should be, — whether such a circumstance,
if it had been true, was inconsistent with it. He preferred,
he said, of free and deliberate choice, to be allowed to sit
only an hour a day by my side, to the fulfilment of the brightest dream which should exclude me, in any possible world."

In the same letter she describes at some length the
life she had lived before she knew Mr. Browning, as
some excuse, if any was needed, for the tendrils of
her affection having been ready to twine around him.
Here are her words: —

" But the personal feeling is nearer with most of us than the
tenderest feeling for another ; and my family had been so
accustomed to the idea of my living on and on in that room,
that while my heart was eating itself, their love for me was
consoled, and at last the evil grew scarcely perceptible. It
was no want of love in them, and quite natural in itself; we
all get used to the thought of a tomb ; and I was buried, that
was the whole. It was a little thing even for myself a short
time ago, and really it would be a pneumatological curiosity
if I could describe and let you see how perfectly for years

together, after what broke my heart at Torquay, I lived on the outside of my own life, blindly and darkly from day to day, as completely dead to hope of any kind as if I had my face against a grave, never feeling a personal instinct, taking trains of thought to carry out as an occupation, absolutely indifferent to the *me* which is in every human being. Nobody quite understood this of me, because I am not morally a coward, and have a hatred of all the forms of audible groaning. . . . A thoroughly morbid and desolate state it was, which I look back now to with the sort of horror with which one would look at one's graveclothes, if one had been clothed in them by mistake during a trance."

What followed can only be understood by explaining the character of Mr. Barrett, and the utter hopelessness of trying to move him by any appeals to his reason or his parental love. He had long since constituted himself absolute dictator in his family, and no one ever questioned his will in the smallest matter. The year previous to Mr. Browning's declaration of his love, his daughter Elizabeth for the first time came into something like collision with him on the subject of her own health. She had been told by her physicians, and had long felt herself, that her only hope of betterment lay in seeking a warmer climate in the winter season. So she desired to go to Italy for the winter, and took all the preliminary steps for doing so, — never once doubting that her father would desire to have her go if she wished. But the mere mention of it, the thought that she had even dared to think of such a thing for herself without his taking the initiative, excited his anger to such an extent that not only did she have to give up the thought of making the journey, but he treated

her with such harshness that it prostrated her for
many months. She knew well enough his exaggerated notions of authority, but she had never before
doubted his affection. Now he did not come to her
room, except for five minutes in the morning, and
showed her his displeasure in every way he could.
She had always loved him for father and mother
both, and she tells us that " he had always had the
greatest power over my heart, because I am of those
weak women who reverence strong men. By a word
he might have bound me to him hand and foot.
Never has he spoken a gentle word to me or looked
a kind look which has not made in me large results
of gratitude, and throughout my illness the sound of
his step on the stairs has had the power of quickening
my pulse, — I have loved him so and love him."
Now there was set up against this hardness and cold-
ness, this isolation and despair, the warmth of a great
love, the promise of that tenderness which her heart
so needed, and that understanding of her nature for
which she had always yearned. Her whole impulse
was to yield; but the habit of a lifetime was against
her, — she was so accustomed to yield to her father
that she found it almost impossible to resist his will.
And she was well aware that he would show her
no favor. As soon as he had suspected that Mr.
Browning had any special interest in visiting his
daughter, he had frowned sternly upon him. It had
long been understood in the family that no member
of it would ever be allowed to marry, and retain the
affection of the father. He considered his children
as his property, and never admitted that any one of
them had any individual rights. So from the first

there was no thought of taking him into their confidence. It would have been the signal for his casting his daughter off forever, and she was too weak to go through that terrific ordeal. She says in regard to it: " That I was constrained to act clandestinely, and did not choose to do so, God is witness, and will set it down as my heavy misfortune, and not my fault." She was privately married to Mr. Browning on September 10, 1846, and immediately crossed the Channel to Havre, and so on to Paris. Even her sisters did not know of the time of her marriage, though they knew of her engagement. She had kept it from them for their own sakes, fearing to draw upon their heads their father's displeasure. But they entirely approved her action, and one of them, a few years later, was obliged to take similar action in her own case, her father refusing to allow her to be married, after an engagement of several years' standing. He behaved in the same manner to all his children when the time for their marriages came around. From the moment of Elizabeth's marriage he cast her off and disowned her. She wrote to him regularly for years, only to find out in the end that he never opened one of her letters, even those sent in black-bordered envelopes, which might have contained the news of the death of her husband or child. He returned them all to her after many years, when she had made one final appeal to him, in order to have her understand the impossibility of any relenting on his part. This was a life-long grief to her, and one great cause of her never returning to England, except for brief visits. Her father never did relent, but died as he had lived, —harsh and implacable.

The newly married couple met their friend Mrs. Jameson in Paris, and after spending a few weeks there, they journeyed on with her to Pisa. She was the greatest possible comfort to them in that anxious time. Of course there was great anxiety about Mrs. Browning's health at first, but she bore the journey wonderfully well, not suffering from it in the least, except from fatigue. In October they reached Pisa, and settled down there for the winter. The mild climate, as she had anticipated, agreed with her, and she remained permanently much better than she had ever been in England. She was able to go about from the first, guardedly of course, and was never reduced to a state of complete invalidism from that time. Her friends regarded it as a miracle, and she herself called it the miracle of love. She grew to love Italy, and even in the heat of its summers was well and happy. From the first her letters are a record of delight, and that note is never lost through all the long years. In one of the first letters written from Pisa she says:—

" I was never happy before in my life. Ah, but, of course, the painful thoughts recur ! There are some whom I love too tenderly to be easy under their displeasure, or even under their injustice. Only it seems to me that with time and patience my poor dearest papa will be melted into opening his arms to us, — will be melted into a clearer understanding of motives and intentions; I cannot believe he will forget me, as he says he will, and go on thinking me to be dead rather than alive and happy. So I manage to hope for the best; and all that remains, all my life here, *is* best already, could not be better or happier."

Again she says : —

"I have been neither much wiser nor much foolisher than all the shes in the world, only much happier, — the difference is in the happiness. Certainly I am not likely to repent of having given myself to him. I cannot, for all the pain received from another quarter, the comfort for which is that my conscience is pure of the sense of having broken the least known duty, and that the same consequence would follow any marriage of any member of my family with any possible man or woman. I look to time, to reason, and natural love and pity, and to the justification of the events acting through all; I look on so and hope, and in the meanwhile it has been a great comfort to have had not merely the indulgence but the approbation and sympathy of most of my old personal friends — oh, such letters!"

The marriage was undoubtedly an ideal one, and the happiness of it very great, as was evidenced by all her letters to the very end of her life, and by all the accounts which friends and relatives have given of it. The situation was rather trying too; the perpetual *tête-à-tête*, the solitude of a new and strange land, the need of a life of exile, the comparative poverty, the delicate health, — all these things offered opportunity for discontent, if the deep feeling had not more than counterbalanced them. The cheapness of living in Italy at that time, was one inducement to live permanently there. For three hundred pounds a year they enjoyed advantages which they could not have had for twice that sum in England, and they always needed to consider the money question. Neither of them made much money by their poems for many years, and it was not until after they received a legacy of eleven thousand pounds from her cousin Mr. Kenyon, that they were at all independent in their resources. This was many years after her marriage.

It was during their stay at Pisa that Mr. Browning first saw his wife's " Sonnets from the Portuguese." It was their custom to write alone, and not to show each other what they had written. But one day she stole up behind him and, placing a packet of papers in his pocket, told him to read them, and tear them up if he did not like them. Then she ran lightly away, and he seated himself to their reading. He read, and considered them the finest sonnets since Shakespeare's. They were certainly the best of her own work, up to that time, if we need to make even that exception. Delighted beyond measure, he insisted upon their publication, though that had not been her intention. They were written out of her heart, with no thought of the outside world, and their exquisite delicacy was a revelation of her soul, such as she had never before given. All the faults of previous poems had been overcome, and they were more nearly faultless in style and finish than any of her other poems. When they were published privately in 1847, and publicly in 1850, they were accepted at once as among the finest love-poems of the language, and they have never lost that rank. Mr. Browning himself is perhaps her most formidable rival in that line of writing. We have only to recall " By the Fireside," " Evelyn Hope," " The Last Ride Together," " The Statue and the Bust," " Any Wife to Any Husband," among the many fine ones, to make this clear, though none of these have quite the charm of the Sonnets. In April, 1847, they left Pisa and journeyed on to Florence, where they settled in furnished rooms in the Palazzo Guidi, which continued to be their home during the remainder of Mrs. Browning's life, though such was far from their intention at the time. They made the old palace known to all the world, and it is eagerly sought out now by all travellers through Italy. The city government has marked it by a tablet which tells of the illustrious poetess who lived there and formed " a golden ring between Italy and England." They travelled more or less as the years went on, and once or twice lived in Paris for several months; but here was their home, where the greater part of their beautiful years was spent. Here their child was born and reared, and added the one thing wanting in their early married life. He was a beautiful boy, strong and active, and a great favorite, as he grew up, with the Italians of the neighborhood. He was named Robert Wiedemann Barrett Browning. Their joy in their first born was somewhat dimmed by the death of Mr. Browning's mother a few days later.

The Browning family had received Mrs. Browning with the utmost love and kindness, and she had become devotedly attached to them. Mr. Browning's sorrow for his mother was very deep, and only the lapse of time tempered it. At first even the advent of the little son could not wile him away from it. They left Florence that year for the mountains, during the heat of summer, but were very happy to get back to Casa Guidi as soon as the autumnal winds began to blow. Here Mr. Browning wrote his " Christmas Eve " and " Easter Day," and Mrs. Browning prepared a new edition of her poems for the press. Here they read the best of the new books that came out in England, and took the deepest interest in all that went on in the literary world there. Tennyson and Carlyle were their favorites, and elicit the highest praise in the letters. But all the notable books, from " Shirley " and " Jane Eyre " to " Vanity Fair," are noted. They also read Balzac diligently and with great delight, as they did George Sand and Alexandre Dumas. It was rather difficult to procure books in Florence, and the lack of them was sometimes felt rather deeply by people who went out as little as the Brownings, and had as little in the way of amusement. Florence was rather dull, and Mr. Browning felt it seriously sometimes, particularly after passing nine months in Paris the year of the *coup d'état*, when the excitement was so intense, and into all of which he entered with the utmost enthusiasm. Mrs. Browning also enjoyed the Paris visit very much, and it was thought for a time that they might make their home there, but she was so much better in health in Florence than elsewhere, that the project was abandoned. They made their first visit to England at that time, but she was quite unwell there, and the attitude of her father, and even of some of her brothers, caused her so much pain that she almost resolved never to see England again. In a letter written after they had returned to Paris in October she says : —

" With such mixed feelings I went away. Leaving love behind is always terrible, but it was not all love that I left, and there was relief in the state of mind with which I threw myself on the sofa at Dieppe, — yes, indeed. Robert felt differently from me for once, as was natural, for it had been

pure joy to him with his family and his friends, and I do believe he would have been capable of never leaving England
again, had such an arrangement been practicable for us on
some accounts. Oh, England! I love and hate it at once.
Or rather, where love of country ought to be in the heart,
there is the mark of the burning iron in mine, and the depth
of the scar shows the depth of the root of it."

It was at this time that Mrs. Browning's admiration
for Louis Napoleon began. She was always greatly
interested in public questions, and Italian politics had
already occupied much of her attention, and she
became almost equally engrossed in French affairs
while residing in Paris. Liberty was the passion of
her soul, and during the long years of the struggle
for Italian independence and unity, which followed
the upheaval in France, she became completely
absorbed in the burning question. Because Napoleon
promised and gave aid against Austria, she believed
in him implicitly, made him the hero of her heart,
and was almost heart-broken after Villafranca. She
could not bear to have any one differ with her on
this subject. It was not enough to sympathize with
Italy, and to wish her freed of her Austrian tyrant,
but her friends must worship with her her heroes
Victor Emmanuel and Louis Napoleon. When war
was actually declared, and the Austrian troops had
crossed the Ticino, her excitement knew no bounds.
Her husband did not entirely agree with her as
regarded Napoleon, but his interest in the cause of
Italian freedom was as great as her own. He was
less surprised than she when Napoleon's zeal for
Italian independence stopped short at the frontiers
of Venetia, or when he made his demand for Nice

and Savoy, but he sympathized to the utmost in her
passionate disappointment and grief on these two
occasions. In her poem "First News from Villafranca" she gave vent to her sorrow and dismay, —

> " Peace, peace, peace do you say?
> What ! — with the enemy's guns in our ears?
> With the country's wrong not rendered back ?
> What ! — while Austria stands at bay
> In Mantua, and our Venice bears
> The cursed flag of the yellow and black ?
>
> .   .   .   .
>
> Peace, peace, peace do you say?
> What ! — uncontested, undenied ?
> Because we triumph, we succumb ?
> A pair of Emperors stand in the way
> (One of whom is a man beside)
> To sign and seal our cannons dumb ?
>
> .   .   .   .
>
> Hush ! more reverence for the dead !
> *They* 've done the most for Italy
> Evermore since the earth was fair.
> Now would that *we* had died instead,
> Still dreaming peace meant liberty,
> And did not, could not mean despair."

But she was still inclined to give Napoleon credit
for what he had actually done, though she afterward
wrote of him these lines, —

> " Napoleon - as strong as ten armies,
>   Corrupt as seven devils — a fact
> You accede to, then seek where the harm is
>   Drained off from the man to his act,
> And find — a free nation ! Suppose
>   Some hell-brood in Eden's sweet greenery
> Convoked for creating — a rose !
>   Would it suit the infernal machinery ?"

When Victor Emmanuel entered Florence in April, 1860, she greeted him with a song beginning, —

> " King of us all, we cried to thee, cried to thee,
>   Trampled to earth by the beasts impure,
>   Dragged by the chariots which shame as they roll:
>   The dust of our torment far and wide to thee
>   Went up, dark'ning thy royal soul.
>   Be witness, Cavour,
>   That the king was sad for the people in thrall,
>   This king of us all !"

Perhaps the best of the Italian poems — and there was a whole volume of them — is " Mother and Poet," which is also by far the best known. It was written after the news from Gaeta in 1861, and begins : —

> " Dead ! one of them shot in the sea by the east,
>   And one of them shot in the west by the sea.
>   Dead ! both my boys ! When you sit at the feast,
>   And are wanting a great song for Italy free,
>   Let none look to *me !* "

It told the story of Laura Savio, of Turin, a poetess and patriot, whose sons were killed at Ancona and Gaeta. These poems were not well received in England, but found more friends in America. Indeed, all her poems, as well as those of Mr. Browning, met at first with a warmer reception in America than they did in England.

Long before the Italian poems were written, Mrs. Browning had begun her longest and most popular poem, " Aurora Leigh." The idea of writing a novel in verse dates back at least to 1844, — a novel embodying her ideas of social and moral progress. It was not, however, until 1856 that it was completed,

during Mrs. Browning's third and last visit to England. Its success was immediate. A second edition
was required in a fortnight, a third in a few months.
In America it was one of the most successful books of
that decade. It had more of the elements of popularity than any of her other poems, and perhaps less
of her distinguishing mannerisms. All of her human-
itarian impulses are embodied in it. It is a heart
book, and sent a thrill through the world. Some of
the very best of her poetry is contained in it, though
it is not as exquisite as the " Sonnets from the Portuguese," nor as thrilling as the " Cry of the Children."
It was, of course, a very great delight to her to receive
this warm recognition at last, particularly in England.
But her beloved cousin, Mr. Kenyon, died on the
very eve of its publication, and her grief for him
mingled in her own personal joy. Mr. Browning,
too, had won his audience by this time, fit though
few. A small portion of the cultivated public had
always regarded him as the prophet of a new school
of poetry, and a larger portion as an original thinker
and accomplished writer; but now a larger portion of
the lovers of poetry came to be his admirers, and
there was less talk of his perverse obscurity and
obstinate faults than there had been. The two poets
evidently did not help each other much in matters of
style. It seems they were not much tried with the
faults so apparent to others, and which remain such
a drawback to the pleasure of their readers. The
substance of poetry was never lacking in their work,
but for elegance and smoothness we look almost in
vain. In the places where we do find them, we have
the grandest poetic expression of their time.

For several years Mrs. Browning had been interested in the subjects of Swedenborgianism and spiritualism. She was naturally of a deeply religious nature, and interested in all high themes. She was a diligent Bible student in her youth, and devotional to the end of her life. She became a believer, first in the doctrines of Swedenborg, and afterward in modern spiritualism. In Mrs. Browning's acquaintance with Harriet Beecher Stowe this was the chief bond of sympathy. Mrs. Stowe was at the time very much interested in the subject, and told Mrs. Browning many things which tended to confirm her in her new faith. Of her Mrs. Browning writes in the autumn of 1860: —

"She spoke very calmly of it, with no dogmatism, but with the strongest disposition to receive the facts of the subject with all their bearings, and at whatever loss of orthodoxy or sacrifice of reputation for common-sense. I have a high appreciation of her power of forming opinions, let me add to this. It is one of the most vital and growing minds I ever knew. . . . She lives in the midst of the traditional churches, and is full of reverence by nature ; and yet if you knew how fearlessly that woman has torn up the old cerements, and taken note of what is a dead letter within, yet preserved her faith in essential spiritual truth, you would feel more admiration for her than even for writing ' Uncle Tom.' "

Her correspondence is full of this subject for several years. Her husband did not agree with her concerning it, and was somewhat annoyed at her enthusiasm about it. In " Mr. Sludge, the ' Medium,' " he expresses some of his own views upon the matter.

Mrs. Browning's health had gradually declined

since the publication of " Aurora Leigh." She did little more work, the " Poems before Congress " not occupying much of her time, and lost her strength so gradually that even her husband did not realize how near she was to the end of her earthly course. She made an occasional short journey, — to Rome for the winter, or Sienna for the summer, and once more to Paris, — but she was a good deal confined to her own home, which seemed dearer to her than ever. Her boy was a continual delight to her. No prouder or fonder mother ever lived than she was, from the first to the last. He was indeed a beautiful and gifted child, inheriting something of the genius of both father and mother. His taste for art doubtless came to him from his father, who was somewhat of a connoisseur, and a promising amateur sculptor.

Mrs. Browning's death occurred on the 29th of June, 1861, and was quite unexpected, though she had been ill a week, from one of her accustomed bronchial attacks. She died alone with her husband, with her head upon his shoulder and her cheek against his, entirely unconscious of what was impending.

JOHN RUSKIN.

JOHN RUSKIN, the writer of the finest descriptive prose that the century has produced, was born not in the seclusion of English country life, as would have been fitting, but amid the din and distraction of London life. With the eye of an artist and the imagination of a poet, he was cabined, cribbed, confined, in a smoky suburb where he seldom saw the full light of day. His father was a wine-merchant, a man of fine literary and artistic taste, who read Byron to him when a young boy, concerning which Ruskin said long after: "I never got the slightest harm from Byron; what harm came to me was from the facts of life, and from books of a baser kind, including a wide range of the works of authors popularly considered extremely instructive, — from Victor Hugo down to Dr. Watts." He decided at that early age to make Byron his master in poetry, as Turner in art; not so much, he assures us, for his consummate literary workmanship, as for "his measured and living truth, — measured as compared to Homer, and living as compared to everybody else." Nor must this be considered the opinion of an ignorant child. He had already read Livy, and knew what close-set language was, and had

learned Pope by heart long before. Reading the Bible constantly, too, under his mother's direction, he knew well the majesty and simplicity of language, in the grand poetry of the Hebrew nation. He refers very often to this early familiarity with the Bible as one great source of the incomparable beauty of his literary style, and it was doubtless one of its formative elements.

The mother who insisted so strenuously upon this part of his education was a woman of somewhat severe character, who brought him up in complete isolation from all other children, and with none of the toys or amusements of an ordinary childhood. He says in relation to it: —

"I had a bunch of keys to play with as long as I was capable only of pleasure in what glittered and jingled ; as I grew older I had a cart and ball, and when I was five or six years old two boxes of wooden bricks. With these modest but, I still think, entirely sufficient possessions. and being always summarily whipped if I cried, did not do as I was bid, or tumbled on the stairs, I soon attained serene and secure methods of life and motion, and could pass my days contentedly in tracing the square, and comparing the colors of my carpet. examining the knots in the wood of the floors, or counting the bricks in the opposite houses, with rapturous intervals of excitement during the filling of the water-cart, or the still more admirable proceedings of the turncock when he turned and turned till a fountain sprang up in the middle of the street. But the carpet and what patterns I could find in the bed-covers, dresses, or wall-papers to be examined, were my chief resources."

The artist was embryonic even in the little child, as can be seen by this, and that the poet was also in the soul was shown by his early delight in such glimpses of nature as came to him in his early childhood.

He was once taken to Derwentwater, and he tells of the intense joy, mingled with awe, that he had in looking through the hollows in the mossy roots, over the crag into the dark lake, and which has associated itself more or less with all twining roots of trees ever since. He never lived in the country in childhood, and every small excursion was a most intense delight. He remembers the first time he ever walked on the grass, as other children remember some important occurrence, and every such new introduction to nature was to him a revelation.

His parents occasionally made a journey in their own coach, and these ecstatic periods still linger in his memory. He visited with them many of the famous castles and cathedrals of his native land, and began that study of architecture which has occupied so much of the leisure of his life. He took the greatest interest and pleasure in it from the first, gaining much, no doubt, from the companionship of a man of taste and experience like the elder Ruskin.

John was also taken abroad while quite young by his parents, visited Switzerland and Italy, and learned to revel in the joys of nature and art. He continued the observation of architecture begun among the cathedrals of England, and saw for the first time the incomparable splendor of ancient art. He was already a keen and a minute observer, and came home with many drawings, made with little skill, perhaps, but much truth. His first thought was to be a painter, and he pursued the study of art with much diligence for several years.

We come now to the beginning of his life-work in the " Modern Painters." The first volume was the expansion of a magazine article, affirming that Turner, who had been harshly criticised by leading artists and critics, was right and true, and that his critics were wrong, base, and false. At that time, though he had been several times in Italy, he delighted chiefly in Northern art, beginning when a boy with Rubens and Rembrandt, and going on from them to Turner, who became the idol of a lifetime. The first volume involved him in so much discussion and drew forth such scathing criticism, that he found himself in for a battle, and went at once to Italy to prepare himself more fully.

The result of his study there was a reaction against Rubens, and great delight in Angelo and Raphael. The second volume, like the first, was chiefly written to defend Turner; but Turner had already passed the zenith of his power, and lay ill at Chelsea, embittered by the harsh and unjust criticism of the day, and hardly just even to the man who was endeavoring to do him honor. After his death Ruskin felt no need for haste, and took ten years for the thorough and critical study of art before beginning his work again. Most books would have been forgotten by that time, but the " Modern Painters" was far from being so in the circle it had so stirred, and the third and fourth volumes were received with a new storm of remonstrance and even of defiance. Ruskin contended that it was as ridiculous for any one to speak positively about painting who had not given a great part of his life to its study, as it would be for a person who had never studied chemistry to give a lecture on affinities or elements; but that it was also as ridiculous for a person to speak hesitatingly about laws of painting who had conscientiously given his time to their ascertainment, as it would be for Mr. Faraday to announce in a dubious manner that iron had an affinity for oxygen, and to put it to a vote of his audience whether it had or not.

This was in answer to the cry of his dogmatism, for by this time he did not argue his points, but asserted them. A part of his task of preparation for the position of a dogmatist was a thorough study of the physical sciences, — of optics, geometry, geology, botany, and anatomy. It sometimes required a week or two's hard walking to determine some geological problem; but he never hesitated, and he made journeys to and fro in every direction to verify various points in all these preparatory studies. Then he set himself to a thorough study of all the great artists, and the history of the times in which they lived, travelling much and sometimes giving months of reading and study to one great master. He at the same time was making a real study of classical and mediæval landscape, and sojourning in many different places to do so properly. One whole winter was spent in trying to get at the mind of Titian, going from one city to another for this purpose. The plates for the illustrations, all drawn by his own hand, were also a matter of infinite detail and difficulty.

It was seventeen years before the fifth volume of "Modern Painters" was published. Ruskin had changed much in that time, and his art opinions had changed, but in the main principle of the book, as he says in the preface, there is no variation from the first syllable to the last. It declares the perfection and eternal beauty of the work of God, and tests all work of man by concurrence with, or subjection to that. In other words, he judged of art by its truth to nature, truth being the one cardinal principle of all Ruskin's teachings upon art or morality. In regard to the changes time had made in his opinions, he said: " Let a man be assured that unless important changes are occurring in his opinion continually, all his life long, not one of those opinions can be, on any questionable subject, true. All true opinions are living, and show their life by being capable of nourishment, therefore of change."

In the interval between the fourth and fifth volumes another great task had fallen to him, — the arrangement of all the Turner drawings belonging to the nation. "In seven tin boxes," he says, " in the lower rooms of the National Gallery, I found upwards of 19,000 pieces of paper drawn upon by Turner. Many on both sides, some with four, five, or six subjects on each side; some in chalk which a touch of the finger would sweep away, some in ink rotted into holes, others eaten by mildew, some worm-eaten, some mouse-eaten, many torn half-way through. Dust of thirty years accumulated upon all." With two assistants he was at work all the autumn and winter of 1857, every day, all day long, and often far into the night. The task completed he was left in a state of complete exhaustion. But he had saved the precious relics, of unspeakable value, as showing the complete unfolding of Turner's great mind; and no one else living could have done it. They will be visited by fascinated thousands while a remnant of them remains. To rest himself he started off to Germany and Switzerland, to visit many of the spots shown in the drawings, in order to understand them more fully.

He was never afraid of labor, and was constantly collecting materials and planning out new enterprises. This remained the case even to old age. At fifty-six he wrote: —

"I have now enough by me for a most interesting history of thirteenth century Florentine art, in six octavo volumes; analysis of the Attic art of the fifth century B. C. in three volumes; an exhaustive history of Northern thirteenth century art, in ten volumes; a life of Turner, with analysis of modern landscape art, in four volumes; a life of Xenophon, with analysis of the general principles of education, in ten volumes; a life of Walter Scott, with analysis of modern epic art, in seven volumes; a commentary on Hesiod, in nine volumes; and a general description of the geology and botany of the Alps, in twenty-four volumes."

In "Proserpina" and "Deucalion" he published some of the material upon geology and botany, beginning to see that the limit of an earthly life would preclude the doing of some of the work he longed to do.

It is much to be regretted that he was not able to write the life of Scott, a labor of love which doubtless would have been an enduring monument to the great Wizard of the North. He gives, probably, the truest estimate of the genius of Scott written by any contemporary. While placing him at the head of romancers in his best work, and finding it everywhere ringing true, he perceives the deterioration of his genius in the latter overworked period of his life, and regards as almost worthless some of his hurried work. The books he considers to be of the first rank are the ones produced before the almost fatal illness of Scott in 1819. They consist of "Waverley," "Guy Mannering," "The Antiquary," "Rob Roy," "Old Mortality," and "The Heart of Midlothian." "The Bride of Lammermoor," the first written after his recovery, he ranks in the second class, with "Ivanhoe," "The Monastery," "The Abbot," "Kenilworth," and "The Pirate." He attributes the prevailing melancholy and the fantastic improbability of these to his broken health. He says: "Three of the tales are agonizingly tragic, 'The Abbot' scarcely less so in its main event, and 'Ivanhoe' deeply wounded through all its bright panoply; while even in 'Ivanhoe,' the most powerful of the series, the impossible archeries and axe-strokes, the incredibly opportune appearances of Locksley, the death of Ulrica, and the resuscitation of Athelstane, are partly boyish, partly feverish." Of the others he accepts "Redgauntlet" and "Nigel," "Quentin Durward" and "Woodstock," as sound work, and throws all the others away. The whole essay from which this estimate of Scott is taken, called "Fiction Fair and Foul," is of surpassing interest, and many other original conclusions of the author might be cited. He considers

"the very power to imagine certain characters and incidents as a mark of a diseased condition of the brain," and instances "all the deaths by falling, or sinking, as in delirious sleep, to be found in Scott, as Kennedy, Eveline Neville, Amy Robsart, and the Master of Ravenswood in the quicksand.

"In Dickens it gives us Quilp, Krook, Smike, Smallweed, Miss Mowcher; and the dwarfs and wax works of Nell's caravan; and runs entirely wild in 'Barnaby Rudge,' where the *corps de drame* is composed of one idiot, two madmen, a gentleman fool who is also a villain, a shop-boy fool who is also a blackguard, a hangman, a shrivelled virago, and a doll in ribbons, — carrying this company through riot and fire, till he hangs the hangman, one of the madmen, his mother, and the idiot, runs the gentleman fool through in a bloody duel, and burns and crushes the shop-boy into shapelessness. He cannot yet be content without shooting the spare lover's leg off, and marrying him to the doll in a wooden one, the shapeless shop-boy being finally also married in two wooden ones. It is this mutilation which is the very sign manual of the plague."

This skeleton of "Barnaby Rudge" will no doubt shock the admirers of Dickens, but it is a needed, though scathing *exposé* of much that is unhealthy in modern literature. It will surprise those admirers also to hear that he "separates the greatest work of Dickens, 'Oliver Twist,' with honor, from the loathsome mass to which it typically belongs." "That book," he says, "is an earnest and uncaricatured record of states of criminal life, written with didactic purpose, full of the gravest instruction, nor destitute of pathetic studies of noble passion."

His detestation of those "anatomical preparations for the general market, of novels like 'Poor Miss Finch,' in which the heroine is blind, the hero epileptic, and the obnoxious brother is found dead with his hands dropped off in the Arctic regions," is both violent and amusing.

His abhorrence of the latest *fin de siècle* novels is

truly refreshing, and worthy of being imitated by us all. He says : —

" It is quite curious how often the catastrophe or the leading interest of a modern novel turns upon the want, both in maid and bachelor, of the common self-command which was taught to their grandmothers and grandfathers, as the first elements of ordinarily decent behavior. . . . But the automatic amours and involuntary proposals of recent romance, acknowledge little further law of morality than the instinct of an insect or the effervescence of a chemical mixture."

While he was at Oxford the movement which resulted in the modern High Church and Broad Church parties was already in its incipient stages, but Ruskin took no part and little interest in it. It seems strange that a man who had been brought up on constant Bible-reading and sermon-hearing, who was destined for the Church, and whose life-long business it had been to refer everything to the language and principles of religion, should have looked on unmoved while great questions were being agitated, consciences wrung, and souls torn asunder between faith and doubt.

But his religion had never been a matter of speculation. He had accepted humbly what he had been taught, and, being of a deeply religious nature, he had found its practice not only a duty but a delight. He seems to have had no genius for doubting. It was only after he was separated from his parents that he wandered away from their teachings. But the scientific movement at Oxford, led by Dr. Buckland and Henry W. Ackland, took firm hold of him, and eventually led him away from his attachment to the Church of England. He gave up studying for the priesthood, nominally on account of ill-health, but in reality on account of unsettled belief. He underwent many years of great mental suffering, and at last emerged what might be called a pious agnostic, if such a term is allowable. His deep religious feeling never left him, as all who have studied his works must have remarked; but in the creeds of the churches he had little belief. In old age he became interested in spiritism, and derived great consolation from some of its teachings. His doubts of a future life changed to firm belief therein, and a singular happiness settled upon him, which at first it was thought betokened renewed health and strength.

But his mind had by this time begun to fail, and his first period of insanity came on, which it was feared would blot out forever the great intellect. He recovered after a time, and renewed his labors. But he has been subject to periods of aberration of mind ever since. Settled melancholy is the form it commonly takes, and his visions of life become distorted and threatening, and he lives at all times in an atmosphere of fear and of distrust. He is cared for by his cousin Mrs. Arthur Severns, who has long had charge of his home. He was married in his youth, and lived for a few years with the woman of his choice; but she was not a person well calculated to yield her life to the care of an eccentric man of genius, and was unhappy in that position. There had not been, perhaps, much love in the beginning, on her part, and she decided to live apart from him, to which he gave his consent in a friendly manner, and has lived alone since that time.

This domestic trouble was a blow from which it is thought he never recovered. He lived in great seclusion for a long time, scarcely seeing his nearest friends. Mrs. Ruskin was afterward married to Millais the artist, which event revived much of the gossip which had attended her separation from her husband. That a man proud, sensitive, and devotedly fond, should have been irremediably wounded by such a catastrophe, needs not to be said. But when well advanced in middle life he met another woman for whom he entertained a very warm feeling, and whom he would gladly have brought to his home, as companion and comforter of his declining years. She was said to have been much attached to him also, but she refused to marry him on account of his religious opinions, she being of the straitest sect of the Pharisees, while he was, in her eyes, an unbeliever. One of his most serious illnesses followed the waking from this dream, and from that time he has been almost a recluse from the world. He retired to his country-place, Brantwood, where he spent much time and money in improving it, and where he still lives. But he was very sad even there, and writes at intervals in strains such as follows : —

" Morning breaks, as I write, over these Coniston Fells, and the level mists, motionless and gray beneath the rose of the moorlands, veil the lone woods and the sleeping village, and the long lawns by the lake shore. Oh, that someone had but told me in my youth, when all my heart seemed to be set on these colors and clouds, that appear for a little while and then vanish away, how little my love of them would serve me when the silence of lawn and wood in the dews of morning should be completed, and all my thoughts should be of those whom, by neither, I was to meet more."

Of the large fortune left him by his father little or nothing remains. He gave the greater portion of it away, and used the remainder in working out his impracticable philanthropic schemes, of which he has had many. He spent large sums on the Sheffield Museum, in which he took great pride and interest. He also started St. George's Guild, and it became a considerable expense to him, as did many other of his schemes for the benefit of working-men. For them he wrote the " Fors Clavigera," publishing them in numbers, at intervals, for several years; and he lectured for them a great deal, on many and varied subjects. These letters and talks to working-men, and the miscellaneous letters written to the newspapers throughout his life, contain some of the most valuable of his opinions upon practical subjects. Two or three specimens will show their quality. He writes thus on fox-hunting : —

" Reprobation of fox-hunting on the ground of cruelty to the fox is entirely futile. More pain is caused to the draught-horses of London in an hour by avariciously overloading them, than to all the foxes in England by the hunts of the year ; and the rending of body and heart in human death, caused by neglect, in our country cottages, in one winter, could not be equalled by the death-pangs of any number of foxes. The real evils of fox-hunting are that it wastes the time, misapplies the energy, exhausts the wealth, narrows the capacity, debases the taste, and abates the honor of the upper classes of this country ; and instead of keeping ' thousands from the workhouse,' it sends thousands of the poor both there and into the grave."

Of drunkenness he says : —

" Drunkenness very slightly encourages theft, very largely
encourages murder, and universally encourages idleness. . . .
Drunkenness is not the *cause* of crime in any case. It *is*
itself crime in every case. A gentleman will not knock out
his wife's brains while he is drunk ; but it is nevertheless his
duty to remain sober.

" Much more is it his duty to teach his peasantry to remain
sober, and to furnish them with sojourn more pleasant than
the pot-house, and means of amusement less circumscribed
than the pot. And the encouragement of drunkenness, for
the sake of the profit on sale of drink, is certainly one of the
most criminal methods of assassination for money hitherto
adopted by the bravos of any age or country."

On almsgiving he wrote in 1868 : —

" No almsgiving of money is so helpful as almsgiving of
care and thought ; the giving of money without thought is
indeed continually mischievous ; but the invective of the
economist against *in*discriminate charity is idle, if it be not
coupled with pleading for discriminate charity, and, above
all, for that charity which discerns the uses that people may
be put to, and helps them by setting them to work in those
services. That is the help beyond all others ; find out how
to make useless people useful, and let them earn their money
instead of begging it."

He was Professor of Art at Oxford for many years,
and his " Lectures on Art " fill a valuable place in his
collected writings. They were the cause of a great
volume of controversy, and he was obliged to defend
his opinions and his statement of them many times.
All this discussion was valuable as a means of art
education to the English people, who have made
rapid progress during Ruskin's day. The excitement

that attended the publication of the first two volumes of " Modern Painters " marked an era in the education of the people. That interest was renewed when the " Seven Lamps of Architecture and Painting " appeared. These early works won readers for " The Stones of Venice," and the concluding volumes of " Modern Painters," when they appeared, and for all his books on art or morals that have since been offered to the public. He lives now on the income received from the sale of his books. He has always been opposed to the taking of interest for the use of money, and refused to take it himself. For many years he published his own books, and only in expensive editions with drawings by his own hand. But of late his works have been brought out in cheap editions, and have circulated among all classes. His drawings are of the most exquisite delicacy, and their finish as nearly perfect as human hand can give. He has had great delight in them all his life. In literary workmanship he has not been excelled in his day, and perhaps, in his best work, not equalled. His vocabulary is unrivalled, and he uses every word with a due sense of its meaning and importance. He is perhaps in equal parts artist and poet; his prose poems are pictures, and his illustrations poems. The high character of the man shows in all his literary and critical work. Sincerity and truth are his watchwords throughout, and some of his phrases, like " being wholly right," have become catchwords.

His almost unequalled devotion to the service of mankind, and his pure and passionless life are known to all, and add intensity to the sympathy for his peculiar affliction, felt throughout the world.

Long ago his hand had lost its cunning. The feeble utterances of his later years are sad evidence of a more than natural degeneration and decay. The sweet bells have been jangled in his brain for a long time, and human life has assumed huge and distorted shapes to his fevered vision. That touch of madness which is in all genius has spread beyond its bounds, has assumed control of the whole man at times. It is long since his majestic books were written, whose stately sentences will be his enduring monument. The last superfluous years are a blank in literature, and a blank to friendship also. They remind one of Emerson's saying that life is unnecessarily long. He is the Sir Galahad of modern times. The light that never was on sea or land has led him, and poetry and romance have been his native air. He, too, has followed, yea, seen, the Holy Grail clothed in white samite, mystic, wonderful; and those of us who, like Lancelot, may have followed but not seen, can but pray that its splendor may illume his dying dreams.

THOMAS HENRY HUXLEY.

THOMAS HENRY HUXLEY was born on May 4, 1825, at Ealing, then a small village near London, now a populous suburb of the great city. He was educated chiefly at home, by his father, who was master of a large public school. He attended the school two or three years, and learned some useful lessons in his contact with the boys, particularly to look out for himself, and stand up for his rights. His characteristic traits in after life were inflexible determination and a tenderness that never failed. Here among his earliest companions these final characteristics could have been plainly discerned. He had a hot temper, and he was always ready to fight a bully and to defend a smaller or weaker boy. He was afterwards denominated the fighting scientist, from his readiness to meet in open battle any one who attacked his own opinions or those of his scientific friends. Perhaps he was a little more likely to defend his friends, particularly Darwin, than to take up arms in his own defence. When Darwin published "The Origin of Species," he was bitterly denounced in almost every pulpit in the land as an infidel. Darwin paid little attention to his opponents,

but went on with his researches. But Huxley, who was already a well-known scientist, sprang at once to his defence, and fought his battles in the arena from that time on. He was a brilliant debater and a most powerful adversary. Sometimes it happened that his own discoveries were thrown into the shade for a time by his dashing advocacy of the evolution theory of his friend. He studied medicine at the Charing Cross School, interested especially in physiology. Here he endangered his life in a post-mortem examination, and did not entirely recover from the poisoning for many years. That hypochondriacal dyspepsia which afflicted him throughout life was always attributed to this cause. The asceticism of his life was due partly to this, no doubt, but he was too great a physiologist not to be an advocate of moderation in all things.

In 1845 he received the degree of M. B. from the University of London, being placed second in the list of honors for anatomy and physiology. He began contributing to the " Medical Times and Gazette" while he was yet a student. He was in 1846 appointed assistant surgeon to H. M. S. " Victory," for service in Haslar Hospital, and entered upon his duties with characteristic zeal and industry. Like his friend Darwin, he desired to go on a scientific exploring expedition. Sea-life had, in prospect, a great fascination for him, and he could not be dissuaded from the undertaking by his friends. He secured the appointment as assistant surgeon to H. M. S. " Rattlesnake," bade farewell to family and friends, and sailed away in the highest spirits. He had foreseen some of the inevitable hardships of the long voyage, but the reality far outstripped his liveliest imaginings. But he was a young man, and privations and discomforts sat upon him rather lightly, after all was said; and his work, to which he was supremely devoted, compensated for all. He undertook a systematic study of such branches of natural history as the voyage afforded facilities for, and embodied the results in memoirs afterwards contributed to the Linnæan and Royal Societies, and in a work called "Oceanic Hydrozoa, a Description of the Calycophoridæ and Physophoridæ Observed during the Voyage of H. M. S. 'Rattlesnake.'"

The greater part of the period of his absence from England was spent off the eastern and northern coasts of Australia. Those years were full of absorbing interest to him, and the results of his labors made him, on his return in 1850, a fellow of the Royal Society, and brought him one of the Royal medals. In 1855 he was appointed Professor of Natural History at the Royal School of Mines, and his life-work seemed to be clearly mapped out for him. Honors and emoluments of various kinds followed him, from this time on. He who had had no university education received honorary degrees from the leading universities of Europe, and he was made a member of nearly all the scientific societies of the world, and took active part in their proceedings. At first his work was published principally in the journals of the Royal, the Linnæan, the Geological and Zoölogical Societies, and of course was read mostly by scientific men. But among them his reputation was soon established, and from them spread to the outside world. He has done as much as any living investigator to advance the science of zoölogy, and the world is indebted to him for many important discoveries in each of the larger divisions of the animal kingdom. His Pacific voyage gave him a minute knowledge of the lower marine animals, which had been imperfectly described before his day. His labors in the comparative anatomy and the classification of the vertebrata have been of the first importance. To him, also, is due the vertebral theory of the skull.

Outside of purely scientific circles he is perhaps best known by his three lectures on " Man's Place in Nature," delivered in 1863, wherein he applied the evolution theory to man, and asserted that " the anatomical differences between man and the highest apes are of less value than those between the highest and lowest apes." Of course this assertion brought upon him a perfect storm of denunciation and personal abuse. " Infidel " was one of the mildest names by which he was assailed. The conservative press and the pulpit vied with each other in attacking not his theory alone, but himself. He was soon known as " the man who says his mother was an ape." All the pugnacity of his nature was aroused, and he proved that he could hurl epithets with the best. Ridicule, satire, and invective were in turn employed against his assailants. The defence of Darwin was a sham battle beside this doughty conflict. He did it all with real glee, and not one of the poisoned arrows of his enemies seemed to cleave his mail. The scientific camp itself was divided on this question, but many of his friends came to his support. Always great in controversy, he here outdid himself, and thousands of readers who had never read a scientific work before became his obstinate partisans from that time on. George W. Smalley, who writes most entertainingly of Mr. Huxley, says on this point : —

"Huxley made no attack on religion, and religion none on him. But the Scribes and Pharisees encompassed him about. The self-constituted defenders of the old order of things assailed him. He claimed the right to think for himself on subjects as to which Rome and, following Rome, the Church of England as her spiritual or apostolic successor, had delivered to the world a final decree. That was offence enough. Call him an infidel at once, as Darwin had been called. The result was to engage Huxley in a series of discussions on the mixed and always debatable ground which the Church claims as its private domain, and upon which free thought had steadily encroached. I will not say that in such discussions he was at his best, for scientific experts tell you that he was at his best in pure science, or in the exposition of pure science. But I will say that he was better than anybody else. Whom will you put beside him? Who met and vanquished so many very eminent antagonists? Mr. Gladstone, Ward, Dr. Wall, the Duke of Argyll, Mr. Frederic Harrison, — these are but a few of the most distinguished men who attacked Huxley and were worsted. Ecclesiastical thunders rolled harmlessly about his head. Theology and biblical criticism, cried his opponents, are not Mr. Huxley's ground ; why does he intrude on our pastures? The answer is to be found in the published volumes which contain the essays and discourses on these subjects. It is to be found not less clearly in the existing state of public opinion, due as it is so largely to these very encounters. The emancipation of thought, — that is Huxley's legacy to his century, that was his continual lesson of intellectual honesty."

In 1868 he raised another storm by his lecture "On the Physical Basis of Life." In it he advances the idea "that there is some one kind of matter common to all living beings; that this matter, which he designates as protoplasm, depends on the pre-existence of certain compounds, carbonic acid, water, and ammonia, which when brought together under certain conditions give rise to it; that this protoplasm is the formal basis of all life, and therefore all living powers are cognate, and all living forms, from the lowest plant or animalculæ to the highest being, are fundamentally of one character." The changes which have been rung on the word "protoplasm" from that day to this are infinite, and show the importance the world attached to the idea. The controversialist was obliged to don his armor again and engage in another tilt with his adversaries, from which, as usual, he came out unscathed, and ready for another tourney. In fact, whenever a bugle sounded anywhere throughout the world, he was wont to put on his spurs.

His connection of two years' length with the London School Board was another opening for bitter controversy. He was chairman of the committee which drew up the scheme of education adopted by the Board schools. He was very deeply interested in education all his life, and this was an opportunity to do something practical for its furtherance. He was a splendid worker along his favorite lines, and became a very active member of the Board. His chief battle in the educational field was fought out over the subject of denominational teaching, and his fierce denunciation of the doctrines of the Roman Catholic Church led to much acrimonious debate

That conflict has become historic, and his gallant behavior under fire is still proudly contemplated by his supporters. Of course he made bitter enemies by his intrepid attitude, but such fearless and dashing free lances as he never live long without enemies. He was compelled by ill-health to retire from the Board in 1872. He was then elected Lord Rector of Aberdeen University, and served there for three years. In 1883 he was chosen President of the Royal Society. On the advice of Lord Salisbury, Queen Victoria called him at last to be sworn of the Privy Council, an honor carrying with it the title Right Honorable. He considered it a recognition of the claims of science rather than as a personal honor, and accepted it, knowing it would dignify his chosen work in the minds of the multitude. Largely by his efforts the standing of scientific men had been raised socially in England during his lifetime, and without abating a jot of his native pride and independence, he accepted the recognition of his own labors which the appointment carried.

The popularization of science had been one of the most important works of his life, and some recognition was due it by the government which had benefited by it. Being chosen President of the Royal Society was indeed an honor worthy even of Huxley, but it was a recognition of his purely scientific work in physiology and biology, without regard to what he had done for the mass of his countrymen. Original research is the one thing honored by the Royal Society.

He was long a member of a metaphysical society, and fond of its discussions. Here he used to meet

Mr. Gladstone, and break a lance with him on occasion. He did not hesitate in the least to crumple him up in controversy, scarcely ever agreeing with him in his premises. It was an amusement to the members to see the great high-priest of Orthodoxy in the toils of the scientific expert. Mr. Gladstone, it is well known, could discourse for hours upon any subject of which the mind of man can conceive; and when he was once launched it was almost impossible to bring him to shore any time within the limits of an ordinary gathering of men. To the adroitness of Huxley the Metaphysical Club owed many such skilful landings of the old statesman's craft in bygone days. He was too impatient to listen to any man whose talk goes on forever, in unruffled calm. Still he was a popular man in society, and amazingly prized by his friends. Darwin was far from being the only man who found him "splendid fun." Men regarded him with real affection, and defended him right valiantly when he was attacked. He had as close a personal following as any man of his day. He lived for the greater part of his life in London, and his house in St. John's Wood was the resort of literary and scientific men, who found it a most informal and delightful rendezvous. He gave every Sunday evening a dinner followed by a reception. George Eliot for many years held her little court in the same neighborhood. In both houses there was plain living and high thinking, and utter fearlessness in the expression of opinion. Your ideas might be controverted, they were very likely to be so, but you would be listened to with respectful attention. Many people found out at these gatherings that there were more things in heaven and earth than had been dreamed of in their philosophy. But the meetings were not haunted by the wrangling daw to any great extent. Discussion there was always, seldom dispute. Huxley hated compromise, but in his own home he often smoothed down rough places in the interest of social enjoyment. Herbert Spencer sometimes touched a jarring lyre, in the belief that the right must always be defended, and the wrong always combated.

The gatherings were truly notable ones. Few houses in England assembled such distinguished guests habitually. Tyndall was almost always there, Huxley's one chum, whose impassioned logic never wearied, when he discoursed of the glorious insufficiencies of everything save science, but before whom the flippant quailed and the brazen were awed into silence. Sir Henry Maine, Lord Arthur Russell, Norman Lockyer, were frequent guests. Then the artists came in force; Alma Tadema, Frederick Leighton, Burne-Jones, most frequently. All of the lesser-known scientific men were there, and representative lords and ladies, and even ecclesiastics. Huxley had a

> " High nature amorous of the good,
> But touched with no ascetic gloom,"

and here hilarity was not forbidden, but rather encouraged, and fun and frolic were not unknown.

He was always interested in education and in literature, and he who had the latest word on these themes was always listened to with profound attention; and he loved the society of literary men, who gladly thronged his house. He was a scholar himself,

and greatly prized learning in others. Largely self-
taught, he had acquired Latin, German, and French
as indispensable to his scientific work, and he read
much history and general literature in his small leisure. He was an indefatigable worker, loving to dig
sixteen hours a day, and doing so during much of
his life. His children saw little of him during their
early years for this reason, and felt that a Sunday
walk with him was the choicest of their pleasures.
He used to delight them with sea-stories, and tales of
animals, and occasionally geological sketches suggested by their surroundings, but he gave them no
real scientific instruction. His oldest son graduated
with honors in the classics, which pleased him very
much. He was fond of saying that he could have
done it himself had he had the opportunity. On
these walks his love for animals was frequently shown.
He was fond of dogs, but cats were the nearest to his
heart. His assortment of pet felines was well known
to all his intimates. They followed him up and down
garden walks and terraces, and he was never tired of
their attendance upon him. Children also were great
favorites with him, especially in later life. When
young, he was too much absorbed in his work to give
them much attention. We are told by his son: —

"Spirit and determination always delighted him. His
grandson Julian, a curly-haired rogue, alternately cherub and
pickle, was a source of great amusement and interest to
him. The boy must have been about four years old when
my father one day came in from the garden, where he had
been diligently watering his favorite plants with a big hose,
and said, 'I like that chap; I like the way he looks you
straight in the face and disobeys you. I told him not to go

on the wet grass again. He just looked up boldly straight at me, as much as to say, "What do you mean by ordering me about?" and deliberately walked on to the grass.' The disobedient youth who so charmed his grandfather's heart was the prototype of Sandy in Mrs. Humphry Ward's 'David Grieve.' When the book came out my father wrote to the author, 'We are very proud of Julian's apotheosis. He is a most delightful imp, and the way in which he used to defy me on occasion, when he was here, was quite refreshing. The strength of his conviction that people who interfere with his freedom are certainly foolish, probably wicked, is quite Gladstonian.' Next spring, however, there was a modified verdict. It was still, ' I like that chap ; he looks you straight in the face. But there 's a falling off in one respect since last August, — he now does what he 's told.' Happily this phase did not last too long. In the autumn he writes to me : 'I am glad to hear that Julian can be naughty on occasion. There must be something wrong with any of my descendants, even if modified by his mother's notorious placidity, who is as uniformly good as that boy used to be. "

The humorous side of his nature came out strongly when with children, as it did in intercourse with intimate friends. It was a delightful element of his character, which shows itself at times in his writings, but was much more prominent than his writings would lead one to believe. His family have many charming recollections of how it irradiated the home life. Though not handsome he was easily the most distinguished-looking man in almost any assembly he frequented. He had a commanding air, and a face intensely alive, and soul illuminated. The square forehead, the square jaw, the large firm mouth, the flashing dark eyes, the long gray hair, in later years, combined to form a picture very pleasing, and, when his smile was added to it, very lovable. He was an excellent speaker, and his lectures gained much from his delivery. He frequently had very large audiences at his lectures for working-men, and he was always well heard by the interested auditors. He spent much time in such work as this, talking in a perfectly simple off-hand way that always charmed. He opened his address on " Technical Education " before the Working Men's Club in London in this informal manner: —

" Any candid observer of the phenomena of modern society will readily admit that bores must be classed among the enemies of the human race ; and a little consideration will probably lead him to the further admission, that no species of that extensive genus of noxious creatures is more objectionable than the educational bore. Convinced as I am of the truth of this great social generalization, it is not without a certain trepidation that I venture to address you on an educational topic. For in the course of the last ten years, to go back no farther, I am afraid to say how often I have ventured to speak of education, from that given in the primary schools to that which is to be had in the universities and medical colleges ; indeed, the only part of this wide region into which, as yet, I have not adventured is that into which I propose to intrude to-day. Thus, I cannot but be aware that I am dangerously near becoming the thing which all men fear and fly."

In proof that he had a right to address them, being also a handicraftsman, he said further on:

" The fact is, I am, and have been any time these thirty years, a man who works with his hands, a handicraftsman. I do not say this in the broadly metaphorical sense in which fine gentlemen, with all the delicacy of Agag about them, trip to the hustings about election time, and protest that they too are working-men. I really mean my words to be taken in their direct, literal, and straightforward sense. In fact, if the most nimble-fingered watchmaker among you will come to my workshop, he may set me to put a watch together, and I will set him to dissect, say, a blackbeetle's nerves. I do not wish to vaunt, but I am inclined to think that I shall manage my job to his satisfaction sooner than he will do his piece of work to mine. In truth, anatomy, which is my handicraft, is one of the most difficult kinds of mechanical labor, involving, as it does, not only lightness and dexterity of hand, but sharp eyes and endless patience."

Going on, he gives his ideas of what the education of boys should be who desire to be professional anatomists, and, incidentally, upon many vital questions of general education. He says: —

" Above all things, let my imaginary pupil have preserved the freshness and vigor of youth in his mind as well as his body. The educational abomination of desolation of the present day is the stimulation of young people to work at high pressure by incessant competitive examinations. Some wise man (who probably was not an early riser) has said of early risers that they are conceited all the forenoon and stupid all the afternoon. Now, whether this is true of early risers in the common acceptation of the word or not, I will not pretend to say ; but it is too often true of the unhappy children who are forced to rise too early in their classes. They are conceited all the forenoon of life, and stupid all its afternoon. The vigor and freshness which should have been stored up for the purposes of the hard struggle for existence in practical life, have been washed out of them by precocious mental debauchery, — by book gluttony and lesson-bibbing. Their faculties are worn out by the strain put upon their callow brains, and they are demoralized by worthless childish triumphs before the real work of life begins. I have no compassion for sloth, but youth has more need for intellectual rest than age; and the cheerfulness, the tenacity of purpose, the power of work which make many a successful man what he is, must often be placed to the credit, not of his hours of industry, but to that of his hours of idleness in boyhood. Even the hardest worker of us all, if he has to deal with anything above mere details, will do well, now and again, to let his brain lie fallow for a space. The next crop of thought will certainly be all the fuller in the ear, and the weeds fewer."

That this doctrine is just as good now as many years ago, and even more applicable to America than to England, who can doubt?

In 1876 Mr. Huxley visited America, and gave four lectures, three on Evolution and one "On the Study of Biology." He is said to have been very much interested in the tugs in New York harbor, and to have remarked, "If I were not a man, I think I should like to be a tug." He was very enthusiastically received in this country, where his books had been and still are much read. His lectures on Evolution made an important addition to his published works. In 1883 the condition of his health induced him to resign his various appointments and to settle in the country. He went to Eastbourne by the sea, where he built a house and created a lawn and gardens, to which from that time on he devoted a great deal of time and thought. They became a sort of hobby with him, and all his friends became interested. His son tells us that —

"his chief occupation in the garden was to march about with a long hose, watering, and watering, especially his rockeries of Alpines in the upper garden and along the terraces lying below the house. The saxifrages and the creepers on the house were his favorite plants. When he was not watering the one he would be nailing up the other, for the winds of Eastbourne are remarkably boisterous, and shrivel up what they do not blow down. . . . To a great extent this pottering round the garden took the place of the long walks on the bracing downs which had been one of the chief inducements to settling in Eastbourne. After a spell of writing or reading, the garden lay always handy and inviting a stroll of inspection for as long or as short a time as he liked; indeed, my mother was not quite so well satisfied with the saxifrage mania, and declared he caught cold pottering about his plants."

He could no longer stoop over the microscope, but he loved to bend his back over his flowers, some of which caused him real grief by not thriving in the raw sea-air. He loved to give cuttings to his friends, and to receive them in return, after the manner of loving florists the world over, and he loved to proclaim his triumphs, which were considerable in spite of his unfavorable location, and he was "more inconsolable than Jonah" when he lost a clematis.

With a family of seven children he could not escape many parental anxieties, and the periods of illness in his family were a great drain upon his life forces. His eldest boy was taken from him at the age of four years, and his daughter Marian later in life. These sad events made a profound impression upon him, yet he felt that his own grief was slight and of short duration beside that of his wife, who remained inconsolable to the end.

His own health had usually been good, but failed in 1886, when he went to Switzerland in hopes of benefiting it, and retired from active life. He however continued his writing for some years. He enjoyed his well-earned freedom to the fullest extent, and was especially charmed with life in the country. His last illness was of several months' duration, but he was able to be about his garden a portion of that time. When he could no longer visit it he made daily inquiries about its progress, and took extreme pleasure in the flowers which were brought him. He died in 1895.

When he was gone the world burst into panegyrics. Many who had denied him his due in life, laid chaplets upon his grave. Some through his teachings had grown up nearer to his stature and were better able to appreciate his labors ; some rendered acclamations because of the multitude. His beloved doctrine of evolution had become largely an accepted fact, though the forms in which it was held were many and varied. Few, however, were left to question that

> " The grapes which dye the wine are richer far,
> Through culture, than the wild wealth of the rock ;
> The suave plum than the savage-tasted drupe ;
> The pastured honey-bee drops choicer sweet ;
> The flowers turn double, and the leaves turn flowers ; "

and this was the better part of his contention.

HARRIET BEECHER STOWE.

ON the stern background of old New England life, the Beecher family are cut like silhouettes. Each member, individual and distinct, occupies its own allotted space, and the group as a whole is very remarkable. They are a typical family in some ways, and yet altogether extraordinary. Highly intelligent, well cultured for the time, sternly religious, and affectionate though undemonstrative, — these characteristics were common to all the best New England blood, but in the Beecher family there was superadded a strain of genius, which did not touch all, but raised the general level of the family in the eyes of the world.

The ancestors of the Beechers came early to this country, only eighteen years after the landing of the Pilgrims from the " Mayflower; " and Mrs. Beecher and her son John were highly respected members of that early colony in New Haven. The members of this illustrious family had many traits in common; love of learning, public spirit, playful temper, and moods of deep depression, marked all the generations of them of whom we have any account.

Dr. Lyman Beecher, the father of Mrs. Stowe, was one of the best-known New England preachers of his

day, noted for eloquence, for faithfulness to all the exacting duties of his profession, for moral courage that never quailed when the situation became difficult, and for a vein of poetry that ran through all his nature, alongside of the deeper vein of honest common-sense for which he was famed. He lived very near to nature when a boy, and his love for all her varied phenomena lasted him through life. Mrs. Stowe once asked him if he was not afraid of the terrible thunderstorms which broke over the fields where he was working alone when a boy. "Not I," he answered gayly. "I wished it would thunder all day;" this, despite the religious teaching of his time, which made death a horror and a dread to so many. Their part of New England was an unsettled country in those days; and his first parish, East Hampton, Long Island, was a wild secluded spot on the seashore, whither he took his wife soon after his marriage, when twenty-four years old.

Harriet was born in Litchfield, Connecticut, June 14, 1811. She was hardly four years old when her mother died. This mother had been a beautiful and lovable woman, gifted in many ways. She had made an ideal home, and an irreproachable minister's wife. Dr. Beecher regarded her as the better and stronger portion of himself, and said that after her death his first sensation was one of terror, like that of a child suddenly shut out alone in the dark. With his family of eight children he was left to face the world alone, at a time when his position in the ministry was a peculiarly trying one. Mrs. Stowe had scant recollection of her mother, but she writes: —

"Then came the funeral. Henry was too little to go. I remember his golden curls and little black frock, as he frolicked like a kitten in the sun in ignorant joy. I remember the mourning dresses, the tears of the older children, the walking to the burying-ground, and somebody's speaking at the grave, and the audible sobbing of the family; and then all was closed, and we little ones, to whom it was so confused, asked the question where she was gone, and would she never come back."

Little Henry was discovered soon after digging in the ground, and upon being asked what he was doing, lifted up his curly head, and answered joyfully, "Why, I 'm going to heaven to find ma." Two years after, a new mother was brought home to this houseful of children, who appears to have come as near to filling the vacant place there as any woman could. Harriet writes of her coming : —

"A beautiful lady, very fair, with bright blue eyes, and soft auburn hair bound round with a black velvet bandeau, came into the room smiling, eager, and, happy-looking, and, coming up to our beds, kissed us, and told us that she loved little children, and that she would be our mother."

She won the love of the little motherless group, and the home was once more a happy place in which to live.

Harriet attended the Litchfield Academy until her eleventh year, and after that her sister Catharine's school at Hartford. She regretted Litchfield very much, but did not return to it for any lengthened stay. She says : —

"My earliest recollections of Litchfield are those of its beautiful scenery, which impressed and formed my mind long before I had words to give names to my emotions, or could analyze my mental processes. I remember standing

often in the door of our house and looking over a distant
horizon, where Mt. Tom reared its round blue head against
the sky, and the Great and Little Ponds, as they were called,
gleamed out amid a steel-blue sea of distant pine groves.
To the west of us rose a smooth bosomed hill called Prospect
Hill; and many a pensive, wondering hour have I sat at our
playroom window, watching the glory of the wonderful sunsets that used to burn themselves out, amid voluminous
wreathings, or castellated turrets of clouds, — vaporous
pageantry proper to a mountainous region. Litchfield sunsets were famous because perhaps watched by more appreciative and intelligent eyes than the sunsets of other
mountain towns around. The love and notice of nature
was a custom and habit of the Litchfield people; and
always of a summer evening the way to Prospect Hill was
dotted with parties of strollers who went up there to enjoy
the evening."

During these years of attendance upon school in
Hartford, Harriet began to try her pen. It was her
dream to be a poet, and she began a drama, called
" Cleon." The scene was laid, she tells us, " in the
court and time of the Emperor Nero, and Cleon was
a Greek lord residing at Nero's court, who, after
much searching and doubting, at last comes to the
knowledge of Christianity." This choice of a theme
is remarkable for so young a girl, its great literary
and dramatic possibilities showing her intuition in
such things. It remained for a genius of a later day
to fully develop the great theme in " Quo Vadis,"
but this child saw as clearly as did Sienkiewicz what
a picture could be painted on this broad canvas;
and the execution, judging by the few samples given
us, was as remarkable as the conception. Her sister
Catharine, however, considered this writing a waste

of time, and set her to the study of Butler's Analogy and the reading of Baxter's Saint's Rest.

It was at this time that she first believed herself to be a Christian. Most of her father's sermons she tells us were as unintelligible to her as if spoken in Choctaw, but he preached one simple and eloquent one from the text, "Behold, I call you no longer servants but friends," which for the first time made her think of Christ as a friend, and to love him. Her heart was filled with great joy, and she communicated her feeling to her father after their return home from church. "'Is it so?' he said, holding me silently to his heart, as I felt the hot tears fall on my head. 'Then has a new flower blossomed in the kingdom this day.'" "If she could have been let alone," her son writes, "and taught 'to look up and not down, forward and not back, out and not in,' this religious experience might have gone on as sweetly and naturally as the opening of a flower in the gentle rays of the sun. But unfortunately this was not possible at the time, when self-examination was carried to an extreme that was calculated to drive a nervous and sensitive mind well-nigh distracted. First, even her sister Catharine was afraid that there might be something wrong in the case of a lamb that had come into the fold without being first chased all over the lot by the shepherd; great stress being laid, in those days, on what was called 'being under conviction.'" It was not long before these anxious friends had her as unhappy as their hearts could wish, and she writes to her brother Edward: "My whole life is one continued struggle: I do nothing right. I yield to temptation almost as soon as it assails me. My deepest feelings are very evanescent. I am beset behind and before, and my sins take away all my happiness."

About this time Catharine lost her lover, Professor Fisher of Yale College, who was drowned at sea. "Without this incident," writes Rev. C. E. Stowe, "'The Minister's Wooing' would never have been written, for both Mrs. Marvyn's terrible soul struggles, and old Candace's direct and effective solution of all religious difficulties, find their origin in this stranded storm-beaten ship on the coast of Ireland, and the terrible mental conflicts through which her sister afterward passed, for she believed Professor Fisher eternally lost." One can imagine what an impression this incident made upon the already morbid mind of Harriet, and how her internal conflicts increased, until her whole soul was encompassed by great darkness. That she was obliged to work hard was her safety, for she now began to teach, as well as to study, in Catharine's school. The need of her beginning to work thus early will be understood, when it is stated that Dr. Beecher's salary had at first been from three to four hundred dollars a year and his firewood, and afterward eight hundred. Dr. Beecher was impelled, partly by his poverty, to remove to Boston at this time. This was the period when Harriet felt that she drew nearer to her father than at any other, though she did not go to Boston with the family.

Her religious conflicts lasted through months and even years, and we are told "that the terrible arguments of her father and her sister Catharine were sometimes more than she could endure." Her unhappiness was so deep and so apparent as to become a source of worry to her family, who tried in vain to cheer her aching heart. Her dark sorrows and melancholies were often discussed in their letters. Her health, never very good, suffered. As she grew older she showed plainly the strain of all her childish years. Overwork had produced its inevitable result, and through all her after-life she was a woman delicate and nervous, and subject to much suffering. This was a continual drawback to her in her literary work all through her years of most strenuous toil, and her lack of strength was made manifest at many great crises of her life. That old life of Puritan New England was indeed hard upon the young. Relaxation was frowned upon and deemed unnecessary. Hard work was the order of the day. Recreation was a word almost unknown, and what it stands for was very scant, and occupied but little of the time of the community. The youth of the Beecher family was a time of storm and stress, mainly from mental and religious conflicts. Outward temptations, or ordinary follies of youth, formed scarcely any part of it. But the intensity of their natures caused struggle and suffering in attaining that spiritual peace they longed for, and deemed so vital. The goal they sought was the feeling thus expressed : —

> " Come ill or well, the cross, the crown,
> The rainbow or the thunder,
> I fling my soul and body down,
> For God to plough them under."

Harriet after a few years thought she had attained this, and became calmer and happier.

After the removal of the whole family to Cincinnati, where she helped her sister in her school, we find her hard at work, but enjoying more of a social life, and broadening out in many ways. Here she met Dr. Stowe, who was then living with his first wife, and formed a strong friendship for both.

Dr. Beecher had what became a beautiful home on Walnut Hills. It was at that time two miles from the city, and the drive a very charming one through beech groves, and up and down hills, covered with rich turf, and shaded by magnificent trees. Here she began to write for the public. Her first success was taking a prize of fifty dollars offered by the editor of " The Western Magazine " for a story. From that time she devoted herself to literature, and entered into literary society in Cincinnati with as much zest as her health would permit.

About a year after her arrival in the West, her attention was first called to the subject of slavery. She made a visit to the plantation afterwards described as Colonel Shelby's in " Uncle Tom's Cabin." It was situated in Kentucky, and was one of the sources of her knowledge of negro character, though at the time she was there she did not appear to notice much of what was going on about her. But the subject was beginning to fill the minds of all morally earnest people, and though subordinate to other things up to this time, in her mind, her convictions were already strong as to the evils of slavery. It was not until after her marriage, however, that this subject assumed unusual prominence in her life. Professor Stowe's first wife having died two years before, she was married to him Jan. 6, 1836.

He was a professor in Lane Theological Seminary, a thorough scholar, eager for learning, and very proficient in Hebrew, Greek, and German. His memory was remarkable, and his learning exact. Although possessed of a keen sense of humor, he was extremely subject to depression of spirits, and needed above everything cheerful companionship. Harriet had been one of his wife's earliest friends, and had been a good deal in his family since her arrival in Cincinnati. This calm friendship had ripened into love through her sympathy in his affliction, and his need of care and tending.

Soon after her marriage her husband received an appointment as Commissioner to go abroad and report upon the common schools of Europe, especially those of Prussia. The opportunity was too fine a one to be rejected, and Harriet urged his acceptance of the appointment; so he left her for several months, and she remained in her father's home. These few months proved to be very eventful to the abolitionists. Mr. Birney and Dr. Baily came to Cincinnati and started an antislavery paper there. Kentucky slave-owners came over the border and destroyed the press. There was mob rule for the first time in Ohio. The Beecher family were naturally found on the side of law and order, and Harriet wrote to Dr. Stowe: " For a day or two we did not know but there would actually be war to the knife, as was threatened by the mob, and we really saw Henry depart with his pistols with daily alarm; only we were all too full of patriotism not to have sent every brother we had rather than not have had the principles of freedom and order defended." But here the tide turned. The mob, unsupported by a now frightened community, slunk into their dens and were still. "Pray, what is there in Cincinnati to satisfy one whose mind is awakened on this subject?" she continues. "No one can have the system of slavery brought before him without an irrepressible desire to *do* something; and what is there to be done?" Thenceforth it became one of her chief thoughts to find this something which she could do, and, her whole family feeling with her, they soon became a prominent factor in the abolition cause. They were an accession of infinite importance to the little band who were already pledged to this unpopular cause.

Before Professor Stowe had returned from his long stay in Europe Mrs. Stowe had given birth to twin daughters, and a year later a son was given them. Of course her domestic cares became almost overwhelming, her health suffered very much from this overstrain, and outside affairs became secondary for a brief period. In one of her off-hand letters she writes thus at this time: —

"Well, Georgy, this marriage is — yes, I will speak well of it, after all; for when I can stop and think long enough to discriminate my head from my heels, I must say that I think myself a fortunate woman both in husband and children. My children I would not change for all the ease, leisure, and pleasure that I could have without them."

Domestic help was hard to get at that time, and with their slender means almost impossible to them, and this was the time when she began her real acquaintance with the negroes. She could procure colored help, and began to do so early in her married life, and she was quick to note all their peculiar characteristics. This was done unconsciously at the time, but served a great purpose in after years. When the domestic vortex was in a comparative calm, she would even in this most trying time seize her pen and throw off some story or sketch, for which she received a slight remuneration, very welcome to her in her sore need. Four years and a half after her marriage she was possessed of four children, the resources of the family had not been increased, and her health seemed absolutely broken. After the birth of the fourth child she was confined to her bed for many weeks, and could not bear the light of day, owing to severe neuralgia in her eyes. That year they also had much other sickness in the family, Mrs. Stowe herself having been laid up fully six months out of the twelve.

But as soon as she was slightly recuperated she began to plan once more for literary work, the need of money was so very pressing. It is pathetic to read her appeal to her husband for a little room to herself in which to do her writing, — this delicate, nervous, highly strung woman with four children on her hands, and driven by want to undertake to add to the family income. One would think that the luxury of a study was an indispensable one. But she had written heretofore in all the tumult of the living-room, and with the babies tumbling about her. She writes : —

"There is one thing I must suggest. If I am to write I must have a room to myself, which shall be my room. I have in my own mind pitched on Mrs. Whipple's room. I can put a stove in it, I have bought a cheap carpet for it.

and I have furniture enough at home to furnish it. All last winter I felt the need of some place where I could go and be quiet and satisfied. I could not there, for there was all the setting of tables, and clearing up of tables, and dressing and washing of children, and everything else going on ; and the continual falling of soot and coal-dust on everything in the room was a continual annoyance to me, and I never felt comfortable there, though I tried hard. Then, if I came into the parlor where you were, I felt as if I was interrupting you, and you know you sometimes thought so too."

One does not wonder much to find her adding : —

" One thing more in regard to myself. The absence and wandering of mind and forgetfulness, that so often vexes you, is a physical infirmity with me. It is the failing of a mind not calculated to endure a great pressure of care ; and so much do I feel the pressure I am under, so much is my mind often darkened and troubled by care, that life seriously considered holds out few allurements, — only my children. In returning to my family, from whom I have been so long separated, I am impressed with a new and solemn feeling of responsibility. It appears to me that I am not probably destined for long life; at all events, the feeling is strongly impressed upon me that a work is put into my hands which I must be in earnest to finish shortly."

She had been absent at this time for some months on account of her failing health. Within a few months another daughter was born to her, and she writes to her brother: " Our straits for money this year are unparalleled even in our annals. Even our bright and cheery neighbor Allen begins to look blue, and says six hundred dollars is the very most we can hope to collect of our salary, once twelve hundred dollars." Things went on in much

this way for some years. Once she was obliged to
be away from her family for eleven months, at a
water-cure establishment, where she could at least
rest. She now had six children left to her, one
having died during Dr. Stowe's absence in the
east, the year of the cholera epidemic in Cincinnati. Many times she complained of her brain
giving out, and was much alarmed at this serious
symptom, due no doubt to her extreme weakness. She
was much depressed at this period of her life, and
needed all her strong faith and religious earnestness
to carry her through. At last there came a break in
the clouds, a call to Bowdoin College, which Dr.
Stowe accepted with peculiar pleasure, because he
had graduated there and passed there his happiest
years. He had given seventeen of the best years of
his life to Lane Seminary, and it was still a poor and
struggling institution. The removal to Brunswick,
Maine, marked that tide in the affairs of men which
leads on to fame and fortune. They were more
prosperous, happier, and less overworked from this
time. Mrs. Stowe's health gradually improved, and
she resumed her literary work, — though that had
never been entirely dropped.

On her way to Brunswick she stopped at the
home of her brother Dr. Edward Beecher. The
hearts of men were stirred, as never before, by the
Fugitive Slave Law, then being debated by Congress,
and there was fierce and fiery discussion of this measure during her visit. Both brother and sister knew
slavery by this time, having received and forwarded
fugitives many times, and heard heartrending accounts of what had befallen them as slaves. Mrs.

Beecher was the first one to appeal to Mrs. Stowe to use her pen in defence of the helpless people; and Mrs. Stowe responded with a promise to do something if she lived. Soon after being settled in her new home, she began her slave story in a white heat of passionate enthusiasm. It was to come out in the " National Era," and be written from week to week, as domestic matters would allow. This was usually her way of working during all her literary life. When driven to the last extremity, she dropped everything else, and became completely absorbed in her work, producing copy in an incredibly short space of time, seldom revising, or even punctuating, the sheets thus thrown off. Her publishers were sorely tried by her sometimes, but she had so many other cares, all her life, that it seemed impossible for her to improve her literary methods.

In writing " Uncle Tom's Cabin " she had no choice in the matter. There was still a baby in her arms, and a brood of young children in the nest, and only fragments of time could be used for her writing. But her subject possessed her, she did not have to beat about for ideas, or search long for plot or characters. Her whole being was saturated with the theme, her hot indignation ever welling up, her deep pity a part of her inmost soul. To make her circumstances a little easier while writing, the editor of the " Era " sent her one hundred dollars in advance, and with this encouragement she began. She wrote to friends in different parts of the country to place all the reliable information in their possession at her command, and received a great deal of ready-made pathos and horror. She worked upon the story for a year, writing an instalment every week, sometimes under almost insurmountable difficulties. The death of Uncle Tom was the first part written. This scene, we are told, " presented itself almost as a tangible vision to her mind while sitting at the communion-table in the little church in Brunswick. She was perfectly overcome by it, and could scarcely restrain the convulsion of tears and sobbings that shook her frame. She hastened home and wrote it, and, her husband being away, she read it to her two sons of ten and twelve years of age. The little fellows heard it with a passion of weeping, one of them saying through his sobs, ' Oh, mamma, slavery is the most cursed thing in the world.' From that time the story can less be said to have been composed by her than imposed upon her. Scenes, incidents, conversations, rushed upon her with a vividness and importunity that could not be withstood. The book insisted upon getting itself into being, and would take no denial. . . . In shaping her material the author had but one purpose, to show the institution of slavery truly, just as it existed."

The book appeared March 20, 1852. Ten thousand copies were sold in a few days, and over three hundred thousand within a year, and eight power-presses, running day and night, were barely able to keep up with the demand for it. It was received with acclamations throughout the North, and awakened the moral sense of the nation. People who had viewed the subject with indifference before, from that day became the haters of the system. It was eagerly read by all classes, young and old,

rich and poor, religious and irreligious. It stirred
the comatose Church like a blast from the final
trumpet, and it no longer lagged in the rear of
progress. It penetrated the walls of Congress and
made the politicians tremble. It startled statesmen,
who scented danger near. It reinforced the ranks
of the unpopular reformers, who had taken their
lives in their hands in this struggle, and filled up
their ranks with sturdy and enthusiastic recruits. It
made itself heard where no words of the abolitionists
had ever penetrated before. For years they had
rehearsed these appalling facts and made these
impassioned pleas in their meetings, but the people
would not come to hear, nor would they read the
papers in which they proved their allegations and
tried to stir an unresponsive world. But this book
spoke as one having authority and not as the
Scribes. It read itself, and no one who opened its
covers could escape unchanged. It was the marvel
of the time, and the wonder of succeeding generations. It was the beginning of the end, and no one
person contributed so much toward the downfall of
slavery as did its author. Even Whittier's fiery
lyrics paled their ineffectual fires before it, and
Sumner's words, which were half-battles, seemed
tame. The fiery eloquence of Phillips and Parker,
of the Beechers, father and sons, and all that innumerable company of orators and saints, fell short of
this miracle in conversions. Mrs. Stowe, the poor
overburdened mother, the careworn wife of a discouraged, unsuccessful minister, — she whose simple,
unpretending life had been passed in obscurity, —
from that day was the most famous woman in the

world. From over the sea, in a very short time, came the greetings of the great of all nations. Lord Carlisle, Charles Kingsley, the Earl of Shaftesbury, Archbishop Whately, Arthur Helps, Frederika Bremer, and George Sand were among the first to write and warmly congratulate her on her triumph. The book was soon translated into other languages, and the masses of the people in Europe read it, as they had done in America. Its phenomenal success abroad was the second great surprise its author had at that time. But all this has passed into history, and needs not to be retold.

A year after the book was published Mrs. Stowe visited England, and was received at Stafford House, there meeting all the best-known people in England, and receiving a perfect ovation from them, and thenceforth from all classes wherever she went in that country and in Scotland and Ireland. Addresses were made in every town she visited, and public meetings and demonstrations of sympathy were universal. The lordliest homes in the land were thrown open to welcome her, and none were too great or powerful to do her reverence. She received all these demonstrations with modesty and dignity, and although entirely new to scenes of this nature, comported herself well.

On her return to America she wrote of her experience abroad, in a series of sketches called "Sunny Memories of Foreign Lands," and soon after this composed her second great book, "Dred." Previous to this, however, she had written her "Key to Uncle Tom's Cabin," giving in detail all the facts upon which the book was founded. "Dred" was regarded by many of the best critics as a greater book than "Uncle Tom's Cabin," but its success was less pronounced, though great in itself. She made another visit to Europe after its publication, and met with the same cordial reception as before, alike from the great and the humble.

She returned home, and suffered, soon after, the loss of her eldest son Henry, who was drowned while bathing in the Connecticut River at Hanover, where he was pursuing his studies at Dartmouth College. The family were now living at Andover, and it is from this place that the letters to her friends announcing this sad news were written. She was more nearly crushed by this blow than by anything which had befallen her theretofore, but was sustained by that deep religious feeling which was a part of her nature, and was able to write: "These weary hours, when sorrow makes us for the time blind and deaf and dumb, have their promise. These hours come in answer to our prayer for nearness to God." To her youngest daughter she writes: —

"The fact is, pussy, mama is tired. Life to you is gay and joyous, but to mama it has been a battle in which the spirit is willing, but the flesh weak ; and she would be glad, like the woman in St. Bernard, to lie down with her arms around the wayside cross, and sleep away into a brighter scene."

She began at this time the publication, in the "Atlantic Monthly," of "The Minister's Wooing," one of her best pieces of work. She was cheered on by such letters as Lowell wrote her, wherein he says : —

"I am sure that 'The Minister's Wooing' is going to be the best of your products hitherto, and I am sure of it because you show so thorough a mastery of your material, so true a perception of realities, without which the ideality is impossible. . . . There is not, and never was, anybody so competent to write a true New England poem as yourself, and have no doubt that you are doing it. The native sod sends up the best inspiration to the brain, and you are as sure of immortality as we all are of dying, — if you only go on with entire faith in yourself."

In 1859 she went abroad once more, visiting Italy this time, and meeting in Rome Mr. and Mrs. James T. Fields, who became thereafter her closest personal friends, and from whom she received the kindest attentions and sympathy throughout life. Their home in Boston became her home also, whenever she chose to go there for rest or change; and, as her publisher, Mr. Fields was as kind and patient and helpful as a publisher could be. Mrs. Fields became the editor of Mrs. Stowe's life and letters, after her death, and executed the work with exquisite taste and perfect fidelity.

The stay in Rome was enjoyed exceedingly, although there were dark clouds gathering at home in the national sky, which betokened the long, dreadful storm of war which soon broke over the country. After her return her whole soul became bound up in the affairs of the nation, and for many years all her personal history became secondary to that of her country. No truer patriot ever lived than this weak, delicate woman, who had done so much for her country and had yet so much to do. One of her sons was among the first to respond to the President's call for volunteers. He enlisted in Company A of the First Massachusetts Volunteers. She went to see him off when the regiment left Jersey City, where she parted from him with a grave yet cheerful face, and returned home to her severe labors, as serene outwardly as before. What she felt in her heart it would be vain to try to describe. Of all her various labors at this time it is needless to speak in detail, but she was active from morning till night, and all days in the week, throughout the entire war. Visiting Washington at one time, and being introduced to President Lincoln, she was greeted in this way: "Is this the little woman who made this great war?" In many other ways a sense of deep responsibility was pressed home upon her which awed, but did not daunt her. Her lofty spirit is shown in the following words written in one of the darkest hours of defeat:

"If this struggle is to be prolonged till there be not one home in the land where there is not one dead, till all the treasure amassed by the unpaid labor of the slave shall be wasted, till every drop of blood drawn by the lash shall be atoned by blood drawn by the sword, we can only bow and say, 'Just and true are thy ways, thou King of Saints.'"

Lieutenant Beecher received a wound in the head early in the war, from which he never recovered. After months of intense suffering it healed, but imperfectly. He was never himself again. After the war his mother bought a plantation in Florida, where he was placed in hope of benefit to his health; but he grew worse rather than better, and never ceased to be the heaviest cross his mother bore. After a time he went to New York and sailed from there to San

Francisco; they knew that he arrived there in safety, but from that moment they never heard of him again. The terrible suspense and anxiety of the after years cannot be depicted in words. Two children she had already buried, but she had never known real sorrow before, as she often said to her friends.

But still another heavy blow awaited her in the trouble which befell her almost idolized brother Henry Ward Beecher. Scandal for the first time attacked this vulnerable man, who had made hosts of enemies by his antislavery work, his independent course in war-time, his outspokenness at all times, his increasingly liberal religious views, which brought him into great odium among the most conservative people of the Church, and in other ways, during a long and intensely exciting ministerial life. Such men walk at all times with their heads in a cloud of poisonous flies, and at last they settled upon Mr. Beecher at the very summit of his fame and usefulness.

We are not concerned with this matter except as it bears upon his sister's life, but no one can really understand that, without knowing her attitude upon this trying occasion. Her confidence in her brother was never shaken for a moment, and her love grew with her sorrow and her sense of wrong and cruel outrage. Her strength failed visibly. She resorted to Florida in order to avoid the newspapers and the hearing of torturing details. But she could not run away from the harrowing thoughts that encompassed her like a cloud, and made life for a time unendurable. She was hardly her old self after this to the close of her life.

Since the close of the war she had written a good deal, and during the reconstruction period exerted her powerful influence in many ways; but she had reached the summit of her greatness as a writer by that time, and though she still wrote well for many years, she never achieved another exceptional success. It is needless to recapitulate the long list of her books; they are familar to the literary world, although not known to the masses, as was "Uncle Tom's Cabin." She lived largely at the South for a few years, although she had a home also in Hartford, whither the family had removed after Professor Stowe had retired from his work at Andover. She was a weary woman by this time, and enjoyed the free pleasant life in the open air which she lived while at Mandarin. Here she had a well-tended orange-grove, and a lovely cottage of many gables, overlooking the beautiful St. John's River, which is five miles wide at this point. The piazza was built around one of a group of superb live-oaks, hung with the gray moss which gives such a ghostly air to Southern trees. After a time, however, the health of her husband confined her to her home in Hartford. Here he died in 1886. She was now seventy-six years old, and had earned her release from further active service. She had written thirty books, and performed almost incredible labors in many lines, often in pain and portentous weariness. She had been the principal bread-winner in the family during all her later life. She was always driven to write for money, in spite of the large sums she received from her books. Many works were executed under this pressure, when inspiration was lacking, which showed brain weariness rather than the gushing fervor of her earlier work.

But during the period following her husband's death, until her own in 1896, she performed no more labor. Her brain force was spent, and she lived a quiet dreamy life, reverting mostly to the past, and unable to remember from day to day the events which passed around her. She herself expressed it in this wise: —

"My mind wanders like a running brook, and I do not think of my friends as I used to, unless they recall themselves to me by some kind action. . . . I have written all my words and thought all my thoughts, and now I rest me in the flickering light of the dying embers, in a rest so profound that the voice of an old friend rouses me but momentarily, and I drop back again into repose."

Gradually she faded away from the great mystery of life, into the great sweet mystery of death.

ROBERT LOUIS STEVENSON.

ROBERT LOUIS STEVENSON.

THE words which follow might appropriately have been placed over the grave of this pure and gentle spirit, on the far-off mountain-top which overlooks the boundless Western Sea: —

> " I have trod the upward and the downward slope;
>   I have endured and done in days before;
>   I have longed for all, and bid farewell to hope;
>   And I have lived and loved, and closed the door,"

But he wrote his own requiem in other words: —

> " Under the wide and starry sky
>   Dig the grave and let me lie.
>   Glad did I live, and gladly die
>   And I laid me down with a will.

> " This be the verse you grave for me:
>   Here he lies where he longed to be;
>   Home is the sailor, home from sea,
>   And the hunter home from the hill."

Like the grave of Helen Hunt on the lonely mountain-top in Colorado, this poet's grave in distant Samoa will serve as a sort of beacon-light to pilgrims who love to pay tribute to genius. Every year other gifted spirits will seek it out to honor it. For Stevenson was a much loved man, by unknown readers as well as by personal associates, and all will feel an interest in him in death, as they followed him with the deepest sympathy in life to the palm-fringed beaches of the southern seas. But from the top of Mt. Vaea, as from the height where the Tennyson beacon burns, the poet's cheery call can yet be heard crying, " Follow the Gleam."   For —

> " Bright is the ring of words
>   When the right man rings them,
> Fair the fall of songs
>   When the singer sings them.
> Still are they caroled and said —
>   On wings they are carried —
> After the singer is dead
>   And the maker buried.

> " Low as the singer lies
>   In the field of heather,
> Songs of his fashion bring
>   The swains together.
> And when the west is red
>   With the sunset embers,
> The lover lingers and sings,
>   And the maid remembers."

This brilliant, gay, buoyant, and witty, though sick and sorrowful man has made at last his Outward Voyage, and in his own mournful words, —

> " Spring shall come, come again, calling up the moorfowl,
>   Spring shall bring the sun and rain, bring the bees and
>   flowers;
> Red shall the heather bloom over hill and valley,
> Soft flow the stream through the even-flowing hours;
> Fair shine the day as it shone on my childhood —
> Fair shine the day on the house with open door;
> Birds come and cry there and twitter in the chimney —
> But I go forever and come again no more."

He died at the age of forty-four. In that brief period of working years, he had in feebleness and pain produced a long list of works, upon every one of which is the brand of his peculiar genius. Poems, novels, essays, travels, short stories, biography, history, we view them with astonishment, as the work of a man who never knew a perfectly well day. Written in all parts of the world, for he was driven here and there constantly in search of health, they have a cosmopolitan air, though of course the dominant note is Scotch. The breath of the heather is in most of them, and the wild free air of the moors.

There was something exquisitely capricious in his life, as there was in his works. He never lived in the world of conventionalities. He loved "the lees of London and the commonplace of disrespectability." Unshackled freedom was the very breath of his nostrils, and the prosaic life of the average literary man would have been fatal to his genius. He was half the time afloat upon the sea which he loved, watching "the skippers' daughters," blown by gentle wind or wild tempest, half the time in forests, or upon heights overlooking rude seas. Sometimes, of course, in cities, but not for long. He crossed the Atlantic as an Amateur Emigrant, and made a true western Journey across the Plains. He made an "Inland Voyage from Antwerp to Boom, and onward to La Fere of Cursed Memory," and other spots where rivers ran. He made journeys with donkeys, and their annals are as thrilling as Scott's Lays of the Border. He knew by heart the promontories and islands of Scotland, and he loved to hear "the Roost roaring like a battle where it runs by Aros, and the great and fearful voices of the breakers which we call the Merry Men." He especially loved the woods, and says in his " Inland Voyage " : —

" Heine wished to lie like Merlin under the oak of Broceliande. I should not be satisfied with one tree; but if the wood grew together like a banyan grove, I would be buried under the tap-root of the whole ; my parts should circulate from oak to oak ; and my consciousness should be diffused abroad in all the forest, and give a common heart to that assembly of green spires, so that it also might rejoice in its own loveliness and dignity. I think I feel a thousand squirrels leaping from bough to bough in my vast mausoleum ; and the birds and the winds merrily coursing over its uneven, leafy surface."

He had the happy knack of giving the whole outline of a landscape in a few words, and has made "impressionist" pictures for us of many scenes far and near. In his travels there are many superb examples of poetic and sensuous description.

But after all it was man in whom he most delighted, and he was the most beloved writer of his day to men, especially to young men. All the younger literary men of the day belonged to his *claque*. All have written of him with the utmost sympathy and tenderness. Edmund Gosse but voiced their thought when he said : —

" What courage, what love, what an indomitable spirit, what a melting pity ! He had none of the sordid errors of the man who writes — no sick ambition, no envy of others, no exaggeration of the value of this ephemeral trick of scribbling. He was eager to help his fellows, ready to take a second place, offended with great difficulty, perfectly appeased by the least show of repentance. Stevenson was the most exquisite English writer of his generation; but those who lived close to him are apt to think less of that than of the fact that he was the most unselfish and the most lovable of human beings."

He truly " had a taste for other people, and other people had a taste for him."

Robert Louis Stevenson was born in Edinburgh November 13, 1850, the son and grandson of famous lighthouse engineers. One fancies that somehow their adventurous lives got into his blood, and that their knowledge of the sea became a part of his birthright. His childhood was all passed under the shadow of ill health; he was only able to pursue in the most desultory manner his studies, and for sports he had no strength. He was a dreamy boy, and loved to idle about Edinburgh, and wander into the surrounding country, where his eyes, which were emphatically made for seeing, doubtless stored up much which passed into literature in after days. He showed deep insight into child-life in later years, and no doubt some of this was due to memories of his somewhat unhappy, deeply imaginative childhood.

He attended the University of Edinburgh, but was not a brilliant scholar, and no one even suspected him of genius. This is not uncommon, of course, but usually such a youth will be known as a scribbler, which appears not to have been the case with him. He studied law and was admitted to the Scotch bar, but never practised in his profession. He had neither the taste for it nor the necessary health. He gradually drifted into literature, partly under the auspices of Sidney Colvin. His first paper appeared just after he was twenty-three, in "The Portfolio." It was called "Roads." The second, written the next winter at Mentone, was, "Ordered South." His first story of any note, "Will o' the Mill," was written in France. His first book was "An Inland Voyage," which attracted little attention, though it is a charming narrative of travel. His first novel, "Treasure Island," was written, he tells us, in two bursts of about fifteen days each, his quickest piece of work, and thought by many his best. Who does not remember the hold the story took upon him, from the moment when the brown old seaman with the sabre-cut came to the Admiral Benbow Inn? This tall, strong, heavy, nut-brown man, with his hands ragged and scarred, with black broken nails, and the sabre-cut across one cheek, which was a dirty, livid white, who sang, —

> "Fifteen men on the dead man's chest —
> Yo-ho-ho, and a bottle of rum !
> Drink and the devil had done his best —
> Yo-ho-ho and a bottle of rum,"

held us like the Old Man of the Sea from that moment; and we shared in all the terrors of poor Jim as they were unfolded to our view. How we shivered when Black Dog came, and so startled the old buccaneer; and those shiverings were scarcely over for us until the last page of the fascinating book was turned. Here was story-telling pure and simple, vivid, absorbing, poignant. It took hold of the heart of the world, which still loves these thrilling stories of adventure; and Stevenson was no longer an unknown scribbler, but a power in the literary world. The book reminded the older people of the piratical tales in yel-

low covers they had read in their youth, " The King
of the Sea " and " The Queen of the Sea," and their
ilk; but they recognized the difference between them
all the same. " Kidnapped," which Stevenson at the
time thought " his best, and indeed his only good
story," was written at Bournemouth in about five
months, and left him quite exhausted from the labor.
Of this story R. H. Stoddard said : " The fight in the
Round House is as unforgetable as any of the fierce
combats in the Iliad; " and many other high authori-
ties gave praise almost as enthusiastic. This applause warmed the heart of Stevenson, and inspired
him to put forth greater effort. He rewrote certain chapters of " Prince Otto " five or six times,
taking infinite pains, but was still dissatisfied with
his work. Ill health, which so often hampered him,
was doubtless the cause of his waning inspiration.
He was all this time flitting from place to place,
scarcly two of the stories having been written in the
same environment. He had been to America by
this time, and finished " The Pavilion of the Links "
in Monterey, California. It was in 1879 that he took
passage in the steerage of a transatlantic liner to New
York, and afterward made the California journey in
an emigrant train. This was a quest for health, as
most of his journeys were. He made books about
the sea-voyage and the journey across the plains,
which did not at the time attract the attention they
deserved, but are now considered very delightful reading. As an " intermediate " traveller across the Atlantic, he saw a kind of life that was new to him, and,
always a Bohemian, he entered into it with spirit,
and began to study his fellow passengers with his

usual zest. They were, he tells us, for the greater part
" quiet, orderly, obedient citizens, family men broken
by adversity, elderly youths who had failed to place
themselves in life, and people who had seen better
days; and as far as I saw, drink, idleness, and incom-
petency were the three great causes of emigration."
He talked with them a great deal, and was rather
chagrined to find that they did not suspect him of
being of a different grade in life from themselves.
He says : —

" Here I was among my own countrymen, somewhat
roughly clad, to be sure, but with every advantage of speech
and manner; and I am bound to confess that I passed for
nearly anything you please except an educated gentleman.
The sailors called me 'mate,' the officers addressed me as
'my man,' my comrades accepted me without hesitation for a
person of their own character and experience but with some
curious information. . . . They might be close observers in
their own way, and read the manners in the face ; but it was
plain they did not extend their observation to the hands."

His descriptions of his fellow-passengers were
graphic, including that of the old lady on her way
to Kansas : —

" We had to take her own word for it that she was married ; for it was sorely contradicted by the testimony of her
appearance. Nature seemed to have sanctified her for the
single state ; even the color of her hair was incompatible
with matrimony, and her husband, I thought, should be
a man of saintly spirit and phantasmal bodily presence.
. . . They had heard reports, her husband and she, of
some unwarrantable disparity of hours between New York
and Glasgow, and with a spirit commendably scientific had
seized on this occasion to put them to proof. It was a good

thing for the old lady, for she passed much leisure time in studying the watch. Once, when prostrated by sickness, she let it run down. It was inscribed on her harmless mind in letters of adamant that the hands of a watch must never be turned backwards; and so it behooved her to lie in wait for the exact moment ere she started it again. When she imagined this was about due, she sought out one of the Scotsmen. She was in quest of two o'clock; and when she learned it was already seven on the shores of the Clyde, she lifted up her voice and cried 'Gravy!' I had not heard this innocent expletive since I was a young child; and I suppose it must have been the same with the other Scotsmen present, for we all laughed our fill."

Pictures of this kind are drawn of many of his fellow-passengers, bright bits of humorous description, such as occur in all his writings. Landing in New York, he left at once for California across the plains. While in San Francisco he was married to Mrs. Osborne, who with her two children, the son the Lloyd Osborne of whom from that time we hear so much, especially at Samoa, returned with him to Europe. This lady is described as a small woman, with clear-cut delicate features, but with a face of unmistakable strength. Her hair is black, and her complexion rather dark. She is alert and vivacious, and was the best of good company for Stevenson from that time on. At that time he was described as a young man with a face of extreme pallor, long and oval, with wide-set eyes, straight nose, sensitive mouth scarcely shaded by a light mustache, and long dark hair straggling with an irregular wave to his neck.

On his return to Europe Stevenson lived alternately in Scotland and on the Continent, as his health permitted. All the usual winter resorts were tried; but his weak lungs did not improve, and the shadow of death hung over him many times. He loved the beautiful blue Mediterranean, and would gladly have lived beside it, but fate warned him to "move on," at short intervals. He envied average mortals with ordinary health most heartily, and would have given his genius in exchange for the body of any ploughman with pleasure. Could he have been idle it would have gone better with him; but work he must, and did, sick or well, suffering or at ease, even to the last Vailima days. He had not apparently had a very happy youth, but he now began to look back to it with regret; for, though ill and suffering when young, he still had boundless hope which lightened his heart. Now he began to sing of the old days regretfully, as in this little song: —

> " Sing me a song of a lad that 's gone,
>   Say, could that lad be I?
>   Merry of soul he sailed on a day
>   Over the sea to Skye.
>
> " Mull was astern, Egg on the port,
>   Rum on the starboard bow;
>   Glory of youth glowed in his soul:
>   Where is that glory now?
>
> " Give me again all that was there,
>   Give me the sun that shone;
>   Give me the eyes, give me the soul,
>   Give me the lad that 's gone.
>
> " Billow and breeze, islands and seas,
>   Mountains of rain and sun,
>   All that was good, all that was fair,
>   All that was me is gone."

In these years he produced "Virginibus Puerisque,"
" Familiar Studies of Men and Books," " Memories
and Portraits," and other famous essays. The treas-
ures of humor and pathos, of tenderness and wit,
unfolded in these were a surprise to many who had
known him chiefly by his stories. Indeed, his essays
would assure him a lasting place in the literature of
the day had he never written anything else. The
felicity of phrase in them, the cameo-like finish, the
exquisite delicacy, the hearty courage with which
they face life and all its inevitable terrors, — these
render them unique among the productions of recent
years.

In these years also were written " Kidnapped " and
" Dr. Jekyll and Mr. Hyde," both at Bournemouth,
" The Merry-Men and Other Tales," and many
sketches. His literary activity was truly wonderful.
Of these books, " Dr. Jekyll and Mr. Hyde " produced the most marked sensation. Thousands who
knew nothing of Stevenson before, read that book
and were his bond slaves ever after. Its fascination
was for all, though, despite that, it was utterly repel-
lent to many. The theme was as old almost as
time itself, and had many times been treated much
more delicately and even powerfully, but there was
a literalness in this which, though rather clumsy,
took hold of the ordinary reader with more power
than former delineations of the dual life had done.
It was grotesque and horrible to a degree, especially
when rather unskilfully put upon the stage, as was
afterwards the case.

Here is his own account of the origin of the
book : —

"I had long been trying to write a story on this subject, to find a body, a vehicle, for that strong sense of man's double being, which must at times come in upon and over-whelm the mind of every thinking creature. . . . For two days I went about racking my brains for a plot of any sort; and on the second night I dreamed the scene at the window, and a scene, afterwards split in two, in which Hyde, pur-sued for some crime, took the powder and underwent the change in the presence of his pursuers. All the rest was made awake and consciously. . . . The meaning of the tale is therefore mine, and had long pre-existed in my garden of Adonis, and tried one body after another in vain. Mine too is the setting; mine the characters. All that was given me was the matter of three scenes, and the central idea of a voluntary change becoming involuntary."

In 1887 he grew rapidly worse, and it became imperative for him to make some change in his sur-roundings. He came to America, and passed the winter in the Adirondacks, near the Saranac River. Life in the pine woods revived him somewhat, and he spent a part of the spring in New York and New Jersey. In New York he met for the first time our leading literary men, whom he charmed by his vivacity, his cordial manners, and his keen interest in every new phase of life. His life in the woods had delighted him, and he enjoyed relating his expe-riences to his new acquaintances, and declaring his belief in the savage state as against civilization. This was in reality a cardinal doctrine in his creed of life, though his whimsical way of asserting it did not always give this impression to his hearers. He hated the shams and shows of conventional life right heartily, and dreamed always of a life like that depicted by Tennyson, —

" Or to burst all links of habit — there to wander far away,
On from island unto island at the gateway of the day.

" Larger constellations burning, mellow moons and happy skies,
Breadths of tropic shade and palms in cluster, knots of
Paradise.

" Never comes a trader, never floats an European flag,
Slides the bird o'er lustrous woodland, swings the trailer from
the crag ;

" Droops the heavy-blossomed bower, hangs the heavy-fruited
tree —
Summer isles of Eden lying in dark-purple spheres of sea.

" There, methinks, would be enjoyment more than in this march
of mind,
In the steamship, in the railway, in the thoughts that shake
mankind."

No doubt there was also great pleasure to one of
his feeble body in the thought of men " iron-jointed,
supple-sinewed," in contrast to those he knew so
well " with blinded eyesight poring over miserable
books."

This ideal life he soon attained, going to Samoa
during a cruise in the South Sea, and becoming so
fascinated with it, and finding it suiting him so well,
that he remained there to the end of his life. It was
one of his dreams come true. His residence there
undoubtedly prolonged his life, though he was far
from well even there. He purchased a large estate
in the hills beyond Apia, and took great interest in
developing the plantation. He succeeded in the end
in making it a source of some profit. The name
Vailima was suggested by the streams which run
down from the mountains. " An island home in the

heart of a mountain forest" it has been called, and the words convey to us an enchanting picture. It is easy to divine that Stevenson soon loved the secluded spot, and that life became better worth the living than it had been to him in all the years of his wandering. He had scarcely ever felt at home before; but now, as he sat under his own trees, and planted and picked his own fruits, that sort of content came to him which comes only of the true home feeling. A pilgrim and a sojourner he had been heretofore, a dweller in tents; now beneath his own roof-tree he sang in his heart the songs he had never been able to sing in a strange land. His family were almost his only companions. Occasionally a guest came to him from a passing steamer, who was received with great applause, and shown all the sights of the island in the most hospitable manner. But stranger tourists who also came at intervals were not so hilariously received. If busy upon a new book, he would not waste his precious time upon them. He had learned the best manner of getting rid of bores, by long practice, and defended himself valiantly from them to the end. Even in Samoa the species were to be found and fought off, sometimes, to his great amusement.

He wrote a number of books here, frequently doing it in bed, though at the last he dictated while walking rapidly up and down the room. Here he wrote "The Dynamiter," "The Wrong Box" in collaboration with Lloyd Osborne, and "Three Plays" in collaboration with W. E. Henley, "The Wreckers" and "Ebb Tide," both with Lloyd Osborne. He also wrote several books without help from others; among them, "David Balfour" and a book of ballads. He was always busy, very often hurried, and no sooner had one work off his hands than he began another. It is little wonder that his health did not improve much. Overwork and an infinite number of cigarettes effectually prevented that. In the Vailima letters which he wrote so intimately to Mr. Colvin, he sometimes spoke of his weariness of it all, and deplored the need of it. It is sad to read such a paragraph as this : —

"I sometimes sit and yearn for anything in the nature of an income that would come in, — mine has all got to be gone and fished for with the immortal mind of man. What I want is the income that really comes of itself, while all you have to do is just to blossom and exist and sit on chairs. Think how beautiful it would be not to have to mind the critics, and not even the darkest of the crowd, — Sidney Colvin."

That this delicate master of humor and of pathos must toil like a cart-horse that he might have bread to eat, was a sad commentary on the emoluments of literature.

After the heat and languor of a June day, he writes again : —

"I wonder exceedingly if I have done anything at all good ; and who can tell me? and why should I wish to know? In so little a while I, and the English language, and the bones of my descendants, will have ceased to be a memory. And yet — and yet — one would like to leave an image for a few years upon men's minds — for fun. This is a very dark frame of mind, consequent on overwork and the conclusion of the excruciating ' Ebb-Tide.' "

Shortly before his death he wrote : —

"I know I am at a climacteric for all men who live by their wits, so I do not despair. But the truth is, I am pretty nearly useless at literature. Were it not for my health, which made it impossible, I could not find it in my heart to forgive myself that I did not stick to an honest, common-place trade when I was young, which might have supported me during all these ill years. But do not suppose me to be down in anything else; only, for the nonce, my skill deserts me, such as it is or was. It was a very little dose of inspiration, and a pretty little trick of style, long lost, improved by the most heroic industry. So far I have managed to please the journalists. But I am a fictitious article, and have long known it. I am read by journalists, by my fellow novelists, and by boys; with these, *incipit et explicit* my vogue. Good thing, anyway, for it seems to have sold the Edition. And I look forward confidently to an aftermath; I do not think my health can be so hugely improved, without some subsequent improvement in my brains. Though, of course, there is the possibility that literature is a morbid secretion and abhors health : I do not think it is possible to have fewer illusions than I. I sometimes wish I had more. They are amusing. But I cannot take myself seriously as an artist; the limitations are so obvious. I did take myself seriously of old, but my practice has fallen off. I am now an idler and cumberer of the ground; it may be excused to me, perhaps, by twenty years of industry and poor health, which have taken the cream off the milk."

But these last letters are not all of this complexion. They are sprinkled with fun and little personal details which, though trivial, are not wearying to the true devotees of this Samoan exile. The pleasantest things to dwell on in these later years are the long cruises among the islands, which he loved to make, and which were his only real recreation. One can fancy him standing on his own deck and crying, like Ulysses : —

"Come, my friends,
'T is not too late to seek a newer world.
Push off, and sitting well in order smite
The sounding furrows; for my purpose holds
To sail beyond the sunset, and the baths
Of all the western stars, until I die.
It may be that the gulfs will wash us down :
It may be we shall touch the Happy Isles,
And see the great Achilles, whom we knew."

That he loved the sea, we know, and the tropic islands with feathery-branched cocoa-palms, with trees hung with glorious orchids and ghostly mosses; and all that tangled undergrowth of nameless flowers and vines, how he must have loved them we can well imagine. The very clouds of the south and the stars of the sky must have been a deep joy to him, in that land of streams and lapsing waters and sweet airs.

But the time came when he was weighed upon with heaviness, even in this land of amaranth and moly, and he could only " muse and brood and live again in memory." The fires were burning low. The last spark would soon go out. On the evening of December 3, 1894, he breathed his last. The call came suddenly, as he had so often wished that it might come. A stroke of apoplexy fell in the midst of unusual good health, and he survived but two or three hours. He had been working very hard, having in hand two novels, both of which were left unfinished. One called " St. Ives" was nearly completed; the other, which he called " Weir of Hermiston," was thought by Mrs. Stevenson to be his strongest piece of work.

One calls to mind the following words written by him many years ago, in connection with his sudden death: —

" And does not life go down with a better grace, foaming in full body over a precipice, than miserably struggling to an end in shady deltas? In the hot fit of life, a-tiptoe on the highest point of being, he passes at a bound on to the other side. The noise of the mallet and the chisel is scarcely quenched, the trumpets are hardly done blowing, when, trailing with him clouds of glory, this happy-starred, full-blooded spirit shoots into the spiritual land."

Also one thinks of his wish in that little poem sent out shortly before his death, — a wish that was not to be granted like the other. Here are the lines: —

" Blows the wind to-day, and the sun and the rain are flying —
    Blows the wind on the moors to-day and now,
  Where about the graves of the martyrs the whaups are crying,
    My heart remembers how!

" Gray, recumbent tombs of the dead in desert places,
    Standing stones on the vacant, wine-red moor,
  Hills of sheep, and the homes of the silent vanished races
    And winds austere and pure!

" Be it granted me to behold you again in dying,
    Hills of home! and to hear again the call —
  Hear about the graves of the martyrs the pee-wees crying,
    And hear no more at all."

Not on those hills of home was he destined to look when the swift release came to him, but on alien mountain heights and sad solemn seas, known but too well to his homesick heart; yet we doubt not that even on the top of Mt. Vaca the weary soul sleeps well.

WILLIAM DEAN HOWELLS.

WILLIAM DEAN HOWELLS.

THE grandfather of William Dean Howells, who was of Welsh extraction, came to this country early in the century, and settled in Ohio. At the point where he started his new home, it was an almost unbroken wilderness, in which fact he rejoiced, as it would keep his children farther from the temptations of the world which he dreaded for them, and enable them to attend primarily to the salvation of their souls, — a point upon which he felt a life-long solicitude; not the languid interest of these more faithless times, but the heartfelt agony of a strong soul over the danger of eternal ruin to those whom he most dearly loved. Here Mr. Howells' father was brought up, and after a season of scepticism became a religious man, but not in the fashion of his father. Mr. Howells tells us that " my father, who could never get himself converted at any of the camp-meetings where my grandfather led the forces of prayer to his support, and had at last to be given up in despair, fell in with the writings of Emanuel Swedenborg, and embraced the doctrine of that philosopher with a content that has lasted him all the days of his many years." The grandfather had certain literary tastes, mainly for poetry of a gloomy sort; and this taste was much accentuated in his son, who had a decided literary bent, and whose library was composed principally of poetry and theology. He was the editor of a country newspaper, and his very limited collection of books was increased in William's childhood by a few which were given him to review. He was fond of reading aloud to his family, as were many thoughtful men and women of that generation, whose lives were secluded, and not full of the haste and harry of the present day. His son owns that he was sometimes wearied with these readings, which were not always suited to his years; but as he grew older he appreciated the fact that they had deepened and developed his natural taste for reading. He heard in this way such books as Thomson's "Seasons," Cowper, Goldsmith, Burns, Scott, Byron, and even Moore. There was no fiction in the collection, and none apparently in the town; at least William was some time in finding any. He was not very much in school, but began working in the printing-office at a very early age. He had a passion for books, however, and educated himself, principally through reading. He acquired a reading knowledge of the German, Spanish, French, and Italian languages, and an average schoolboy's acquaintance with Latin, while he was still a young man, by his own almost unaided efforts; spurred on to this by his strong desire to read the masterpieces of literature, which he saw so continually referred to in English books.

The family were poor, though happily almost unconscious of the fact, as all the people about them were poor also, and they suffered no real privations. William continued in the printing business in one place and another all through his early youth, reading voraciously, and writing a great deal in imitation of the writers he most prized. He was very happy in this life, but injured his health by his confinement to the printing-office and the little study, where he pursued his reading with such ardor. His first literary idols were Goldsmith, Cervantes, and Irving; but these idols gave way to others in due time, and he has continued to worship at new shrines, at uncertain intervals, all through life.

He first attracted public attention as a newspaper correspondent from Columbus, during succeeding sessions of the State Legislature, and grew into editorial work through that. Very little of his early work found its way into print, which was probably a bit of literary good fortune more appreciated by him in after days than at the time. The first position on a paper offered to him was that of a reporter, but one night's round with other reporters to the police stations satisfied him, and he declined the offer of the place. He afterward regretted it, as the training of a reporter and the variety of life which he would have seen would have been valuable to him in his later work; but he did not appreciate this at the time. Soon after, however, he had another offer of a place on a paper at Columbus, which was more to his liking, as it included the literary notices and book reviews. He accepted this place, and enjoyed his work and the society of the city very much. A constant round of dances, suppers, with music and cards, and talk about books, gave him his first taste of gayety, and took him from his beloved books. He had mixed but little in society up to this time, had been too busy and too absorbed in study to care for it. When one works in a printing-office the greater part of the day, and is so in love with books that he passes the remainder of it and all the evening over them, he has little desire for the companionship of the outside world. He had always had some single friend whose tastes were like his own, with whom he had read and discussed books, and who was interested in his experiments in making literature himself, and he had been satisfied with this intellectual companionship. At one time it was an organ-maker who lived in the village, and who made organs, from the ground up, every part of them with his own hands. He had the most unstinted admiration for Dickens, and this was the one thing in common between the two friends. He was an Englishman, about fifty years old, and he revered the Book of Common Prayer, while he disputed the authority of the Bible. This rather strange friendship was a source of much pleasure, and no doubt of profit also, to the young author. Then he came upon a young poet who looked after the book half of the village drug-store. From him as from all his youthful friends he borrowed books, for they were scarce in the Ohio village at that time, and the money with which to purchase them scarcer still. With this young poet he spent many happy hours during the brief acquaintance which preceded the early death of the gifted young man. Afterward he made friends with a book-binder who helped him with his German, and shared in his infatuation with Heine. This man, being alone, with no companionship outside his own family, doubtless prized his intimacy with the young enthusiast very highly, and the interest and affection were warmly reciprocated. They met every evening in the editorial room, and by candlelight pored over their Heine, and the dictionary. It seemed to the young men a true intellectual banquet, and Mr. Howells has enjoyed nothing since, more fully. He had also congenial friends occasionally among printers, and after a time the acquaintance of John J. Piatt, the young Ohio poet, with whom he afterward published a volume of poems. This is a goodly list of congenial friends for any man, and we cannot but feel that he was richer than many whose social circle was much wider. The deep enthusiasm for literature among the better class of young men was a very pleasing feature of the life of that early day. The very scarcity of books seemed to serve the purpose of making them highly prized. Many people, young at that time, remember the day when they acquired a certain book as a date of importance, an area almost in their intellectual lives, and the passing of these from hand to hand among the little circle of friends was considered a favor not to be lightly estimated. Thus, Mr. Howells remembers who lent him a book, to this day, and regards it still as a distinct act of friendship, and is duly grateful for it. Many others feel the same. In these days of the multiplicity of books and of their cheapness, this feeling can hardly be appreciated by those well to do;

but there are still places in country districts where the conditions are much as they were fifty years ago.

Mr. Howells regards his two winters in Columbus as the heyday of life for him, as he was beginning then to find opportunity and recognition. After that he received the appointment as Consul to Venice, from Mr. Lincoln, and started for that city almost immediately. He arrived in Venice one winter morning about five o'clock, and it was in the coldest winter that Venice had known for many years. Yet that appalling hour and that coldest winter did not at all interfere with his enjoyment of the first glimpses of that glorious city in the sea. Doubtless he was saying to himself, as he entered his gondola and glided up the Grand Canal, the words that are always in the mind of the newly arrived traveller:

> " The sea is in its broad, its narrow streets,
>   Ebbing and flowing ; and the salt sea-weed
>   Clings to the marble of her palaces.
>   No track of men, no footsteps to and fro
>   Lead to her gates.   The path lies o'er the sea,
>   Invisible; and from the land we went
>   As to a floating city — steering in
>   And gliding up her streets as in a dream,
>   So smoothly, silently, — by many a dome
>   Mosque-like, and many a stately portico,
>   The statues ranged along an azure sky."

For does not every one associate Rogers and Byron with Venice still, though Mr. Ruskin told us long ago that —

"The Venice of modern fiction and drama is a thing of yesterday, a mere efflorescence of decay, a stage-dream, which the first ray of daylight must dissipate into dust.   No prisoner whose name is worth remembering, or whose sorrows deserved sympathy, ever crossed the Bridge of Sighs which is the centre of the Byronic ideal of Venice ; no great merchant of Venice ever saw that Rialto under which the traveller now pauses with breathless interest ; the statue which Byron makes Faliero address as one of his ancestors was erected to a soldier of fortune a hundred and fifty years after Faliero's death."

And Mr. Howells himself, after a four years' residence there, destroyed many more of our illusions. But at the time of his first entrance he also was a romantic traveller, full of the glamour which youth monopolizes, and brimming over with that poetic emotion which the thought of Italy, of Venice, inspires in the poetic temperament. And so he tells us : —

"I think there can be nothing else in the world so full of glittering and exquisite surprise, as that first glimpse of Venice which the traveller catches as he issues from the railway station by night, and looks upon her peerless strangeness.

"There is something in the blessed breath of Italy (how quickly, coming south, you know it, and how bland it is after the harsh transalpine air !) which prepares you for your nocturnal advent into the place ; and oh, you ! whoever you are that journey toward this enchanted city for the first time, let me tell you how happy I count you ! There lies before you for your pleasure the spectacle of such singular beauty as no picture can ever show you nor book tell you, — beauty which you shall feel but once, and regret forever."

And again he says : —

"So I had arrived in Venice, and I had felt the influence of that complex spell which she lays upon the stranger. I had caught the most alluring glimpses of the beauty which cannot wholly perish while any fragment of her sculptured walls nods to its shadow in the canal ; I had been penetrated by a deep sense of the mystery of the place, and I had been touched already by the anomaly of modern life amid scenes where its presence offers, according to the humor in which it is studied, constant occasion for annoyance or delight, enthusiasm or sadness."

The first days in Venice were perhaps the most enchanting of all, and we shall get one more brief look at them through the eyes of this Western poet, this unknown genius from the heart of Ohio. Take this : —

" I found the night as full of beauty as the day, when caprice led me from the brilliancy of St. Mark's, and the glittering streets of shops that branch away from the Piazza, and lost me in the quaint recesses of the courts or the tangles of the distant alleys, where the dull little oil lamps vied with the tapers burning before the street-corner shrines of the Virgin in making the way obscure, and deepening the shadows about the doorways and under frequent arches. I remember distinctly, among the beautiful nights of the time, the soft night of late winter, which first showed me the scene you may behold from the Public Gardens at the end of the long concave line of the Riva degli Schiavoni. Lounging there upon the southern parapet of the Gardens, I turned from the dim bell-towers of the evanescent islands in the east (a solitary gondola gliding across the calm of the water and striking its moonlight silver into multitudinous ripples), and glanced athwart the vague shipping in the basin of St. Mark, and saw all the lights from the Piazzetta to the Giudecca, making a crescent of flame in the air, and casting deep into the water under them a crimson glory that sank also down and down in my own heart, and illumined all its memories of beauty and delight. Behind these lamps rose the shadowy masses of church and palace; the moon stood bright and full in the heavens; the gondola drifted away to the northward; the islands of the lagoons seemed to rise and sink with the light palpitations of the waves like pictures on the undulating fields of banners; the stark rigging of a ship showed black against the sky; the Lido sank from sight upon the east, as if the shore had composed itself to sleep by the side of its beloved sea, to the music of the surge that gently beat its sands; the yet leafless boughs of the trees above me stirred themselves together, and out of one of those trembling towers in the lagoons one rich, full sob burst from the heart of the bell, too deeply stricken with the glory of the scene, and suffused the languid night with the murmur of luxurious, ineffable sadness."

The idleness of the population was at first a wonder to him, as to all visitors from Western lands, and he writes: —

"When, however, I ceased (as I must in time) to be merely a spectator of this idleness, and learned that I too must assume my share of the common indolence, I found it a grievous burden. Old habits of work, old habits of hope, made my endless leisure irksome to me, and almost intolerable, when I ascertained fairly and finally that, in my desire to fulfil long-cherished but, after all, merely general designs of literary study, I had forsaken wholesome struggling in the currents where I felt the motion of the age, only to drift into a lifeless eddy of the world, remote from incentive and sensation."

Mr. Howells, in spite of the enervating influences of Venice, did some good literary work there, and the two volumes of sketches called " Venetian Life " made him many readers and admirers at the time of publication, and have remained popular to this time. His volume of " Italian Journeys " also was a fascinating narrative, and though somewhat overshadowed by his novels, still finds readers who enjoy its delicate humor and bits of poetic description. One of the illusions which he destroyed for some of us was that of the charm of an Italian winter. Mrs. Hawthorne had already attacked that, and it remained for Mr. Howells to reinforce her testimony. He said in one place: —

" In fine, the winter climate of North Italy is really very harsh, and though the season is not so severe in Venice as in Milan, or even Florence, it is still so sharp as to make foreigners regret the generous fires and warmly built houses of the North. There was snow but once in my first winter, 1861–62; the second there was none at all; but the third, it fell repeatedly to considerable depth, and lay unmelted for many weeks in the shade."

Mr. Howells was married during his residence in Venice, and tried housekeeping in an old palace. He had had enough of lodgings during his first year there, and had the American longing for, and expectation of a home; and here he realized his fond expectations. He says of himself and his wife: —

" They were by nature of the order of shorn lambs, and Providence, tempering the inclemency of the domestic situation, gave them Giovanna.

" The house was furnished throughout, and Giovanna had been furnished with it. She was at hand to greet the newcomers, and ' This is my wife, the new mistress,' said the young *paron*, with the bashful pride proper to the time and place.

"Giovanna glowed welcome, and said, with adventurous politeness, she was very glad of it. '*Serva sua ?*' The *parona*, not knowing Italian, laughed in English. So Giovanna took possession of us, and, acting upon the great truth that handsome is that handsome does, began at once to make herself a thing of beauty."

Although he spent so much time, during his stay in Venice, in looking at and studying the art and architecture of the place, he very modestly disclaims the idea of being capable of such art criticism as passes current in the world, and one respects him more highly for the disclaimer. By foregoing much art talk in his pages, he " so rests happy in the thought that he has thrown no additional darkness on any of the pictures half obscured now by the religious dimness of the Venetian churches." He remarks also that "just after reading Mr. Ruskin's description of St. Mark's Church, I, who had seen it every day for three years, began to have dreadful doubts of its existence." Some of his confessions as to his enjoyment of pictures there are of great interest, as this final summing up : —

" I have looked again and again at nearly every painting of note in Venice, having a foolish shame to miss a single one, and having also a better wish to learn something of the beautiful from them ; but at last I must say that, while I wondered at the greatness of some, and tried to wonder at the greatness of others, the only paintings which gave me genuine and hearty pleasure were those of Bellini, Carpaccio, and a few others of that school and time."

At last the pleasant years came to an end, the years of dreaming and idling, and gazing at the thousand beauties of art and of nature, the moonlit nights, the sunsets, and the glorious panorama of the charmed Adriatic; all faded out into the harsh realities of travelling, and of settling themselves in a new home on the other side of the sea. He was sad for what he was leaving, happy in that to which he was returning.

After his return to America, his literary work was for some time book-reviewing, largely for the "Nation" in New York. He brought to that work the results of very wide reading, — for the years in Venice had been fruitful in that way, as well as the years that had gone before, — a delicate taste, and a fair-mindedness not always to be found in critics. There was a certain catholicity, too, in his tastes; he was never partial or one-sided, and he was too young to have outgrown his native enthusiasm. Indeed, he has not to this day outgrown that, but always has some author for whom he cherishes a passion. When he became assistant editor of the "Atlantic Monthly," he wrote the book notices for that periodical for some years. He had many favorites in Italian literature, had a peculiar admiration, almost adoration, for Heine, loved certain French books fervently, and after a time became infatuated with the Russian novelists, particularly with Tourguenief and Tolstoi.

During his residence in Venice, he had read much relating to its history, and was charmed with Italian poetry, — not the classics, but the works of the modern poets. He read there, also, the current English novels, "Our Mutual Friend," "Philip," "Yeast," and "Romola" among the number. He says of "Romola": —

"I had brought 'Romola' with me, and I read that again and again with that sense of moral enlargement which the first fiction to conceive of the true nature of evil gave all of us who were young in that day. Tito Melema was not only a lesson, he was a revelation, and I trembled before him as in the presence of a warning and a message from the only veritable perdition. His life, in which so much that was good was mixed with so much that was bad, lighted up the whole domain of egotism with its glare, and made one feel how near the best and the worst were to each other, and how they sometimes touched without absolute division in texture and color."

If anything could destroy a taste for reading, it would undoubtedly be book reviewing, continued for too long a time. When reading becomes forced it is nothing less than drudgery, and all drudgery becomes hateful in time. Many fine readers have been ruined by becoming critics. Fortunately Mr. Howells was not one of this number, though he continued that work for some years after he became editor-in-chief of the "Atlantic." But he was better able to choose what he would write, after that event, and usually wrote only of the books he enjoyed reading. These were not necessarily the great books, for he was fond of many writers who never gained any great audience, even upon his recommendation. Some of these past favorites cause him amusement now as he recalls them, but he has usually been faithful to his literary loves. He fell in love with Henry James at first sight, and has held to his admiration with great steadiness through all the years. He says: "I have read all that he has written, and I have never read anything of his without an ecstatic pleasure in his unrivalled touch. In literary handling, no one who has written fiction in our language can approach him, and his work has shown an ever-deepening insight." While living in Cambridge during his connection with the " Atlantic Monthly," he had a severe sickness, and during his convalescence he continued his life-long reading of books. He says:—

"In those days I made many forays into the past, and came back now and then with rich spoil, though I confess that for the most part I had my trouble for my pains ; and I wish now that I had given the time I spent on the English classics to contemporary literature, which I have not the least hesitation in saying I like vastly better."

We may quote here a few more of his opinions concerning modern books, which we are able to do, as he has recently presented them to us in a volume called " My Literary Passions," from which much of the material of this sketch has been obtained. He says:—

"In those years at Cambridge my most notable literary experience without doubt was the knowledge of Tourguenief's novels, which began to be recognized in all their greatness about the middle seventies. I think they made their way with such of our public as were able to appreciate them before they were accepted in England ; but that does not matter. It is enough for the present purpose that 'Smoke,' and ' Lisa ' and ' On the Eve,' and ' Dimitri Rondine,' and ' Spring Floods,' passed one after another through my hands, and that I formed for their author one of the profoundest literary passions of my life.

" I now think there is a finer and truer method than his, but in its way Tourguenief's method is as far as art can go ;

that is to say, his fiction is in the last degree dramatic. The persons are sparsely described, and briefly accounted for, and then they are left to transact their affair, whatever it is, with the least possible comment or explanation from the author. . . . When I remembered the deliberate and impertinent moralizing of Thackeray, the clumsy exegesis of George Eliot, the knowing nods and winks of Charles Reade, the stage carpentering and lime-lighting of Dickens, even the fine and important analysis of Hawthorne, it was with a joyful astonishment that I realized the great art of Tourguenief."

It is needless to say that criticism of this kind was not accepted by the reading world without a protest. Readers flew to the defence of their idols, and such adjectives applied to the great masters were repeated with great scorn throughout their ranks. These writers had appeared to them almost above criticism for many years, and that they had faults of artistic construction was an unwelcome revelation to many. We must quote one more passage from the very beautiful account of Mr. Howells' acquaintance with Tourguenief : —

" Life showed itself to me in different colors after I had once read him ; it became more serious, more awful, and with mystical responsibilities I had not known before. My gay American horizons were bathed in the vast melancholy of the Slav, patient, agnostic, trustful. At the same time nature revealed herself to me through him with an intimacy she had not hitherto shown me."

Mr. Howells himself gives a whole chapter to Tolstoi, all of which is very delightful reading ; but we must content ourselves with a few extracts showing the spirit of the whole. He calls Tolstoi his noblest enthusiasm, and finds it difficult to give a notion of his influence without exaggeration. He says : —

"As much as one merely human being can help another, he has helped me ; he has not influenced me in æsthetics only, but in ethics, too, so that I can never see life in the way I saw it before I knew him. Tolstoi awakens in his reader the will to be a man ; not effectively, not spectacularly, but simply, really. He leads you back to the only true ideal, away from the false standard of the gentleman, to the Man who sought not to be distinguished from other men, but identified with them, to that Presence in which the finest gentleman shows his alloy of vanity, and the greatest genius shrinks to the measure of his miserable egotism. I learned from Tolstoi to try character and motive by no other test, and though I am perpetually false to that sublime ideal myself, still the ideal remains with me, to make me ashamed that I am not true to it. Tolstoi gave me heart to hope that the world may yet be made over in the image of Him who died for it, when all Cæsar's things shall be finally rendered to Cæsar, and men shall come into their own, into the right to labor and the right to enjoy the fruits of their labor, each one master of himself and servant to every other. He taught me to see life not as a chase of a forever impossible personal happiness, but as a field for endeavor toward the happiness of the whole human family ; and I can never lose this vision, however I may close my eyes, and strive to see my own interest as the highest good."

The light which this long extract throws upon the character of Mr. Howells must be the excuse for making it, as is the case in most of the extracts from his writings already given. They show the man far

better than any mere description of his qualities
could, and the charm of their diction will be recognized by all. Those constant readers who followed
Mr. Howells through all his novels, remember distinctly the time when he changed from one who
set art above humanity in literature, to one " who set
art forever below humanity," though they did not at
that time realize, perhaps, that it was Tolstoi who had
wrought this " sea change into something new and
strange." Whether he gained or lost as a literary
artist by this change, will depend upon the reader's
point of view. It was the generally despised ethical
works of Tolstoi that made the change in his spiritual horizon, as he tells us further on : —

"As I read his different ethical books, 'What to Do,'
'My Confession,' and 'My Religion,' I recognized their
truth with a rapture such as I have known in no other reading, and I rendered them my allegiance, heart and soul,
with whatever sickness of the one, and despair of the other.
They have it yet, and I believe they will have it while I
live. . . . I have spoken first of the ethical works of Tolstoi,
because they are of the first importance to me, but I think that
his æsthetical works are as perfect. To my thinking they tran-
scend in truth, which is the highest beauty, all other works
of fiction that have been written. and I believe they do this
because they obey the law of the author's own life."

During all these years of which we have been
speaking, Mr. Howells had been writing and publishing his own important books. If the little book
of poems already referred to, " The Poems of Two
Friends," cannot be called really important, because
it " became instantly and lastingly unknown to fame,"
it seemed of great importance to him at the time, and

was a part of the literary preparation for the greater successes of after years. Then came the "Venetian Sketches," which gave him a literary standing when he returned to this country, and helped him to a place in which to work. There was a great literary ferment at the close of the war. Some of our best work had been done shortly before and during the war, and the high level was maintained for some years thereafter. Mr. Howells had missed the high excitement, sitting in Venice and watching for privateers that never came, and getting late and often unreliable news from home. But he could not escape the echoes of that transcendent period, after his return, for the great reconstruction period was hardly less exciting than the war itself. But he did not turn to either for his literary material, and few books were more uneventful and lacking in excitement than his earlier novels. They were thought tame by the perfervid public, and were only admired by cultivated and literary readers. How their names recall to us the quiet humor, the delicate description, the rather shadowy portraiture, the finished artistry of them all, from "Their Wedding Journey" down. That was an enormous favorite at the time with his select circle, as were "A Chance Acquaintance" and "The Lady of the Aristook." The circle began to widen, his reputation was established, and for many years he was the most popular writer in this country. He worked hard to keep up with the demand for his books, and after a while went abroad again for a year of rest. His duties as editor, interfering with his making of new books, were abandoned, though he has continued to be connected with magazines during all the past years. Many of his stories have been published serially in them. It is not necessary to mention the names of these novels. The list is long, and they are all familiar to the reading world. Perhaps the " Rise of Silas Lapham " and " A Modern Instance " caused as much comment as any, though each one has been the favorite of a coterie.

His magazine work has come nearer to the work of George W. Curtis than that of any other writer since the death of that gifted and deeply lamented man. Latterly his farces have afforded great amusement and delight to the younger generation. The change in literary purpose already referred to, lost him some of his earlier admirers, but doubtless increased his following among the more earnest people of his day. People who, like himself, had begun to discern their relations to the race, considered that the supreme art in literature was the much decried "purpose." For the rest there is always the faultless fluency, the even flow, the perfect taste and finish of the whole, and almost always the quiet, charming story, which in these days of literary blood-letting and hysteria is a comfort and a relief.

Mr. Howells is fond of Shakespearian titles, and has returned to them in his latest story, which is called "A Circle in the Water." Others will be recalled, like "The Quality of Mercy," "A Hazard of New Fortunes," "A Foregone Conclusion," and "The Undiscovered Country."

He has lived mostly in cities since his early youth, — in Venice, Boston, Cambridge, and New York. His boyhood was passed in Hamilton, Dayton, and Ashtabula, Ohio, and he spent one year in a log-house near to some mills in which his father was interested, and which he and his brothers enjoyed vastly. The village life of that day was very charming, with its ease and freedom and its perfect equality, and he has written of it very delightfully in "A Boy's Town" and in other places. But his early life was not so much outward as inward; he worked for several hours every day in a printing-office, but he really lived in the realm of books. Shakespeare and Tennyson, Cervantes and Chaucer, Dickens and Thackeray, were his intimates, and he had little time for poorer acquaintance. When he shut himself up in his little room, or wandered away into the deep woods, with one of his favorite friends in his pocket, his delight was greater than the society of kings could have given him. The wine of new thought exhilarated him, the glamour of imagination colored every event; the sweet, sad music of his poet friends set the rhythm of his life. His thought, no doubt, was like that of another: —

> " These are my friends, loved for so many years
> That scarce I can remember when loved not,
> Found ever faithful, in no stress forgot,
> Changing to smiles oft-times my bitter tears,
> And drawing me to ever-widening spheres,
> Opening soul-spaces o'er a narrow lot.
> Can I be poor with Shakespeare in my cot,
> And at my board all whom my soul reveres?
> Who would leave Homer's side to sup with kings,
> Or Dante for the chambers of the great?
> With Milton or with Shelley shall I part
> To chat with little men on common things,
> Or seek for power in a degenerate state,
> Or show to babbling fools a wounded heart?"

LOUISA MAY ALCOTT.

LOUISA MAY ALCOTT.

WHEN Nora, in " The Doll's House," is about to
leave her home, and her husband recalls to
her her duties as a wife and mother, she answers:
" I have other duties equally sacred, — my duties
toward myself." In recalling the life of Louisa
Alcott one is tempted to wish that she had considered a little more her duties toward herself, that
her self-abnegation had not been quite so complete;
and to wonder whether utter self-sacrifice is indeed
the greatest of all virtues, as she considered it. To
the sympathetic heart the long sad story of her
struggle to care for others, her final worldly success,
but complete physical break-down, as a result of
over-care and overwork, is one of the saddest chapters in literary history. One turns away from it with
a pang of heart-break for this gifted woman, " Duty's
faithful child," who was cut off in the midst of her
years, worn out before her time, by loving labors for
others, by cares too great for her, by heroic self-
sacrifice throughout a lifetime. One wishes for her
the brightness that was her due; for nature had endowed her with great capacity for enjoyment, for
pure delight in life, of which circumstances had cruelly
defrauded her.

But she took small thought for herself, loyally obeyed the voice at eve obeyed at prime, and the record will stand for all time as that of one of the bravest battles that ever was fought in this stern campaign of life. For

> " No heart more high and warm
> Ever dared the battle storm ;
> Never gleamed a prouder eye
> In the front of victory ;
> Never foot had firmer tread
> On the field where hope lay dead,"

than are hid within that lonely grave on that hill-top hearsed with pines, in that sacred spot, the rustic burying-ground at Concord. Her friend and master, Emerson, was laid there before her, having gained that " port well worth the cruise" but a few years sooner than she, who was so much younger, and still had the expectation of so many full years of service and of joy. Hawthorne also lies under the mosses and ferns of Sleepy Hollow, — a sad heart glad of the still retreat; and Thoreau, with his face to the sky he loved, and shaded by the pines, to whom he was a brother. There too, best of all, were the dear mother, whose life she had blessed and in whom her own soul was bound up, and the darling sister, for whom she felt both a mother's and a sister's love, who fell so early by the way, when the path of life became difficult.

But could she have done otherwise than she did? Apparently not in the earlier years, for the straits were too great, the need too urgent, the failure to exert every power would have been too disastrous to those whom she loved. But in later years, we wish that she could have spared herself a little, while there was yet time to regain health by long repose and quietude. Even that did not seem possible to her, and so the tired brain was driven at full speed to the very end, and the world was soon the poorer for the passing of a great heroic soul.

Louisa Alcott was born in Germantown, Pennsylvania, November 29, 1832. She was the second of a family of four daughters, born to A. Bronson Alcott and his wife, Abba May, a daughter of Colonel Joseph May, of Boston. Mr. Alcott, the transcendental philosopher and seer, had removed from New England to Germantown, shortly before her birth, to take charge of a school there, but returned to Boston in 1834, where he opened a school, which was afterward quite famous, but which brought very small pecuniary returns. The family lived in extreme simplicity, the children's food being plain boiled rice, and graham bread without milk or butter. This was partly on account of Mr. Alcott's being a strict vegetarian, but largely on account of his poverty. No meat was ever eaten in the family during Louisa's childhood, but fruit was allowed when it could be obtained. Fruit meant apples in New England at that time, and little else, and apples were the chief luxury in the household during all those early years. Louisa grew up sturdy and strong on this plain fare, but the two younger children were more delicate, and did not thrive so well on it.

In 1840, Mr. Alcott's school having proved unsuccessful, the family removed to Concord, where they passed the remainder of their lives; at least that was the home, from which they went forth at different times on their various ventures. Louisa had very little schooling. Her father taught her and the others, having for a long time no regular employment, and being a finely gifted teacher, curiously interested in the minds of children. One of her early remembrances was of a fugitive slave hidden in the brick oven; this experience made her an abolitionist, and very proud to be one, in the early and unpopular days of that great reform. She knew the best of these reformers familiarly in her childhood, and became the life-long friend of such men as Theodore Parker, Emerson, and Phillips. Her youthful companions in Concord were the children of Emerson, Hawthorne, and Channing; her relatives were the noble family of Mays; so she knew the best society from her earliest days, though not the society of wealth or fashion. They were far too poor for that, having indeed no reliable means of support throughout Louisa's childhood and youth. But they continued to live somehow, Mrs. Alcott being as practical as Mr. Alcott was unpractical, and toiling early and late to keep her family in as much comfort as was possible. She was proud of her gifted husband, and loved him with a romantic affection which lightened all the hardships of her lot; but she felt the deprivations of her children keenly, having come from a well-ordered and comfortable home herself, when she linked her fortunes to this dreamer and enthusiast. Although Emerson considered him one of the greatest philosophers since Plato, he had no following, could get neither readers nor listeners, but lived apart in a sort of world of his own, an idealist, a mystic all his days.

Louisa always spoke of her childhood as a happy one, and drew upon it as from a storehouse for much of the material she afterwards used in her books for children; and the family life is very truthfully depicted in "Little Women," where it has charmed the heart of youth. Like all imaginative children, they lived in a world of their own. She describes it thus: " Pilgrims journeyed over the hill with scrip and staff and cockleshells in their hats; fairies held their pretty revels among the whispering birches, and strawberry parties in the rustic arbor were honored by poets and philosophers, who fed us on their wit and wisdom while the little maids served more mortal food." All the fairy tales were dramatized and acted, Louisa being author and leading actor in most cases. She led a perfectly free, active, out-of-door life all these years, laying up stores of strength for the coming time when she would need it all. She enjoyed superb health in her youth, was able to walk twenty miles a day and enjoy it, or — what she did much more frequently — do the family washing, baking, and cleaning in the morning, write a story in the afternoon, and be ready for a frolic in the evening.

While she was yet a child, the co-operative experiment of the Fruitlands Farm was tried, with some English friends who sympathized with Mr. Alcott's ideas. Like all his practical undertakings, it came to naught, and brought great hardship to his family. Mr. Emerson visited them while there, and wrote thus in his journal : —

" The sun and the sky do not look calmer than Alcott and his family at Fruitlands. They seem to have arrived at the fact, — to have got rid of the show, and so are serene.

Their manners and behavior in the house and in the field were those of superior men, — of men at rest. And it seemed so high an attainment that I thought — as often before, so now more, because they had a fit home, or the picture was fitly framed — that these men ought to be maintained in their place by the country for its culture. . . . I will not prejudge them successful. They look well in July; we will see them in December."

The children rather enjoyed this experiment, which, like the similar but more famous one at Brook Farm, soon faded into thin air, and Louisa afterwards wrote her version of it in a story called " Transcendental Wild Oats," where she brought out the comic side of it with great distinctness. But to Mrs. Alcott the affair had no comic side, but was one of bitter disappointment, though she had not really had much faith in it from the beginning. But she had tried hard, and was utterly discouraged at the outcome.

It is needless to relate all the pathetic shifts and changes of the family during Louisa's childhood; it is sufficient to say that by some means they managed to live until she and her elder sister were old enough to begin to try to earn a little for themselves. In 1841 Colonel May, Mrs. Alcott's father, died and left her a small amount of property. Mrs. Alcott decided to purchase with this a house in Concord; and the addition of five hundred dollars from Mr. Emerson enabled her to buy the place called Hillside. They now were a little easier, as they had a home of their own; but there was little for either the father or mother to do in Concord, and in 1848 they removed to Boston, where Mrs. Alcott found employment, and her husband began to hold Conversations. He attracted the attention of some thoughtful people, and enjoyed his work, but brought little money to the family in this way. At a very early age Louisa resolved, as soon as she was old enough, to support the family and relieve her mother, and to make this her life-work. She never lost sight of this purpose to the end. It absorbed her thoughts, inspired her ambitions, and reined in all her personal desires. The family first, herself afterward, was the motto of her life.

When success came after weary years of waiting, they enjoyed its fruits, while she toiled on harder than ever to keep up the new scale of living. Only with death did she give up her charge. In 1850 she began to teach a small school in Boston, and her sister Anna went as a nurse into the family of a friend. After that her labors never ended. At this time she writes in her journal: —

"I often think what a hard life mother has had since she married, — so full of wandering and all sorts of worry; so different from her early easy days, the youngest and most petted of the family. I think she is a very brave, good woman; and my dream is to have a lovely, quiet home for her, with no debts or troubles to burden her. But I am afraid she will be in heaven before I can do it. Anna, too, is feeble and homesick, and I miss her dreadfully. She must have a good time in a nice little home of her own some day, as we often plan. But waiting is so *hard.*"

Again she says: —

"Anna wants to be an actress, and so do I. We could make plenty of money perhaps, and it is a very gay life. Mother says we are too young, and must wait. A—— acts splendidly. I like tragic plays, and shall be a Siddons if I can."

She had in truth a great longing for the stage, and some dramatic talent. She acted frequently in private theatricals all her life, and always enjoyed it exceedingly. At the time of which we are speaking, she wrote many plays which with the help of young friends were performed before a few families of their acquaintance. One or two of them were produced at the Howard Athenæum, and won their meed of praise from the critics and of applause from the audience. At this time the necessities of the family were such that, the school being closed, she went regularly out to service. The experience, she afterward described in a story " How I went out to Service." She was treated with great indignity in the place she tried first, and after two months gave it up in despair and returned home. Her experiment was a pretty good answer to that class of people who wonder why self-respecting young girls do not try domestic service as a means of livelihood. But she was forced to accept such work more than once, before she achieved success with her pen. She would not allow her pride to stand in the way, and bravely endured all sorts of humiliation in the effort to help her family. The work she did not dread, but she resented the treatment she received, with her whole soul.

For several years she taught school when she could, at starvation wages, sewed all the evening, and during school vacations, to earn a little more, filled up any intervals between engagements, with attempts to endure domestic service, and occasionally wrote a little story. She was paid five dollars for her first, and she tried very hard after that to sell others, but did not succeed for some time in doing so. She really had no leisure for writing, and the first attempts were not very well executed, though usually well planned. During the years passed in this way, the money she earned went into the home fund. The amount was pitifully small. At one time she records working at housework from May to October, and bringing home thirty-four dollars, which looked to her like a little fortune. It did buy many comforts for the family, and helped to clothe her for the next experiment. Such extracts as the following might be made from her letters and journals during all these years : —

" I am grubbing away as usual, trying to get money to buy mother a nice warm shawl. I have eleven dollars, all my own earnings, five for a story, and four for a great pile of sewing. I got a crimson ribbon for a bonnet for May, and I took my straw and fixed it up nicely with some little duds I had. Her old one haunted me all winter, and I want her to look neat. . . . I hope the little dear will like the bonnet, and the frills I made her, and the bows I fixed over from bright ribbons which L. W. threw away. I get half my rarities from her rag-bag. . . .

" For our good little Betty, who is wearing all the old gowns we left, I shall soon be able to buy a new one, and send it with my blessing to the cheerful saint. To father I send new neckties and some paper ; then he will be happy, and able to keep up the beloved diaries though the heavens fall."

To her sister Anna, who is also working, she writes : —

" Keep the money you have earned by so many tears and sacrifices, and clothe yourself ; for it makes me mad to know that my good little lass is going round in shabby things, and looked down upon by people who are not worthy to touch her patched shoes or the hem of her ragged old gowns."

When twenty-two years old she received thirty-two dollars for her first book, and felt very well paid. It was called "Flower Fables," and was but a slight affair, but its publication encouraged her to go on writing, at such times as she could. The book had really been written at sixteen and laid by until now. An edition of sixteen hundred was sold.

All this time Mr. Alcott was trying in vain to earn money, and there are many pathetic pictures of his failures in Louisa's journals. During this Boston life in 1854 she writes: —

" School for me month after month. Mother busy with boarders and sewing. Father doing as well as a philosopher can in a money-loving world. Anna at S. I earned a good deal sewing in the evening."

" In February father came home. Paid his way, but no more. A dramatic scene when he arrived in the night. We were waked by hearing the bell. Mother flew down, crying ' My husband.' We rushed after, and five white figures embraced the half-frozen wanderer, who came in hungry, tired, cold, and disappointed, but smiling bravely and as serene as ever. We fed and warmed and brooded over him, longing to ask if he had made any money ; but no one did till little May said, after he had told all the pleasant things, ' Well, did people pay you ? ' Then, with a queer look, he opened his pocket-book and showed one dollar, saying with a smile that made our eyes fill, ' Only that. My overcoat was stolen and I had to buy a shawl. Many promises were not kept, and travelling is costly ; but I opened the way, and another year shall do better.' I shall never forget how beautifully mother answered him, though the dear, hopeful soul had built much on his success; but with a beaming face she kissed him, saying, ' I call that doing *very well.* Since you are safely home, dear, we don't ask anything more.' Anna and I choked down our tears, and took a little lesson in real love which we never forgot, nor the look the tired man and the tender woman gave one another."

In October, 1857, the family returned to Concord, and lived once more in the old Orchard House, a picturesque old place near Mr. Emerson's, who liked to have them near, that he might "see to them" and enjoy Mr. Alcott's society, which he always prized. He was their unfailing friend, who always came to their rescue in their cruellest straits, and whom Louisa worshipped with a full heart. From a child she regarded him with a romantic affection, writing letters to him after the manner of Bettine to Goethe, in her early girlhood, though she never sent these effusions, but contented herself with admiring him from afar. He was a great help to her intellectually and spiritually, as she grew older, and the tie of loving friendship was never broken. In his modest, delicate way, when he knew the family must be hard pressed, he would visit them, and place his offering of money under a book on the table or in some similar place, say nothing about it, and go his way. This was always appreciated, though it galled Louisa cruelly, as she grew older, to be under the necessity of accepting these offerings. Mr. Emerson's beautiful character nowhere shines more brightly than in his dealings with the family of his impracticable but beloved friend. He tried in every way to secure for Mr. Alcott the recognition which he felt that he deserved, and it was mostly through his influence that in the later years, particularly at the West, Mr. Alcott gathered a little circle about him who enjoyed his Conversations and did him honor. But this partial recognition came too late to be of much comfort to his family.

Soon after their return to Concord, little Beth was taken from them. She died from the remote effects of scarlet fever, which Mrs. Alcott had brought home from the tenements of Boston, where she had been visiting and helping the poor people suffering from the infection. In her charitable labors for others she had introduced small-pox into her own family, a few years previous to this, but fortunately all recovered from the dread disease. Louisa was at home for a long time caring for her sister, and, in the intervals of labor, writing stories to keep the family purse supplied. But in spite of all her efforts they got into debt, and it was many years before she paid the last of these obligations. She accepted her sister's loss with deep resignation. She had no dread of death, and never had experienced that feeling, and life was so hard for her, that she almost gratefully found the sweet and delicate young sister freed from its burdens. But how she missed the dear child, none but her sympathetic mother ever knew. She was a person of deep religious feeling, and though she had been brought up among the transcendentalists, she had a simple faith of her own, apart from any of their subtleties, which comforted her throughout her life. She loved to listen to Theodore Parker, and became one of his intimate friends and followers, and his earnest, almost impassioned, religious fervor strengthened her own convictions, and was a great support to her at this time, and always. She believed in a Heavenly Father and Mother, in all good work, and in its ultimate reward. She prayed fervently, and sometimes writes in her journal in this way : —

" I don't often pray in words; but when I set out that day with all my worldly goods in the little old trunk, my own earnings ($25) in my pocket, and much hope and resolution in my soul, my heart was very full, and I said to the Lord, ' Help us all, and keep us for one another,' as I never said it before, while I looked back at the dear faces watching me, so full of love and hope and faith."

Some time after the death she writes thus in her journal : —

" I don't miss her as I expected, for she seems nearer and dearer than before ; and I am glad to know she is safe from pain and age in some world where her innocent soul must be happy. Death never seemed terrible to me, and now is beautiful ; so I cannot fear it, but find it friendly and wonderful."

Soon after this Anna was married, and also left the home. Louisa rejoiced greatly in her sister's happiness, and went on her own way, with no thought of such happiness for herself, though she was still young. She had set herself a stern task, and she never flinched from its full execution. There is no record that her heart was ever greatly touched, but she had opportunities to marry, which she graciously declined, and apparently without regret. But it is unnatural to suppose that this lovable and loving woman went to her grave with no romance of her own. But if she had one, she was one of the voiceless as regarded it, and the great world never knew. Perhaps it was with her as with so many others, Fate denied her the supreme good. For do we not know that often —

> " Two shall walk some narrow way of life,
>   So nearly side by side that should one turn
>   Even so little space to left or right,
>   They needs must stand acknowledged face to face,
>   And yet with wistful eyes that never meet,
>   With groping hands that never clasp, and lips
>   Calling in vain to ears that never hear,
>   They seek each other all their weary days,
>   And die unsatisfied ; and this is Fate."

One cannot but regret this outcome, for she was so warm-hearted and tender a woman, that life to her lost half its beauty when she walked its ways alone.

It was about this time that she took to writing sensational stories for the cheap story-papers, and found she could make more money by it than in trying to do better work. Such entries as this are quite frequent in her journal: " Got thirty dollars for a story. Sent twenty home." But she well knew that this work was unworthy of her, and dropped it as soon as she could get anything accepted in better places. That time was now approaching. After one of the most depressed periods which she had ever suffered, a period when she came very near to despair, in 1859 she had a story accepted by the " Atlantic Monthly," and it cheered her very greatly. She writes : —

" Hurrah ! my story is accepted : and Lowell asked if it was not a translation from the German, it was so unlike most tales. I felt much set up, and my fifty dollars will be very happy money. People seem to think it a great thing to get into the 'Atlantic'; but I've not been pegging away all these years in vain, and may yet have books and publishers, and a fortune of my own. Success has gone to my head, and I wander a little. Twenty-seven years old, and very happy. The Harper's Ferry tragedy makes this a memorable month. Glad I have lived to see the antislavery movement, and this last heroic act in it. Wish I could do my part in it."

She now wrote "Moods," her first novel. She says : —

"From the second to the twenty-fifth I sat writing, with a run at dusk, could not sleep, and for three days was so full of it I could n't stop to get up. Mother wandered in and out with cordial cups of tea, worried because I could n't eat. It was very pleasant and queer while it lasted; but after three weeks of it I found that my mind was too rampant for my body, as my head was dizzy, legs shaky, and no sleep would come."

This was her most unfortunate book, but the one dearest to her own heart. It waited long for a publisher, and was only floated at last, by the success of " Little Women."

In 1862 she went to the hospital in Georgetown, District of Columbia, as a nurse. She had longed to do this for some time, but had yielded to the judgment of others in delaying to do so. She had a taste for nursing, and had always cared for the sick ones of the family, and for some friends. She was not entirely unprepared for her work, therefore, and was useful from the first day. Some extracts from her journal tell the brief story of her undertaking : --

"We had all been full of courage till the last moment came; then we all broke down.   I realized that I had taken my life in my hand, and that I might never see them all again.   I said, 'Shall I stay, mother?' as I hugged her close.   'No, go, and the Lord be with you,' answered the Spartan woman;   and till I turned the corner she bravely smiled and waved her handkerchief on the doorstep.   Shall I ever see that dear old face again?   So I set forth in the twilight, with May and Julian Hawthorne as escort, feeling as if I were the son of the house going to war. . . . A most interesting journey into a new world full of stirring sights and sounds, new adventures, and an ever-growing sense of the great task I had undertaken.   I said my prayers as I went rushing through the country white with tents, all alive with patriotism, and already red with blood.   A solemn time, but I'm glad to live in it; and am sure it will do me good whether I come out alive or dead."

Again she writes:—

"Up at six, dress by gaslight, run through my ward and throw up the windows, though the men grumble and shiver; but the air is bad enough to breed a pestilence; and as no notice is taken of our appeals for better ventilation, I must do what I can.   Poke up the fire, add blankets, joke, command, and coax, but continue to open doors and windows as if life depended on it.   Mine does, and doubtless many another, for a more perfect pestilence box than this house I never saw, — cold, damp, dirty, full of vile odors from wounds, kitchens, wash-rooms, and stables.   No competent head, male or female, and a jumble of good, bad, and indifferent nurses, surgeons, and attendants to complicate matters."

She was right about the pestilence, for she had been there but six weeks, when she was taken with typhoid fever, and her father summoned to take her home.

The fever was very malignant, she was delirious for three weeks, and was in mortal danger, and it left her with shattered nerves and weakened constitution, and she never knew her old abounding health and unusual strength, after this sad experience. Just as life was about to present success and appreciation to her, she lost her power fully to enjoy and make the most of it. The irony of fate could go no further. After her recovery from the fever she brought out her " Hospital Sketches," which were almost literal reproductions of her letters to her family during her brief absence. The book attracted unusual attention from its timeliness, and introduced her to a different audience from that to which her stories had appealed. Soon after, she wrote other stories born of her experience; among them, " My Contraband," one of her best stories. She began to get praise in high quarters, and to have letters from publishers asking for contributions. Such men as Higginson, Hale, Henry James, and even Charles Sumner expressed their appreciation of her genius. The tide had turned, and its flood would lead on to fame and fortune.

From this time she was able to earn enough to keep the family in comfort, but she denied herself almost as severely as of old. She began to be something of a lion in society, and went out more than she had ever done. She was able to help her sister May in her art studies, which was a great delight to her, and from this time the dear old mother gave up her hard work, and took her ease in her armchair, as Louisa had all along declared she should do some day. This was the sweetest drop in the cup of prosperity, to the loving daughter. She also rejoiced that her father could now be happy in his own way, and not be harassed by poverty and debt.

In 1865 an opportunity offered itself for her to go abroad as a companion to an invalid lady. She was not yet able to spend the money herself, for even small journeys, and she accepted this place, though with some hesitation. She remained abroad nearly a year, travelling about some of the time, and making long stays, at intervals, in places that suited the invalid. She got a good deal out of it, though she chafed sadly at the limitations which the circumstances placed upon her freedom of movement. The unproductive year left her in debt, and she worked harder than ever, after her return, to repay all obligations.

In May, 1868, Roberts Brothers asked her to write a girl's story for them, and she began to depict the adventures of the Pathetic Family, as she always called the Alcotts, and the result was "Little Women." She did not at all appreciate the excellence of the work, and was amazed at the success the book achieved. The struggles of the family, which had been so hard to her in the living, now became her literary capital. She drew on them in many of her books from this time, and they always touched the heart of the world. "Little Women" was received with acclamations by girls everywhere, and they were far from being its only admirers. When it entered a home, the entire family read it, and enjoyed it about equally. She was now the most popular writer for girls in the world, and she continued to be so as long as she lived.

The sales of some of her books were quite phenomenal. They were translated into French, German, and Dutch. In England also they were very largely read. They followed each other in rapid succession, — "Little Men," "Jo's Boys," "An Old-Fashioned Girl," "Eight Cousins," "Rose in Bloom;" they were written with great ease and rapidity. Had she been as well as formerly, the labor would not have worried her in the least. But now she was often ill, and the work told upon her. She usually spent the winter in Boston and the summer in Concord. She could work better in the city, and she had never been fond of Concord. She needed quiet and solitude; and curious people had begun to intrude themselves upon her in the village, whom she escaped in the city. She began to do her work rather wearily after a time. She writes thus, after finishing "An Old-Fashioned Girl": —

"I wrote it with my left hand in a sling, one foot up, head aching, and no voice; yet, as the book is funny, people will say, 'Didn't you enjoy doing it?' I often think of poor Tom Hood as I scribble rather than lie and groan. I certainly earn my living by the sweat of my brow."

In 1870 she found herself much in need of rest and change, and went abroad again for a pleasure-trip. This time she was able to plan her own journey, to visit friends, and to forget the worries of former years. May was with her, and some of their early dreams came true. She wrote bright and witty letters home, which afterward entered into the composition of "Shawl Straps." In Rome she received news of the death of Anna's husband, Mr. Pratt, which shocked her greatly. He had been in every way a brother to her, and she had depended upon him in many things. After hearing of his death her thoughts turned at once to the support of his family, and from that time she planned for them as well as for the others in all she did. They became members of the Alcott family, and all lived together for a while. The entries in her journal are pathetic at this time. She writes in this wise: —

"I have no ambition now but to keep the family comfortable and not ache any more. Pain has taught me patience, I hope, if nothing more. . . . Home and begin a new task. Twenty years ago I resolved to make the family independent if I could. At forty that is done. Debts all paid, even outlawed ones, and we have enough to be comfortable. It has cost me health, perhaps ; but I still live ; there is more for me to do, I suppose."

She sent May to Europe once more, to pursue her art studies, in 1873. While residing in London she made acquaintance with a young Swiss gentleman named Nieriker, became much attached to him, and was married to him in 1878. He was of a German-Swiss family of high standing, and the marriage proved one of almost ideal happiness. This idyl of true love, whose course ran smooth, was a great joy to Louisa in the midst of her labors, and the anxieties of looking after her mother, who was now old and very feeble. She died in 1877, before the happy love marriage had been consummated, but the brightness of the prospects of her baby girl had cheered her last weary months. Her death was the hardest blow Louisa had yet received, and she says of it in her journal: —

"I never wish her back, but a great warmth seems gone out of life, and there is no motive to go on now. I think I shall soon follow her, and am quite ready to go, now she no longer needs me."

But others still needed her, and her cares were even to be increased, before the end. In 1879 her sister May died, in Paris, and her infant daughter was sent to Louisa to be brought up. She became a great comfort to her devoted aunt, who cared for her till her death, after which event the child was returned to her father in Switzerland. Louisa wrote of her sister's death : —

" In all the troubles of my life I never had one so hard to bear, for the sudden fall from such high happiness to such a depth of sorrow finds me unprepared to accept or bear it as I ought."

And afterward of the baby's coming she said : —

" She always comes to me, and seems to have decided that I am really ' marmar.' My heart is full of pride and joy, and the touch of the dear little hands seems to take away the bitterness of grief. I often go at night to see if she is really *here*, and the sight of the little head is like sunshine to me. Father adores her, and she loves to sit in his strong arms. They make a pretty picture as he walks in the garden with her to ' see the birdies.' . . . A hard year for all, but when I hold my Lulu I feel as if even death had its compensations. A new world for me."

In 1882 Mr. Emerson died, — a great sorrow to her, and a severe blow to Mr. Alcott. No greater reverence and gratitude had ever repaid kindness than that which was felt toward Mr. Emerson by the Alcott family. After his death life seemed poorer to all of its members who survived.

In the same year Mr. Alcott suffered a stroke of paralysis, from which he never fully recovered, and his daughters shared in his care to the end, or almost to the end, for Louisa was herself so ill at the moment of his death that she was not with him, and was never conscious of her loss. She had continued to work to the last, although very ill. But the work had been done with difficulty, and was doubtless a great injury to her. She was not conscious during her violent but brief last illness, the trouble being of the brain.

Who can match the record of this life, so briefly sketched, for steady purpose, for self-abnegation, for unwearied kindness and devotion, for ceaseless labor, for lofty purpose, and for high ideals? Of her literary work one can truthfully and gratefully say, that it was the best work of its kind that was done in its day, perhaps in any day. And was it not an important work, to enliven and amuse, to instruct and inspire, a whole generation of young people; to redeem the literature of childhood from its stupidity and its cant, from its priggishness and unnaturalness, and to put into the hands of children books which it was a joy to read, an education in humanity to pore over, and a keen delight to remember in later days? Their influence was unbounded, and it made for righteousness in every instance. And it was an influence which will not wane, for it had in it the most enduring elements, and appealed to the universal in the heart of man. One cannot feel for her death even so light a pang as nature feels when a blossomed bough is broken, for she was weary and only thus could rest be won.

LYEFF TOLSTOI.

LYEFF TOLSTOI.

IN literature the coming man is, in all probability, a Russian. From no nation have we at present reason to expect as much, in the near future, as from the dwellers in that still half-mysterious land. Greece had its Homer, Italy its Dante, England its Shakespeare, Germany its Goethe, and if one might predict where the next universal genius or world-man would arise, he would be justified in looking to Russia, first of all, for that unique product of the best world force. We shall hardly produce such a genius in the New World. There is too much equality, too much prosperity, too much general intelligence. We cannot expect giants where the average stature of mankind is so high; we shall look in vain for one man than his brethren taller and fairer.

He may be already born among the steppes of Russia. In some bleak settlement, on the far plains of Siberia, or in the wilds of the stern Caucasus, or on the banks of the lonely Neva, or in some little communal village in the Northern forests, the child may now be playing who will voice the sorrow of that sorrowful land, in a song or a story which will touch the universal heart, and add one more to the roll-call of the great immortal names. Perhaps he is even now trying his unaccustomed hand on some work, which will picture the passion and the pain, the misery and the mystery of life in Russia, in colors which the whole world will recognize as those of a master-hand, — a Michael Angelo or a Titian painting in words. There have been many fore-runners of this genius, John the Baptists, crying, " Prepare ye the way;" and the world has begun to recognize them, and to put itself in an attitude of expectancy whenever a new Russian star rises in the sky. The fascination of the country to the mind of the outside world is deep and strong. Those dreamy solitudes of virgin forest or virgin plain, those distant mountain peaks with their purpling glooms, those impassable morasses, and those in-tensely sad, widely separated little villages, all appeal to the imagination with a powerful charm. So, too, do its inhabitants. The romantic back-ground for the novelist is already prepared. The stillness, the solitude, the mystery, the despotism, the discontent, the continual tragedy of life there, — all these elements combine to give even to writers below the great, much advantage over the novelists of our own favored land, where life is not romantic or tragical, but matter-of-fact and rather prosaic.

The sternness and sadness, the listlessness and apathy of Russian life, with its eternal monotony of card-playing ; its one excitement of intoxication ; its occasional fierce outbursts, which show that even ages of repression cannot entirely subdue the spirit of man ; its continual intrigue, its frequent treachery, its constant danger, — all these things lie ready to the writer's hand, and he cannot justly be accused of unreality or exaggeration if he freely uses them. So it comes about that the Russian writers are strong, virile, primitive, — brutal realists, but with the realism of Homer and not of Howells, not even of Zola, though many times they are not more delicate than he.

A man like Gogol, descended from those Zaparog Cossacks whose heroic exploits the author of " Taras Bulba " celebrates, and brought up on the marvellous legends of the Malo Russians, if he prove to be a writer at all, will be no snowy-handed dilettante, singing to a lute, but a strong, fantastic, half-diabolical realist, such as Gogol really was. Count Tolstoi was, perhaps, his intellectual heir. At any rate, he belongs to the succession, but has far outdone his predecessor.

Tolstoi was born in 1828, and reckons among his ancestors one of the best servitors of Peter the Great, Count Piati Tolstoi. The family has come down in unbroken line from that barbarous time, and its annals are full of exciting adventures. The young Lyeff was born at Tuba, and was educated partly at home and partly at the University of Kazan. We are told little of his life at the university, but he doubtless made acquaintance there with brilliant young men from various parts of the empire, who scattered words which grew into opinions, and influenced his later life. He entered the army in 1851, and served until the end of the Crimean War. He was shut up in Sevastopol during the siege, and was greatly distinguished for his bravery. His description of the siege is one of his most powerful pieces of writing. No painter of war and battle has been more revoltingly realistic than he. He was afterward Adjutant to the Emperor, and a writer who knew him at that time describes him thus: —

"He was the wildest young guardsman in Petersburg. His life at that time would certainly have been outside the tests of even the mildest morality; he could jest in half-a-dozen languages and jest well; he was brilliant, fascinating, universally admired; everything seemed within his reach. He had been named for the government of an important province; was heir to a vast property, a whole district of the richest land, the dowry of an ancestress, a Tartar princess, bearing his name."

He had written a number of things while in the army, and " The Cossacks," while staying with a brother in the Caucasus. It narrowly escaped the condemnation of the censor, and created a sensation in reading circles. After this, his whole mind was upon literature for a few years. His great novel of " War and Peace " was published in 1860, and soon translated into other languages. Its length is enormous (eighteen hundred pages), but its interest intense. It gave him a European reputation. But the culmination of his literary success was, doubtless, " Anna Karenina," which followed " War and Peace." In this most powerful novel we have an appalling picture of that retribution which has been the theme of so many of the great masterpieces of literature. In modern times few stronger delineations of the inevitable punishment which follows sin have been made. The motto of the book, " Vengeance is mine, I will repay," gives the whole motive of the work.

The story is of thrilling interest, and the genius of
the author is shown most strongly in the manner in
which the retribution is brought about. Not from
the outside, but from within; the sin punishes itself,
as is the method of nature, or of God, as you choose
to phrase it. It is the story of an adulterous amour,
and the end is a tragedy, as the result of such *liaisons*
is apt to be, if the parties to it, as in this case,
are persons capable of a sincere, profound, and solemn passion. The heroine, Anna Karenina, loves
Vronsky, for whom she has left her husband, an
ambitious and absorbed, perhaps also an unlovable
man, with a perfect passion. For him she has sacrificed even her son, whom she loved with all the
intensity of her nature; her reputation, which was
almost equally dear, for she was a proud as well as
a passionate woman; and at first she feels satisfied
with her sacrifices, and lives in a feverish dream of
joy. Her lover takes her to his distant estates,
where his high position insures her a certain respect,
as he installs her mistress of his splendid domain.
Vronsky's family treat her with consideration, and
outwardly she is not subjected to those humiliations
which in real life, and in most works of fiction, attend
such a connection. She refuses the divorce which
her husband offers her, preferring that the bond which
binds her to Vronsky shall be one of mutual love only,
and she maintains this exaltation of feeling for a considerable time. She has now a daughter, whom she
does not love, all her motherly affection being centred
in the son whom she has deserted, and whom she
mourns with unavailing sorrow. Soon the punishment of guilty love sets in. " All the illusions which

exalted the senses as long as they were postured in love's shadow," vanished. Her life seemed a feverish dream, unreal, terrible, though filled with a kind of joy in the sweetness of her love, and the certainty of its being fully reciprocated by her lover.

But the feeling of moral decadence which was within her, made the dream almost hideous at times, even in the earlier days. She felt, we are told, "the impossibility of expressing the shame, the horror, the joy which were now her portion. Rather than put her feelings into idle and fleeting words, she preferred to keep silent. As time went on, words fit to express the complexity of her sensations still failed to come to her, and even her thoughts were incapable of translating the impressions of her heart." She hoped that calmness and peace might come to her, but they held aloof. With a relentless hand Tolstoi describes all the torments of her lot. This is the keen and bitter interest of the book, the agonies of a soul making expiation for a grievous wrong. "What agonies of remorse," says another, "this illegal union so passionately desired, brings upon the guilty woman! What deep mortification and what vulgar discomfitures; what deadly humiliations and what prosaic irksomeness spring from this false situation, and ultimately make it so odious, so painful, that way of escape has to be found, by an act of madness, in a moment of despair." These same fears and doubts worry Vronksy, who is noble and high-minded, and single in his devotion to her; and the estrangement has begun. "These two beings, starting on the bright and free pinnacles of love, have descended, without being themselves aware of it, into the dark and suffocating regions of hate."

The terrible end of the beautiful woman is pictured with the same ruthless fidelity with which the whole story is told. She sees, when in the midst of her agonies one day, "a freight train coming; she goes to meet it. She looked under the cars, at the chains and the brake, and the high iron wheels; and she tried to estimate with her eye the distance between the fore and back wheels, and the moment when the middle would be in front of her. Then she said, looking at the shadow of the car thrown upon the black coal-dust which covered the sleepers, 'There in the centre he will be punished, and I shall be delivered from it all — and from myself.'" The full description is almost too terrible to be transcribed, and, indeed, the whole story is pitiless in the unflinching manner in which the expiation is wrought out. No stroke of the brush that would deepen the shadows or add intensity to the tragedy has been spared. Tolstoi the artist is also Tolstoi the moralist in this marvellous book. And yet it is under ban as an immoral book in many quarters. Like Goethe's "Elective Affinities," it was, however, considered by its author as the most pointedly moral of all his works.

With it he closed his career as a novelist pure and simple, and soon after entered upon the third stage of his career, his religious and socialistic propaganda.

What subtle change had come over his spirit, what awakening of the latent fanaticism of his nature, we can only guess. The transformation seemed startlingly sudden to the world, but may have been long in the making, for aught we know; it was radical and lasting. The gay young soldier and courtier, the absorbed man of letters, the seeker after honors and fame, had passed away. The conversion of Saul of Tarsus was not more surprising to his circle, than that of this aristocrat and grandee to his little world, and to the world at large. A new man was born,—a reformer, an ascetic, an extremist. A madman too, it was thought among his old coterie; and the fate of Gogol, who ended his career in a madhouse, was often cited in speaking of him. Gogol, even in his earlier works, displayed something akin to the hyperæsthesia of seers and of the insane. It lent a thrilling charm to some of his poetical descriptions. On the track of witches he took us through the awful solitudes of Russian forests, showing us also the wide stretches of waste country and the sky of the steppes. There is a wild grace and woodsy flavor in all the pictures he points out to us, and the Rusalka we are following may disappear at last in a silver mist, or hide among the rushes and nenuphars, in a marsh lighted by fireflies. That a half-insane man could write as well as Tolstoi, they tried to prove by quotations from his books such as his description of the Dnieper, which is not finer than many other poetical passages in his works: —

"Marvellous is the Dnieper on a warm summer's night, when all things are asleep, both man, and beast, and bird; God only from on high looks down majestically on sky and earth, and shakes with solemnity his chasuble, and from his priestly raiment scatters all the stars. The stars are kindled, they shine upon the world; and all at the same instant also flash forth from the Dnieper. He holds them every one, the

Dnieper, in his sombre bosom ; not one shall escape him, unless indeed it perish from the sky. The black forest, dotted with sleeping crows, and the mountains rent from immemorial time, strive, as they catch the light, to veil him with their mighty shadow. In vain. There is naught on earth can veil the Dnieper. Forever blue, he marches onward in his restful course by day and night. He can be seen as far as human sight can pierce. As he goes to rest voluptuously, and presses close unto the shore by reason of the nocturnal cold, he leaves behind him a silver trail, flashing like the blade of a Damascus sword, and then he yields to sleep again. Then also he is wonderful, the Dnieper ! and there is no river like him in the world."

Some members of his astonished circle traced close resemblances to Gogol in Tolstoi's work, and read into them something more than the natural similarity of kindred genius, thus accounting for his mental attitude.

His first book after the change of which we are speaking was " My Religion," and he has been proclaiming the ideas embodied in it ever since in one form or another. His religion was the religion of Jesus Christ carried out literally in thought and action, even to the washing of the feet of menials, and the sharing of all the toils and privations of the humblest. " Sell all that thou hast and give to the poor," he took to mean just what it said, and so with all the other teachings of Jesus. The Church scarcely knew what to say to a disciple like this, and the world opened its eyes in grave wonder.

Non-resistance was one of his leading tenets, and is so still. A recent writer, who has visited him, gives this account of his present ideas : —

"He strongly asserted the doctrine of non-resistance, and in support of his argument he mentioned an instance of some peasants, who, to test the sincerity of some Stundists, gradually robbed them of all their movable property. One day they took away the horses, another the cows, the third day the furniture, until finally there was nothing left for them to take. Then they waited a day or two to see whether the Stundists would be false to their profession. Finding, eventually, that the Stundists did not move in the matter, and being conscience-stricken, they returned all the stolen property."

The Count's sincerity was such that the people came to have faith in him, and he soon had followers in almost all ranks of Russian life. Mr. Francis Prevost visited a Tolstoi colony in 1891, and writes in "Temple Bar" about "The Concord of the Steppe": —

"That small village of the Steppe was a State, ideally independent. Men came to it from every quarter of the Empire, — soldiers, tchinovniks, lawyers, priests, artists, peasants, and petty tradesmen ; men often of delicate nurture, whose feet had grown black with travel, and their backs bent with the spade ; the clothes they wore and the tools of their trade were their sole possessions, and their tenure even of these was always terminable by another's greater need."

There was a teacher there, we are told, "a man, splendidly made, and with the face of a Jewish prophet, who had left the first society of Moscow, where his wife remained to spend his millions, to wander barefoot without a home. We spent many days and nights together thereafter, he and I, back to back for warmth in the straw of country carts, under the frosty moon, and later, in the night dens of thieves and plotters of all kinds in Moscow, but I never heard a word from his lips of which the purest saint could be ashamed. Yet he was but one of many there, and no exception."

To one visitor Tolstoi talked in this wise: —

"But why should a man sleep on a bed, if he can do without one by sleeping on the ground? You would increase their wants and make them luxurious. If a man is happy without a bed, why should he have one? Marcus Aurelius used to sleep on the ground. Why should n't the muzhiks?"

Visitors from all parts of the world seek him out in his retirement, and many and various accounts are given of his mode of life. That his wife still retains his estates, and lives in comfort with her nine children, is often spoken of with reproach. But she has never followed him to the extreme in his vagaries, and has succeeded in retaining a hold upon him which has somewhat curbed the impracticability of his action. She is only in partial sympathy with him, and asserts "that he changes his opinions once in two years, and with each new conviction plunges with a characteristic impetuosity into the task of converting the world to the new belief." But she denies the assertions that he is not sincere in practising his own doctrines; and we are told "that whatever break has occurred in the severity of his life has been on her importunity and that of his children; that when the long absences from his daily peasant toil come, they are caused by illness brought on by excessive abuse of his physical powers." The figure of this wife is a very pathetic one. Torn from the congenial life of her earlier years, obliged to manage large estates, to rear her children, to watch over and strive to restrain her eccentric husband, to aid him in . the more practical part of his work for others, — one watches with interest and with sympathy the noble woman thus situated.

During all these later years Count Tolstoi has added nothing to his literary output which the world has regarded with favor. A series of what have been well called Latter-Day Pamphlets, bearing about the same relation to his best work that Carlyle's Pamphlets bear to his "Hero-Worship" or his earlier Essays, have been issued from time to time; the "Kreutzer Sonata," which was never regarded by impartial critics as the work of a really healthy or even perfectly sane mind; "The Epilogue," and the treatise on Life, are about all that attracted attention outside of Russia. But we are told that the year 1891 found him with vast plans for future literary effort, of what sort we are not informed. Whether he could with his broken health have produced any- thing corresponding to his old work, may well be doubted. But the effort would have been interesting to his old following, and it is a source of regret to them that, the year of famine coming on, he aban- doned entirely his own plans, and set to work with characteristic enthusiasm to aid the sufferers by every means in his power. E. J. Dillon writes of his labors thus : —

"While absorbed in these literary labors he heard the peasants' piteous cry for bread, and throwing up all work and leaving his home and his family, he sallied forth in peasants' garb to help them. He is now in the Dankovsky district, moving about from house to house, from village to village, from canton to canton, gathering information about the needs of each family and individual, feeding the hungry, tending the sick, comforting those who have lost their bread-winners, and utterly forgetful of himself. From morning until night he is on his legs, distributing, administering, organizing, as if endowed with youthful vigor and an iron constitution. Hail, rain, snow, intense cold, and abominable roads are nothing to him."

The Countess was equally busy in Moscow. A letter she wrote in the "Russian Gazette" produced the result described as follows: —

"People of all classes and conditions were coming up on foot or in carriages, entering the house, crossing themselves before the icons, putting packets of bank-notes upon her table, and going their ways. In a short time the table was literally covered with bank-notes. The Countess was engaged in sealing up these offerings, and sending them off at once to her sons and daughters, who are in the tea-stalls and corn-stores in the famine-stricken districts."

The whole family were employed throughout the period of the famine, in making known the condition of the people to the world, in collecting money, and personally attending to its distribution, and, one adds very reluctantly, in bearing the harsh criticism and blame of a certain portion of the Russian press and people.

A man like Tolstoi in a country like Russia could not live long without becoming "a suspect." During the famine "the high-born family of his excellency" were made the objects of many fierce onslaughts, as well as the Count himself. In a country so much governed as Russia, it was regarded as extremely suspicious for "private persons, perhaps forming a private society," — that great dread in despotic governments, — should go about collecting information about the famine; and "conspiracy" was at once charged by some journals. But his later writings have at last been published in his native country, and are said to exert a great influence; so it was not possible to make great headway against him at that critical time, and he was able to keep on with his work. That there is much that is revolutionary in his teachings no one can deny, especially upon the subject of marriage. But his latest evangel, that of manual labor for all, need not be regarded as dangerous, even in Russia. And certainly there is nothing alarming in his new golden rule, which he states thus: "Get others to work for you as little as possible, and work yourself as much as possible for them; make the fewest calls upon the services of your neighbors, and render them the maximum number of services yourself."

One would be glad to hear that his work is satisfying to himself, and that he, who has sacrificed so much for an idea, is not haunted by doubts of its real usefulness. But we are told by a late visitor that he, at parting, uttered the following sad and remarkable words: —

"I do not know whether what I am doing is for the best, or whether I ought to tear myself away from this occupation. All I know is that I cannot leave this work. Perhaps it is weakness; perhaps it is my duty which keeps me here. But I cannot give it up, even if I should like to. Like Moses on Mt. Horeb, I shall never see the fruit of my labors. I shall never know whether I have been acting for the best or not. My fear is that what I am doing is only a palliative."

One is reminded of Ruskin's old age by that of
Tolstoi. Like Ruskin, he did brilliant and valuable
literary work in youth and middle age, and received
his meed of fame. But in his later years he has
poured forth much that is irrelevant and almost
childish, though always in brilliant fashion, and has
lost his hold upon the attention of the world. But
Tolstoi's is the happier lot, in that he has a devoted
wife and sympathizing family, while Ruskin sits by a
lonely fireside, and is not even cheered by the memory of happy domestic days. That these men wrought
for others in the day of their strength, loved the
world with surpassing love, and strove to make it
better, happier, nobler, must somehow lighten the
burden of their years; and though the shadows be
very deep about them as they go down the western
slope of life, that thought must light their pathway
like a star. In Russia the work to be done is so vast,
the reforms needed so many and radical, the changes
which the times in which we live demand so revolutionary, that the patriotic and public-spirited grow
hopeless and are unnerved, and the constant danger
is that only babblers will come to the front. Stronger
practical men than Tolstoi must do the great work;
but it will be his glory that he tried in his own way
to do something; forgot his ease, his prospects, and
his fame, and became a servant to all; suffered for
his convictions, and roused many other noble souls
to aid in the supreme struggle. Not what he has
done, but what he sought to do, will be his lasting
monument. He goes swiftly now, —

> "Upwards towards the peaks,
> Towards the stars,
> And towards the great silence."

RUDYARD KIPLING.

RUDYARD KIPLING is one of the latest of the young men of genius to awake in the morning and find himself famous. Far across the plains and the jungles of India his name had flown in the night. The little book printed on brown paper, and passed from hand to hand, had done it. Only a handful of barrack-room ballads had wrought the spell. Very soon they flew across the seas, and the larger world of Europe read and laughed, and began to criticise. In the language of his own "Conundrum of the Workshop," —

"When the flicker of London sun falls faint on the club-room's
        green and gold,
    The sons of Adam sit them down and scratch with their pens
    in the mould —
    They scratch with their pens in the mould of their graves, and
    the ink and the anguish start,
    When the Devil mutters behind the leaves: ' It 's pretty, but
    is it art ? ' "

But the period of questioning did not last long, and the literary world soon decided that it was art, and with a pungent new flavor which they relished. The daring young Englishman had carried more than the outer entrenchments, he had raised his flag over the fort. Perhaps, if one said he had stormed the barri-

cade, it would be a better simile, for there was something of French dash and theatricality about the *coup.* The literary men and the critics had been captured among the rest, and soon two continents were ringing with " The Road to Mandalay," and quoting Mulvany. No such storming of the Malakoff of public opinion has occurred since Byron's famous onset long ago. Without any of Byron's stage properties it had been accomplished. Neither wide manorial halls, nor titled ancestors, nor romantic love affairs, nor beauty that was half divine, nor fascinating qualities such as the world has seldom seen, belonged to this young aspirant, who had made an almost insolent success. Bret Harte's sudden and reckless dash at the literary outworks amid the wild Sierras, was more nearly akin to Kipling's theatrical storming of the breastworks.

Mr. Kipling thus describes his first book: —

" There was built a sort of a book, a lean oblong docket, wire-stitched, to imitate a D. O. government envelope, printed on one side only, bound in brown paper, and secured with red tape. It was addressed to all heads of departments and all government officials, and among a pile of papers would have deceived a clerk of twenty years' service. Of these books we made some hundreds, and, as there was no necessity for advertising, my public being to my hand, I took reply post-cards, printed the news of the birth of the book on one side, the blank order-form on the other, and posted them up and down the Empire from Aden to Singapore and from Quelta to Colombo. The money came back in poor but honest rupees, and was transferred from the publisher, the left-hand pocket, direct to the author, the right-hand pocket. Every copy sold in a few weeks, and the ratio of expenses to profits, as I remember it, has since prevented my injuring my health by sympathizing with publishers who talk of their risks and advertisements."

It was not many years before it took forty thousand copies of his new "Jungle Book" to satisfy the first demand in England and America.

The spirit of the East had somehow penetrated the blood of this Englishman, who was born in Calcutta in 1865. But the hearts of the parents had never left their native land, and they went back to the little lake by which they had wandered in the days of their young love, for a name for the child, and called him Rudyard. The name of his mother was Alice McDonald.

India is not a good place in which to educate children, and the boy was sent to England, where he spent several years, returning to India when he was sixteen years old. His bent for letters was shown thus early, and he spent seven years in newspaper reporting. This training, for a story-writer was superb, and we have been enjoying the fruits of those years of uncongenial toil, ever since he began to write for the outside world. His work upon the "Civil and Military Gazette" had been that of proof-reading, scissors-and-paste work, and the boiling down of blue-books into summaries. It was distasteful, and his days long. But he wrote beyond hours, and produced such sketches and poems as soon made his name known in the more intelligent circles of Anglo-India. A too robust imagination is not much liked in a newspaper office, and many efforts were made to curb the exuberance of this boy, who was irrepressible, but who finally settled down to routine work in his own office, and to sending his poems and sketches to other publications, where they were admired and paid for.

It is significant, too, that when the proprietors finally decided that it was necessary to put more "sparkle" into the paper, they did not apply to Kipling for that purpose, but to E. Kay Robinson, who was afterward the editor of the paper. But Mr. Robinson applied to Kipling at once for assistance in enlivening the "rag," and the two worked together very harmoniously. Mr. Robinson says: —

"The amount of 'stuff' that Kipling got through in a day was indeed wonderful; and though I had more or less satisfactory assistants after he left, and the staff grew with the paper's prosperity, I am sure that more solid work was done in that office when Kipling and I worked together than ever before or after."

Throughout the terrible heat of summer, when almost every white family had gone to the mountains, Kipling remained at his post, toiling incredibly. He explored all the reeking haunts of the great city, and photographed some of them, as in the "City of Dreadful Night." He had the most intimate acquaintance with the life of the natives, and knew the army people, the government officials, and all classes of English residents by heart. He acquired all this knowledge apparently without effort,— a glance seemed to photograph everything upon his brain. The sadness and the homesickness of the English impressed him very much, although there is in India much gayety of a feverish sort.

He always felt himself an exile, and spoke of the English as exiles, and was always longing for the fuller life of the Western world, of which he had had a glimpse in his school days. A very beautiful poem, "Christmas in India," reveals this feeling as well as anything he has written: —

" Dim dawn behind the tamarisks — the sky is saffron yellow —
    As the women in the village grind the corn,
  And the parrots seek the river-side, each calling to his fellow
    That the day, the staring Eastern day, is born.
  Oh the white dust on the highway! Oh the stenches in the
    byway !
    Oh the clammy fog that hovers o'er the earth!
  And at home they 're making merry 'neath the white and scarlet
    berry —
    What part have India's exiles in their mirth ! "

There is a note of bitterness in some of the lines: —

" High noon behind the tamarisks — the sun is hot above us —
    As at home the Christmas day is breaking wan.
  They will drink our health at dinner, those who tell us how they
    love us,
    And forget us till another year be gone.

" Oh the toil that knows no breaking! Oh the heimweh, cease-
    less aching !
    Oh the black dividing sea, and alien plain !
  Youth was cheap — wherefore we sold it; gold was good —
    we hoped to hold it;
    And to-day we know the fulness of our gain.

" Gray dusk behind the tamarisks — the parrots fly together —
    As the sun is sinking slowly over home ;
  And his last ray seems to mock us shackled in a life-long
    tether,
    That drags us back, howe'er so far we roam.

     .   .   .   .

> "Black night behind the tamarisks — the owls begin their
> chorus —
> As the conches from the temple scream and bray,
> With the fruitless year behind us, and the hopeless years before
> us ;
> Let us honor, O my brothers, Christmas day !"

Although he felt so keenly the pangs of the exile, he was far more favored in his life than the majority of the young men, his companions; for his own family were with him, and he had a delightful home life, as a background to his wearisome days. John Lockwood Kipling, his father, was a man of fine artistic tastes, literary gifts, and quiet humor; his mother a charming woman, witty and cultivated; and his sister a person also of literary gifts and attainments. Their home at Lahore was a charming retreat from the uncongenial office, and Rudyard the life and light of it. Here he gave vent to his high spirits, and satirized to his heart's content the " society " of the place. He could be as caustic as he liked, and repression had always irked him rather sorely. Indeed he had not always repressed himself, and the originals of his satirical portraits of men and women were pretty well known throughout the land. Despite this, he was a pronounced favorite with the very society he so rashly satirized. He was allowed to be, in peace,

> "The prophet of the Utterly Absurd,
> Of the Patently Impossible, and Vain,"

and many times " when the thing that could n't had occurred," he had only to apologize lightly, smile, and be forgiven. In after years he addressed his Indian friends thus : —

> " I have eaten your bread and salt,
>   I have drunk your water and wine,
> The deaths ye died I have watched beside,
>   And the lives ye led were mine.
>
> "Was there aught I did not share
>   In vigil or toil or ease, —
> One joy or woe I did not know,
>   Dear hearts across the seas?
>
> " I have written the tale of your life
>   For a sheltered people's mirth,
> In jesting guise — but ye are wise,
>   And ye know what the jest is worth."

The sadness of some phases of the life of India does not lend itself very readily to mirth, and that Kipling had felt the pathos of the lives of the Indian women, he shows more than once. When Lady Dufferin raised a fund for medical aid for them, he voiced the gratitude of the poor dumb creatures, in a poem called " The Song of the Women," of which we append a part: —

> " How shall she know the worship we would do her?
>   The walls are high, and she is very far.
> How shall the women's message reach unto her
>   Above the tumult of the packed bazaar?
> Free wind of March, against the lattice blowing,
> Bear thou our thanks, lest she depart unknowing.
>
> " Go forth across the fields we may not roam in,
>   Go forth beyond the trees that rim the city,
> To whatsoe'er fair place she hath her home in,
>   Who dowered us with wealth of love and pity.
> Out of our shadow pass, and seek her singing —
> ' I have no gifts but Love alone for bringing.'

"Say that we be a feeble folk who greet her,
    But old in grief and very wise in tears;
Say that we, being desolate, entreat her
    That she forget us not in after years;
For we have seen the light, and it were grievous
To dim that dawning if our lady leave us.

.   .   .   .

"If she have sent her servants in our pain,
    If she have fought with Death and dulled his sword;
If she have given back our sick again,
    And to the breast the weakling lips restored,
Is it a little thing that she has wrought?
Then Life and Death and Motherhood be naught.

"Go forth, O wind, our message on thy wings,
    And they shall hear thee pass and bid thee speed,
In reed-roofed hut, or white-walled home of kings,
    Who have been holpen by her in their need.
All spring shall give thee fragrance, and the wheat
Shall be a tasselled floor-cloth to thy feet."

If ever the pathos and the pain of woman's life in India shall find a voice, it will be the beginning of the deliverance from her thraldom of ages, and there is no one so well fitted for uttering this cry of souls in prison as Rudyard Kipling. We might well spare a few stirring tales and dashing ballads, we might well leave the jungle to its wild beasts and serpents, and the Seven Seas to their own monotony, if he would utter for us The Cry of the Human, which has been repressed for centuries in the Orient.

The soldiers never appeal to him in vain, and he depicts, as no one else has ever done, that army life,

"Where there are n't no Ten Commandments, an' a man can
    raise a thirst."

He gives their message to the world in their own choice language through Tommy: —

> "We are n't no thin red 'eroes, nor we are n't no blackguards too,
> But single men in barricks, most remarkable like you ;
> An' if sometimes our conduck is n't all your fancy paints,
> Why, single men in barricks don't grow into plaster saints."

His keen eye takes in even the Zulus, and the inhabitants and fighting men of the Soudan, and half the world is now familiar with the name of Fuzzy-Wuzzy, the big black bounding beggar who "bruk a British square," and who, though he was "a pore benighted heathen," was a "first-class fighting man." Even in drawing-rooms now you may hear of this "bloomin'" patriot, who is

> "All 'ot sand and ginger when alive,
> And generally shammin' when 'e 's dead."

A royal favorite with his creator, too, is Gunga Din, the water-carrier who saved the lives of men in battle by filling up their helmets.

But with all this knowledge and insight about India, which no one else possesses or will probably ever accumulate, we are not sorry to have our Englishman leave India, "where a woman is only a woman, but a good cigar is a smoke," and return to England in 1889. He published almost immediately "The Record of Badalia Herodsfoot," and his first novel, "The Light that Failed." Soon a book of poems followed, entitled "Mine Own People." Thenceforward a new story or book at brief intervals up to this time. In 1891 he met Wolcott Balestier, a promising young American writer, in London, and formed a strong friendship for him. He visited him afterward, in Vermont. In 1892 Mr. Kipling was married in London to Caroline Balestier, a sister of his new friend. They sailed for this country soon afterward, and established their home in Brattleboro', Vermont, and spend a part of every year there, or near by at Waite. His home is called "The Naulahka," and there he hides himself from lion-hunters and produces "copy." "Captains Courageous" and the "Seven Seas" are his latest books, each done, if internal evidence proves anything, for the "joy of the working." That his best work will be done in the future is not to be doubted, yet, as the years go on, we fear that he will scarcely

> " recapture
> That first fine careless rapture."

It is almost too much to hope that he can combine that with the more studied work of his maturer years.

His greatest danger is that the commercial spirit shall master him, and that he shall outwrite his vein, resort to collaboration as in "The Naulahka," or to play-writing, or to the mere making of "copy," the scrawling strange words with a barbarous pen for pay. This is the danger of the day to all literary idols, but the strong savor of good sense in Mr. Kipling's nature may save him from the common fate of fortune's favorites. Thus far his natural force is not abated by reason of his versatility.

Some of the more striking traits of his character have been discussed in the periodicals from time to time. Among these, self-confidence is most often mentioned by scribblers. To read some of these, you would think he was like Ben Jonson's hero who thought that at each step he took his advanced head knocked out a star. That he has the vanity of a man of genius is not to be denied, but that it is as extreme as described, may well be doubted. But he has the poet's frankness also, and, like Dr. Holmes, who admits that

> "He sometimes sits beneath a tree
> And reads his own sweet songs,"

would proclaim it, if such were the case. This, the Kipling "cult" would delight in; but the scornful world might smile, as they smiled at Tennyson's impassioned words to Amy, —

> " Having known *me*, to decline
> On a range of lower feelings, and a narrower heart than mine,"

in the far-away days when " Locksley Hall " was new.

The next quality is given by his friends as mental alertness, sensitiveness, receptivity. He sees everything, hears everything, feels everything, absorbs everything. Then, when he is ready to write, all that he has seen or heard or felt rolls in upon him, and he has no lack of striking words in which to clothe his dramatic conceptions. His bits of landscape are like Turner's, and his descriptions of places like photographs, in their realism. His men stand out like statues, but his women are rather shadowy. He is most at home in writing of India, but in all his books England appears as the pleasant place of all festivity, and much wonder was felt when he settled down in America instead of England. But his stay may not be permanent, for already we hear of him as again in London, and even in South Africa. Industry and perseverance are among his most striking characteristics, and account for the number of publications already signed with his name.

His dread of the interviewer and dislike of personal publicity have been much commented on in America; but these are English traits, and perhaps not unusually marked in Kipling. That he would dread having his privacy invaded by Miss Henrietta Stackpole is undeniable, but that he would get rid of her in the most polite manner possible is unquestionable also. He has the reticence of a gentleman, and he would prefer to have a wall about his villa, after the manner of his countrymen, and to choose his visitors, and not to be overrun by the curious mob. This his friends admit, but, otherwise than this, he is a perfectly accessible and very delightful gentleman. That he often rides a tilt at propriety, that he is as indelicate as a soldier sometimes in his expressions, must be admitted. But, in his own words, —

> " You could n't raft an organ up the Nile
> And play it in the Equatorial swamps,"

and it is the life he has lived, that has given him his qualities, and the defects of those qualities. You cannot " travel with the cooking-pots and pails," and be " sandwiched 'tween the coffee and the pork," and not get an occasional smudge upon your spotless apparel. But if in his pages we live a good deal with maids of matchless beauty and parentage unguessed, yet the heart of the whole is clean, and in the Descent into Hell which has been made in recent years by the new generation of writers, Kipling, if he did not ascend into Heaven, surely remained in the Purgatorio. That he sees a high ideal before him, and will sometime follow it, we believe for many reasons, and partly from the hymn, " To the True Romance," in the " Seven Seas," from which we quote, —

> " Thy face is far from this our war,
>   Our call and counter-cry;
> I shall not find thee quick and kind,
>   Nor know thee till I die:
> Enough for me in dreams to see
>   And touch thy garment's hem;
> Thy feet have trod so near to God
>   I may not follow them."

Such poems as the " Recessional," written at the time of the Queen's Jubilee, promise us in the future much better poetry than he has yet written. That he should have been Laureate when Tennyson died, his admirers strongly argued, though in vain; but, with Swinburne living, that claim was hardly just. But that he represents the imperial instinct of the British race better than any other living poet is true. If to cheer her on in war, to praise her great exploits on land and sea, to commemorate her heroes, and the virtues of her patriots living and dead, be the work of a Laureate, he might fitly be called to wear the crown of bay. Read his Jubilee poem and see if you can recall a nobler : —

> " God of our fathers, known of old
>   Lord of our far-flung-battle line,
> Beneath whose awful Hand we hold
>   Dominion over palm and pine —
> Lord God of Hosts, be with us yet
> Lest we forget — lest we forget!

"The tumult and the shouting dies —
  The captains and the kings depart.
Still stands Thine ancient Sacrifice.
  An humble and a contrite heart.
Lord God of Hosts, be with us yet
Lest we forget — lest we forget!

"Far-called our navies melt away —
  On dune and headland sinks the fire ;
Lo, all our pomp of yesterday
  Is one with Nineveh and Tyre !
Judge of the Nations, spare us yet,
Lest we forget — lest we forget !

"If, drunk with sight of power, we loose
  Wild tongues that have not Thee in awe —
Such boasting as the Gentiles use
  Or lesser breeds without the Law —
Lord God of Hosts be with us yet,
Lest we forget — lest we forget!

"For heathen heart that puts her trust
  In reeking tube and iron shard —
All valiant dust that builds on dust,
  And guarding calls not Thee to guard —
For frantic boast and foolish word,
Thy mercy on Thy people, Lord !
                    Amen."

But it is as a story-teller, and not as a poet, that
Kipling is best known, and probably will be in the
future. "The Barrack-room Ballads" were many of
them stories, and, in the highest sense, not poetry
at all. They are rough descriptive sketches, marred
by the coarseness of the life they depicted, and too
much sprinkled with profanity; but they have the
true poetic quality, spite of all defects, and their
swing and verve haunt the reader, and he puts many
of them to tunes of his own making, and hums them

as he rides or walks. Indeed, Kipling wrote many of them to music of his own, — first caught the melody and fitted the poem to it. But the vividness, the power, the strength of the stories are a higher test of his genius. Some enthusiasts call them the best short stories in the English language. However this may be, they are probably the best now being produced; and if pitched in a little lower key, and pruned of some hysterical tendency to be what the new novelists call " relentless " or " unflinching," they would come near to being what his admirers claim. Vividness and strength, however, may be bought at too high a price.

CHRISTINA ROSSETTI.

CHRISTINA ROSSETTI.

THE Rossetti family, with their genius and their striking individuality, have occupied a large space in current literary history. There has been a fascination connected with the very name, with its foreign associations, and mysterious hints as to the "conspiracy" which had placed them upon English soil. Gabriele Rossetti, the father of Dante Gabriel, William Michael, Mary Francesca, and Christina Rossetti, was born in Vasto, on the Adriatic coast, in the kingdom of Naples in 1783. Secret societies were a part of the very life of the Italians at that period of their history, the only vent for their patriotism, and almost the only stirring interest of their lives. Proscribed by the government, they flourished more and more, and every thoughtful and daring soul was irresistibly drawn into their communion. Gabriele Rossetti was no exception. Literature and patriotism were the interests of his life. Proscribed while still young for Carbonarism, he left Italy, and settled in London, as a teacher of Italian, in 1824. Here he mingled chiefly with that body of exiles who had preceded him for like cause, and kept his burning zeal for Italian liberty alive by fiery meetings, where plots and counterplots formed the chief subjects of impassioned harangues. He married a Miss Frances Mary Polidori, whose mother was an Englishwoman, and whose father was of Italian blood. He became Professor of Italian in King's College in 1831, but devoted all his leisure time to studying and writing of Dante. He was a writer of stirring verses himself, mostly of a political character. His house was thronged with exiles during the early years of his London residence, and the earliest recollections of the children were of these waifs and strays, in whom their parents took such deep interest and unqualified delight.

The children themselves were a good deal wearied with the endless discussions and fervid appeals, the snatches of impassioned poetry introduced on all occasions, the continual denunciations of Louis Philippe, which were a commonplace of their childhood. Gabriele Rossetti's declamation, which their mother always listened to with such reverent attention, had its ridiculous side to the irreverent young group, who never dared to smile at it openly. Even the Dante Commentary on which the father spent so many years came to be regarded in somewhat the same manner. William Rossetti tells us: " The Convito was always a name of dread to us, as being the very essence of arid unreadableness. Dante Alighieri was a sort of banshee in the Charlotte Street house; his shriek audible even to familiarity, but the message of it not scrutinized." A sort of dislike of the family bogy grew up in the minds of all, and instead of reading him, they railed at him violently in secret.

From the first Gabriel meant to be a painter, and as soon as his limited school days were over he entered a drawing academy, where he remained four years, drawing from the antique, dabbling in anatomy, and doing all things in an individual way which perplexed his teachers. After that he went to the Royal Academy School. Holman Hunt writes of him at this time as follows: —

"A young man of decidedly foreign aspect, with long brown hair touching his shoulders, not taking care to walk erect, but rolling carelessly as he slouched along, pouting with parted lips, staring with dreaming eyes. He was careless in his dress. So superior was he to the ordinary varieties of young men that he would allow the spots of mud to remain on his legs for several days. . . . With his pushing stride and loud voice, a special scrutiny would have been needed to discern the reserved tenderness that dwelt in the breast of the apparently careless and defiant youth. . . . In these days, with all his headstrongness and a certain want of consideration, his life within was untainted to an exemplary degree, and he worthily rejoiced in the poetic atmosphere of the sacred and spiritual dreams that encircled him, however some of his noisy demonstrations at the time might hinder this from being recognized by a hasty judgment."

In 1848, when twenty years old, he entered the studio of Ford Madox Brown, and became one of his friends, — an acquaintance which led to his being introduced to Holman Hunt and Millais, and to the foundation of their famous Preraphaelite Brotherhood.

Maria Francesca was a gifted woman, who showed fine poetical promise in " The Shadow of Dante," but who subordinated literary achievement to religious and charitable work. She entered, as a novice in 1873, a sisterhood of the Anglican Church, and in 1874 joined it as a fully professed member. Her devotional feelings were a strong part of her nature, and she was glad to lead a religious life, separated in a measure from the world. William Michael was by nature a scholar, and has spent his life in various literary activities, but gained his greatest laurels as a critic. This family with their various gifts were bound firmly together by the bonds of family affection, and were helpful and comforting to each other to the last.

Christina, whose life we are chiefly to consider, was born in 1830, at the home in Charlotte Street, London. Her godmothers were Lady Dudley Stuart and Miss Georgina Macgregor. The family income was small, and shared with unfailing generosity with all the needy exiles who frequented the home. Some of these were artists, some sculptors, some poets, and the talk was of art and literature, interspersed with patriotism, as they grew older, though it had been chiefly of patriotism when they were children. They spoke Italian always, and loved the language. The education of all the children was rather desultory. Christina was taught at home, principally by her mother. But the children with their brilliant minds helped to educate each other. They were constantly reading and writing together. They were early acquainted with Shakespeare and Scott and with the Iliad. The mother, being a member of the Church of England, and of somewhat High Church opinions, brought the children all up in that belief. The father was nominally a Catholic, though a good deal of a free-thinker withal. Christina had naturally an irritable strain in her disposition, which she seems to have entirely conquered in later life. She, as well as Maria, had a strong religious nature, and both were very devout from their earliest youth. One of her earliest recorded opinions was stated in this wise: " Is it quite certain that no day will ever come when even the smallest, weakest, most grotesque, *wronged* creature will not in some fashion rise up in the Judgment with us to condemn us, and so frighten us effectually once for all? "

She was Dante Gabriel's first model, and there is a portrait of her by him executed when she was about seventeen. She also sat to her brother for the Virgin in his picture of " The Annunciation." We are told that " the tender almost deprecating look mingled with simplicity, the almost childlike beauty on the Virgin's face, was very characteristic of her in girlhood and early womanhood." Other friends of her early youth speak of her pensive beauty. She sat to Mr. Holman Hunt for the face in his picture called " The Light of the World," and artists all delighted in the fascinating mystery and soft melancholy of her eyes. But her admirers were chiefly artists and poets. Ordinary people saw no beauty in her pallid face and unfathomable eyes. Her brothers were called her adorers in early life, and remained almost that throughout life. Her health was extremely precarious in youth, and it was hardly expected that she would live to attain to womanhood. This state of health very naturally induced melancholy, and she was subject to that through all her early years. The family resources becoming more and more straitened,

Mrs. Rossetti and Christina opened a school in 1851, while Maria went out as a daily governess. The London school, not proving a success, was removed to the country, and they made there another effort. But at Frome in Somersetshire, they did little better, and the knowledge of country life which Christina obtained there was almost the only advantage derived from the change. Soon after their return to London her father died, and she felt the need of earning money by her pen if possible. She wrote a good many of her poems during the next few years; but her first volume, " Goblin Market and Other Poems," did not appear until 1862, and even then was not remunerative. But her brothers were more prosperous by this time, and she and her mother were relieved of pecuniary anxiety. About the year 1849 the romance of her early life was enacted, in quietude and almost secrecy. She was exceedingly reticent by nature, and her family hardly knew of it before it was over. Maria was possibly an exception, for the sisters were affectionately devoted to each other. A young painter of their little social circle had for some time been a secret admirer of her poetic face and of her sweet imaginative nature. He had heard much talk of her in his circle of artist friends, and was familiar with the repressed life she was leading. She was also secretly attached to him. But she had many religious scruples to contend with in harboring this affection. Her mind was somewhat narrow at best, and her sense of duty the supreme passion of her soul. The lover was a Roman Catholic, and her prejudices were strong against those of that faith. When he finally declared his love, the struggle was very desperate between affection and what she esteemed duty. She was of an intense nature, and capable of a passionate devotion, and this was the first time she had known the meaning of the word "love." But the indecision did not last long, and the lover was sacrificed. She was very unhappy for a long series of years, and put some of her pain into her poems. There are several in the volume called "New Poems" which relate to this matter. One entitled "What?" may be recalled: —

> "Glorious as purple twilight,
>   Pleasant as budding tree,
> Untouched as any islet
>   Shrined in an unknown sea:
> Sweet as a fragrant rose amid the dew: —
>   As sweet, as fruitless too.
> A bitter dream to wake from,
>   But oh, how pleasant while we dream!
> A poisoned fount to take from,
>   But oh, how sweet the stream!"

There are one or two of her short poems only in which a hint of the happiness of love is given. One of them is the exquisite little song, "A Birthday": —

> "My heart is like a singing bird
>   Whose nest is in a watered shoot;
> My heart is like an apple-tree
>   Whose boughs are bent with thickest fruit.

> "My heart is like a rainbow shell
>   That paddles in a halcyon sea;
> My heart is gladder than all these
>   Because my love is come to me.

> " Raise me a daïs of silk and down ;
>   Hang it with rare and purple dyes ;
>   Carve it with doves and pomegranates,
>   And peacocks with a hundred eyes ;
>
> " Work it in gold and silver grapes,
>   In leaves and silver fleurs-de-lys ;
>   Because the birthday of my life
>   Is come, my love is come to me."

When we read this and a few other brief and simple lays which she wrote, easily it seems, and naturally as a bird sings, we cannot but deplore the fact that they are so few, and that she lived in the strained and affected atmosphere of a mystical æstheticism, and sought so diligently for far-fetched imagery and artificial and morbid phases of thought. There are scarcely a handful of her poems where she is content to develop the genuine pathos of which she is capable, in a simple and unaffected manner.

These poems are almost the only ones which are known to the great body of readers, even to those of real poetic taste. Among them we may place the following : —

> " When I am dead, my dearest,
>   Sing no sad songs for me ;
>   Plant thou no roses at my head,
>   Nor shady cypress tree :
>   Be the green grass above me
>   With showers and dew-drops wet ;
>   And if thou wilt, remember,
>   And if thou wilt, forget.
>
> " I shall not see the shadows ;
>   I shall not feel the rain ;
>   I shall not hear the nightingale
>   Sing on as if in pain ;

> And dreaming through the twilight
>   That doth not rise or set,
> Haply I may remember,
>   And haply may forget."

Another is the familiar " Is the Road Up-hill?"—

> " Does the road wind up-hill all the way?
>   Yes, to the very end.
>   Will the day's journey take the whole long day?
>   From morn to night, my friend.
>
> " But is there for the night a resting-place?
>   A roof for where the slow dark hours begin?
>   May not the darkness hide it from my face?
>   You cannot miss that inn.
>
> " Shall I meet other wayfarers at night?
>   Those who have gone before.
>   Then must I knock or call when just in sight?
>   They will not keep you standing at that door.
>
> " Shall I find comfort, travel-sore and weak?
>   Of labor you shall find the sum.
>   Will there be beds for me and all who seek?
>   Yes, beds for all who come."

Of Dante Gabriel Rossetti the same thing might
be said. He was capable of being the best beloved
poet of his day, if he had been content to express
in honest English verse the deep-seated feelings
which are common to human nature under all the
varying circumstances of time and place. Fantastic
originality is a poor substitute for genuine feeling
expressed with truth and sincerity. In the poem
" Jenny " he for once complied with our demand,
and he treats the subject of woman in her utmost
degradation, in so delicate a manner that the most

prudish need not be repelled, and takes into the high realm of poetry one of the most persistent of the moral problems of the race. This poem is not marred by even a word we might wish omitted. When we consider how open he is to criticism upon the subject of erotic poetry, we almost wonder how he reached this height upon such a theme.

But in making these demands upon brother or sister, we ought to keep in mind, in regard to both, the fact that they are not really English poets, but Italian, as only one quarter of English blood ran in their veins, and in youth their environment was largely foreign. Their father spent his life over old forgotten folios, writing a learned and ponderous commentary on Dante, and their own studies ran a good deal in the direction of the merely quaint and obscure.

Christina lived quietly in London, though she made occasional visits to friends in the country, for the years following the life sacrifice we have narrated so briefly, but which was of such prominent importance in her life. Being a first and quite youthful affection, it was apparently outgrown in the course of a few years. But again visions of golden futures began to dance before her eyes, and the one real passion of her mature life claimed her for its own. An air inviolate surrounds the details of this epoch of her existence, but imagination can fill out the bare outlines, knowing the nature of the high heroic soul with whom we deal. This time the lover was a distinguished scholar and man of letters, and she was very sincerely attached to him. But she again did violence to her own nature by refusing to marry him, because he was not a Christian according to her ideas of what a Christian meant, having undefined and heterodox views. She dismissed him with the feeling in her heart, —

> " I could not love thee, dear, so much,
>   Loved I not *duty* more ; "

and tried thereafter to feel as loveliest

> " The hour of sisterly sweet hand in hand."

She loved no more, but led a lonely life, entirely devoted to her mother, whose chief comfort she was in her declining years. The pity of it all was infinite. A warped womanhood resulted, a narrow life, the life of a zealot and recluse, where gracious motherhood and sweet marital companionship, might have widened the nature and deepened the insight of this true, though limited poet, in some senses one of the finest of her day.

In 1861 and in 1865 she went to the Continent, visiting France, Switzerland, and Italy, and enjoying for the first time grand mountain scenery, which she found very saddening, though so inexpressibly beautiful. Her poem " En Route " contains these lines :

> " Farewell, land of love, Italy,
>   Sister-land of Paradise ;
>   With mine own feet I have trodden thee,
>   Have seen with mine own eyes :
>   I remember, thou forgettest me,
>   I remember thee.

> " Blessed be the land that warms my heart,
>   And the kindly clime that cheers,
>   And the cordial faces clear from art,
>   And the tongue sweet in mine ears :
>   Take my heart, its truest tenderest part,
>   Dear land, take my tears."

In 1871 she had a serious illness, and for two years her life seemed in danger. After this she lived for a while at the Convalescent Hospital connected with the Anglican Sisterhood of All Saints, where her sister Maria devoted herself to the care of the sick and suffering. She went to this retreat several times between 1870 and 1883, not as a patient, nor yet as a sister, but from love of the life there, and companionship with her sister. Her brother calls her "an outer sister," for she was interested not only in this sisterhood, but in an institution for redeeming fallen women, in district visiting, and various kinds of evangelical work. She delighted in making scrap books for hospital children, and in getting up treats for them, and had always on hand some private charities which filled a share of her time and attention. She was also nurse in her own family, all her life, sometimes injuring her own health in caring for others. To her brother Gabriel in particular she ministered unceasingly. In 1867 he was attacked by insomnia, and his eyesight was threatened. It was a weary, dreary time, and his family entered into his troubles with the most devoted sympathy. His wife, to whom he was romantically attached, had died after the two brief years of wedded life which followed many long years of troublous waiting and uncertainty. He had buried his poems in her coffin, "putting the volume between her cheek and beautiful hair." "I have often," he said, "been writing these poems when Lizzie was ill and suffering, and I might have been attending to her, and now they shall go." The lovers had become what he had foreseen, Severed Selves: —

> " Two separate divided silences,
> Which, brought together, would find loving voice;
> Two glances which together would rejoice
> In love, now lost like stars beyond dark trees ;
> Two hands apart whose touch alone gives ease ;
> Two bosoms which, heart-shrined with mutual flame,
> Would, meeting in one clasp, be made the same ;
> Two souls, the shores wave-mocked of sundering seas : —
> Such are we now.   Ah, may our hopes forecast
> Indeed one hour again, when on this stream
> Of darkened love once more the light shall gleam ? —
> An hour how slow to come, how quickly past, —
> Which blooms and fades, and only leaves at last,
> Faint as shed flowers, the attenuated dream."

Now indeed his query became pertinent : —

> " Why does Sleep, moved back by Joy and Ruth,
>   Tread softly round, and gaze at me from far ? "

And he often invoked the night in tones of despair :

> " Oh, lonely night ! art thou not known to me,
>   A thicket hung with masks of mockery,
>   And watered with the wasteful warmth of tears ? "

She had become to him through death " a sweetness more desired than Spring," " a music ravishing
more than the passionate pulse of Philomel," and he
held her thus in his heart till his life ended.

During all this time it was his sister who was his
comfort and his stay.   His poems had in 1869 been
exhumed by his friends, and they were published in
1870, and received with great favor by the reading
world.   The only adverse criticism was directed
against the love poems, particularly " The House of
Life," which was held " to express the languors of
sickly and unwholesome passion, in language little

short of absolute pruriency." The severity of this criticism, though not undeserved, cut his loving sister to the heart, and aggravated to a decided extent the ailments of her brother. He had, as a palliative of insomnia, begun taking chloral some time before, and now he was reaping the bitter fruits of that fatal mistake. His sufferings were excruciating, and drug added to drug brought not sleep, but delirium. Mr. Gosse states that " no case has been recorded in the annals of medicine in which one patient has taken so much, or even half so much, chloral as Rossetti took." No brain could withstand poisoning to this extent, and horrible depression took possession of him, accompanied by a turmoil of distempered fears and fantasies. The mental collapse soon became complete, and his life ended in the utmost bitterness and despair. Upon him in his last days came, even in an exaggerated degree, that

> " Wild pageant of the accumulated past
> That clangs and flashes for a drowning man."

And no change or peace could be looked for by the devoted friends, but the last great change of all, the peace that passes understanding. To his sisters, with their passionate religious feeling, their brother's last days were the sorest trial, particularly his attempt at suicide by the drinking of laudanum; but every one who knows the facts must regard that as the act of an irresponsible person, driven to desperation by suffering. Concerning Christina's influence upon her brother, Mr. Watts-Dunton says: —

" It was the beauty of her life that made her personal influence so great, and upon no one was that influence exer-

cised with more strength than upon her illustrious brother
Gabriel, who in many ways was so much unlike her. In
spite of his deep religious instinct and his intense sympathy
with mysticism, Gabriel remained what is called a free-thinker
in the true meaning of that much-abused phrase. In religion as in politics he thought for himself; and yet when
Mr. W. M. Rossetti affirms that the poet was never drawn
toward free-thinking women, he says what is perfectly true.
And this arose from the extraordinary influence, scarcely
recognized by himself, that the beauty of Christina's life
and her religious system had upon him."

In spite of the severity of her religious views, one
almost fancies that these lines were written to this
beloved if erring brother: —

> " Up the high steep, across the golden sill,
>   Up out of shadows into very light,
>   Up out of dwindling life to life aglow,
>   I watch you, my beloved, out of sight; —
>   Light fails me, and my heart is watching still,
>   My heart fails, yet I follow on to know."

Of religious poetry she wrote a great deal, and a
good deal also of devotional prose. Her first volume
of the latter was called " Annus Domini;" the second
" Called to be Saints." Then there were " Letter
and Spirit," " Time Flies," and " The Face of the
Deep." Mingled with the prose of these books are
some beautiful religious lyrics. In " The Prince's
Progress and Other Poems " there is a devotional
section, containing " The Lowest Place," one of the
world's favorites. In it occur the well-known lines :

> " If I might only love my God and die !
>   But now He bids me love Him and live on."

There is much devotional poetry in each volume of her verse, even " A Pageant and Other Poems," the only one which contains no separate section of such poems.

Her sister Maria Francesca died in 1876, and was buried in Brompton Cemetery according to the simple rules of the sisterhood to which she belonged. She was a woman of the highest ideals, and strove to carry out in practical life the virtues which she admired, and that sacrifice of self which she deemed a duty. Like Christina, she had deliberately sacrificed all hopes of personal happiness in domestic life, because the person on whom her heart was set could not profess, as she thought was essential, her views of evangelical religion. Christina mentions the matter in these words: " One of the most genuine Christians I ever knew, once took lightly the dying out of a brief acquaintance which had engaged her warm heart, on the ground that such mere tastes and glimpses of congenial intercourse on earth wait for their development in heaven." We are told, in the memoir of Christina, that the person who had thus engaged the warm heart of Maria Francesca was Mr. John Ruskin. In the memoir of that gentleman the story is told of his love for some woman, who loved, but refused to marry him, on grounds of religious differences between them; and Maria Francesca Rossetti is presumably that person.

Christina's death took place after many months of severe suffering, in December, 1894. It is sad to be obliged to relate that her mind was in a troubled state during this time of intense physical suffering. But her brother writes concerning it in these words : —

" In the last three months or so of her life she was most gloomy on the subject (of her spiritual state), some of her utterances being deeply painful. This of course was beyond measure unreasonable, but so it was. I *believe* the influence of opiates (which were indispensable) had something to do with it. . . . Assuredly my sister did to the last continue believing in the promises of the Gospel, as interpreted by Theologians; but her sense of its threatenings was very lively, and at the end more operative on her personal feelings. This should not have been. She remained firmly convinced that her mother and sister are saints in heaven, and I endeavored to show her that, according to her own theories, she was just as safe as they; but this — such was her humility of self-estimate — did not relieve her from troubles of soul. If there is any reality in the foundations of her creed, she now knows how greatly she was mistaken."

So gloomy were her religious views, and so melancholy her nature, that one almost fears that even in her chamber beneath the moss she will continue to hear

" the nightingale sing on as if in pain."

But a more robust and cheerful faith rebukes the morbid fancy.

HENRY DAVID THOREAU.

CONCORD, although noted as the residence of many famous people, can be called the birthplace of but one man who has really achieved greatness. That one is Henry David Thoreau, who was born there in 1817. Here throughout boyhood he

> " watched the green fields growing,
> The reaping folk and sowing,
> The harvest time and mowing,"

and the sleepy world of streams.

His home was an old-fashioned New England house of the humbler sort, with gray unpainted boards, and damp mossy roof, standing in an unfenced dooryard, which had the neglected look common to such places in those days. Unattractive as it was, in its neighborhood were pleasant sunny meadows, with beds of peat, old picturesque orchards, mossy brooksides, and clumps of native trees, the resort of many birds. These were sufficient attractions for a boy like Henry Thoreau, who, when " weary of days and hours," as he often was weary, ran off to these favorite haunts and dreamed his accustomed dreams in their solitude. The Concord River became very early his daily haunt; tramping along its banks, or floating upon its bosom,

he passed the happiest hours of his boyhood. He never remained indoors when there was a possibility of being in the outer air, and the mere fact of being out of doors seemed happiness enough for him through all his early years. He was not consciously observing things in those days, but he was open-minded, and many things came to him which he afterwards deemed of importance. To roam through the woods, to paddle his boat up the streams, to watch the phenomena of dawn and of dusk, of the clouds and the dew, of growing things and of living things, — this was his joy, this his work. He did not change much from boy to man; this was still his work while life lasted. More important work, too, than friends and neighbors thought, when, after he was gone, the books so full of himself were given to a sympathetic world. Once more we were taught what we are so slow to believe, that genius must take its own course, and cannot walk in the old trodden paths of men. If it likes a hut and a handful of beechnuts better than a mansion and a stalled ox, then let it to the hut, and sleep under "the wide and starry sky," as long as that mood lasts. And do not be too solicitous about its losses and gains; time will balance the ledger, and, if not time, then eternity. The years spent by Wordsworth at Rydal Mount were not lost, though he did little more of practical import there, than Thoreau at Walden. Emerson's year, when he seemed only to have planted an orchard, was a fruitful year in other ways, and Tennyson's long solitude by the sea had the deepest significance of any part of his long life. When quite young, our embryo philosopher wrote of a fallow field he noted in his walks:

> " There is one field beside this stream
>   Wherein no foot does fall,
> And yet it beareth in my dream
>   A richer crop than all."

During Henry's childhood his father earned the living of the family by pencil-making, and his boys were early called upon to assist him in his labors. Henry acquired great skill in it, and resorted to it at intervals all his life, when he had no other means of subsistence. The business in time grew to be mainly the preparation of fine-ground plumbago for electro-typing. This he supplied to publishers, and among others to the Harpers, for several years. He was fitted for Harvard College at the village academy. Here he studied Greek, and when he entered college in 1833 was proficient in it. He learned this, like most other things, with ease, and took great delight in it. At sixteen his reading had already been quite extensive, and in college also he read as well as studied, but was rather indifferent to the ordinary college motives for study. He did not rank very high, for that reason.

After leaving college he made some attempts at school-teaching, and lectured in Concord and neighboring towns. His originality as a writer was already apparent, and soon attracted the attention of Mr. Emerson, and the other transcendentalists who were just coming upon the stage. Emerson was as yet almost unknown. He had published his first volume, " Nature," but it had attracted little attention except among a little Boston coterie. Carlyc was but little known as yet in America, Margaret Fuller was a novice in literature, Alcott laughed at as a dreamer, Ripley unknown.

That Thoreau was affected by their atmosphere is doubtless true, but it is equally undeniable that his originality is as marked as theirs, and that he did his own thinking on independent lines. In his very first writings there were passages which were said to resemble Emerson, and which proved to have been written before he had read the essays he seemed to imitate. We can now perceive that the time was ripe for such utterance as theirs, and that it sprung up of itself in different quarters of the world, like seed that had been sown, broadcast. In fact, such seed had been sown by Wordsworth, Coleridge, Richter, Goethe, Kant, and their followers, and our New England transcendental period was the time of blossoms. It was a far more rich and pleasing time than its forerunner, but of it could still be truthfully said, as of Tennyson's followers in poetry, " All can have the flowers now, for all have got the seed."

This was the period of Fourierism, and there were other men beside Alcott and Thoreau, who had only scorn and commiseration for people who went about bowed down by the weight of broad acres, and with great houses on their backs. The Brook Farm experiment was made ; the similar, but less noted one, at Fruitlands, and some Fourier settlements started at different points. It is noticeable, however, that Thoreau was never drawn toward any of these. His individuality was too distinct for that; and having made up his mind to do with the bare necessaries of life, and having no desire to secure a competence by any of the ordinary methods of procedure, he found it easy enough to live according to his desire, without the co-operation of any community. It was different with Alcott, whose large family suffered for his opinions. Thoreau lived among his farmer friends a life homely and rugged as their own. He surveyed their wood-lots, laid out their roads, measured their fields and pastures, when that became necessary; he helped toss their hay or raise their barns, or draw their winter's wood; and such scanty earnings sufficed for his scanty needs. One of his maxims was, " From exertion come wisdom and purity; from sloth, ignorance and sensuality." In a letter he refers, as he frequently does, to this subject: —

" How shall we earn our bread is a grave question; yet it is a sweet and inviting question. Let us not shirk it, as is usually done. It is the most important and practical question which is put to man. Let us not be content to get our bread in some gross, careless, and hasty manner. Some men go a-hunting, some a-fishing, some a-gaming, some to war; but none have so pleasant a time as they who in earnest seek to earn their bread. It is true actually as it is true really, it is true materially as it is true spiritually, that they who seek honestly and sincerely, with all their lives and strength, to earn their bread, do earn it, and it is sure to be very sweet to them. A very little bread — a very few crumbs are enough, if it be of the right quality, for it is infinitely nutritious. Let each man, then, earn at least a crumb of bread for his body before he dies, and know the taste of it, — that it is identical with the bread of life, and that they both go down at one swallow."

In the same letter are these sentences: —

" So high as a tree aspires to grow, so high it will find an atmosphere suited to it. . . . The heavens are as deep as our aspirations are high. . . . If one hesitates in his path, let him not proceed. Let him respect his doubts, for doubts, too, may have some divinity in them. That we have little faith is not sad, but that we have little faithfulness. By faithfulness faith is earned."

He has his occasional flings at Concord in his letters, and at the things which occupy its attention. Thus, he says: —

"Concord is just as idiotic as ever in relation to the spirits and their knockings. Most people here believe in a spiritual world which no respectable junk bottle which had not met with a slip would condescend to contain even a portion of for a moment, — whose atmosphere would extinguish a candle let down into it, like a well that wants airing; in spirits which the very bullfrogs in our meadows would blackball. Their evil genius is seeing how low it can degrade them. The hooting of owls, the croaking of frogs, is celestial wisdom in comparison. If I could be made to believe in the things which they believe, I should make haste to get rid of my certificate of stock in this and the next world's enterprises, and buy a share in the first Immediate Annihilation Company that offered."

In Concord, too, they had many lectures, which leads him to exclaim: —

"I was surprised when the farmer asked me, the other day, if I was not going to hear Dr. Solger. What! to be sitting in a meeting-house cellar at that time of day, when you might possibly be out of doors! I never thought of such a thing. What was the sun made for? If he do not prize daylight, I do. Let him lecture to owls and dormice. He must be a wonderful lecturer, indeed, who can keep me indoors at such an hour, when the night is coming in which no man can walk."

And at another time he promulgates his beatitudes:

"Blessed were the days before you read a President's Message. Blessed are the young, for they do not read the President's Message. Blessed are they who never read a newspaper, for they shall see Nature, and, through her, God."

And —

"Where is the 'unexplored land,' but in our own untried enterprises? To an adventurous spirit any place — London, New York, Worcester, or his own yard — is 'unexplored land,' to seek which Frémont and Kane travel so far. To a sluggish and defeated spirit even the Great Basin and the Polaris are trivial places."

Again he says: —

"If a man is in love, he *loves;* if he is in heaven, he *enjoys;* if he is in hell, he *suffers*. It is his condition that determines his locality. . . . The principal, the only thing a man makes, is his condition or fate; though commonly he does not know it, nor put up a sign to this effect, 'My own destiny made and mended here.'"

He had always longed for a home of his own in the woods near Concord, where he could read and write, and be alone with nature, as much as he wished; and in 1845 he built a cabin on Walden Pond, and retired to it. The reason he gave was "because he wished to live deliberately, to front only the essential facts of life, and see if he could not learn what it had to teach, and not, when he came to die, discover that he had not lived." Here he remained two years, though he did not confine himself closely at all, but visited his family often, sometimes every day, and was quite as social as during the years when he lived at Mr. Emerson's house before going there, or after his return to the village when the two years were over.

He wrote here his book "Walden," and read and studied much; he also tilled a patch of ground, and raised nearly everything which he ate. He was never weary of singing the praises of solitude, and here from day to day no one interfered with his mood. He did not miss a sunset because some one was with him, or a moonlight night because of the noisy people on the street. Here he did not have to throw away his precious walks on some companion, but could have first nights at all the spectacles of nature, with the box to himself. He had opportunities during his life of seeing some of the great show-places of the earth, if he would but have gone as companion to another, — to South America, where the tropic vegetation would so have entranced him, to the West Indies, to the Yellowstone River, — but he would not have the great things at that price. He preferred Concord and the Merrimac all to himself. He had travelled a great deal as he remarked to a stranger "in Concord;" and he saw more in that circumscribed area, than many men do who go around the world — in sixty days. As soon as he had exhausted the advantages of a solitary life at Walden, he abandoned it, and the book he wrote there was the foundation of his fame. From that time he began to write quite industriously, and by the help of Mr. Greeley and other friends his writings were advantageously placed, though they brought him but little money. He now had many opportunities to lecture, and went to the towns round about Boston quite frequently for that purpose. He was called a good speaker, and some of his best-known essays were used first as lectures.

In 1856 Mr. Greeley, who had conceived a warm interest in, and liking for him, invited him to come and live with him at Chappaqua, as tutor to his children. Thoreau, who felt a sincere friendship for the man, and under great obligations to him as well, at first thought favorably of the proposition, but it resulted only in a brief visit being paid to the great editor. He was never destined to get much into the world. His longest journey was one to see the Mississippi. He made short excursions, of which he wrote delightfully, to Canada and to the Maine woods; but he moved in a narrow orbit, and had no great desire to enlarge it. How he felt in regard to it can be seen by his poem " The Fisher Boy," one of the most beautiful he ever wrote : —

> " My life is like a stroll upon the beach,
>   As near the ocean's edge as I can go ;
>   My tardy steps its waves sometimes o'erreach,
>   Sometimes I stay to let them overflow.
>
> "My sole employment is, and scrupulous care,
>   To place my gains beyond the reach of tides,
>   Each smoother pebble, and each shell more rare,
>   Which Ocean kindly to my hand confides.
>
> " I have but few companions on the shore ;
>   They scorn the strand, who sail upon the sea ;
>   Yet oft I think the ocean they 've sailed o'er
>   Is deeper known upon the strand to me.
>
> " The middle sea contains no crimson dulse,
>   Its deeper waves cast up no pearls to view ;
>   Along the shore my hand is on its pulse,
>   And I converse with many a shipwrecked crew."

Upon the subject of society and solitude he writes in a letter : —

"As for the dispute about society and solitude, any comparison is impertinent. It is an idling down on the plain at the base of the mountain, instead of climbing steadily to the top. Of course you will be glad of all the society you can get to go up with. Will you go to glory with me? is the burden of the song. I love society so much that I swallowed it all at a gulp, — that is, all that came in my way. It is not that we love to be alone, but that we love to soar, and when we do soar, the company grows thinner and thinner till there is none at all. It is either the tribune on the plain, a sermon on the mount, or a very private ecstasy still higher up. We are not the less to aim at the summits, though the multitude does not ascend them. Use all the society that will abet you."

It has often been asked if he ever felt the passion of love, if he ever knew in his own heart that flame of holy fire of which he speaks so reverently. Has a poet ever lived without love? Love is the poet's native air, and he scarcely lives in any other atmosphere. When he ceases to love, he lives only automatically. Thoreau felt this passion but once, and it was in early youth. We are told that he and his brother John loved the same maiden, and we are left to wonder if that was the reason why neither claimed her for his own. It is not to be questioned that this love had a profound influence upon him. If it had come to a happy issue, his whole life might have been changed. His youthful peculiarities would under its influence have been gradually softened down, he would have been forced into more conformity to the ways of the world, and been obliged to think more of others and less constantly of himself. A fortunate marriage, like that of his friends Emerson and Alcott,

would have widened the horizon of his life. The
poem called " Sympathy," which was first published
in " The Dial " was addressed to this maiden, although
a thin disguise is adopted : —

> " Lately, alas ! I knew a gentle boy,
>   Whose features all were cast in Virtue's mould,
> As one she had designed for Beauty's toy,
>   But after manned him for her own stronghold
>
> " On every side he open was as day,
>   That you might see no lack of strength within ;
> For walls and posts do only serve alway
>   For a pretence to feebleness and sin.
>
> .   .   .   .
>
> " Each moment as we nearer grew to each,
>   A stern respect withheld us farther yet,
> So that we seemed beyond each other's reach,
>   And less acquainted than when first we met.
>
> " We two were one while we did sympathize,
>   So could we not the simplest bargain drive ;
> And what avails it, now that we are wise,
>   If absence doth this doubleness contrive ?
>
> " Eternity may not the chance repeat ;
>   But I must tread my single way alone,
> In sad remembrance that we once did meet,
>   And know that bliss irrevocably gone.
>
> " The spheres henceforth my elegy shall sing,
>   For elegy hath other subject none ;
> Each strain of music in my ears shall ring
>   Knell of departure from that other one.
>
> " Make haste and celebrate my tragedy ;
>   With fitting strain resound, ye woods and fields :
> Sorrow is dearer in such case to me
>   Than all the joys other occasion yields."

Rather more like the ordinary lover's poetizing is another, from which we can only make extracts: —

> " The trees a welcome waved,
> And lakes their margin laved,
> When thy free mind
> To my retreat did wind.
>
> .   .   .   .   .
>
> It was a summer eve —
> The air did gently heave,
> While yet a low-hung cloud
> Thy eastern skies did shroud ;
> The lightning's silent gleam
> Startling my drowsy dream,
> *Seemed like the flash*
> *Under thy dark eyelash.*
>
> .   .   .   .   .
>
> I 'll be thy Mercury,
> Thou Cytherea to me, —
> Distinguished by thy face
> The earth shall learn my place.
> As near beneath thy light
> Will I outwear the night,
> With mingled ray
> Leading the westward way."

There are occasional stanzas on this subject, all written near this time. Afterward there appear to be no allusions to it. Here are one or two: —

> " Implacable is Love, —
> Foes may be bought or teased
> From their hostile intent, —
> But he goes unappeased
> Who is on kindness bent."

> " There 's nothing in the world, I know,
> That can escape from love,
> For every depth it goes below,
> And every height above."

The greater number of his poems were written between 1837 and 1841. The best of them appeared in "The Dial," which he helped to edit, and to which he contributed regularly for several years, receiving no remuneration for his work. That journal of high quality appealed to but a very limited audience, and scarcely paid the cost of its making, although the matter it contained was not paid for. In it, however, a good many famous men sowed their transcendental wild oats, and gained experience both in writing and in the conduct of life. Many of them were led out into other lines of work, and became a power in the land. Poor Margaret Fuller met a tragic death before her genius had really come to flower. Alcott, who had great promise in his youth, never reached any higher altitude. Thoreau died before his meridian. Only Emerson expanded and developed, until his fame spread abroad through the earth; and only his works will probably remain to stand for the New England Renaissance, in time to come.

Although Thoreau had a scorn for politics, and never even voted, and was sent to jail for refusal to pay his poll-tax, he always paid the tribute of his respect to the antislavery party. He believed, indeed, not only in the abolition of slavery, but in the abolition of tariffs, almost the abolition of government. Naturally he could work with no party, and he had a chronic quarrel with so-called reformers. He sympathized with Hawthorne in his dislike of men who were bent upon reforming other people, and always suggested to such the duty of beginning at home. But he admired a hero when he saw one,

and was the first man openly and publicly to
approve of John Brown, after his raid on Harper's
Ferry. He gave out word that he would speak on
that subject in Concord, almost as soon as the news
of Brown's arrest had reached the North, and though
even the antislavery men tried to persuade him to
wait, he would not do so, and addressed the multitude who gathered, earnestly eulogizing the rude old
man who had struck the first blow for Freedom.
"For once," he cried, "we are lifted into the region
of truth and manhood. No man in America has
ever stood up so persistently and effectively for the
dignity of human nature; knowing himself for a man,
and the equal of any and all governments. The only
government that I recognize — and it matters not
how few are at the head of it, or how small its army
— is that power which establishes justice in the land."
F. W. Sanborn says of this declaration: "Words like
these have proved immortal when spoken in the cell
of Socrates, and they lose none of their vitality coming from the Concord philosopher."

Thoreau was very fond afterward of quoting
Brown's address from the scaffold, to the members
of the Northern Church whom he considered dere-
lict in their duty toward the antislavery movement.
Brown said: " I see a book kissed here, which I
suppose to be the Bible, or at least the New Testament. That teaches me that whatsoever I would
that men should do unto me, I should do even so to
them. It teaches me, further ' to remember them that
are in bonds, as bound with them ; ' I endeavored to
act up to that instruction. I say that I am yet too
young to understand that God is any respecter of

persons. I believe that to have interfered as I have done in behalf of his despised poor was not wrong, but right." Moral courage was one of Thoreau's most prominent traits. He acted upon his convictions, and refused conformity wherever he lacked entire belief, as in the matter of church-going. He belonged, he said, to the Church of the Sunday Walkers, and that church was often named in enumerating the churches of Concord. He felt that individually he got greater benefit from a day spent in the woods than in the churches, and he did not hesitate to carry out his preferences, though the opinion of the entire community was against him. Yet he was of a reverent nature, and a believer in that natural religion to which he gave so much time and study. These are some of his sentences on this high theme : —

"The perfect God in his revelations of himself has never got to the length of one such proposition as you, his prophets, state. Have you learned the alphabet of heaven, and can count three? Do you know the number of God's family? Can you put mysteries into words? Do you presume to fable of the ineffable? Pray, what geographer are you, that speak of heaven's topography? Whose friend are you that speak of God's personality? . . . Tell me of the height of the mountains of the moon, or of the diameter of space, and I may believe you; but of the secret history of the Almighty, and I shall pronounce you mad. . . . The reading which I love best is the scriptures of the several nations, though it happens that I am better acquainted with those of the Hindoos, the Chinese, and the Persians than of the Hebrews, which I have come to last. Give me one of these Bibles and you have silenced me for a while."

"There are various, nay, incredible faiths; why should we be alarmed at any of them? What man believes, God believes. Long as I have lived, and many blasphemers as I have heard and seen, I have never yet heard or witnessed any direct and conscious blasphemy or irreverence; but of indirect and habitual, enough. Where is the man who is guilty of direct and personal insolence to Him that made him?"

"If it is not a tragical life we live, then I know not what to call it. Such a story as that of Jesus Christ, — the history of Jerusalem, say, being a part of the Universal History. The naked, the embalmed, unburied death of Jerusalem amid its desolate hills, — think of it."

"You can hardly convince a man of an error in a lifetime, but must content yourself with the reflection that the progress of science is slow. If he is not convinced, his grandchildren may be."

"Men reverence one another, not yet God."

"This fond reiteration of the oldest expressions of truth by the latest posterity, content with slightly and religiously retouching the old material, is the most impressive proof of a common humanity. . . . All men are children and of one family."

Emerson tells us "that he thought that without religion or devotion of some kind nothing great was ever accomplished; and he thought that the bigoted sectarian had better bear this in mind." Yet so extreme was he in the statement of his position, so iconoclastic as regarded the received opinions of his day, so exaggerated in denial, so coarse sometimes in ridicule, that he excited only horror and dismay, scarcely anywhere sympathy, or even toleration. The more gentle and serene Emerson, clothing his thought in classic phrase, and keeping himself sweet to the core, could utter as revolutionary sentiments as his audacious young friend, but they crept into men's hearts and nestled there, while the rough and somewhat rowdy words of the young man repelled, and excited only antagonism. He expended the native force which might have made him the captain of great enterprises in these attacks upon the idols of his time. He had such energy and such practical ability that it seemed a great loss to his friends that he had no ambition for the world's work, but was content to be a dreamer.

He might have been great in science, in education, in oratory, in great works of practical importance to the nation. But, as Emerson remarks, wanting ambition, " instead of engineering for all America, he was the captain of a huckleberry party." Emerson adds: " But these foibles, real or apparent, were fast vanishing in the incessant growth of a spirit so robust and wise, and which effaced its defeats with new triumphs." Had he lived longer, it is not likely that he would have changed much outwardly, but we should doubtless have had a literary product which would have better represented his genius and his maturer thought. He would have grown away from that youthful folly of trying to take the world back into the state of nature it had but half emerged from, would have learned that the world goes forward and not back. As Lowell says, he thus far had been " converting us back to a state of nature ' so eloquently,' as Voltaire said of Rousseau, ' that he almost persuaded us to go on all fours,' while the wiser fates were making it possible for us to walk erect for the first time." Time would perhaps have changed him in this regard. Still he was no longer a young man, being forty-five at the time of his death. But he was still a growing man, and great changes might have taken place in his literary workmanship, if not in outward life or character.

He died on the 6th of May, 1862, of pulmonary consumption. This disease, his friends thought, was brought on by the exposures to which he had often subjected himself in his trips and excursions, — particularly in sleeping on the ground in cold weather, insufficiently protected. The last few months he passed quite cheerfully, confined mostly to the house. On March 21st he wrote to a friend: "You ask particularly about my health. I *suppose* that I have not many months to live; but, of course, I know nothing about it. I may add that I am enjoying existence as much as ever, and regret nothing." When Parker Pillsbury essayed to talk to him upon the subject of a future life, his life-long reticence about sacred things prompted him to reply, " One world at a time," though his belief in immortality had been firm and unfaltering all his life. Upon his coffin was placed the inscription : " Hail to thee, O man ! who hast come from the transitory place to the imperishable." For the comfort of his friends he left verses like these : —

> " Now chiefly is my natal hour,
>   And only now my prime of life :
>   I will not doubt the love untold,
>   Which not my worth or want hath bought,
>   Which moved me young, and moves me old,
>   And to this evening hath me brought."

BAYARD TAYLOR.

TO the older generation of readers Bayard Taylor was a unique and fascinating figure. His was an attractive personality, and his readers were likely to become his friends. Those who followed him through his first journeys took almost a romantic interest in him to the end. Those who ever saw him were captivated with him, for he was a man of splendid physique and hearty and joyous nature. All of our literary men felt the charm of his acquaintance, and were his loyal friends. Whittier, who had spent a part of a summer with him in the "Tent on the Beach," thus sang of him: —

" One whose Arab face was tanned
  By tropic sun and boreal frost,
  So travelled there was scarce a land
  Or people left him to exhaust,
  In idling mood from him had hurled
  The poor squeezed orange of the world,
  And in the tent-shade, as beneath a palm,
  Smoked cross-legged like a Turk, in Oriental calm.

" His memory round the ransacked earth
  On Ariel's girdle slid at ease ;
  And, instant, to the valley's girth
  Of mountains, spice isles of the seas ;
  Faith flowered in minster stones, Art's guess
  At truth and beauty found access ;
  Yet loved the while, that free cosmopolite,
  Old friends, old ways, and kept his boyhood's dreams in sight."

Soon after the publication of "Views Afoot" Taylor visited Boston, and was received with applause by the literati of that city. He was but an unknown youth who had made his first venture in literature. Now that writing books has become so almost universal, that little volume would attract slight attention; but then the body of writers was small and compact, — a New England group, for the greater part, — and their dictum made or marred a man's career. But they welcomed new talent gladly, and crowned some immortals who have already passed into forgetfulness. James T. Fields, the most loving and generous of men, who helped every new writer who appeared, with judicious praise and advice, and personal friendship as well, greeted and entertained Taylor, and introduced him to the charmed circle. After that his personal graces made his way for him. So it was in New York, and so abroad, among litterateurs and savants, wherever he went all his life long. He records very early, an evening with Lowell, a night with Longfellow, a ramble with Whittier, and a glimpse of Webster in the pine woods of Abington.

Taylor was of German descent, on his grandmother's side, and was born at Kennett Square, Pennsylvania, in 1825, the year of the first successful locomotive. The family was of Quaker origin, descended from Robert Taylor, who came over with Penn, and settled near Brandywine Creek. He was one of ten children, though but half that number lived much beyond babyhood. He was brought up with Quaker strictness, especially as to non-resistance and the sin of swearing. He was occasionally rebellious as to his moral teachings, and "once, after a homily upon swearing, he was seized with such a desire to swear that he went forth alone into a field, and there 'snatched a fearful joy' by cleansing his stuffed bosom of all the perilous oaths he had ever heard." It is not probable that these were of a very startling nature in that Quaker environment, but he wrote long afterward, of those

" Moral shibboleths, dinned in one's ears with slaverous unction,
  Till, for the sake of a change, profanity loses its terrors."

The reader may recall the similar feeling of Henry Ward Beecher, who in early youth experienced such a reaction from the repression under which his gay and jocund temperament chafed, that one day he went out behind the barn, and roared out " Damn it " in the most stentorian voice. But Mr. Beecher was overtaken with instant remorse, and truly felt that he had imperilled his soul's salvation, and was correspondingly alarmed.

Taylor early showed his roving disposition, and was hardly to be contained within the limits usually set for boys. He also showed quite early his passion for books, and his desire to be a poet.

He was early apprenticed to a printer at West Chester, and began to write for the papers. He made the acquaintance of N. P. Willis and Rufus W. Griswold through letters, and they were both of use to him in his literary career. He began to write for " Graham's Magazine," a notable publication in its day, and soon made a little reputation, which he put to use in forwarding his scheme of foreign travel, which had by this time quite taken possession of him. But he had no money, had not finished his apprenticeship, and his scheme seemed utterly fool-hardy to all his friends. But he would not be daunted by difficulties. He was now nineteen years old. He wrote to some shipowners in Philadelphia to ascertain if he could work his passage, and took some other preliminary steps as to his project. He sought for engagements as foreign correspondent to several papers, and at last succeeded in making engagements with the " Saturday Evening Post," and the " United States Gazette," and they paid him something in advance, to enable him to go. He started with the sum of one hundred and forty dollars. He was accompanied by a cousin who wished to study at Heidelberg, and a young man named Barclay Pennock.

He saw Horace Greeley before embarking, and he also made some conditional agreement as to pay-ment for letters, should any be received worth the publication.

Of that voyage and its sufferings in the ship " Oxford," beginning on the first day of July and ending at Liverpool on the twenty-ninth, he never liked to talk, and touched but lightly on it in his letters. It was, like Stevenson's trip to New York, a steerage passage, but he did not, like Stevenson, analyze and describe it. It was too full of inconceivable misery for that. There being one more passenger than there were berths, he and his cousin had generously offered to sleep together, hardly realizing at the moment what that meant, but finding it the most serious tor-ture of the torturing voyage. Youth and perfect health carried them through unharmed, but they never liked to talk of their first voyage. They made a journey through Ireland and Scotland, then descended into England, walking much of the way. It was no mere holiday ramble that he had undertaken. It was to be his university education, his preparation for literature, the beginning of his acquaintance with the world. He stayed abroad for two years, very scantily supplied with money all that time, and occasionally penniless. He tried type-setting at intervals, to enable him to live in the cities, he received a little money for his correspondence, and he learned how to live in the most primitive and abstemious manner. On the Continent he spent the greater part of his time in Germany and Italy. In Florence he made his longest stay.

Fifteen francs remained, upon leaving Marseilles, to carry him to Paris. His shoes were worn out with his constant walking, and severe storms came upon France at that time. Walking until dark, he could make but thirty miles a day. After leaving France he returned to London. He says : —

"I stood upon London Bridge in the raw mist and the falling twilight, with a franc and a half in my pocket, and deliberated what I should do. Weak from seasickness, hungry, chilled, and without a single acquaintance in the great city, my situation was about as hopeless as it is possible to conceive."

On the 1st of May, 1846, he landed in New York, glad, triumphant, though he had hardly a cent in his pocket. His letters were collected and published. Willis christened the book " Views Afoot," and it was a successful venture. All the literary coterie rallied to his support, and his name became worth something to editors thereafter. He returned to Kennett, and soon his engagement to Mary Agnew, a friend of his childhood, was announced. There had been a romantic affection existing between these two for some years, and a diligent correspondence carried on while he was away. Grace Greenwood once described her as " a dark-eyed young girl, with the rose yet unblighted on cheek and lip, with soft, brown, wavy hair, which, when blown by the wind, looked like the hair often given to angels by the old masters, producing a sort of halo-like effect about the head." There could be no thought of marriage for a long time, and he went up to New York to try his fortunes there, while she waited with great devotion at home. He enjoyed the metropolis as only an ambitious young man seeing success ahead could, and he worked fifteen hours a day. He found good friends there among the literary and journalistic set. Richard Henry Stoddard became his closest friend, though they seldom met except Saturday nights, when their week's work was over. A place was made for him on the " New York Tribune " in 1848, and he remained connected with that paper for many years. In 1849 he was sent to California to write up the great gold regions. He took passage in a crowded steamer for Panama, and after a terrible experience in crossing the Isthmus, arrived at San Francisco in the midst of the fiercest excitement of those exciting years. His letters were very eagerly read, and he enjoyed the new adventures with all the fervor of a young man, but was rejoiced to get back to his editorial work again. He had hastened home on account of the illness of Miss Agnew. She had been in delicate health for some time, and now was failing rapidly from consumption. He found her but a shadow; the long months of absence had been a time of worry and of suffering to her, and he saw at once that she would not be with him long. But it was his desire that their marriage should take place at once, and it was so arranged. On October 24, 1850, they were married, and on the 21st of the following December she died. Mr. Taylor was utterly bereaved, and almost despairing for a time. She had been his early idol, and he the only thought of her young heart. They had been long separated, but their mutual devotion knew no abatement. It was for her that he toiled and suffered, she was the centre of all his future dreams, without her he hardly cared to continue the battle of life. Great regret, too, mingled with his loneliness and sense of loss, that he had strayed so far away from her and been absent so long. Though he had done it as a preparation for their future together, it now seemed to him selfish and wrong, and he reproached himself bitterly. It was many years before he recovered from this cruel blow, and his poetry was for a long time full of the echoes of his grief. A year after her death he wrote a poem entitled " Winter Solstice," in which he recalls her : —

> " For when the gray autumnal gale
> Came to despoil the dying year,
>   Passed with the slow retreating sun,
> As day by day some beams depart,
>   The beauty and the life of one
> Whose love made Summer in my heart.

> " Day after day, the latest flower,
>   Her faded being waned away,
> More pale and dim with every hour, —
>   And ceased upon the darkest day !
> The warmth and glow that with her died
>   No light of coming suns shall bring ;
> The heart its winter gloom may hide,
>   But cannot feel a second spring.
>
> " Oh darkest day of all the year !
>   In vain thou com'st with balmy skies,
> For blotting out their azure sphere,
>   The phantoms of my Fate arise :
> A blighted life, whose shattered plan
>   No after fortune can restore ;
> The perfect lot, designed for man,
>   That should be mine, but is no more."

He went back to his work a sorrowful man, the bloom of whose youth was gone. Long after he wrote, —

> " But my heart grows sick with weary waiting,
>   As many a time before :
> Her foot is ever at the threshold,
>   Yet never passes o'er."

His vision of love and home had passed, and

> " Now toiling day and sorrowing night,
>   Another vision fills his sight :
> A cold mound in the winter snow ;
> A colder heart at rest below ;
> A life in utter loneness hurled,
> And darkness over all the world."

He worked heroically for several months, even beyond his strength, and then was advised to go abroad once more, which he did the summer following his great loss. He decided upon visiting Africa, and embarked for Alexandria, Egypt, from Smyrna in November, 1851. His journey up the White Nile was perhaps his most exciting adventure, but adventures were not wanting in any kind of African travel in that day. His letters describing this long and eventful journey were eagerly read at home, and increased his reputation, which was already nearly at its height, though he was but twenty-seven years old. He finally turned away from the silent fiery world of tawny sand and ink-black porphyry mountains, in the heart of Nubia, and reached Cairo in April, 1852. He proceeded to Jerusalem, Damascus, Aleppo, and through Asia Minor to Constantinople, where he arrived in July. In October he reached London, but it did not have for him the charm of the earlier years. He had always loved the sun, and after his tropical journeyings London seemed dark and forbidding. He echoed Landor's saying, that "one might live comfortably in England if he were rich enough to possess a solar system of his own." He then proceeded to Spain, and by the India mail-steamer reached Bombay in December. When in Constantinople in July, he had found a proposition awaiting him, to accompany Commodore Perry's expedition to Japan, the "Tribune" to supply the funds and to obtain for him a place on board the flagship if possible. He had accepted the offer, and now, after his journey through India, he met Commodore Perry at Shanghai, and spent four months as master's mate on board his vessel. The rules of the service prevented his writing a line for publication. He kept a careful journal, however, which he delivered to the Navy Department, but which he was never permitted to recover. In December, 1853, he arrived in New York. He found remarkable changes in social and literary life, and felt that still greater changes had taken place in himself.

He had grown to be a wanderer, and he was not long satisfied to keep to the dull routine of editorial work on the "Tribune." He was again off, in 1856, for a trip to the Far North, which furnished the material for a book of Northern Travel; and after that he visited Greece and Russia. His descriptions of Norway were very delightful, and inspired in Tennyson, among others, a desire to visit the Northern lands, which was gratified in later life. He had now seen life in almost all known lands, and had become a true cosmopolitan. His life had greater breadth of view, his imagination had been fed from many fruitful sources, he had become a finished writer, and a famous man. When he afterward published his "Poems of the Orient," he expressed his feeling about his wandering life in these lines : —

> "For not to any race or any clime
>> Is the completed sphere of life revealed.
> He who would make his own that round sublime
>> Must pitch his tent on many a distant field."

Between 1854 and 1860 he was largely engaged in lecturing, a profitable but exhausting occupation. He had fully determined upon building a mansion at his old country home in Kennett, and of residing there a large part of every year. To gain the money for this outlay, he travelled and lectured extensively. He received large prices for his lectures. James T. Fields once told the story of his own experience, and that of Dr. Holmes, who at first received five dollars a night for their lectures. Upon one occasion the lyceum refused to pay Fields because, as the chairman said, " it wa'n't as good as we expected." Taylor was always as good as was expected, and received higher and higher prices year after year. But the toil was excessive, the travelling repugnant after the splendid journeys he had made in distant lands, and the monotony of repeating the same lecture over and over intolerable. In 1854 he delivered two hundred and thirty lectures, and for many years he kept up this profitable new enterprise. He built a large and handsome house costing him seventeen thousand dollars, and bought a large tract of land about it for a park. He called the place Cedarcroft, and installed his father and mother and sisters there. He considered himself a prosperous man now, and in fact was so. Yet this large outlay, and the expense of keeping up such an establishment, became a great burden to him after a time, and it was one cause of the overwork which finally undermined his health. The home he had so longed for, and which he had enjoyed so much in anticipation, became rather a trouble than a delight, when his brain flagged, and his body refused to do all that he required of it.

In October, 1857, he was again married to Marie Hansen, daughter of Peter Andreas Hansen, the eminent astronomer and director of the Ducal Observatory in Gotha. He went to Greece in December of that year, and passed one of the pleasantest winters of his life there and at other points in the Mediterranean. Excursions were made to Crete, to the Morea, and to Thessaly, and through Mycenæ and Tiryns. The next fall he brought his bride home to America.

They soon began a life of lavish hospitality at his country-seat, and all visitors were charmed with the beauties of the place, and the good cheer which was maintained there. He was a delightful host, and his wife a charming and lovely woman. They had one daughter, who was named Lillian. For the first time he was able to entertain the friends who had been so much to him in all his troubled early years. Here came Boker, and Stedman, and the Stoddards, Dr. Furness, and hosts of other faithful friends; and here merriment was contagious, and festivity perpetual.

Conviviality was a part of his creed of life, and his country neighbors were sometimes shocked at the consignments of wines and liquors which were sent down to Cedarcroft. Some criticisms of this kind caused unpleasant feelings between him and the old settlers, and he satirized them severely in his novels which were written at that place during the succeeding years. They retorted in kind, and he became less contented in his country home than he had been at first. The charge of intemperance was many times made against him, but his biographers all deny that he ever drank to excess. He had undoubtedly become a beer-drinker, but he had never made any pretensions to total abstinence. Further than this, his biographers admit nothing. A guest at Cedarcroft once asked Mr. Taylor why he had created a pond at the foot of the lawn. He replied that in it he intended to drown his disagreeable neighbors. This playful answer covered a real feeling, for he did not find his environment congenial there. He liked better the gay evenings he spent with brilliant, if erratic, Bohemian friends in New York. There, were gay converse, loud laughter, jolly singing, the making of verses, and the talk of the town, to say nothing of the conversation of the craft, in which he delighted.

Stoddard, Taylor, and O'Brien were frequently amiable rivals in the making of burlesque verses. Some of these Taylor afterward published in the "Atlantic Monthly," calling them "Diversions of the Echo Club," and they were the source of much mystification as well as amusement to its readers. They were not parodies of single poems, but burlesques of the general style of the poets. Here are a few specimens. That on Aldrich began: —

"I lay in the bosom of the sun,
  Under the roses dappled and dun.
  I thought of the Sultan Gingerbeer,
  In his palace beside the Bendemeer,
  With his Afghan guards, and his eunuchs blind,
  And his harem that stretched a league behind.
  The tulips bent in the summer breeze
  Under the broad chrysanthemum trees,
  And the minstrel playing his culverin
  Made for my ears a merry din.
  If I were the sultan and he were I,
  Here in the grass he should loafing lie,
  And I should bestride my zebra steed,
  And ride to the hunt of the centipede;
  When the pet of the harem Dandeline
  Should fill me a crystal bucket of wine,
  And the kislar aga, Up-to-Snuff,
  Should wipe my mouth when I sighed 'enough.'
  And the gay court poet Fearful-Bore
  Should sit in the hall when the hunt was o'er,
  And chant me songs of silvery tone,
  Not from Hafiz — but mine own.

> Ah me! sweet love, beside me here,
> I am not the Sultan Gingerbeer,
> Nor you the odalisque Dandeline,
> Yet I am yourn and you are mine."

And is not this a real echo of Mrs. Browning:—

> " When I beheld his red-roan steed
> I knew what aim impelled it;
> And that dim scarf of silver brede,
> I guessed for whom he held it:
> I recked not, when he flaunted by,
> Of love's relentless vi'lence,
> Yet o'er me crushed the summer sky
> In thunders of blue silence.
> His hoof-prints crumbled down the vale,
> But left behind their lava;
> What should have been my woman's mail,
> Green jellied like guava:
> I looked him proud, but 'neath my pride
> I felt a boneless tremor;
> He was the Beër I descried,
> And I was but the Seemer."

One of the best echoes was of Taylor himself, of which a verse will suffice: —

> " The cockatoo upon the upas screams;
> The armadillo fluctuates o'er the hill;
> And like a flag incarnadined in dreams,
> All crimsonly I thrill!"

Taylor was not only editorially connected with the "Tribune," but was also a small stockholder in the property. Among his associates on that paper were Sidney Howard Gay, Charles T. Congdon, Edward H. House, and William H. Fry. Among his most intimate friends were George Ripley and Charles A. Dana.

At the beginning of the war he sold one share of his "Tribune" stock to enable his youngest brother to enlist in the army. The war years proved to be a trying time for all literary men; lecturing did not pay, no new books were called for, and few published, and copyrights on old ones were unprofitable. Taylor had written many books of travel, almost every journey he had taken having furnished material for one; he had also written two or three books of poems, and done a good deal of hack work like the "Cyclopædia of Modern Travel," but he had only a small income from his books. The "Tribune" stock went down in value a little later, and he had no dividends from that for many years. So the year 1862 found him in Washington as war correspondent for the "Tribune." He was also zealously engaged in promoting the Union cause in every way in his power. A little before this, he had delivered his lecture in Philadephia, girt about by policemen; and he had roused great indignation in Brooklyn by defending his friend Curtis, who had been mobbed in Philadelphia.

A lecture bureau in the South cancelled its engagements with him after hearing of the course he was taking, and all these incidents but made him more outspoken and fearless. He had only begun his work as war correspondent, however, before it was proposed to him to accompany Simon Cameron to Russia, as Secretary to the Legation.

He accepted with great pleasure, as it was understood that Mr. Cameron would return in the fall, leaving him acting *chargé d'affaires*, and that the ministry might ultimately be his own. He sailed in May, 1862. He remained in Russia a year, when

Cassius M. Clay arrived, he having been appointed
minister instead of Mr. Taylor. He was seriously
disappointed, but could not regret the glimpse he
had had of what is called diplomacy. He also had
great satisfaction in the thought that he had been
able to really do his country some service in Russia,
in the short time he had been connected with the
embassy there. It was undoubtedly true that he
influenced the Czar somewhat, and the court also;
and the friendly attitude of Russia during our great
national trial has been remembered with gratitude,
and will continue to be so remembered for all time
to come. It was for party reasons alone, that the
office of minister had been withheld from him and
given to another; and a special mission to Persia was
talked of, to be filled by him. Upon his return in
September, President Lincoln expressed surprise,
and said he thought he was in Persia. Secretary
Seward alone knew why he was not there.

In deep grief for the death of his young brother
upon the field of Gettysburg, he took up the burden
of literary work once more. He had brought back
from Russia a completed novel, partly written before
his residence there; and it was published in 1863.
It was called " Hannah Thurston," and it was received with great favor, though criticised very severely
in some publications, for misrepresentation and exaggeration of certain features of our national life.
The next year he published another somewhat similar novel of American life, called " John Godfrey's
Fortunes." He was a very rapid writer, although a
painstaking one, and composition did not seem to
exhaust him. Both novels showed evidences of

haste in construction, and this is not to be wondered at, when we consider that the latter was written between the middle of March and that of August. He reserved his best strength and his careful finish for his poems, upon which alone he depended for literary reputation. The crudity of his novels, and the ephemeral nature of his works of travel, were well known to him, all of them having been written under the spur of necessity; but he felt that his poems did justice to his powers as a writer, and would give him some permanent place in his country's annals. "The Poet's Journal," was little more than a record of personal sorrow, and Tennyson had fully occupied that ground before, and his poem could not bear the test of comparison with "In Memoriam." The "Poems of the Orient" were a great advance upon the first volumes, and were very warmly received.

If any of his work is lasting, it will doubtless be that, and his translation of Faust, which was his greatest work, and one of which his country has reason to be proud. This was a labor of love, and he gave to it the strength of his maturity, and the long preparation which such a work requires. He had mastered the German language, and could use it like his native tongue. His vocabulary was singularly rich, and his command of metrical measures complete. His Faust was received with a chorus of praise from all critical quarters, and his satisfaction with it was entire. He seemed to have become completely possessed by the spirit of his master, comprehended in fuller measure than any other who had essayed translation, the great conception of Goethe, and, enamoured of his work, held to it with such rare and long devotion that when it was done, it seemed to have been done finally.

This was not a popular work, like the stirring lyrics, full of the fire of youth and passion, which constituted the " Poems of the Orient." But it gave him his place among scholars, and came nearer satisfying his heart than any other work he had done. After this a new ambition took possession of him, and remained with him to the last, although he was never able to complete the work he planned. This was to write the Lives of Goethe and Schiller, and to make them the crowning work of his lifetime. This was the one hope to which he clung, the one interest paramount to all others, in the closing years of his life.

He had written three dramatic poems, the " Masque of the Gods," " The Prophet," and " Prince Deukalion; " this latter, his latest published book, coming out but a month before his death. There was a great deal of literary work done of which no mention has been made, nor could be in so short a sketch, many journeys of which no account has been given, and much that was of deepest interest in his poetry and in his life, which has scarcely been touched upon. That life was a pure and noble one, so much so that Longfellow, who knew and loved him, wrote : —

> " Thou hast sung with organ tone
> In Deukalion's life thine own ;"

and Lanier, —

> " In soul and stature larger than thy kind."

His generous and genial spirit, his high moral atti- tude, his open and hearty expressions of his friendship, and his constant gentleness in dealing with his friends under all varying circumstances, had endeared him to all who came into personal relations with him, and some echo of this feeling had found the reading world. He was now nearing the close of his eventful life. His health had been failing for some years, and in 1877 serious symptoms began to show themselves. But he continued to work hard, and finished " Deukalion " in October. He had already collected a large amount of material for his Life of Goethe, and wrote of it: " My biography of Goethe is my sole absorbing interest. . . . I cling to my plan with such tenacity that I surely must be allowed to finish it before I die."

On the 15th of February, 1878, President Hayes sent his name to the Senate as Minister to Germany. This recognition of his fitness to represent his country at that important point, was a great delight to him, when other delights had begun to pall upon his jaded heart. Nothing left in the world could probably have afforded him the same satisfaction. And the expression of the nation concerning the appointment added greatly to his joy. No appointment was ever better received in this country. Now he felt he could write his great work, the Life of Goethe; he would have the leisure and the environment he had so much longed for. He enjoyed the dream, but it was never destined to be fulfilled. Until he sailed in April, one demonstration after another was made of the delight of his friends. Banquets, dinners, balls, followed each other, until, quite worn out with festivity, he sailed away. The excitement had been too much for him, and dangerous symptoms followed. He was threatened with brain fever, and only quieted with opiates. But this danger was tided over, and he reached Germany, somewhat improved, but far from being a well man. He was received with the utmost cordiality there, and entered upon his new duties with enthusiasm. Some important matters came before him almost immediately, which he managed with ability and tact. But the disease he labored under made rapid progress from the time of his arrival at Berlin, and before a year had passed, his death was announced to his startled friends and countrymen. He died sitting in an arm-chair in his library, without warning, although his death was not entirely unexpected. " I must be away," were the last words he uttered.

> " Friend, but yesterday the bells
> Rang for thee their loud farewells;
> And to-day they toll for thee
> Lying dead beyond the sea,
> Lying dead among thy books,
> The peace of God in all thy looks ! "

JAMES MATTHEW BARRIE.

IAN MACLAREN recently related the following incident, illustrating the pride of the common people of Scotland in their most popular author. He said:—

"Not long ago, I was travelling from Aberdeen to Perth. A man sitting opposite studied me for a minute, and then, evidently being convinced that I had average intelligence, and could appreciate a great sight if I saw it, he said, 'If you will stand up with me at the window, I will show you something in a minute; you will only get a glimpse suddenly and for an instant.' I stood. He said, 'Can you see that?' I saw some smoke, and said so. 'That's Kirriemuir,' he answered. I sat down, and he sat opposite me, and watched my face to see that the fact that I had had a glimpse of Kirriemuir, or rather of its smoke, was one I thoroughly appreciated, and would carry in retentive memory for the rest of my life. Then I said, 'Mr. Barrie was born there.' 'Yes,' he said, 'he was; and I was born there myself.'"

This intense loyalty to every thing Scotch, this pride in the achievements of any countryman, this appreciation of the national element in literature, is one of the most pleasing traits of the Scotch character, though it has its humorous side, and has

roused inextinguishable laughter in its day. Much as the outside world praises and prizes the best work of such men as Stevenson, Barrie, Ian Maclaren, and others, it is only people who have lived with and loved the bracken and the heather, who feel its subtlest charm. This fragrance is in every leaf of these Scottish stories, and it cannot stir the alien heart as it does that of the native. What a classic land its writers have made of Scotland, the wild and rugged, and barren little spot! The land touched by the pen of Scott is as classic as Greece, that connected with the life of Burns no less so, and the home and haunts of Carlyle, if loved by a lesser number, are loved just as passionately. And now we have a new Delphian vale in Thrums or Kirriemuir, and still another in Drumtochty. Time will test the fame of these new men, and prove their staying qualities, but at present they really seem to have made a high bid for continued favor, in the hearts of so steadfast a people as the Scotch.

James Matthew Barrie was born in Kirriemuir on May 9, 1860. Kirriemuir is sixty miles north of Edinburgh, and Mr. Barrie has made all the world familiar with the little secluded hamlet, by his descriptions of Thrums and its inhabitants. We know these people as we do our personal friends, and if we could but sit at the window in Thrums we could call many of their names as they pass by. Leeby and Jess, las! we should not see; they are asleep under the bracken and the moss on the hill overlooking Kirriemuir, and that little burgh seems thinly inhabited now that they are gone.

Th day of James Barrie's birth was always remembered in his family by the fact that six hair-bottomed chairs were brought into the house upon that day, — chairs which had been longed for, and waited and worked for, by that capable and ambitious woman, Margaret Ogilvie, his mother. He heard the description of the coming of the chairs so often afterwards, and shared in the toil and saving to get other things to place beside the chairs, for so long a time, that he feels as if he remembered the event for himself; and this is the case with many of the incidents of his mother's life which had been conned over so often in his hearing. From six years old he takes up the thread of memory for himself, and sees his mother's face, and knows that God sent her into the world to open the minds of all who looked to beautiful thoughts. His life was very closely bound up with hers from this time on, and the history of the one is that of the other. What she had been and what he should be, were the great subjects between them in his boyhood, and the stories she told him, for she was a born story-teller, took such hold on his memory, and so stirred his imagination, that they afterward laid the foundations of his fame, when he published them in his first volume of "Auld Licht Idylls." Never were such friends as he and his mother all through his youth, and her mark was indelibly set upon him by that time. She had a numerous family of children, but Jamie seemed to be different to her from the others. " Some peculiar mystic grace had made him only the child of his mother," and it was a worshipful love on the part of both that held them together. This mother was a great reader, and they read many books together when he was a boy, " Robinson

Crusoe" being the first. This led to his writing stories himself, and reading them to her. She was a sharp critic, and he served his apprenticeship under her. They were all tales of adventure, he tells us; the scene lay in unknown parts, desert islands, and enchanted gardens, and there were always knights in armor riding on black chargers at full tilt. At the age of twelve he made up his mind to be an author, and she aided and abetted him in all the ways known to a loving mother's heart. About this time, or a little later, he was sent to the Dumfries Academy, where his brother was Inspector of Schools. He was a bright scholar, and very happy there, where he made unusual progress in his studies.

At eighteen years of age he entered the University at Edinburgh, and devoted himself especially to the study of literature. He went but little into the society of the place, and made but few friends among the students, being considered " reserved." But he had opportunity for more reading than ever before, and became quite absorbed in the multitude of books to which he had access for the first time. He also began the writing of literary criticisms for the " Edinburgh Courant " at this time. He showed a true touch even in his first writing, which may have been owing somewhat to his years of practice in the garret at home, on stories which must be made to please his mother. Carlyle, whom he had sometimes seen while at Dumfries, and who became his hero, exerted a great influence upon him at this time. He began to look upon life through the eyes of his mentor, and to value the sturdy virtues which form so large a part of his discourse. He caught some of his phrases, which were a stumbling-block to his mother, — although she too was an ardent admirer of the rugged Scotchman. Sincerity, truth, courage, strength, these became his watchwords, and their influence can be seen in his writings to this day. The poetry of common life, the hardy virtues of the humble, the sweetness of the domestic life in many lowly cottages, the humorous side of petty religious controversy, — these became his theme, and the world turned away from the conventional novel about Lady Arabella and Lord Vincent Vere de Vere, and the vicar and the curate, and the old family solicitor of the Tulkinghorn type, to read about " The Courting of T'nowhead's Bell." He heeded Longfellow's advice, although very likely he had never heard of it, in the verse which says, —

> " That is best which lieth nearest,
> Shape from this thy work of art."

How many times of late we have seen the wisdom of this course exemplified! Instead of going back to the past, or flying to the ends of the earth for some new and impossible theme, we have seen our most popular writers sitting down on their own doorsteps, and describing what actually passed before their eyes, with the result that the whole reading world wanted to see just what they saw, and with their eyes. Miss Murfree among the Tennessee mountains, Miss Wilkins in hackneyed New England, Olive Schreiner on a South African Farm, Mr. Cable among the Creoles of Louisiana, Kipling with the British army in India, Thomas Nelson Page in the New South, Mary Hallock Foote in the Western mining-camps, and many others who have achieved late successes, have done so on their own ground, in reporting the actual life of the people with whom they were familiar. That repulsive realism which concerns itself only with disease and vice and abnormal conditions will be crowded out by the better realism of the new school. While we have among the younger writers a few who follow the lead of Ibsen and of Zola, and insist upon dragging into the light all the hidden things of life, and whose writings consequently are redolent of decay, this newer group give us novels of character, and our interest lies in its development amid the varied circumstances depicted, and not in some hidden crime or adulterous amour, which is exploited with all its disgusting details, till the revolted reader throws it into the fire, which alone can purify its poisonous pages. That our presses have teemed with this kind of books for a few years past, is a well-known fact. About them we could say as Thoreau said about certain poems of Walt Whitman, —

" He does not celebrate love at all. It is as if the beasts spoke. I think that men have not been ashamed of themselves without reason. No doubt there have always been dens where such deeds were unblushingly recited, and it is no merit to compete with their inhabitants."

But in the very midst of this passing phase of the gospel of dirt, were flung such books as "A Window in Thrums" and "The Bonnie Brier Bush," and their reception proved that the heart of the reading world is sound, although it is sometimes beguiled into the haunts of leprosy for a season.

Graduating from the University in Edinburgh in 1882, Barrie necessarily began to look at once for work, for his father had already done perhaps more than he was able to do for him, and there was a numerous family whose needs had to be considered. The famous managing of Mrs. Barrie had been put to many hard tests in its time, and her son knew too well the inner details of the home life, to wish to live a moment longer than was necessary at the expense of his parents. He tells us in one place about the little parlor which was the pride of his mother's heart: —

" Every article of furniture, from the chairs that came into the world with me, and have worn so much better, though I was new and they were second-hand, to the mantel-border of fashionable design which she sewed in her seventieth year, having picked up the stitch in half a lesson, has its story of fight and attainment for her; hence her satisfaction."

The furnishing of the family wardrobe also had been with her a series of skirmishes, in which she had plucked from every well-dressed person she had chanced to see, ideas for the making or re-making of garments for one or another of the family. And she made very good imitations indeed of the clothing of the better dressed people, out of the poorer resources of her cottage. She would imitate the cut of a garment, if only she could get one long satisfying look at it, in a manner that would have been the envy of some famous dressmakers. And as to patterns and colors her taste was perfect. Her son dwells lovingly on all these details, in his memorial of her, which is in part a history of his own life, so interwoven were their existences. He made what haste he could to earn money for himself and her. For the greatest of his pleasures in the earning came to be what he could do for her to gratify her innocent pride and her generous impulses toward others. At this time his sister saw an advertisement for a leader-writer by the Nottingham "Daily Journal," and with great trepidation and excitement the family awaited the result of his application for the place. Great was the rejoicing when he received the appointment, at what seemed to them the magnificent salary of three guineas a week. For this sum he was to write an article, and notes on political and social topics every day. This journalistic training was doubtless of great value to him, and he describes it somewhat in a novel written some years afterward, called "When a Man 's Single." In it he narrates how the young man, who had accepted a place on the paper, first appeared at the office of the "Daily Mirror." He says: —

"During the time the boy took to light Mr. Licquarish's fire, a young man in a heavy overcoat knocked more than once at the door in the alley, and then moved off as if somewhat relieved that there was no response. He walked round and round the block of buildings, gazing upward at the windows of the composing-room ; and several times he ran against other pedestrians, on whom he turned fiercely, and would then have begged their pardons had he known what to say. Frequently he felt in his pocket to see if his money was still there, and once he went behind a door and counted it. There were three pounds seventeen shillings altogether, and he kept it in a linen bag that had been originally made for carrying worms when he went fishing. . . . Rob had stopped at the door a score of times and then turned away. He had arrived in Silchester in the afternoon, and come straight to the 'Mirror' office to look at it. Then he had set out in quest of lodgings, and having got them, had returned to the passage. He was not naturally a man crushed by a sense of his own unworthiness, but looking up at these windows and at the shadows that passed them every moment, he felt far away from his saw-mill. What a romance to him, too, was in the glare of the gas, and in the 'Mirror' bill that was being reduced to pulp on the wall at the mouth of the close! It had begun to rain heavily, but he did not feel the want of an umbrella, never having possessed one in Thrums."

The new reporter finally made his way in, and was introduced by the editor to the reporters' room, where the following conversation took place: —

"'What do you think of George Frederick (the editor)?' asked the chief, after he had pointed out to Rob the only chair that such a stalwart reporter might safely sit on. 'He was very pleasant,' said Rob. 'Yes,' said Billy Kirker, thoughtfully, 'there's nothing George Frederick wouldn't do for any one if it could be done gratis.' 'And he struck me as an enterprising man.' 'Enterprise without outlay, is the motto of this office,' said the chief. 'But the paper seems to be well conducted,' said Rob, a little crestfallen. 'The worst conducted in England,' said Kirker, cheerfully. Rob asked how the 'Mirror' compared with the 'Argus.' 'They have six reporters to our three,' said Kirker, 'but we do double work and beat them.' 'I suppose there is a great deal of rivalry between the staffs of the two papers?' Rob asked, for he had read of such things. 'Oh, no,' said Kirker, 'we help each other. For instance, if Daddy Welsh, the "Argus" chief, is drunk, I help him; and if I'm drunk, he helps me.'"

This initiatory conversation was closed by Kirker asking Rob to lend him five bob, and after that Rob took two books, which had been handed him for review, and made his way to his lodgings. He sat up far into the night reading one of the books, "The Scorn of Scorns," and writing a murderous review of it, and upon the effect of that review hangs the rest of the story.

However literal this description of his first adventures as a journalist may or may not be, there he was, at last, engaged in the profession of literature. No prouder or happier man walked the earth. He remained in Nottingham about two years, and during that time he began sending articles to various London publications. The first paper to accept any of these contributions was the "Pall Mall Gazette." But others were accepted after a while, and the young man began to think seriously of leaving his position in Nottingham and going up to London. The great city was calling to him, as it calls to so many young men of talent and ambition every year. He began to hear his days before him, and the music of his life. He was

"Yearning for the large excitement which the coming years
    would yield,
Eager-hearted as a boy when first he leaves his father's field."

And it was not long after he began hearing the voices, before he " saw the lights of London flaring in the dreary dawn." The "St. James Gazette " accepting a couple of articles was the decisive event with him. After that he concluded to make the rash venture, although his mother gave way to her fears, and protested earnestly against it, fearing he would have to sleep in the parks, and be robbed or murdered whatever way he might turn. Mr. Barrie says : —

" While I was away at college she drained all available libraries for books about those who go to London to live by the pen, and they all told the same shuddering tale. London, which she never saw, was to her a monster that licked up country youths as they stepped from the train ; there were the garrets in which they sat abject, and the park seats where they passed the night. Those park seats were the monster's glaring eyes to her, and as I go by them now she is nearer to me than when I am in any other part of London. I dare say that when night comes, this Hyde Park, which is so gay by day, is haunted by the ghosts of many mothers, who run, wild-eyed, from seat to seat looking for their sons. . . . ' If you could only be sure of as much as would keep body and soul together,' my mother would say with a sigh. ' With something over to send to you.' ' You couldna expect that at the start.' "

He says further of this time : —

" In an old book I find columns of notes about works projected at this time, nearly all to consist of essays on deeply uninteresting subjects ; the lightest was to be a volume on the older satirists, beginning with Skelton and Tom Nash — the half of that manuscript still lies in a dusty chest. The only story was one about Mary Queen of Scots, who was also the subject of many unwritten papers. Queen Mary seems to have been luring me to my undoing ever since I saw Holyrood, and I have a horrid fear that I may write that novel yet. That anything could be written about my native place never struck me."

The " St. James Gazette " continued to take his articles after he went up to London, though the editor had advised him not to come, and he began writing his "Auld Licht Idylls." The first book which he put forth was a satire on London life, called "Better Dead," which was not a success. But his newspaper articles had begun to attract attention, and by the time "Auld Licht Idylls" appeared, he had achieved a reputation, — at least a local one. This book had an immediate success, and ran rapidly through several editions. His mother had been an Auld Licht in her youth. They were a very small but fierce sect who had seceded from the Presbyterian church, and maintained themselves in isolation from all other Christians for some time. Mrs. Barrie, knowing them from the inside, could tell all sorts of quaint and marvellous tales about them, whose humor was sure to please. It was from her stories that the Idylls were mainly drawn, so she was in a sense a collaborator with her son in their production. But she had no faith in them as literature, and considered an editor who would publish them as "rather soft." When she read the first one she was quite alarmed, and, fearing the talk of the town, hid the paper from all eyes. While her son thought of her as showing them proudly to all their friends, she was concealing them fearfully in a bandbox on the garret stair. It amused her greatly, from that time on, that the editors preferred the Auld Licht articles to any others, and she racked her brain constantly for new details. Once she said to her son : "I was fifteen when I got my first pair of elastic-sided boots. Tell the editor that my charge for this important news is two pounds ten." And she made brave fun of those easily fooled editors day after day. The publishers were very shy of the book when it was offered to them, and it went the round of their offices before it found a purchaser. But at last a firm sufficiently daring was found by a good friend, an editor, and Mrs. Barrie had the great satisfaction of seeing her son's name really on a book-cover, and in knowing in her inmost heart that the book was largely her own, though that she would never admit, even in the home circle.

When the next book was ready, there was no looking for a publisher, all were eager now to use his material. A few months only, elasped before the second successful book was published. It had run serially through a weekly paper, and was republished from that. It was called "When a Man's Single," and embodied some of his journalistic experiences, as has been told. In rapid succession came "A Window in Thrums," "My Lady Nicotine," and "The Little Minister." In the first-named he went back to his childhood's home, and gave pictures of the life in it and in the village, with his mother and sister for two of its leading characters. He opens it with a description of the House on the Brae : —

"On the bump of green ground which the brae twists, at the top of the brae, and within cry of T'nowhead Farm, still stands a one-story house, whose whitewashed walls, streaked with the discoloration that rain leaves, look yellow when the snow comes. In the old days the stiff ascent left Thrums behind, and where is now the making of a suburb was only a poor row of dwellings and a manse, with Hendry's house to watch the brae. The house stood bare, without a shrub, in a garden whose paling did not go all the way round, the potato pit being only kept out of the road, that here sets off southward, by a broken dyke of stones and earth. On each side of the slate-colored door was a window of knotted glass. Ropes were flung over the thatch to keep the roof on in wind.

" Into this humble abode I would take any one who cares to accompany me. But you must not come in a contempt- uous mood, thinking that the poor are but a stage removed from beasts of burden, as some cruel writers of these days say ; nor will I have you turn over with your foot the shabby horse-hair chairs that Leeby kept so speckless, and Hendry weaved for years to buy, and Jess so loved to look on."

The window at Thrums was that of Jess : —

" For more than twenty years she had not been able to go so far as the door, and only once while I knew her was she ben in the room. With her husband, Hendry, and her only daughter, Leeby, to lean upon, and her hand clutching her staff, she took twice a day, when she was strong, the journey between her bed and the window where stood her chair."

Again he writes : —

" Ah, that brae ! The history of tragic little Thrums is sunk into it like the stones it swallowed in winter. We have all found the brae long and steep in the spring of life. Do you remember how the child you once were sat at the foot of it and wondered if a new world began at the top? It climbs from a shallow burn, and we used to sit on the brig a long time before venturing to climb. As boys, we ran up the brae. As men and women, young and in our prime, we almost forgot that it was there. But the autumn of life comes, and the brae grows steeper ; then the winter, and once again we are as the child, pausing apprehensively on the brig. Yet we are no longer the child ; we look now for no new world at the top, only for a little garden, and a tiny house, and a hand loom in the house. It is only a garden of kail and potatoes, but there may be a line of daisies, white and red, on each side of the narrow footpath, and honeysuckle over the door. Life is not always hard, even after backs grow bent, and we know that all braes lead only to the grave."

It was the plainest and simplest of books, all about a handful of peasants who spoke in broad Scotch, which many times the reader did not fully understand, but it caught the eye of the world, and it went to its heart. It was the literary success of the year, and Margaret Ogilvie should have been satisfied. But there was a thorn in her side, and that was the name of Robert Louis Stevenson. She had great fear that he was still considered the superior of her Jamie. At first she refused to read a word he had written, deriding him every time his name was mentioned. Then, her curiosity getting the better of her prejudice, she read him secretly, to convince herself of her son's superiority, but not getting great comfort from the experiment. Then she scoffed more than ever at " that Stevenson man," and tossed her head, and her soft tender face became hard. " I could never thole his books," she would say vindictively. But at last she was caught in the act of reading " The Master of Ballantrae " by her son, who peeped through the keyhole, and " muttering the music to herself, nodding her head in approval, and taking a stealthy glance at the foot of each page before she began at the top." But that was nothing to the enchantment which " Treasure Island " had for her, when once she had opened its fascinating pages. They had not dared to laugh at her, for fear she would give up her pleasure entirely, and so it was understood in the family that she only read him to make

sure of his unworthiness. But the night when she
became so absorbed in it that she did not know when
bedtime came, and they remonstrated with her, and
coaxed her to give it up and go to bed, she exclaimed
quite passionately, " I dinna lay my head on a pil-
low this night till I see how that laddie got out of the
barrel; " and the secret was told, and they knew that
Stevenson had conquered his last enemy. But never
in words did she admit it. To the last she disliked to
see letters come to her son with the Vailima post-
mark on them.

" The Little Minister " came as a revelation of Mr.
Barrie's sustained power, to many people who had
read his sketches. It is probably his finest piece of
work thus far. Its success was overwhelming; many
people were fascinated with it who cared little for his
first efforts. One must be something of a humorist
himself to thoroughly appreciate his earlier work, and
all readers are not endowed with that quality. But
most readers enjoyed the new story, and its author
became the drawing card in periodical literature.
Suddenly in the midst of his fame, and a young
man's delight in it, he left London and went back to
Kirriemuir to remain. The long invalidism of his
mother had taken on dangerous symptoms, and the
faithful daughter, who had no breath, no being, but
in hers, could not care for her alone, for she was
herself smitten with a lingering but fatal disease.
For a long time the two faithful watchers tended the
dying mother, doing everything themselves, for she
would not allow any one else even to touch her, and
at last the worn-out daughter — as her brother describes it — " died on foot," three days before the

mother. They were buried together, on her seventy-sixth-birthday. Her son writes: "I think God was smiling when He took her to Him, as He had so often smiled at her during those seventy-six years."

Mr. Barrie continued to live on at Viewmount House, the little villa built in recent years on the outskirts of Kirriemuir. It was there that he was married, in 1894, to Miss Mary Ansell, an English girl, and really began life for himself, at the age of thirty-four. His last novel, "Sentimental Tommy," deals largely with the boyhood of the hero, and the scene is laid in London and in Thrums alternately. Whether that locality will serve much longer as literary material is a question which readers will answer differently, according to whether they really belong to the Barrie cult or not. On those who worship at the inner shrine it never palls, but the general reader may perhaps complain of monotony, and yearn for a new setting for the coming tales.

His latest work is "Margaret Ogilvie," a memorial of his mother from which we have quoted largely in · this article.